Praise for *Beggar's Feast*

"A post-colonial Gatsby ... A rags-to-riches picaresque about the clash of worlds and the revenge of empires, about fate and history and harbours and birthright and brothels and moneylenders and metal-benders ... Boyagoda, a sharp and subtle writer, slips easily into many different characters' heads and their internal rhythms, and lyrical lines abound ... A satirical feast."

—*The Globe and Mail*

"Let us neither over nor under-state the case—this is a beautifully written book. It reads like a hot curry balanced against a mango relish. The central flavour is dark and filled with fire, while all about it is a sweetness that keeps the palate happy and willingly engaged. *Beggar's Feast* is so finely etched and filigreed that it actually causes me to consider a new literary theory. Which is this: I'm finding that the books I read by authors from or within a generation of the Asian sub-continent have a certain elegance, a means of describing the events of day-to-day life in terms that are not mundane and unnecessary but rather fresh, well-chosen and illuminating of one's own life. In other words, what books are supposed to do ... *Beggar's Feast* is a triumphant entry into the classic genre of the multi-generational epic ... There is a whiff of Charles Foster Kane about Sam Kandy ... It takes a great writer to conjure up a loving portrait of an unlovely man. Mordecai Richler of course did it pretty much every book and in some ways Sam Kandy is Randy Boyagoda's Duddy Kravitz ... An excellent novel. You could knock me over with a feather if it doesn't end up on various prize lists."

—*The Winnipeg Review*

"Sam's life—Boyagoda keeps us fascinated if not always sympathetic—powers the narrative ... Magical language, rhythmic

storytelling and telling gestures ... Sam Kandy's century burns very
brightly indeed."   —*Toronto Star*

"[Boyagoda] has a flair for concision ... Rags-to-riches narratives
seldom have much humbler starting points than the Ceylon village
where *Beggar's Feast*'s protagonist is born ... Against all better
judgment, the reader warms to him and his single-minded drive
to transcend his origins. He's Naipaul's Mr. Biswas as unapologetic
success rather than embittered failure, Richler's Duddy Kravitz
followed far past his apprenticeship. If you've found a place in your
heart for either of those complicated figures, make way for Sam
Kandy."   —*The Gazette* (Montreal)

"As lush as the tropical landscape of Ceylon ... The language is also
charged with vitality and allows for the emergence, from time to
time, of stark human truths."   —*National Post*

"The figure of Sam Kandy and the feverish, often hallucinatory
quality of the prose in *Beggar's Feast* suggest the influence of William
Faulkner."   —*Quill & Quire*

"One heck of a story arc ... Rollicking!"
                          —Shelagh Rogers, host of *The Next Chapter*

"Richly researched, the novel goes deep into another culture in
another era, beginning in 1899, which is a pleasure in itself. But
what gives this book its power is the character of Kandy himself.
He's not exactly likeable ... [Boyagoda] does, however, succeed in
making you care."   —*NOW* magazine

"Wonderful ... has at its heart a metaphor at least as old as the
Talmud."   —*Pique NewsMagazine*

Praise for *Governor of the Northern Province*

Longlisted for the 2006 Scotiabank Giller Prize

"*Governor of the Northern Province* is one of the funniest books ever written about federal politics in Canada ... Boyagoda's humour is astoundingly politically incorrect. With his irreverence, the author crosses lines most would dare not even approach."

—*Ottawa Citizen*

"Boyagoda's language is colourful and alliterative, and his long sentences often dance with a storyteller's rhythm. The characters and their interactions are vividly depicted with choice details ... This is a sharply intelligent novel, both entertaining and disquieting."

—*Winnipeg Free Press*

"Boyagoda's prose is exhilarating."   —*The Globe and Mail*

"[A] boisterously irreverent first novel ... Boyagoda zeroes in on various targets without slackening pace: colonialism, foreign aid, Anglo reserve and the exalted status of hockey all take stinging hits."   —*Toronto Star*

"There is real bravery in approaching such dark, emotionally charged subject matter with humour ... very funny ... the book shines with artistic certainty."   —*Literary Review of Canada*

"Like any accomplished satirist, Boyagoda has a great time with language ... his evocations of human beings ... are completely vivid, full of humour, insight and compassion. Boyagoda really is one of those writers who make you laugh and cry at the same time."

—*The Gazette* (Montreal)

"Richler's successor?"
—*Embassy*

"Scathing and unpredictable, *Governor of the Northern Province* is a novel of considerable accomplishment; Randy Boyagoda's merciless prose marks him as a talent to watch."
—Trevor Cole, author of *The Fearsome Particles* and *Norman Bray in the Performance of His Life*

PINTAIL

BEGGAR'S FEAST

Writer, critic, and scholar RANDY BOYAGODA is a professor of American Studies at Ryerson University. His writing has appeared in *The New York Times, Harper's, The Walrus, The Globe and Mail,* and the *National Post.* His debut novel, *Governor of the Northern Province,* was longlisted for the 2006 Scotiabank Giller Prize. He lives in Toronto with his wife and three daughters.

BEGGAR'S FEAST

randy boyagoda

PINTAIL

PINTAIL
a member of Penguin Group (USA)

Published by the Penguin Group
Penguin Group (Canada), 90 Eglinton Avenue East, Suite 700, Toronto, Ontario, Canada M4P 2Y3
(a division of Pearson Canada Inc.)

Penguin Group (USA) Inc., 375 Hudson Street, New York, New York 10014, U.S.A.
Penguin Books Ltd, 80 Strand, London WC2R 0RL, England
Penguin Ireland, 25 St Stephen's Green, Dublin 2, Ireland (a division of Penguin Books Ltd)
Penguin Group (Australia), 250 Camberwell Road, Camberwell, Victoria 3124, Australia
(a division of Pearson Australia Group Pty Ltd)
Penguin Books India Pvt Ltd, 11 Community Centre, Panchsheel Park, New Delhi – 110 017, India
Penguin Group (NZ), 67 Apollo Drive, Rosedale, Auckland 0632, New Zealand
(a division of Pearson New Zealand Ltd)
Penguin Books (South Africa) (Pty) Ltd, 24 Sturdee Avenue, Rosebank,
Johannesburg 2196, South Africa

Penguin Books Ltd, Registered Offices: 80 Strand, London WC2R 0RL, England

First published in Viking hardcover by Penguin Canada, a division of Pearson Canada Inc., 2011
Published in this edition, 2012

1 2 3 4 5 6 7 8 9 10 (RRD)

ISBN: 978-0-670-06658-2

Visit the Penguin US website at **www.penguin.com**

ALWAYS LEARNING   PEARSON

For Anna,
and for Mira, Olive, and Ever,
the four corners of my earth

O fool, to try to carry thyself upon thy own shoulders!
O beggar, to come to beg at thy own door!

RABINDRANATH TAGORE, "O FOOL"

part one SQUIRREL

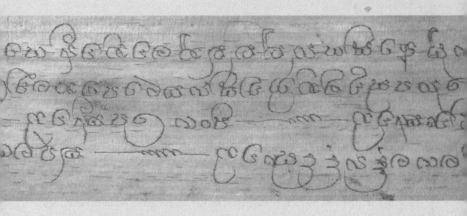

one

Chase away a little bird, putha, only a little bird. It looked more like a winged dog, waiting for him at the far side of the great green clearing. His father was standing beside the man who'd come to the hut and eaten all their lunch the day before. His mother and brothers and sisters and the new baby were also there, and one of his grandmothers, who was given a stool. She carried a little rag and always wiped her mouth before and after she spoke. The baby was crying. His father motioned him over and opened and closed his palm long enough to show him a piece of jaggery. Then he pointed at the bird and the boy ran right at it. On his eighth birthday, the crow was waiting at the same place behind the village. His father showed him two pieces and the boy ran again. As he neared, the bird lifted and jumped forward, directly at him, once more sending him glancing to the side. But this time, when he turned to face his father, he had to watch him feed his promised sweets to two of his brothers, who were jumping up and down at their sudden good fortune. He decided that would not happen again. At nine, they went to the field with a bowl of curd and treacle, and a newer baby crying, and no grandmother, and with everyone cheering he sprinted at the crow through a stretch of limp yellow grass no longer knee high. His heart lifted as the bird went off at his approach but it resettled not ten steps away. He looked to his father, who was looking to the keeper for a ruling. The boy would not wait. He ran at the bird again, who lifted over another few feet, then again, and again, and soon he was running useless figure eights across the great green clearing, his eyes burning with sweat and tears and dirt, and they were all laughing and eventually he fell and the bird, the bird actually hopped closer to him. It seemed to be considering him with its bead-black eyes, as if to say *Hard luck. See you next year*, but it was only watching his father, who knelt beside the boy, lifted his chin, and pointed at the crow. He wanted to say to him *Sorry Appachchi* but instead watched his father dump the bowl of white curd onto the dry brown ground. The bird's beak gleamed.

He'd been six-plus when the dry time had first descended on the village. Every family needed someone to blame. They took him to the astrologer's hut, which always occupied the most auspicious of the four corners of the dry dirt square where the village's two lanes met. Villagers had lately been queuing in greater numbers to see her. She asked less than the nearby temple monks and their bottomless stomachs, and besides horoscopes, she could also read palms. After first uncoiling his birth-hour scroll and showing his parents a future tattooed with empty houses and empty marriages, she took the boy by the wrist and traced the lines already creasing his small hands—hunger, poverty, rage. The boy was then sent from the hut, where he met other families' blights: a granny who peed herself while he waited, and a girl with milk-white eyes, another with a creviced lip, and also an uncle who giggled while smelling his wrists. But he had ten fingers and ten toes. He hunted snakes and could climb almost any tree his brothers could. Why was he here? Meanwhile, the astrologer told his parents that this was a son never meant to be born in the middle of a family. She said he would never give when he could take, never serve when he could be served. He should have been born first or last.

"What will he do to us?" his mother asked.

"Ruin you," she answered.

"What can be done?" his father asked.

"I'll send my husband to see you."

⁓

As was his known habit in the village, the astrologer's husband came calling just as his mother was getting the lunch—rice, a thumb-print of dried fish for his father's plate, dhal, and limp long slices of salt-and-peppered papaya and combs of finger-long plantains. Plantains were the only food the children were allowed to eat as they pleased. His father gave his plate to the visitor.

"He looks too young, I am telling you. I can't take a man's money when he has so many to care for, and at such a terrible time for everyone, no?" The crow-keeper swept his dhal-dripping hand across the reedy children, all of them watching him with mud-brown eyes.

"Doesn't matter," his father answered. "Tomorrow he is seven. We have heard of others who have chased the crow at this age. Who's to say, maybe he will too, no? At least to try, what harm?"

"Only harm is the cost."

"Which is?"

"Not payable with a plate of rice and curry."

"No, it's an honour to have you share our table. About paying, it's like this." His father bagged up his sarong between his legs. "I'd like to pay you, of course. But also, if you're interested—"

"I'm not."

"Right."

His father took him walking that evening. He couldn't think of what for, this private time together. As they passed through the village, dusk and a long day's work draining it of all colour, his father ruffled his hair, then found a piece of sweet jaggery in one of his ears and popped it into the boy's mouth. Joyfully sucking on this hard miracle, he didn't think they were eating such delights even in the great walauwa itself.

"Tomorrow, putha, do you know what day that is?"

"Appachchi," he slobbered, before shifting the sugar rock to the other side of his mouth, "another piece?"

"Soon, baba, soon. Tell me, putha, what day is tomorrow?"

"Birth day."

"And how old are you turning?"

"Se-ven." A gob of sweet spit dripped from his mouth.

"And do you know what that means? It means you must show all of us what a big boy you've become! Tomorrow in the clearing you will see a little bird, putha, only a little bird, and you must run at it like the big boy you are and chase it off. We will all be watching and cheering you. Will you do this for your Appachchi?"

"What will you give me if I chase the bird, Appachchi?"

His father nodded. A son who would never give when he could take.

When he was ten, the village was still in a very bad way. A fourth year of poor paddy: cracked mud lands, the village water tank a puddle of itself, the men broadcasting useless seed, the silo empty of all rice and grain and echoing like bellies. People were accusing each other of evil eyes and bad mouths. Jungle papers covered the tree trunks, so many that when the anonymous accusations were read, the sound was like an army walking through leaves. The astrologer was chased off and brought back, chased off and brought back. Pirith ceremonies became so commonplace that monks were yawning in the middle of their chanting against these dark days. The walauwa people, who had misfortune enough in their own history, as the old ones in the village sometimes lamented, sometimes cackled about, were made to suffer again. A rich fisherman from down south came to buy the family lands, and the servants said the Ralahami had him chased off only because the figure was too low. Then, a few months later, his wife, the pretty Hamine, died in her first childbirth: twins, a boy and girl, Arthur and Alice. The Ralahami cursed both babies.

On his tenth birthday, his father walked him over to the great green clearing wordless and empty handed. Twenty words hadn't passed between them that year. The crow-keeper approached like an old friendly devil. He took the boy close and tried to give him an avocado nut to throw at it. The keeper had grown a grand belly in recent times, which inclined him to be merciful to those he'd seen more than twice. But the boy walked straight past him. This old ugly bird, also slick and fat from years of good work, didn't even watch him coming. Only the boy didn't run this time. After hundreds of nights of plotting under the broadcast stars, the jurying heavens, he had decided that he wouldn't chase this bird into the air. He would stomp it into the ground. He would do it slowly and absolutely. The crow cleared the treetops before cawing its offence. Turning back triumphant, the boy passed the keeper calling after the bird in vain. That night the keeper left the village and was never called back. Alone, the astrologer held out for another week.

His father met him and cupped his chin. He told him that he was such a good boy. His ears burned. His father said more. He said the boy had done an auspicious thing for his family name and that it would be remembered. As they returned to tell his mother, his father said that the next morning he would get his reward. He promised that it wouldn't be more jaggery and curd, and at this they laughed together like men, and the boy almost forgot how he had wanted to grind his heel into that bird until its blue-black wings snapped. The next day, at dawn, in fresh rods of joyful rain, the half-sleeping child was bundled into a bullock cart, his head pressed against his proud father, who murmured of prizes as they went forth. Who broke no branch when they passed from the village into the world. Who, at the gates to the great temple at Kandy town, pressed down on his shoulders until he knelt and then pointed at the dry red ground in front of a smiling saffron man. And when the boy stood and looked back and called for him, it was raining and his father was gone. And so he was taken to robes and shaved to skin to begin a new life of desire and suffering, defeat and triumph, from which would come another, and another, and another, and then, at last, after one hundred years of steel and pride, fever and speed, another.

two

For the three years of his temple life, he was questioned by the other boys after evening prayer. Was it a lady's finger, drumstick, chicken bone, green bean, crab leg, crow's beak, cow's tit, dog's tail, bandicoot? Are they green gram or peppercorns, peppercorns or rambutans, rambutans or thambili, thambili or durians? He would say nothing. They decided his silence meant he actually enjoyed it. When one day he saw his teacher laughing to talk to another apprentice monk, his hand upon *that* boy's head and *that* boy smiling, he had wanted to run and fight him down to the ground. Lying upon his mat that night, black and quiet and thirteen years old, he had stomped and triumphed in his head until it was only he and his teacher again and when he woke it was with a wretched longing, such a wretched longing, and he knew then that there was nothing to do now but wait for another lesson time or once more run and fight and triumph from this life unto the next.

It rained the morning he went forth, the way it did every year in the weeks before the grand relic procession. The sky was blue like an Englishman's eyes. The sun was holy white. Water came down from unknown clouds but it cleaned nothing. It only turned the temple's red grounds darker, a bloody brown, and when the storm finished, the immediate heat warmed it. His feet smudged into that darker redness as he made his way along the stone walkway to the shady timber hall where he knew he would find his teacher alone at the hottest time of day, seated behind a pale yellow pillar scored from centuries of sudden rain. He turned his heels and wiped his soles as he climbed the old chipped steps. The boy wanted his feet stone smooth for what they had to do.

"No lessons just now, Squirrel. Sadhu is cooling," the monk said, as the boy held his breath and knelt on the rough rock floor to give respect. The monk smiled, twittering his toes. A few days after he'd been left at the temple gate, the boy heard another whispering that monks' feet smelled like tins of cheese. It was 1909 and he didn't know what a tin of cheese was, he would not ask, and in his three years of temple life, he never found out.

"Not asking for lessons, Sadhu," he said, rising. "I have come to make you a present."

"But who comes empty handed promising gifts, Squirrel?" the monk asked, resting on his elbows, knees lolling at a wide angle. Considering him. Smiling. Opening things up.

"This is my gift, Sadhu." He dropped his robe and went forward too fast for the monk to slam his knees together. After three years, he knew where to kick. He made sure Sadhu's crusty peppercorns got some of his heel too.

"Ooh sha squirrel … Ackguh … Magee Amma!"

Mother was the last word he heard as he ran down the stone steps bare-bodied save for the white cloth that hung about his waist. He cut across the grounds toward the front gate. Temple flowers lay about from the last Poya day, limp and browned. Rain was falling again, piping through white light and blue sky. Running past the royal lake, his body made a streak upon the still water. Blackbirds were perched upon the highest clutch of a sunken Mara tree. Throats pulsing, eyes black and shining, they watched him pass. When finally he had to stop for breath, he was taken for a most holy young beggar by passersby who noticed that he didn't even have a bowl to beg with. Clasping his hands and dipping his head in taught humility, he was well fed within the hour, cinched a new sarong at his knees, and barefoot went walking down the Kandy Road.

On the way to Colombo, he became a blank slate for bullock cart drivers. The nervous ones decided that he had an honest face and asked that he keep watch for thieves and monkeys. The guilty ones divined his bullet head and beggar's bowl to mean they were gaining merit for their next lives by helping a wayward young monk home to temple. The lonely ones saw their own sons in him. He didn't care, so long as they let him ride. His feet throbbed. His head ached from squinting through long hours of sunlight. Climbing into the carts, he would crawl into straw-smelling narrows where it was darkest and coolest and then stretch his legs in search of lighter air for his feet. More than once, he just moulded his body onto heaped bags of rice. There he'd sleep suddenly, deeply, until someone slapped his ankle and waking in a fragrant rage he was roughly helped down to the ground, rubbing his eyes to life, already walking again.

He took his last ride on a cart loaded with English furniture that once belonged to a planter's favoured servant, a childless hoarder now dead, whose mad passion for northern wood made his nearest relations true believers in its worth. Hoping to marry off their daughters with good dowries, the driver told him as he climbed in, they were now sending all of it to a nephew in Colombo who knew about such things. He found an armchair balanced between the upturned legs of other chairs. He pulled it free and cleared a space at the far side of the cart. From the Kandy side of Ambepussa to the nephew's address in Colombo, he watched as a new green expanded in the cart's creaking wake, a countryside milder in its rise and fall, thinner of trees, brighter in sky and more peopled than the world of home had been. He felt no urgency of what he might do when he reached the city. There were so many people there already. Colombo could take one more.

In the village, everyone always gathered whenever boys actually came home from the city. They always returned in dark trousers and collared white shirts, their arms carrying city things, their mouths too full at last of mother food to answer father questions. They brought a folded set of shirt and pants for their fathers, who either wore the gift to tatters or died before finding a worthy enough occasion. They gave bolts of fabric to their mothers and older sisters, who argued over how many saris were there. They brought bouncy balls for little brothers and yarn-headed dolls for little sisters. They never had anything for their older brothers, only sometimes a handkerchief for their wives, scented with lavender and the hope of envy. They would leave their grandmothers with foreign-stamped envelopes mailed from England itself; their mothers, with chipped china slipped out of Colombo hotel kitchens for their First-of-the-Year milk rice and with shortbread tins smelling of metal and butter—treasure boxes for old proposal letters, coiled horoscopes, morsels of wedding gold. Once, a boy brought home a framed picture of the young Queen Victoria, the cloudy glass cracked above the peak of her beak-like nose. Bugs entered through the break and took up residence along her milk-white collarbone. He remembered his brothers laughing about it. The boys who lived with the Queen heard and challenged. They had fought on the great green clearing behind the village, in a humid birdcall silence. While the others clawed and kicked, he had knelt in damp dirt, pressing his head against his enemy's knee, the bigger boy twisting his arm, burning the skin until he said *Mercy*. He'd bitten his lip until it bled instead. And if all these returning boys could come home each with so much, he knew he would be able to get enough for himself, more even. And were he ever to return to the village, he promised himself, the world, he'd return like it had never been done before.

But what would he call himself in the city? *Malli* had been enough to get from the temple gate to the city outskirts, but he did not want a new life as just another sweet little brother, just another weary smiling street-side boy born to be helpful, waiting to be helped. He had been called Ranjith at home, but no one had called him that since he had been sent to the temple, where he was formally Samanera and less formally, in the empty audience hall those dead afternoons, Squirrel. Shortly before his departure, the other boys had learned of Sadhu's pet name for him. They had used it without mercy. His teacher had told him that he would get a new name upon becoming a full monk. He would be a Sadhu then too, and his priestly surname would be the name of his birth-village. But he would never be a full monk, and he could think of no cause to honour Sudugama, and so when he was asked his name by the Colombo nephew who received the dowry furniture, he just said "Sam."

"And what's your father's good name?"

"My father doesn't have one."

"Why is that?"

"He's not good enough."

"You would disrespect your father to a complete stranger! Who is this tamarind mouth you have working in the back here?" The nephew called over the driver, who had been happy to drink a lime-juice and let Sam unload the furniture.

"He's not mine. Malli only wanted a ride to Colombo."

"What village are you from?" the nephew asked him.

"I'm here now."

"So why have you come?"

Sam jumped off the cart, head down, carrying the furniture into the stall.

"Stop this or I'll give you a thrashing. I have no money for you."

"I only want a little space."

"This is Colombo. There is no space."

"I'll help you in your work."

"And what's my work?"

"The driver says you're to sell this furniture for your family."

"And you think that's my work?" The back half of the nephew's stall was dark. He sounded amused by his own question.

"I don't care what you do for your work."

"Good. This is Colombo."

Those daughters waiting on dowry money must have died spinsters. Nothing was ever sent back to the village. The nephew, who was named Badula and went by B., sold off whatever he didn't keep for himself. B. was a street hustler businessman whose every decision was made to get more money and more mutton, as he called it. He was five or six years older, his every way and feature curved and narrow like the husk of a coconut flower, and they were more than once mistaken for brothers after Sam began trailing him around the glorious cutthroat bedlam that was Pettah. Sam Kandy's education into the world began in those bright and steamy knife-edge streets, where everyone with something to sell was the last honest man in Colombo, where the rest of the city went by tram and rickshaw to look and take what they would and escape home hoping they had not been taken for too much. Pettah stank and gleamed with spices and gold, with fruit money flesh. B. had a finger in anything he could pry open or plug. He borrowed, he lent, he fenced. He immediately liked the look and feel of Sam standing behind him as he conducted his business and so took him everywhere. More, he liked the audience the boy gave him those nights it was only the two of them in the stall, alone with its few moulding and stained pieces of once fine furniture and the mad piles of rusting kettles and crudescent frying pans that were B.'s outward concern. On such nights, B. rose and fell with remembering while they fell asleep on the dank floor. He recounted his sad life in the village as the loyal, wronged son who had had no choice but to leave. It was the same morality play every time, and it was too familiar from the first. *When I was a boy, I thought my father*

B.'s second story, his heroic flight, was Sam's reward for suffering the first. He left his village, near Dambulla, and made his way northeast to Trincomalee, where he eventually found work carrying crates of tea onto British ships. The older boys already on the job tried to scare him away. They told him about a Frenchman's ghost that had haunted the docks since before even the Dutch had come. Sometimes, they said, this bloodied sailor would sway to the sad music of two drowning sisters calling for help in vain, Tamil girls who had kept him back from his departing ship for a dance lesson, none of them knowing that their brothers were watching. But B. kept carrying the crates. One day, a few months into it, he walked up a gangplank and unloaded but this time kept walking forward, an endless banner of sea blue and blue sky stretching before him. He turned at the first quiet corner and tripped over two fellow stowaways. He suggested they move deeper into the ship. One boy whispered back that he was trying to trick them and the other motioned for him to go. Ten minutes later he heard them begging for mercy as they were thrown off. He was himself sent off at Galle, his arms bent back so far he swore his elbows actually touched for a moment.

B. spent a year in that southern city. At the rail station, he fought others as hungry and ready as he was to carry trunks for white people; on starched Sunday mornings he waited outside their fortress churches with a dirty snappy monkey that their children begged money from their fathers to play with; for two days he worked for a buffalo farmer with two pretty daughters; eventually, he ran messages for a blind Moor and his seven miserable sons. They lived and worked along Havelock Street and they always made him shake loose his clothing and curl his tongue before leaving their stalls, even the blind one did.

The next time he tried for that infinite banner of sea blue and blue sky, he was pushed down the gangplank at Colombo harbour. An old uncle helped him to his feet and said that if he tried again, he'd meet the gangplank in Negombo, or Jaffna town, then it would be Trincomalee, then Batticaloa, next Matara, then Galle, and back to Colombo. For years, the uncle whispered, the British had been sailing ships around Ceylon just so boys like them would never see the far white rim of the deep blue water. B. asked the old man how long he'd been trying and he grinned to show the number of teeth he'd had knocked out. And so B. went into the city. Two years later, once he'd taken over a kitchen-goods stall in Pettah under circumstances he never clarified, B. sent word and a biscuit tin to the village: He was presently in Colombo, where he had made a name for himself and could take care of anything.

"Including furniture," said Sam.

"That's right. Of course, you know how furniture lets me take care of my other business!"

"Other business? I thought you called it mutton."

"What Sam, didn't you see the one that came last night? Sha! She was soft as lamb."

Most days they moved around Pettah, hopping piles of bullock dung along the Saunders Place Road and making mad mirror faces at the beaming children riding inside the trams buzzing down Main Street. B. invited any woman who held his glance to come to his stall. He'd tell them to forget Don Carolis and his timber shed: if they visited B. they would see furniture that had once belonged to the Queen of England herself. The kind of women who came on such terms were also the kind of women who didn't mind that a fourteen-year-old boy was lying a few feet away. Early the next morning, after they made B. his tea, the women slipped past Sam looking sunken and sad and also ridiculous—they took dented kettles and rusted hopper pans with them to avoid scandalizing the indifferent street. When Sam officially woke up, B. would sometimes show him how he'd used the furniture the night before, how he'd propped the girl onto the peeling top of a child's dresser or had her hold a washstand's towel rack and lift her blossomy bottom. B. detailed his nightly victories out of boastful charity; he said he knew Sam could only hear, never see. But what Sam could hear was enough. He learned that chairs creaked and sometimes cracked while dresser drawers scraped and eventually shook; he learned that a woman gives a different cry at the beginning, in the middle, and at the end, and, sometimes, a while afterwards, when the only other noise is a sleeping man's innocent sawing. One night B. came over to him with a slip of a Malay girl who had hair that fell past her buttocks in a raven sheaf. B. yawned that he was too tired for a second go but Sam could have a try. The girl jiggered her eyebrows in the carried light of a bottle lamp and he felt something stir but then he felt tight and scalloped around his abdomen and the rest of him felt squeezed and knocked about and so wordless he turned over to their laughing. He fell asleep, eventually, to the girl crying, trying to annihilate memory itself.

Sam decided mutton could wait, but not money. After a year of apprenticeship, he only wanted his mentor to loan him a little so he could lend out himself. And if not a loan to start making and collecting his own, then why not give over one of the yellow-brown stone chains B. was always rubbing in his pockets? Each, as Sam discovered while listening to him conduct his business, had been given to B. by one of his many dead mothers, who had begged him on their assorted deathbeds to sell it to a good man so that any number of poor daughters could be cured buried or married. But the more successful B. became, the more Sam heard promises that he'd get his chance, and in the meantime the more devoted, grateful, and servile he was expected to be: happy to fetch packets for B.'s lunch, proud to be B.'s bucket man.

B.'s stall lost the back quarter of its roof to the southwest monsoon season of 1914 and Sam found a briny stretch of fine green netting blown off some purpose on some ship in Colombo harbour. They hung it across the rough open square that was otherwise gaping daylight. B. said that once Sam found a piece of metal sheeting to hammer into place, he could sell the green netting to whomever he pleased and keep the profits for himself. And so on a hot dead-air day, soon after the monsoon, Sam went squelching through Pettah's junk-bloated alleyways. He could find nothing to fit B.'s roof. His wasn't the only stall the storms had battered. All he came upon were drowned cats until he met a round man squatting in a waterlogged sarong, crowded in by a knee-high metropolis of pottery jugs. His hands were pattering and smacking across the tops of the jugs with the speed sweat and purpose of a tom-tom beater. *Tho tho tho tha tho* Sam began to make a wide arc around some kind of madman.

"Malli, help! They're escaping!"

"What are escaping?"

"Aiyo, all of my beauties are leaving me! Just come see will you!"

Sam swung around, expecting thugs. Such set-ups were commonplace in the backstreets of the market, but they usually involved found gold or waiting flesh. Here seemed neither.

"*Malli!* Pleasewillyoucomehelpme."

Bright colours began catching his eye. Moments later he was happier than he could remember, squatting beside the man, his hands also drumming against the escaping butterflies.

"Not so hard, please. See look, you've just crushed that Black Rajah."

"Uncle, what are you doing?"

"You mean to ask what have I been doing, by myself, since morning? Trying to keep something back of my last six months' patience." *Tho tha* drummed a tired hand in vain. "Aiyo! that was a Blue Mormon that just flew off, no?"

Sam kept drumming while the man, who was called Mahesh, stood and stretched, suddenly indifferent to the bright fleeing papers. Finally here was someone in the city who would listen! An Englishman had been walking in the green behind Mahesh's hut one day, a village down south, some six months earlier. He kept squatting, and Mahesh's mother-in-law had sent him out to see if the man might take gingelly oil to help things along. Mahesh discovered that the man was only crouching to look at butterflies. Standing up, the Englishman declared he'd buy as many living specimens as Mahesh could bring to Colombo harbour six months hence. Mahesh only exaggerated a little in retelling the story to his wife and her mother and soon the entire family was at work upon the village green, ignoring taunts about madness from neighbours while hunting butterflies for half-sovereigns. Only no one told Mahesh how far north the Yala monsoon could reach. He came to Colombo at season's cusp. The Englishmen in the city all looked the same, and none had any notion of paying money for any bloody bow-tie bugs. The bullock cart driver left him and his crates at Pettah. A potter saw and took pity and told him to wait out the monsoon season and then find his Englishman. The potter said Mahesh could even stay in his shop if he had no relations in the city. He would anyway give him enough jugs, at best price, to keep the butterflies safe from the coming rains.

"And you believed this and gave him the rest of your money and now he's sent you back to the street," Sam predicted, feeling streetwise and worldly.

"Malli, what to do? I only know to catch butterflies, not to keep them. Of course now I see I was played the fool. Aiyo half the butterflies died during the rains. I'm telling you, right now, I'd trade the rest for a good blade. If I had a good blade," he said through clenched teeth, "then that potter would know, I promise you that!"

"Truth? You mean you would—"

"Malli, can you blame a man for anything he does in this buzzard's city?"

Sam put his head down and drummed on.

Tho tho tho tho tha

three

After shifting Mahesh's stock into a clay pot apiece, the two of them came to the stall, where Sam asked B. to let him barter for the butterflies. Wordless, B. disappeared into a corner and returned dragging an oak chair by its lion paws. He grandly arranged himself to watch Sam conduct his business, a yawning bored king bemused by his own generosity.

Meanwhile, Mahesh was happy to forsake his muttering for a knife when he saw B.'s piles of kettles and pans. He marvelled at the picture of himself returning to the village, his back made into a shiny metal shell of shiny city things. Sam could tell. He would have been thinking the same, had he a village and family worth the thought. Instead he observed to Mahesh how good it would be, getting down from the cart in front of his house, Colombo-returned with the finest and latest Pettah goods for every woman in his family. Sam said he'd even help Mahesh wipe off the sludge of other people's cooking. And before he left Colombo swearing never to return, Mahesh helped Sam stretch the green mesh netting tight across the stall's monsoon hole to let in light enough to keep the butterflies confined and lively. The leftover mesh was cut and doubled to make a curtain that closed off enough space for four people. B. told Sam to send in six at a time. And so he began to keep a butterfly hall in the back of B.'s stall, making money from city people who had forgotten the village wonder of pretty little papers fluttering in greened light. B. was happy with the arrangement. Sam cared for the butterflies and organized the queues and took the money. This left B. at liberty to visit in the queue itself, where he set the occasional loan and bought and sold and made so many pretty new friends he no longer had to bark along the Saunders Place Road. He was happier still with the returns. He told Sam that they would divide the profits between them, the money "as evenly parted as my Achchi's hair" he vowed the first time he told Sam to hand over the day's take for safekeeping. A long week later, when Sam asked for his share—he lied that he wanted to take his first shave at the Chetty barber's stall up the lane—B. dropped coins in his hand. So few Sam could close his fist around them.

"As agreed. Exactly half," B. said.

"Half," Sam said. He collected this many coins on a Saturday morning. He wiped sudden sweat back into his scalp, pulling his fingers dry through his proud black thatch.

"Yes. This is half," B. said. "Mokatha?"

"How is this half?" Sam demanded, but his voice was hard like a tapped coconut is hard.

"This is half, Sam, after your expenses."

He said nothing. Expenses. He left the stall, B.'s stall, B.'s stall full of B.'s things, things that were stolen, broken, bartered, chipped, rusted and crusted in brown bits and yellow oil, and all his.

He kept giving over money and getting back fistfuls of coins but he wouldn't try what everything—what memory, body, prospects, hunger, justice—wanted him to do, which soon became what

B. himself wanted as well. To drop the money and settle things as men would, not like the perfect parted middle of a granny's hair, but as men would. Sam could feel B.'s regard lowering each time he took the coins without comment, but B. was older, stronger, longer in Pettah than Sam was, and B. was spoiling for it. Why? The butterflies were a greater moneymaker than anything else B. had going, and they were getting him more mutton than ever. He'd lately started to take his women behind the green curtain at night. "Private viewings." He would hold a lantern to show them the butterflies fixed on whatever snapped tree life Sam had been able to find that day. And so at night Sam fell asleep to the sounds of women sucking in their breath at discovered beauty or shrieking, then laughing, at what was suddenly touching them. In the mornings, after they glanced past him with their useless kettles, Sam would go into the hall before the first paying people knocked. He'd rearrange the dragged-down branches and sweep the floor with the hard soles of his feet, so many butterflies dead among the dead leaves.

"If you keep doing this, soon we'll have none," he warned one morning.

"Doing what?" asked B.

"You know."

"Right … and still you don't."

"Every night," Sam continued, ignoring the taunt, the churn it could still give him, "so many die when you go in there with your mutton."

"So?"

"So? So who's going to pay to see a butterfly hall without any butterflies?"

B. shrugged and turned away.

"So then no money, and how will you get your mutton?"

B. switched around and walked straight toward him. Sam took a step back, his legs tight and trilling. Monks lay down and crows hopped away. City men came right at you. But B. stopped short and jabbed a finger at his chest.

"Remember, malli, I was getting money and mutton long before you and your green net and your butterflies, and I'll be getting money and mutton long after you and them are gone."

Sam said nothing.

"More mutton even. Truth! There, I hear someone tapping. Go and see. I'm piss heavy." He grabbed himself and turned around. Before he slipped out to the alley, he called back "Even more money."

Sam began to leave when the women arrived. He learned that Pettah at night was lonely and feral. Cooking fires burned every few stalls but these were always private affairs—a shared cup for pot arrack and palms passing beedis and betel. People had a way of arranging themselves when a stranger lingered at heard laughter. Or they would stare back dumb, glare past, glare until he passed. Sam also tried to join a few streetlight sessions of rajay with boys who looked more his age, even retrieving the rattan ball once, in vain. And so he became but another wanderer in the nighttime city, his act of head down deliberate paces abandoned once he accepted that no one else was even watching, let alone believing, that he among all of them had somewhere to go. But he refused to stand around like the others, wearing mournful twilit faces, leaning against dirty walls, waiting either for something, anything to happen, or for sleep to lower them to their haunches, bottom, back. These were drowsy despairing people he'd never be like, people made lazy at life by pickling themselves in pity. He'd seen them before—in the village, fathers given no sons by their wives, only dowries; in the temple, monks sore with bad heels, creased and cracked and lined up the morning of the long last walking day of a relic procession. But Sam kept moving, thinking about where he could take his butterflies, or where he could go and leave them and their owner. Sometimes he thought about what he couldn't be blamed for doing, a man alone in a buzzard's city like this. Eventually, he decided these nightly walks were in search of a good blade.

The last night he returned to the stall, Sam heard no B. and no woman. Instead, he found an overturned chair with a butterfly perched on a spindle. In the lamplight its wings were a pattern of copper and yellow bands. Past the chair, gathered on the ground, were two black clumps. Rats? He leaned to look, ready to bring his heel down. One was a palm-sized heap of wavy man locks, the other a coil of longer, more delicate strands. Around the hair, the dry dirt floor was a scored record of sudden movement, jagged finger gashes and swirled scuff marks. Whoever it was, whether an angry husband and his brothers or someone B. owed or someone who owed B., had dragged both of them toward the butterflies. He found two more clumps of hair in the ruined hall. Looking up in vain for more butterflies, and turning around in the little space, he suddenly curled his toes. The ground was mucked. It hadn't rained that night. The dead smell of old earth mixed with the iron tang of blood. He held his finger to the light. The tip was covered in a smudge of ground turned reddish brown, and he knew it was from raging life not rain. Only then did he think to turn and make sure he was alone. The double-folded green mesh curtain was gone. Whoever it was, Sam thought, had wrapped B. and the woman in the curtain and taken them away, living or dead. He searched for B.'s stash of money, his money. Instead he caught the last butterfly, righted the chair, and sat down. He decided they must have thrown B.'s body into the harbour. He hoped that B. would someday find his snowfall beyond the blue sea. He hoped that B. would sink and hook onto the anchor of an English ship and be dragged around the island forever. Yawning, Sam looked around the stall a final time before he walked into the bruised blue light of morning in the city, and disappeared.

He curled his tongue and shook out his clothes and asked again.

"Can I go to the harbour and see? I will come back straight away."

"Another boy will ask for your job the moment you leave," Ismail warned.

"You'll keep it for me."

"Ha! Why should I?"

"Who else knows all the village tricks they use on you?" Sam asked. One day, three years after he left B.'s stall, he had passed by the back of a spice shop just as someone was trying to sell the merchant a sack of useless cardamom. The seeds were already out of their pods; the seller must have rubbed a little fresh-ground cardamom into the top layers to hide their failing savour. He had intervened, explained, and the merchant chased the cardamom cheat off. Afterwards, this Ismail told Sam he had centuries of trading in his blood but only decades of selling spice. He took Sam on and let him sleep in the back of the shop instead of the dog he used to keep there. Every night, Sam breathed a pungent smell of burlap and dog's body, piss and spice. He woke only ready to leave the stall and breathe in the first-of-the-day, the seablown air of the city before it combusted into business.

"Do you really have to go and see right now? You know they load elephants onto ships every week at the harbour. See how you're squinting! It's almost noontime sun. There's a sack of peppercorns that needs drying."

"They're taking a tusker on board this time."

"What, just one?"

Sam knew Ismail would try to keep him around with something like that, just as he knew to curl his tongue and shake out his clothes every time he left the spice shop. Sam never told anyone what he did in the time between keeping a butterfly hall and minding spices, only that he remained in Pettah, sixteen and seventeen and eighteen, and in Pettah back then you could always find something to eat so long as you had teeth for bones and a taste for marrow. His new boss was first-person proud of his family's centuries in Ceylon. A few years before he met Sam, Ismail had been beaten to blood and mush by a crowd of Sinhalese men who were running riot against the plague of Coast Moors that had lately come onto the island. Between the blows, Ismail had told the men he hated these new moneychanger Moors as much as they did, that his family had been here as long as any of theirs, longer even, but this last point had made it worse.

But by 1918, the latest Ismail was ten centuries of first-person story, hearsay, memory, and legend. When Sam said two Chinamen had been hanged by the stolen silks they were peddling in Pettah, Ismail spoke of the very first man of his family, a silk merchant who'd escaped Canton in 878 after a new rebel king ordered his subjects to show their loyalty by slaughtering the city's foreigners. That first Ismail had played dead along the way to the harbour, lying in piles of Jews and Christians and Persians. By nightfall, he reached a ship that sailed him to Ceylon, his skin, hair, and clothes soaked with the spent lives of the cosmopolitan dead. When Sam told of a drunken gem trader from Ratnapura who was said to have demanded an entire floor of the Grand Oriental Hotel, hammering on the gilded registry book with a dirty ruby the size of a barbet's belly, Ismail shrugged. "I watched the last king of Kandy weep at his billiards table, shooting ivory balls made from his finest tusker." Another time, Sam described how all of York Street had stopped after three English daughters pulled the tortoiseshell clips from their hair. Ismail snorted. "I have seen twin sisters hang bats from their braids." Sam snorted back. He was from the village. He'd seen his share of bats and long braids. Ismail didn't like that. Sam soon learned to compete only so much with the man who pays you.

"Just lay out the peppercorns and then you can go see your tuskers loaded onto a ship," Ismail allowed, finally. "How many was it again?"

"One."

"Ah, right. You know the Portuguese paraded elephants through Jaffna harbour."

"Once in Kandy they—"

"Head down and spread pepper, Sam, and listen. Then tell me if you still want to see them take your one tusker onto a ship." Sam hauled a burlap sack past the shop's back awning into the nearly noontime sun. He put newspaper sheets onto their drying table, a flat square of shimmery metal they'd mounted onto the cracked base of a pedestal sink some Mount Lavinia Burgher had rubbished.

"Their empty ships would come to Jaffna down from Coromandel," Ismail began, standing in the shade behind Sam as he worked. "We would watch from Point Pedro. The converts among us tried to teach the faith. They said the Portuguese never sank because they sailed the world by the cross. Three masts approaching meant salvation for all, devils and angels alike. What madness. A week later, the ships would leave for Malabar and then on to Portugal, the masts half-fallen from the heavy holds. Christ and his two thieves listing. Now the time I am remembering, I was keeping a shop in Jaffna, near the harbour, and the Portuguese wanted to celebrate a new rebel king, Braganza. From Lisbon the order came for an elephant parade. The ships were to take as many as they could. I closed the shop and went to watch. The last to leave already had tea and spices and king coconut, and it also had to take a mother, a baby, and one, two, *three* tuskers. Did you hear me, Sam? Three. The Portuguese dismissed the mahouts for warning that this was too many, and also for saying that the baby should be with its mother. And so the mahouts walked off the ship into the crowd, making predictions like aunties at an ill-starred wedding.

"The three tuskers and the mother were driven into the hold. The baby was kept on the deck. The ship needed a blessing before it raised anchor, so one of their priests came forward. Even from the shore you could hear the elephants below deck muttering and snuffling through the low slow priestspeech. Finished his prayer, the priest began to throw his water. The sailors knelt and crossed themselves, and then he turned and threw water at the shore and some of us knelt and most of us ducked. Then he began to shake smoke in all directions. Some fool decided the heathen baby should get it before going to the new king. The baby pulled back, more sailors joined to push, and the baby cried out. The priest kept shaking the smoke and she cried again and then, Sam, then the mother answered. Believe it. There was yelling below deck and then a man howling and then the first tusker came up, followed by the others. These poor fellows weren't charging. They were making way. The mother came last, trumpeting and shaking her ears and swinging her trunk along the ship's planks. Everyone ran from the baby and a gun went off but these were now Braganza's elephants so the shooting could only be overhead. The priest tried to run down the gangplank but fell into the water, his chain and ball of smoke too.

"As for the rest of them, those who weren't thrown or trampled crossed themselves and jumped. The ship began to sink, the elephants playing hell along the busted deck. Afterwards, the landside Portuguese called for all pearl divers to come forward, and everyone else went home to tell what had happened and to burn their own incense and hold their own babies. Bodies washed up for days: sailors, elephants, the priest, all covered in seagreens and tealeaves. At night, poor men and thieves came to hack ivory and search for gold and shoes. Someone found a mahout's hook and I traded a bridal sari's worth of silk for it."

Sam still remembered the especially fine elephant hook he'd seen the year before he'd run away from the temple: clean silver, forged with a filigreed handle and a lotus flower hilt, intended only for the ear of the caparisoned tusker who carried the Buddha's tooth in the great relic procession around Kandy town. "You still have it?" he asked, looking up from the pepper.

"Son to son it was passed down," Ismail explained, "until the family split after a 1700s Ismail took a second woman and the first wife demanded it be kept for her son. I have never seen it directly. I came down, first born, but from the second line." Ismail's words fell to bits. The mean exposures of memory. But there wasn't much time. These days they didn't board a tusker so often. This had to be his chance. Sam clapped his hands dry, curled his tongue and shook out his clothes.

"Pepper's finished. Can I go and come?" he asked, then smiled and crooked his head, very like a beggar, and Ismail found centuries of pity for this poor Pettah boy's notion of spectacle. Yes, he could go see his one tusker, but he had to come back in time to turn the pepper. Sam yawned to hide his smile and went. For him tuskers were no greater sight than bats and braids or butterflies. He'd seen enough of them in his life before the city, and by now he'd seen enough of the city itself that he wanted to see only one last part of it: Colombo harbour at midday. Departure time.

four

Before boarding, Sam glanced at the brown buzzing wet spot where the original boy still lay. To his city eyes just another Colombo beauty mark, only no butterflies drying in this blood. Besides, nothing mattered but the heart-ramming prospect before him, certainly not the four village boys already on the great ship, who were glaring at his approach. His fingers still pungent with Ismail's pepper, his ears ringing with his stories, he gave "Sam Kandy" as his full name when the shipping agent asked. He probably could have said George Buckingham without query. It was now past noon and the agent had been up since well before dawn. All he wanted was to watch the yellow-grey mooring ropes fall slack against the ship's hull so he could walk back to his office, hang a sarong across the harbourside window, and sleep until nightfall. Sam was the first boy to come forward and actually stay there when, red-eyed and yawning, the agent called for a volunteer to replace the boy just trampled. He knew he'd catch hell for sending four attendants with the two elephants instead of the five stipulated on the zoo's bill of lading. The white rage for official reality. Ten minutes earlier, one of the boys, stupid fellow, poor fellow, had been standing directly behind the bull when it decided against trying the wide ramp onto the ship. The boy's chest had cracked in the span of a shocked last gasp before a mahout took hold of the elephant by the ear and led it back to the ramp. The bull stepped around the crumpled body like a dainty lady avoiding a mud puddle, its tail swishing at heat and all the greenflies gathering in its wake, their own bodies flashing in the noonlight like a shattered gemstone tossed up in the heavy harbour air that would be Sam's last breath of Ceylon for ten years.

He didn't know how many days had passed when next he saw daylight. They raised and lowered the food and waste buckets before dawn and again at night. And below deck on a ship never meant to sail around Ceylon forever, a ship with so many chimneys and strolling gentlemen it could have been London itself, a ship large enough to carry elephants, time did not slow so much as absent itself. He could tell durance only from his palms, from the sharpness of his fingernails each time he made a fist in vain. Down here, in the hold, it was four against one. The original five boys were from the same village, near the thorn forest where the elephants had been corralled. Tissa had been their leader, their schemer, their storyteller and go-between with grown-ups and white people as they made their way to the city. The great ship was supposed to be next, for all five of them. Instead they had this black-eyed city boy, whose body they made their record of fate's ill treatment while they waited each day for someone to open the hatch and let them out for some time above deck. Sam would begin to climb in their rising, swaying shadows, his chest expanding at these sudden miracles of fresh air, and he would breathe in deeply, greedily, whatever made it past the bodies ahead of him, grateful for anything other than the sweet retched odours of straw and dung and blackened plantains, of animals in close quarters and buckets of their own waste that never even sloshed about—at least that would have meant some movement upon the water.

"I thought you were five down there," he heard a sailor call out just as one of the four, this time Mahinda, jabbed his heel against Sam's fingers. He slipped back down, the thud of the hatch besting the thud of his body. The cow in her pen snuffled and returned to eating. The bull watched him with black eyes.

"Want to trample someone else for me?" Sam asked, getting to his feet once more in the funky blackness, his fingernails digging into his palms. While the others were above, he had to squat in low light and elephant dung, his eyes watering, his face wincing as he worked. The other boys in the hold gave him all the lowest jobs. The beatings were worse if ever they returned and he hadn't already cleared the dung. Enough. He'd be beaten for what he was considering, but he'd be beaten anyway when they climbed back down, windwashed and maybe this time with news of green on the horizon, a destination, not that it mattered. Besides curses and threats, none would speak to him. But, he decided, at least he could do something worthy of the next beating. So Sam felt about in the dark for the heavy egg shapes and broke them and smeared elephant dung on the iron rungs of the ladder. He felt around for more fresh patties and scattered the musky crumble in their sleeping corners, and then did likewise in his own corner for when they tried to sleep there instead. So that at his doing they were all homeless, and all their hands would smell the same, and when the four of them realized what he'd done, understood the hard symmetry of such vengeance, they began to give way. By Sydney they were Sam's boys.

After they were counted alongside the elephants and watched the animals be led away by local men in helmet-looking hats—as if those could save you when the bull decided to turn back to the ship!—the boys were told they had forty-eight hours in Sydney. They were shown to the warehouse where they would be given food and cots in the meantime, provided they gave the name of their ship. They'd smiled and nodded at these instructions and the white man overseeing their stay smiled and nodded back and, as he always did with such boys, reminded them again of when they were to present themselves for the return journey and, as he always did, wished them well knowing he'd never see any of them again. By 1920 Circular Quay was spotted with a hundred brown shades—deckhands, galley grunts, elephant minders, body-servants—young men from all the brown bits of the world carried to and from Sydney harbour on the great ships. And whenever the constables would question them, the boys would make a great show of their unfortunate situation, pantomiming that they were only waiting to leave on the very next ship, their faces grimacing to suggest the hardship of living hundreds of miles away from their fathers and mothers, a hardship of laying about the docks smoking and laughing and sighting parasols twirling to and from the stout ferries. The constables, who were round and thick as barrel and sounded like Englishmen with cows' tongues, would give one or two a crack as warning to the rest to be gone the morrow. When they returned a few days later, everyone knew to look at them with fresh eyes and blank faces, one or two hiding bruises.

The four of them, Mahinda, Mohan, Fat Mohan, and Viresh, assumed Sam was from Colombo—only a city boy could be so strange and bold, proud and profane, as to be called Sam Kandy. He never told them otherwise, and it was he who decided how they would move about Sydney, this skyward puzzle of endless brick and squinting white faces brimmed in black hats. So far, they had left the dock area exactly twice. Both times, the others close behind him in single file, their throats exposed in wonder, Sam had moved with wary Pettah swagger into the busy city, trying not to flinch every few minutes when the world would change from darkness to light and back again at the intersections along Pitt Street. The first time he turned them around, he did it for fear the road they were walking was a world-without-end of looming shadow. Searching ahead, Sam could only see more of the same: broad-faced buildings peaked in a cold recurrence of turrets and clock-faces and steeples, the occasional sceptre-wielding stone queen or sea-goddess borne aloft by petrified knights and mermen. He looked back at the others and shrugged, stretched, yawned, observing they had already seen as much of Sydney as there was, the rest was repetition. The others yawned and stretched and agreed as one and returned to Circular Quay along the same route, only lighter in their steps, their heads more level, feeling like conquerors.

The second time they went into the city, moving again along Pitt Street because they already knew they knew it, they brought with them a coffee-coloured boy with almond-shaped eyes who was younger than even his caterpillar moustache suggested, who would not tell them his name or the name of his island just in case any of these people were in contact with his parents. Mahinda and the other three enjoyed the new boy's company—seeing his exposed throat as he looked up and around immediately made them more experienced, disenchanted. Meanwhile Sam had decided that this time they would turn onto another street, only why this one and that way instead of the next and the other? He never had to decide. You couldn't tell coming clouds from building shadows in this place, and suddenly it was raining fat brown splats. Right away the sixth boy turned back to the harbour and ran, bouncing through the crowd. He looked like a dancing candle disappearing in some nighttime game in the forest. They never saw him again. They were all wearing white cotton, which, soaked through against their bodies, felt like failing bandages. Fat Mohan called ahead to him and pointed to the overhang in front of a hotel where others, where Sydney people, had already gathered. Sam walked toward them, the others following. Toward black shoes and black suits and black vests and black hats all made slick with rain. Toward standing shoulders, broad and square, arranged like statuary and waiting with staring right back at you, too many ever to be scared off or stomped through and suddenly he stopped short, turned and said they'd walked through worse during monsoons back home, so the five stalked back through the rain-sheeted street, droopy tallow too proud and waterlogged to run.

Of various necessities, Circular Quay became their known world. When the ferries on the far-side docks stopped for the day and they could no longer look for parasols and it was too dark for another game of ball, they spoke of their longing for home things, for things that were true green and red, for the shade of trees not buildings, for piles of blush mangoes, for getting the seed to yourself, for the street theatre of rickshaw drivers and cart-men arguing over who was taking up too much road, their necks wrenched at sharper and sharper angles, their curses trailing off in opposite directions. Of course this was longing without end: no one actually wanted to go home to Ceylon. They had discovered that they could live here, in a harbourside Sydney warehouse, until they died toothless old men. They just had to keep their heads down and ears pricked for the ship name the fellow in front of them used in the queues for food and cots. Poor math and bad eyes helped. The men who worked the massive steaming pots were often the same men who pointed the ship-hands to open cots, and they never raised a fuss that the *Sinjin Sailor* seemed to be carrying seventeen little brown men at the lunch hour and seventy-five by dinner. Not a bad life, but Sam and the others were getting notions. You don't come this far in a dark stink beside two elephants, for daily servings of carroty broth and bony bread, for cots that were never but already body-warm and scalp-smelling. The five of them talked up taking a ferry across to the other side of Sydney; they talked up trying Pitt Street again and this time entering one of the stores whose windows were grand new worlds unto themselves, going in perhaps for a pocket-watch or a razor; they talked up the brass foot-rails they'd catch flashes of when the door to a pub would open, which gleamed like holy charms cut from the necks of devout giants. And they began to talk up money, because they had come to understand, not just Sam but all of them, that in a place like this you couldn't ride a notion across the water, you couldn't marvel at its intricacy or weigh it in your palm, you couldn't sip it to waste away an afternoon in a dark murmuring room. Of course they knew how they *could* make money: ships departed daily from Circular Quay, always looking for boys like them to carry and load, to cook, to clean captain's quarters and messes and heads. It was also known that there were paying men, Sydney men, once every now and then even a barrel, who came around the warehouse at the weird hours of night, hats tipped low in low light, pockets full of coin and longing. Sam and the others had witnessed brown boys taken off by both situations—often one was fast followed by the other—and they had agreed that they wouldn't leave this place as servants on a ship, or see more of it by serving any white-bellied nighttime needs. They were in agreement but one time Viresh only wanted to point out that—"That nothing!" Sam cut him off, suddenly vehement and seething. "We're not going to see the world by filling our hands with other people's filth."

Money came, eventually, unexpectedly, after they began to win crowds to their afternoon sessions with the rattan ball. All of them had played the game in the village, and during his nighttime strolls in Colombo, while B. had been busy butchering in his butterfly hall, Sam had also seen boys playing it in the mothy streetlight around Slave Island, everyone too focused to notice a new boy standing at the perimeter hoping for a try, just a touch, looking even for a chance to retrieve an errant throw or dropped ball and be nodded at, if not with invitation or gratitude, then at least with acknowledgement that the ball hadn't floated back to the circle of its own volition but been returned by someone. Someone. But that had been Colombo. Here, in Circular Quay, on the pebbly ground beside their warehouse, Sam not only played, he was in charge. He sent the ball skyward for each in the circle, who then vied to keep it aloft in a competing, scaling show of body music and muscle.

They played with a boy from Java whose ball it was until he left it behind, and occasionally with others who knew the game from their own islands under eccentrically different names. They sent the ball back and forth to him with taps, kicks, elbows, with bounces from the head, hailing and fanning forearms. As each round intensified and more watching white faces ringed their circle, each boy had to top the other until a ball went wide or fell to the ground or, the best times, one of them worked up too fine a combination to be beat and the others knew it and clapped and gave way: as when Sam once threw the ball for Viresh, who took it on one knee and shifted it to the other, then let it drop and drop, nearly to the ground, until a shin kick sent it high enough for a devil-dancer-fast body twirl before the other shin sent it this time waist high for a smiling half-turn finale, a dismissive jolt from the elbow finished with a casual stroll away from the circle, Viresh smiling victory at the crowd, the ball arcing fast and perfectly back to Sam and the others giving a cheer before crouching ready, desperate to beat him on the next throw.

But Viresh always won the most cheers from the other players, and also from their audience and, the time everything changed, he won a florin from someone in the crowd. Studying the sudden silver in his hot palm, he grinned as he flashed it at the others and they all knew it. They had their game. Their sessions now ended not from fatigue or failing light, but always with a dramatic flourish from Viresh followed fast by Sam circulating through the crowd in taught and recalled humility, carrying a battered bowler hat as his beggar's bowl. But the ferry ride to North Sydney was a constant sea-spray and barricade of parasols and fathers, husbands, brothers, suitors, and sons. Their time sipping a pint in the pub was no better. They'd crowded around one open spot at the bar, each trying to get a foot on the rail, their legs raised and shaking forward in a slow, insistent rhythm, shy and smiling like damsel dancers at a village pageant. But around them the other drinkers only squinted and snickered and planned their own prizes. The boys drank bitter and fast and left.

When lining the beggar's hat with spare change was no longer enough for them, Fat Mohan, unanimously the worst player, was chosen for the main role in their new con. He would take a throw from Sam and begin bouncing the ball backward until he fell into the crowd itself, which, with the static intelligence of crowds, didn't make way as he neared but held fast, trusting the notion that he wouldn't actually break the invisible barrier between watched and watcher. But he always did, on one occasion tumbling into a round man with thick red sideburns that had grown to half-moons upon his fat cheeks. Who called out "God and his angels!" as he fell back, Fat Mohan landing on top of him crying "Magee Amma!" and rolling like a pestle on a mortar until Sam came and shoved Mohan and helped the gentleman to his feet, dusting off his coat and making sure he hadn't dropped anything and meanwhile the other boys and spectators crowded in with apologies and concerned noises and offers to call doctors wives and constables, all of it making the mark the more embarrassed of having been so felled and so just to show there were no hard feelings before he walked away never to sight brown boys at their game again, he gave Mohan a florin. Having already given up his pocket-watch.

Within a few weeks they each had one, and then they wanted

more, they needed something else to try for, some other shiny gimcrack to let them believe that they had become conquerors in their new world, not its cowards, that their long days about the docks were days of daring, were days desired more than anything or anyone you could find on open water or down Sydney's canyoned streets. But what? Anxious, agitated, demanding, they looked to Sam, who looked away, not because he didn't know what they should do next, but because why was everything now *they*? Sydney was his latest shadow life, and it had to yield more than shadow because he didn't know what that might mean yet. Not with four others to think of, to worry him with their wanting. But what? He ignored the latest question and Mahinda snapped shut the bright copper halves of a shipping agent's watch and declared it was time to go for their billfolds.

"But a billfold is not simply clipped to a vest," warned Sam.

"You're scared to try? Tissa would have done it," challenged Mahinda, who wasn't looking at him but at the other boys' answering faces, their agreeing nods. *Dung smear squirrel courage*

"Right," said Sam. "You throw." A day later, when Fat Mohan missed the ball and fell and began to pestle and cry out, Mahinda ran over and reached in to help a man in a yellow hat to his feet. Sam waited until just after he saw Mahinda's fingers pulling away a triumphant thickness from the man's vest before he turned Mahinda around and hit him hard in the stomach. Sam picked up the billfold and the man in the yellow hat tapped around inside his coat, then with a black boot gave Mahinda a second to the stomach. Stepping over the curled, cursing boy, the man nodded at Sam. He handed over the money, already wondering if the other boys would catch him before he could jump the next ship out of Circular Quay. But the man in the yellow hat was still staring at him. He pointed at a windowed building beyond the warehouse and walked off. Sam followed.

five

A year later, he slipped climbing the staircase to his new room. His feet had been made modern: they were bound and fine-looking and useless, shod in black leather shoes that were unyielding hard. James Astrobe, the man in the yellow hat, was ahead of him, smoking, his hands free. Sam tried to brace himself against the wall but his nervous hands slid and smeared and he slipped again, pitching forward. Immediately he crouched to make it seem like he was looking between the steps. Astrobe took no notice. Meanwhile, balling his toes in vain, Sam stared down at a world of dark hard wood and yellow lamplight, a world of long windows that rippled their streetscape pictures and rattled in the wind, of muffled voices waiting behind heavy-looking doors that Astrobe hadn't opened and showed him as they'd gone through the grand house of gleaming silver things—knobs and switches on walls, thin knives and little spoons and little mugs arranged on mirrored trays, bells, a clasped book cover, a heavy-looking brush: all of it looking as if washed in silver itself. His hands had touched nothing as he followed Astrobe, but the very idea of it had made them warm and wet like a clam cracked open by a gull and left on a shore rock. They were still damp when to stand up and keep climbing he pressed off the wall, which was itself firm and cold to touch, not home cold, not the earth-smelling soft dampness of the dung-walled house where once he'd been a boy, and not temple cold, not like the shaded stone floor of the audience hall where Sadhu liked to cool his parts, but a cold that was no respite from the world without: late June in Sydney, wintertime. It had already turned black night and hard air when it was time to shut the office for the day and, for the first time, walk home with Astrobe in winds spun up from the great curving bays that ringed the city.

The room at the top of the stairs was an octagon of shuddering windowpanes. It would be weeks before these became sleeping noises for him, by which point he wasn't sleeping anyway. This was to be his graduation from the pallet in Astrobe's Circular Quay office, where he'd been sleeping since that afternoon, a year before, when he'd broken with Mahinda and the others. He may or may not have seen them since: there were always so many brown boys hanging around the harbour, huddled, bruised, staring. Too timid to try anything else. Astrobe motioned for him to come nearer the glass and then he showed Sam the nighttime city. Below them stretching in every direction was a great electrified blackness. Following Astrobe's hand as it pointed past the fine houses of Potts Point, Sam saw broken successions of small blazing squares, where still some office men were working, and also bright clusters and isolated drops, the streetlamps and evening lamps that marked the walkways and warehouses and moored ships of Circular Quay. Sam tapped a finger against the glass. Astrobe tapped just above the faint smudge he'd made and Sam nodded. The office. The tour continued in a gesturing silence. Both of them generally preferred it that way. After a year of acting as James Astrobe's valet shadow and protector against others like himself, Sam had gained a rudimentary sort of English that was daily improving from his errand- and message-running through the city he now knew better than Colombo, but they rarely used English between them. They had been, from the start, so swift and natural with gesture they were loath to give it up, especially when the other way involved the indignities of learning to share a language: the slow long mouths, the patient restatements, the endless reductions from sentence to phrase, from the name for something to the separate sounds that made the name—an ugly primate mimicry.

Astrobe turned on a desk lamp and the starry city disappeared. He stood next to a portrait hanging behind his desk, his back flat against the wall. It was broadsheet-sized and set in a thick frame that was itself a carved busyness of laurel leaves and fruit-studded vines and each sharp corner a crowded garden of blooming flowers and all of it gilded. Looking at Sam with a smile, Astrobe made a face that monkeyed the stern one beside him. He could be this way when it was only the two of them in the office—brothers making faces under father's nose. Sam smiled. He had already decided he would not wonder why Astrobe wanted to be like this with him, this acting like twin mallis though age money and skin said otherwise. He would not wonder because this past year nothing, nothing of his old squirrel life, had happened to make him kick out and run. But he also decided that when he was the one with a young man smiling to serve at his side—and, after a year of watching James Astrobe run a shipping business out of Sydney harbour, Sam knew that somehow, somewhere, he would make this his work as well—he wouldn't ever be so free and friendly and monkeying, wouldn't ever let such a person as he was now feel the pride of place and secret power that he had come to have with Astrobe. Sam liked him, but it was in the way, in the village, you liked an older boy willing to race you along the banks of the paddy fields and at the same time knew to your bones that he was beneath you for doing it.

He stepped closer to study the portrait, his heavy shoes making a rackety footfall against the wooden floors. The face looked about the same age as Astrobe's and was, like his, white as coconut pulp. And the man was also wearing a yellow hat. The resemblance seemed to end there. The hair in the painting was lighter, a reddish orange like the colour of shaved cinnamon trees, regenerate lives. And everything in the face itself looked stouter, rounder, the eyes, nose, the full lips, which were pursed, as if their owner were trying not to laugh at something the painter just said.

"This," Astrobe said, stepping forward, his hand reaching back in a gesture of a formal introduction, "is the late Martin Astrobe, my great-grandfather, as he was painted a hundred-odd years ago, by his wife, when he was a rising gentleman in Rose Hill. Looks like a proper Englishman, don't he?"

Sam said nothing. He stared at the round eyes staring back at his, daggers daring him to disagree.

"But can you guess his secret?" Astrobe asked.

"I cannot say," said Sam, which he thought the greater justice.

"But do you want to know?" asked Astrobe.

"No."

"Not even why the men in my family have always worn yellow hats?"

"No."

"Well then, there's nothing left but for you to meet the rest of us," said Astrobe, a little defeated.

They descended, this time Sam first, the windowpanes warbling behind them. He had wanted to say there was no need to meet anyone. He had already decided he would not stay here a second night, sleeping beneath that portrait's secret gaze, sleeping above what particular secrets of sadness and rage and wrongs were this family's. Which weren't his, weren't anything he wanted to be touched by. For more than symmetry's sake, Sam Kandy would take a man as he asked the world to take him.

⌒

He heard the piano before he entered. And when he went in, something tore open he did not know had been there, something that had been waiting all these years to be torn open. She was turned away from him, concentrating on the playing, as seemed everyone else in the room, which had windows taller than any man he'd ever known and drapes that looked finer than even the finest finery he had watched from Galle Face Parade on Sunday mornings, when it had been English wives walking into Christ Church, their laced throats arching in wonder at the long shadow of the new bell tower. He had to do something else with his eyes and so he inventoried the rest of the room. Heavy chairs, heavy lamps, a large patterned carpet, the cluster of flowers at its centre made yellow beneath a light that looked like a giant drop of perfect water. There was a big black dog sleeping in a corner, on its own carpet, a carpet that was thicker than his father's sleeping mat. A fire was burning at the back of a deep stone square, above it a mantel made of the same grey stone, another promenade for their shiny silver things.

"Everyone, please," said Astrobe. He had talked over her playing! Sam wanted to hate him for it, wanted nothing from the world but to remain in the moment that had just passed, to wither away witnessing the sound and shape of her and her music. But she stopped playing and everyone turned at Astrobe's words—an older woman, a very old woman, a round man about his age, and she did too. She did too.

"Everyone, this is Sam, who's been working for me at the harbour this past year. I may have mentioned him previously. I've decided to let him sleep in the observatory."

"And why?" one of the women asked.

"Because that's what I've decided."

"Yes, I see," she said. Mrs. Astrobe.

"And where is— Sam, is it? Where is Sam from?" asked Astrobe's daughter. Her voice like honey and music.

"Ceylon," answered Astrobe. "And he understands much of what we're saying."

"Oh really, Ceylon?" said Mrs. Astrobe and looked at him, smiled, then turned back to the piano, turning the very old woman at the same time. She never so much as breathed his way again. The very old woman, Astrobe's mother-in-law, spoke to Sam once, a few weeks later, after stopping him in a hallway. "They dance with kangaroos in the bush. And when I was a girl, I watched them shave a bear." And then she walked on.

"Those aren't— Are those Jim's?" asked the round young man, pointing at Sam's shoes but looking at her.

She slammed down on the piano and rushed from the room and the young man followed like some heavy pet, a sloth bear, and also the two women left, and finally Astrobe took a step toward their exit, stopped, then walked away, through yet another doorway, without saying anything to him either. And so Sam was left by himself, the crashing bowel sounds of the piano ringing in his ears, which were burning, wanting more. Everything was. All of it.

six

"Ha! You thought I meant you, yes? That I'm going to box you up and send you home?" Astrobe laughed until it sounded like he was coughing up metal. He dabbed his monogrammed hanky to his eyes. How vengeful was a man's memory, how conspiring his tongue! He hadn't thought of his Jim in days. They were in his harbour office. It was almost time to walk home. He'd only told Sam that he knew of a freighter going to Ceylon with free space in the hold. That something small could be sent along. Not someone.

"What I am proposing," he continued, his voice now milder, chastened, "is that you might want to put together some effects to send to your family back home. Am I presuming too much? Just it's that I thought, and I know it's not for you, and it's months off from December, but people are already getting their parcels ready to send to London for Happy Christmas. There's not much left for ourselves in England, thanks to old Martin Astrobe, but I thought it was something you might want to do. Send something home. We could be of assistance."

Turning over the sudden idea, a year after he'd come to live in Astrobe's house, Sam felt like he'd been walking through a forest watching for songbirds and fallen in a gem pit. "There is family in Ceylon," he began carefully, oh vengeful memory, oh conspiring tongue, "but they do not live near Colombo harbour, in fact they live far from there and I am not sure how something from here would reach them. But I am grateful, yes." Each word was a testing step. There could be a hole within the hole.

"Have you a name for where they do live?"

"Yes. Yes, there is a village name, yes."

"That, and your father's good name, should be enough."

"Yes, I see." He would not tell Astrobe what he had told B. in the greedy gloom of his Pettah stall: that his father wasn't a good enough man for a good name. The week before, one noontime at the office, Astrobe had received a visitor—the bookkeeper from a rival shipping agent, who said he wanted to work for Astrobe because his boss was no good and he knew the company was about to fold. Astrobe had Sam show him to the door and then told Sam to avoid boomerang dealers like that. "You don't tell a man you've burned down the house you lived in and then ask if you can come live in his."

And so Sam wouldn't say a word against his father to Mary's. But he was also, in fact, tempted by the justice and glory of Astrobe's suggestion that he send something to his family, to the village. By the vision of his father opening a crate full of things from a son and a world so far beyond him; things not even the grand walauwa people themselves could have even in the best of paddy and pepper years; things that in an overgrown green emptiness like Sudugama would be worthy of veneration, of shrines, of caparisoned elephants in drummed procession and named first-born sons and declarations of war between houses. Things that, Sam now knew, were to be understood as but trinkets in the great world itself. But as much as Sam wanted this victory, he did not want its cost. Contact. Taint. But he wanted his father, his family, all of Sudugama to know where and what he was now, and he did not. He did not!

"It was just a thought, no matter. Mrs. Astrobe always orders Mary new dresses for Christmas and I'm sure Mary wouldn't mind some of her old ones going to Ceylon this year instead of the mission up at La Perouse. You must have sisters. Maybe a sweetheart? Sam?"

But he wasn't listening anymore. And he wasn't worrying either, about his family, about cost or triumph, contact or taint. He should have been listening. He should have been worrying. But Sam was only waiting for Astrobe to stop talking so they could close the office for the day and go to Mary.

An hour later, her face flashed, then drained of all colour, then flushed red when her father knocked and walked into her bedroom in a single motion, his monkey close behind him. As usual, Cousin Malcolm was in the room already, his face Mary's mirror. He was standing beside her chest of drawers. His elbow looked nailed down.

"Father, why even have doors?"

"Shall we just remove yours then?" Father and daughter smiled at each other, sourly. Sam was smiling too, a wild idiot grin. Shown a mirror, he might have shattered it for shame.

"I see you have company with you, Uncle James." Malcolm nodded at Sam.

"What I was about to say to Mary!" said Astrobe, louder than was necessary, still smiling sour, but now staring at his nephew, who looked down and said nothing else.

"Hello," Mary said to Sam.

"Yes," said Sam to Mary.

"Yes?" asked Mary.

"Yes. Hello," said Sam.

After Astrobe explained that this year's mission crate would be going to Ceylon, she shrugged and disappeared behind the fine-worked door of a large wardrobe. Sam waited and watched. He watched so hard he could have counted the brass flower petals that encircled its knob, unravelled the cardamom-like braid of darker wood running in a square at its centre. Malcolm pried his elbow free from the dresser and went to stand beside her while she sorted her clothes. Sam heard them laugh. She emerged with an armload of frill. She carried it to him. He extended his arms. She gave him a dozen emptied embraces, not even looking at him but already calling back to Malcolm about something else. Astrobe turned to leave and so he had to turn too but then Mary called out "Wait a moment" and Sam Kandy became Lord Buddha's bo tree. She came back to him, bunching up in her hands a long piece of thin fabric, many-coloured. She left it on one of his waiting branches. He held his breath while she placed it there. When she turned he exhaled and it unfurled and Sam tucked his chin to catch it. Standing there in infinite patience, twenty-four sleeves and now this scarf hanging down from his arms, he looked prayer-flagged.

From the first, love had been this suffering, this burning and suffering with knowledge that she was near, which made every triumph of living in Astrobe's dark wood and dog carpet house so much deadwood and ash: the triumph of balancing a cup and saucer on his knee without looking at it, of eating beef, of eating beef with silver, of returning a blue-eyed visitor's gaze straight away, of shaking his ringed white hand. Astrobe told Sam that once a week, every Sunday when the family went to church and then made their calls about town, he could use the family bath. He was to leave no hairs. Even though the tub's taps were explained to him, it had looked to Sam like some mad hunter's trophy, the gutted body of a demon bull, claw-footed and low to the ground, black-hulled and crackled bone-white within. But bathing in heated water late winter afternoons in Sydney, the sunlight streaming through a corner of the facing window and catching the risen steam and making of it a bright angled smoke, was a glory not possible in the world he had known before, a world of bathwater funked and body-warmed by young brother monks, a world of hard and slippery wet stone and furious boring bugs at the bamboo spout in the village, of Colombo seawater that sometimes left you feeling browner, more pungent and pickled than before you'd waded in. But he could not triumph in his Sydney baths as he should have. Each time there was nothing else but to know that she too had been here, Mary's body, like his, waiting in this warm vapoury blanket bottom of the world, like this, just like this. Only she was not here now. She never was and would she ever be? The sun would always fade, the water long since lukewarm, before he stood up, streaming, shuddering from how cold love could be.

As usual, Malcolm came to his room that night. The first time Astrobe's soft heavy nephew had climbed to the observatory, a year before, it had been to explain why his dear cousin Mary had rushed from the music room upon Sam's introduction to the family. Her beloved brother had survived Gallipoli itself, only to die in the retreat from Suvla Bay, stumped at the shins by a landmine. The chaplain's letter home did not advise as such and shoes had been bought and remained boxed until, it seemed, Astrobe had given them to Sam.

Hello, yes, yes, yes, hello—they passed his five Mary words back and forth a thousand different ways, like two dogs running their tongues dry along some common belly sore. And then Sam made his case again and again.

"Never, I'm sorry to tell you," answered Malcolm.

"But look where we are, where *I* have come!" Sam pleaded, his memory open like a conqueror's atlas. "Look at how I've been living with his family this past year! And now this Christmas crate! Also, he has said he wants to speak to me, about my plans, after Wellington. I think that's when I shall tell him. Ask his permission."

"Oh yes, he is off to Wellington isn't he. Remind me when."

"First of next month. And not just him; I am to go too."

Malcolm nodded.

"Also, you have seen how he takes me with him through the city. Doesn't this mean, couldn't it mean that—" he'd never say it outright. In open air, words meant to shape the best possibilities negated them.

"Yes," Malcolm allowed. "But you must know he has done that before."

"You mean with, with—" Sam would never say *Jim* because Astrobe never said his dead son's name, and also out of his own cosmic worrying. Those jurying stars, the broadcast heavens, looked in on the lovelorn shadow he made of his nightly hours in his windowed octagon, high above much of Sydney, just as they'd looked down on his boyhood, those sleepless nights before his birthday runs along the village green.

"Yes, with—" said Malcolm like he was speaking with a child. But by now Sam had talked enough with Malcolm to know a goad. He stayed quiet.

"With Chawkees, yes, he went around Sydney with Chawkees just like he does with you, but that was years ago, when Chawkees was young and strong."

"Chawkees? He called him Chawkees?" Sam asked, confused. Why did men say they wanted to make fellow men of their boys and then call them Squirrel?

"Yes, Chawkees. Oh no, sorry, I didn't mean Jim. Sorry. Is that really what you thought?" Malcolm smiled like he'd been sneaking treacle while the rest of the world was eating sour curd. "Actually, I was referring to that old hunting dog always sleeping in the music room. Chawkees. And sorry to leave you there, but I'm to take tea with Mary and Aunty in the garden."

Sam took Malcolm by the throat, his fingers sinking into the fat folds of his face, his warm pink devil jowls. He choked him to the edge of the staircase. The only decision was whether to send him down without another sterile word spilt between them, or let him apologize and vow he'd make up for it, promise he'd speak to both Astrobe and Mary and make Sam's case for the one with both.

Only he didn't take him at the throat. He didn't send him tumbling down. He extracted no pledge. He only soothed himself with the idea of it as he watched Malcolm leave. There was nothing else to do, twenty-five years old and obsessed with a rich man's daughter, but stare and want and rage. And talk—all these words with her cousin. Talking, staring, wanting: he had discovered hope's darkness, how it endured as the absence of itself. Living in Astrobe's house had made Sam's Kandy chest into a beggar's bowl.

An empty one. She'd given him those dresses to be given, and the next day, Astrobe added some old bed-sheets, an old carpet, an unused set of blue-lined handkerchiefs monogrammed *AJ* by mistake, two old sunbonnets, one of his old yellow bowlers, a pamphlet entitled "Edited for Student Use: Lord Macaulay's *Essay on Warren Hastings*" with DUNTROON stamped on the first and last page, assorted blanched bathing caps. and, pledging Sam to secrecy, a woodcut of Sydney harbour that his friend Preston's wife had done, the ships and buildings outlined in beetle black and coloured broad and bright as from a child's hand. After the crate was packed in a drab salad of shredded newspaper and the father's name and village were extracted for the shipping slip, Astrobe said they were nearly ready and Sam thought, *Nearly?* Astrobe took a slip of paper from his desk and a pen from his vest and handed them down to him crouched on the floor beside this, his triumph or was it his tainting box.

"You'll want to say a few words, I'm sure."

"Right. Yes." Was this a test to see what kind of family man he was or would be?

"Well I'm not about to write it but please, if you would, say something to your father about the family that has sent this along."

"I shall."

"Very good."

But before nailing it shut Sam still would have dropped a match in the box instead of a note. Let them sift in vain, feast on ash. He could have left the page blank and he could have written out a scroll longer than any Pali chronicle or rich man's horoscope, a letter of his life that would touch his father from here, to touch him as Sam could still remember him, waking before dawn and bagging up his sarong above his scuffed doorknob knees to step over their murmuring bodies, to step outside and wake the village with his throat clearing before returning inside to mutter them awake as he made his morning puja. The ink left an indigo pottu mark at the bottom of the letter. He'd kept the pen nib still, deciding not to write out Ranjith, the name they had known him by, or any other. Instead he offered a line of cryptic pride, then nailed the crate shut and wondered again why he was doing this. It was her fault, those emptied embraces, and he was filled with hatred and happiness to think of her while he was here in her father's office, who was seated behind his desk, his own face lost, a cloud of bombsmoke. And meanwhile he imagined something of hers reaching there, the village, passing through the low doorway to the family house, the crate's blond wood split and blooming mould in the upcountry air, the contents shadowed over with so many brown heads bowing as each cast-off and throwaway relic of Sam's faraway place was raised for veneration.

~

July 1, 1924: their ship was scheduled to leave shortly but they were still in Astrobe's office. Sam was watching him shake open the drawers of his desk, muttering that it wasn't ultimately important but he'd like to bring it along anyway, a scrolled menu card for a Federal Conference banquet held forty years earlier at the Menzies Hotel, Melbourne. The New Zealand representative had been a great-uncle of the man Astrobe was going to see in Wellington about securing exclusive agent's rights to the family's sheep concern. Sam was coming along to attest, firsthand, to the firm's care and success in shipping animals—elephants no less. Sam gripped the cool leather and metal handle of the suitcase he had been given for the voyage—he did not ask whose, just as he did not ask why, when Astrobe had presented him with a dark three-piece suit, he recommended Sam change in the coat closet at the office.

"We should make our way down to the ship," said Astrobe, resigned.

"Do you want me to see if you left it upstairs?" asked Sam.

"You think you could run home and back before we left?"

Sam shrugged and both smiled, remembering their old wordless competitions.

"But what about this?" He spread his hands along his chest and down the length of her dead brother's suit, which hung loose on him the way a rice sack hangs loose on a pole in a garden plot.

"This time of day, no one should be about the house. And anyway be quick about it. Leave your kit here. I'll see that it gets on board.

He nodded and went with such great purpose and imagined rewards that he did not stop running until he reached the last step before the observatory. He was breathing so hard he did not hear their breathing within. They were lying together on his own cot, his own sheet bunched high around Malcolm's fat middle, whose body was going like a hammering pink temple. She was lying beneath him.

Mary gasped. Was this her brother Jim, burnt and shrunk by gunpowder death or hell, and anyway returned in his best suit, returned because what she had finally consented to do with their cousin was fit to raise the dead? Malcolm was making noise too, uncontrollably, sighs-into-groaning, his body moving past his mind's stilled sadness, hatred, at discovery. He looked away. She was slapping his shoulders to stop now, where moments before she'd been kneading, breathing deeply in and out with him. This misfortunate little brown fellow would now know why Malcolm had been so good and answering these past months to all his useless Mary-talk, why he had so nodded at Sam's telling him, falsely it seemed, that he and his uncle were going to Wellington this first-of-the-month.

Taking him by a tuft of hair warmed by her skin, oh by her own hair, Sam turned Malcolm's head and yanked him off her body, brought him to his feet and chopped down at his cowardly hands struggling with hers for the sheet. Sam pushed him hard and Malcolm's splotchy pinkness collapsed into itself as he staggered backward against his uncle's desk, his arms and hands scissoring into a V at his privates. Sam rammed an open palm into his nose and when he raised his hands to his blooming bloody face Sam kicked him down. Malcolm fell to the floor, sucking and gurgling. Sam walked over to the desk. He found the scrolled menu card half tucked beneath the blotter and turned to leave. But he had to look again at his cot, at her face, also splotchy. She seemed to be wriggling away, or trying to get herself onto her elbows without the sheet falling. She was cursing as she moved—her cousin, her brother, her father. She leaned and spat in the wastebasket beside his cot. His bed! Suddenly she was staring at him, her eyes diamond bright with confusion and rage and shame, could it be, and thanks-giving? But the creased bed-sheet looked like ten thousand crows' feet. He felt like a paddy field on fire. He felt charred, used up, scoured of past life and all possibility save one. Sam ran.

part two **ALICE**

SEVEN

As promised: from high upon the verandah of the silent walauwa, and from within the dark doorways of Sudugama's silent village huts, a strange new noise was heard coming down the Kurunegala Road. It sounded like distant bees, or ten thousand dragonflies, forty thousand wings, a vibrant hum that became a growl and then a rumble and whine as it neared the village whose people, always ready for omens, checked the time and reminded themselves of the date and squinted over the treetops to consider, in its early-morning fade, how much and malevolent was the moon left in the sky. Malaria, drought, and now this, in 1929, some boxy monster bringing with it dogs barking; birds cawing; boys clapping and calling on friends to come see; older men slack-jawed with shock, women peering from behind husband and brother shoulders, failing to hold on to their own children, who ran to join the mad parade that had gathered around him town after town since Colombo. Sam Kandy was seated in the back of the first motorcar ever to come to the village of Sudugama, a 1928 Morris Minor, black as deep water; his driver, a boy with blue eyes.

The car turned off the main road into a dry dirt laneway cut between the paddy fields. On the left was the reedy pond, now more a brown puddle. Sam remembered how once, before the temple, when he was just another boy in the village, he had been told that this pond was filled with baby turtles, told by a boy who was soaked through and smiling as he described the crawling surface of the water. His wet finder's feet were filmed in dust from running up the laneway. Sam never thought to ask him where his turtle was. He ran down straight away, crouched and squinted across the reed-bent water, waiting for the shimmering surface to tremor with life born to be caught. He was pitched forward by the very boy who had called him down. The leafy surrounds shook with laughter as the other boys, ranging from long dry to still damp, stood to see the latest conned. The boy who had pushed him in pulled him out with rough ceremony and said that now it was his turn to find his own boy to tell about the baby turtles. Sam understood and played the game and played it well. He had been so happy not to be the last boy found, happier still that the boy he ran and called down was Bopea, whom he had once fought and lost to on the great green clearing.

The Morris was moving very slowly now, the surface of lane that led through the village undulant like the bony backs of the men and beasts born to walk it. At Sam's word the car paused at the barren junction that marked the centre of the village. He glanced to the right, toward the now gaping astrologer's hut. He glanced to the left, down the lane past the carpenter's stall, at what, until so very lately, had been his family's own place. And now, twenty years later, always, he looked forward, upward, to the great twin boulders that marked the entranceway to the walauwa itself. Boulders that, in years past, had always barred the way forward, upward, for men like his father and his father and his father too, the men of his family back unto the very first of his line who emerged from untold, unknown history, who appeared on the scene from unnamed and long forgotten geography one morning to spend the rest of his days and his son's and his son's forever more working the mud lands of men born to better horoscopes. Until now and himself, Sam thought, wondered, promised; no, vowed. He had stopped the car so he could ask himself one last time if what was next was in fact what was wanted. And it was, it had to be, it was what everything before this day compelled him now to seek, impelled him, at last un-fathered, to make his own.

⌒

"What are you? A politics? A temperance bugger?" the old man had asked him, days before, when he had stepped into the hut. He'd come by train and then cart, dressed in a simple clerk's outfit, unannounced, unknown, to see what was left of a forgotten family he was certain and outraged and grateful had forgotten him.

"You don't know me?" Sam asked. Yes, he did, he wanted it that way, wanted no ceremony as he returned to the low little room lit only by bottle lamp and any early moonlight and starshine washing in through the side window beneath which he had lain as a little boy. Those jurying stars. While his father studied him, Sam looked around and found nothing of the Christmas crate he had sent from Sydney, four years earlier. He breathed deeply the odour of ages, finding again nothing of himself in it save the earthly sweet smell of ripe plantains, combs as profuse as they and they alone always were, piled on the table. The rest was old dirt and oil, burnt rice, rinds, pot arrack; old man smells.

"I don't owe you any money, I know that! Ask anyone if I owe anyone."

"Are you alone here?" Sam asked. His mother must have died. *Soo sa* he had tried to protect her from muddy snakes when he was a boy and she was pregnant too long and they had gone walking on the great green clearing. *Soo sa* she had taken him to the astrologer and let his father take him to chase the crow and then to the temple. *Soo sa*

"Mokatha?" his father shot back, less with puzzlement than worry.

"You really don't know who I am?" *Appachchi* he hadn't said; the word had curled and disappeared upon his tongue like a singed leaf.

"Justgowillyou" the old man muttered, bagging up his sarong between his legs as he always did. Only now the legs looked thin as cigarettes. Only now the sarong was from an old bed-sheet, bought years earlier by Mrs. James Astrobe at David Jones in Sydney and long since faded and betel- and tea-stained beyond all recognition. "I owe nothing in this village. Just ask any fellow if I owe him still! I have nothing for you."

"Uncle," Sam said, swallowing the rest of it. He would use the first of his two plans, the greener one, to get his father out of Sudugama before he arrived a few days later in the motorcar. "I am here on behalf of someone else, to see your wife about an inheritance matter."

The bunched-up fabric dropped and the old man hooked forward, his eyebrows crumpling. "Aiyo malli-sir, it's like this. I am a poor widower, my beloved wife has passed only recently, and just see all my ungrateful children have left me."

"And where are all your children?"

"They are all ungrateful, all gone and left me."

He was alone. Sam felt nothing.

"There are none remaining in this village? None from your relations? No blood?" Sam asked carefully, his words heavy as links. But he felt nothing. He could not.

"They are all gone and left me!" He would be alone, undiscovered. He could do it.

"And your wife's family?"

The old man waited a beat and bagged himself about the legs again. "No one I can think of, malli-sir."

"Only you?" Sam confirmed, pretending to write something in a ledger, knowing the old man was lying but not worried. He could not remember any of his mother's family save the old one, his grandmother. She was long since gone. None of the rest would remember him. He could do it.

"I have come on behalf of one of your wife's distant relations, from down south, near Matara. Did you know she had family there?"

The old man bobbled his head, knowing it was not true, that no one in his wife's family or his own had ever been, save Kandy town, farther than a dog's trot from Sudugama.

"Right," Sam said. He had lately gone down to Galle to secure a shipping agreement with a family of Muslim traders. Afterwards, he went farther south, as far as he could, and then inland a ways from Matara. He told anyone he met what he wanted and with funny looks was sent to Ankuressa and there he looked until he found what it needed to be, a certain kind of house for sale. No one had lived in it for a long time, no one could chase them away, and it was a bad omen to cut down a Mara tree. Sam had waited past dusk to make sure that what he had been told was true. And yes, oh vengeful symmetry, this great flamboyance of leaves and branches was in fact a roosting tree, where every night the crows beat its branches black.

"What have you come to say from them?" his father asked.

"Not come to say, Uncle, but to give. This relation has died and I have come to show you the deed for the property, a good property, down south with a good strong Mara tree and here is your rail ticket from Kandy—"

"I AM GOING IN THE MORNING!"

When the Morris jumped back to life, something fired out the back. Three boys took off down the lane, racing to see who would first find whatever bullet cannon or fireball this thing just shot out. An older man tripped backward over a dog, one of the many milling about sniffing and barking and considering what part of this thing looked softest to bite. There were yells and screams, laughter terror outrage from the rest of the crowd, which, like some palpitating organ, had surrounded the car when, moments before, it had stopped at the village crossroads. The crowd gave way as the car resumed its course, straight ahead and slower still, moving into a steady incline, deliverance from and deliverance forward, the angle-bodied mutts still nipping at its back wheels in vain and so nipping at each other instead. The crowd reformed as one in Sam's wake, not following but instead watching the black beast drive on to the big house near empty and silent with its own waiting.

Robert had been standing on the verandah sipping tea that had steeped too long when he heard it coming. He forgot about condensed milk; whatever this thing was, it had to be coming for him. If a little surprised, he was, still, not unhappy about this. He might have been, even, relieved. He looked behind his shoulder, into the quiet walauwa. When he was sure there was no one about, he stepped forward to the stone ledge that ran the length of the verandah and ducked down. The hem of his sarong curled and floated in his tea cup. He never noticed. In the gaps between the chipped, veined white pillars, he could only see of his village what he had always seen from this crouch: browns and greens and jumbled thumbprints of black hair; smoke from cooking fires and the burning of spent fields rising to fade into whatever time of day and weather it happened to be. Today what smoke there was was also engine smoke fading into the haze of mid-morning, vellum-covered sunlight.

Holding the pillars between his hands, he remembered how he used to watch this way when his father descended to make his rounds about the village. Sometimes his father walked beneath a white parasol ringed in thick wavy black lines, two cobras swallowing each other at the tail, which he had bought during a pilgrimage to the great temple in Kandy town. Later, his father began going down with a fox-headed walking stick and a stove-black bowler. Both had been presented to him by a Crown Agent who had grandly appointed him to the village headman's position that he and his father and his father before him had all been born to—the white rage for official reality. In the time between his father's death and when Robert felt old enough to try these things himself, the parasol fell to moths, and the walking stick vanished, likely spirited out the kitchen doorway by some servant girl to the boy who had caught her eye or to the husband whose eye she was trying to keep. Robert still had the hat. It sat on a high shelf in a back room, untouched for decades, a dusty palace for whole races of insects.

Robert had been twenty-plus when his father died. That day, instead of watching from the verandah, he was told to go with him, to a meeting held at the crossroads. It had to be called, his father explained to the dark faces gathered, because he, the third Ralahami to rule Sudugama, was being shamed by the men of his village, who had failed to report for Road Ordnance duty as they had been invited, asked, and then ordered to by the Crown Agent. He then declared, once again, that Sudugama was abandoning the old way in the fields. There was to be no more clearing of the King's trees and firing the scrubby flats. No more hope in ruinous fresh soil and friendly moonlight. But his father had chosen the wrong time for the meeting, midday, before the meal, and the crowd, mostly field-hands who loved their hena farming as much as they loathed the prospect of tar-pots, was hungry, heat tired, sullen, and staring stone silent. Besides which, in the paddy fields that morning they had been told that the chief monk of the village temple had ruled that labouring for the British might be a wicked conversion scheme: a good Buddhist carrying timber looked too much like a cross-dragging Christ. But this wasn't Negombo! With devout pride the men in the fields were decided: faith, history, and the high cause of the failing first family itself were in fact on their side in not going to work the roads, the very same roads upon which the British had lately hanged the famous Saradiel, a highwayman who had shown greater courage than any Ralahami in exacting right tribute from the English passing in their coaches—gold and pocket-watches, whole trunks and billiard balls and lady brooches. Their own Ralahami should have been ashamed for asking them to abandon the old ways, the good ways of growing, let alone begging them to report to the Crown.

Sensing their sourness and also beaten by the heat, Robert's father began to sweat. There came a stir at the back of the crowd and a draught of coconut water was passed forward. Conciliation. Instead of hacking open a good heavy coconut and passing it forward, they had drained it into a fine-rimmed glass that some returned son had stolen from a Colombo hotel, a glass passed forward in honour of the Ralahami's smart bowler hat and walking stick and faith in English farming pamphlets. He finished it but for a couple of seeds and, smiling, showed its empty sunlight to the crowd. He handed out betel, tipped his hat, and the men went home for lunch looking pleased as fox.

The bowler fell off when his father staggered upon the stone steps to the big house. Robert, standing behind him, picked it up and stood to the side as the servants looked down and yelled and his mother, screaming, her sari streaming, flew along the stairway to cover the twitching body with her own. She was joined, moments later, by her own mother and by Robert's two sisters, and with all of them crowded around her, she cradled her husband's face in her lap, wiping and wiping the forehead and cheeks with her hands and hair and pleading with him like he was a baby about to break fever. Eventually, and wearing the bowler for the first and last time because he did not know what else to do with it, Robert took his mother at the elbow and half carried, half guided her up the stairs and into the house, her heaving little body swinging against him like a birdcage wrapped in a bed-sheet. He sent a servant for the village doctor, a legendarily fat man, who, when woken from a snatched nap because no one had come to see him for two hours that day, took twenty minutes to dress worthy of a visit to the walauwa. He came, breathing loud as a bullock, his sons at his forearms helping him climb the stone steps. When the doctor finally reached the back room where the Ralahami lay dead, Robert stepped around the body and the crying women and sent him off. On the next auspicious day, mourners from another village were hired in and his father was cremated. The family washed itself with limes and fed the monks. The Crown Agent arrived the next morning and appointed Robert the fourth Ralahami of Sudugama. He then ordered Robert to stand close by and say nothing while he questioned the men of the village. It made for a quiet time. No one knew anything about anything. They would only swallow their lips and stare elsewhere until the white man and his translator let them be. It was as if his father hadn't given the empty glass to another human hand but somehow passed it through some momentary rent in the world itself that had closed as soon as it had opened. Like a lizard had blinked, a chameleon.

His mother's hair changed to white with black ribbon within a week and in the village they said the widow was turning into some witch or ghost to avenge her husband's death. One fool thought her hair must have touched his poisoned skin but he was stared quiet.

Poison? What is poison? Chameleon water. She barely spoke for two years. And when her daughters were to marry, ten days apart, twin brothers with good perches in Mahaiyawa, on the far side of Kandy town, she rose before dawn to feed milk rice to their dry mouths and divide her bridal jewellery between them. The older girl started another fit when her mother said a final time that she would not, could not, attend the wedding. A fibbing aunty intervened, counselling in a whisper that a widow at a wedding was as bad an omen as seeing a lone magpie the morning of. And so the eldest accepted a glass of first milk from her mother at the threshold and they said goodbye and to stop his sister from spending the rest of her life weeping on the verandah Robert arranged for a cow to pass just before she reached her carriage. He had to rush her down the stone steps and between the boulders to make the omen. And so the bridal party began its departure, everything petal-graced, the blue light of before morning beaten through with tom-toms and lit up with torches, and the first bride's eyes shut against the possibility of a magpie, while in the carriage behind her, the bride-of-next-week, worried middle child, was head down and counting, wondering if their mother's jewellery had been divided evenly. Meanwhile Robert's mother dismissed her servant girl for the day and went for a walk in the high green grass behind the big house, toward the old village founder's cave, and that was how she stepped out of frame before full morning and it was hours before anyone knew to look for her, by which time she was a ghost in the back garden.

On his own wedding night, a few years later, Robert and his wife were formal strangers facing each other across a bedroom lit in copper light and faint with jasmine and brazier smoke, a room that felt as empty and echoing as a failed water tank. Eventually, he made her nearly cry but then laugh and come closer by imitating how stiffly she'd stepped on and off the wooden poruwa during the ceremony. She was nineteen years old. But then, without anything more, she moved a step closer. And afterwards, a sheet pulled to her waist in a shared narrow bed, she lay his head upon her stomach, and it was firm and fine like the butter-clay glad kings used for temples in the old epics, and she shaped his face with her fingers again and again, and Robert fell asleep for a perfect moment. She had been warm like wood in the sun. Nine months later the world was rent and bawling. But when those cries from the lay-in room stopped, the universe itself fell silent, and suddenly there were new noises, *eck eck aah* and a pause, then a second *eck eck aah*, but Robert, waiting outside the curtained threshold, couldn't hear any more of it for all the sobbing rolling into sobbing from the women inside. His wife's servant girl, Latha, streaming proprietary tears, eventually came out. Perhaps she had thought it would balance out his grief to bring the babies with her—twins, a boy and girl. He was staring at them when he was told the news, staring at their raw faces, listening to their eyes-shut-screeching at world and time for finding and taking them out as they had. Immediately he envied them the perfect rightness of their pain, the roomful of cupping hands and soothing songs that were theirs now and would be for years, whereas he, almost thirty, an eight-year orphan and ten-minute widower and ruler of a hundred lazy murdering omen gluttons and now father to two *say it, if only to spit it out* two more "Bloody murderers!" he sobbing cursed, staggering past her blotted, sheeted body and out to the verandah, where off to a corner, he fell to his knees and then his stomach and the stone was cold and flat and he remembered hers, before them. A warm banner of fair flat skin. Not one high-caste daughter in all the surround was ever found who wanted bridal gold and walauwa honour enough to have a poisoned ghost for a father-in-law and a garden ghost for a mother-in-law and a sweet gone beauty for her husband's nightly dreaming and mother-taking twins for stepchildren. Robert had been alone for twenty years, crouched low in memory and waiting for what would come next, watching, and also trying to amend words his children had never heard, were never told, words they never but felt in how numb his hand could be upon their waiting brows at night.

eight

What she saw, thinking he could not see her watching, was a flash of silver and then of fire and then the fire was gone. In its place there was a glowing mark in the dark, passing back and forth on a short fast course around what must have been his body, like a burning star fixed upon a wire, like an abacus bead on fire. Eventually there would be more flashes of silver in the otherwise dark front room, where her father was standing to speak with the stranger who had not been asked to sit upon entering their house, at least not immediately. Who, minutes before, when the vertigoed servant had stopped staring at the brown man emerging from the back of a motorcar and had pattered up the stone stairs and back into the big house to present the visitor with a brass tray of the Ralahami's own betel leaves, had bowed from the shoulders but demurred. The servant ducked away and returned, once more bent at the waist, this time to arrange with great satisfaction a low stool before this obviously low man. But placing a black-cased foot on the stool with a firm tap, a foot that had been shod in black leather many times buffed of its own scuffed history, Sam leaned forward to light a cigarette, a habit picked up in the brothel life of Singapore and not forsaken upon his return to Ceylon. From his work in Colombo since that return—his rice dealing and passage- and money-making about the harbour—and also, more recently, from his waiting outside the Fort offices of men who would now envy him his Morris, Sam had overheard the English view of betel chewing. Yet in so choosing to keep his own mouth modern and clean, Sam never knew how close he came to failing at all else, how close he came, just then, to being ordered off his land and out of his village forever. But then he found his lighter.

Robert was by all rights outraged that the visitor had declined his offered betel. But also, if not impressed, he was at least curious what kind of brown man would show up like this, behave like that, look as he did, and own or at least, until the constables found him, have a motorcar in his possession. The last stranger who had entered his village with a bold and wanting eye, many years before, was a money-fat fisherman from down south, who was announced from fifty yards by his aftershave—Portuguese, all shot blooms and sweet wine. Back then, fish oil smiles were suddenly appearing everywhere on the high side of the once impregnable Kadugannawa rock that the English had blasted through so their tea trains and motorcars could pass between Colombo and Kandy town. And then everyone else could come too, and they did come and begin smudging away everything that for centuries had made great the good green country on the high side of the rock—courage for kingdom and honour and history and blood-run lands. Strangers were coming with far more money than the mud flats and weedy tanks and dung floors and daub walls were worth, money that was wiping clean fierce memory.

The bulging fisherman had sat in Robert's front room and accepted his betel happily, openly chewing less than he took and then asking for more, asking loud enough to wake Robert's wife, who seemed otherwise to have slept through the early months of her pregnancy. No doubt the fisherman sold the rest of the betel to his own mother when he returned to Bentota, after making such a low offer that Robert had called for the metal-benders and had him thrown in the back of his loud painted cart, a cracker lit to scare his fat bullock down the lane and gone. Six months later, and such dead and bawling months they were, the same bugger came back and asked if Ralahami was ready now, and then he made the same low bloody offer. Robert would have taken a cracker himself this time and chased him down the steps and thrown it after him, were he not in mourning and the lonely babies, for once, sleeping.

Twenty years on and a new stranger now before him, Robert decided that dressed as he was, carrying himself as he did, this one would make no low offer, this baggy pinstriped suit with a silver flint in one hand and a painted tin the size and colours of a songbird in the other, blowing modern smoke through the shade-drawn room. Moments later, those watching from nearby breathed it in, and Sam stared right at her as she leaned forward and coughed. He thrilled and smiled to himself as she stared at him before disappearing again behind a pillar, where she coughed a second and third time, her long fingers reaching for a blue-lined butterfly as it unravelled across the passageway to the inner court- yard. It was a moment's flight in bright light. He did not recognize its mis-stitched monograph. He offered a cigarette to her father, returning to the business at hand.

"Whose ..."

"—motorcar—"

"... is it that you have taken and brought to my village?" Robert asked, after declining the cigarette. How would it look to the servant, to the crowd coughing back of him, if he took it after his own best betel had just been placed to the side? He made another decision, he made it three times. He would decline, were he offered a ride. Because otherwise he might kiss his daughter on the forehead and tell her to go to her aunties on the other side of Kandy town; he might leave no note for his son because his son was not supposed to come to the village until he was finished his studies, even on English school holidays; he might lie to the servant that the Ralahami would just quickly go and come and command that in the meantime Lal was to sweep through the house morning noon and night until the day he died or his own son took over, and then Robert would ride straight out of this mud and black hat burden he had to call *my village* unto death. A death that he was hoping his son Arthur would avoid, which is why Robert had sent him, nine years earlier, to a Buddhist boys' college in Colombo where the boy had begun his way to a world well beyond his family's own, a world of medical college, of London, of saying, yes, motorcar.

"The motorcar is mine," said Sam, in English. He was asked to sit down.

"But not even the Englishmen I know own such things on this island," countered Robert, who could speak a little English too.

"Some have, in Colombo. The ones I know," said Sam.

"Ah right, of course, the ones you know. Next you will tell me that you take tea on Thursdays with the Governor. You say you have, just like the English. Right. But you are not just like the English, are you. You are like nothing I have ever seen. Don't smile that I say this, because you don't know what I have seen in this place, where my family has been on this land since long before your father's father had a name to call his own. Don't smile. Just tell me. How old are you? Where were you born? What is your good name? You have village colour, that is obvious, but you have taken English from somewhere, from someone else, that is also obvious. Who is it? Where? My son speaks English, but that is because he is reading Medicine at University College London. He, is, in, London."

Arthur had been studying abroad for two years. He had, so far, mailed four letters home, though none as yet had acknowledged Robert's own.

Sam said nothing. Another pile of fine betel offered in vain. *"He is,"* Robert insisted. "But you, dressed like this, come here as you have! What, did you take some planter's tongue and then his suit and then his motorcar? How much did you pass to the driver to dump the body in the well?"

"A crowd gathered round us when we stopped at Ambepussa and were shouting questions," said Sam. "They kept asking without waiting for me to answer. And really, I think they were all asking only one question, every man and boy, even the constable when he came through the crowd."

"Which was?"

"'May I have a ride?'"

"Can you give me even one name? Can you give me your own? Can you tell me where you have come from, what people? Can you tell me why you have come here—to my village?"

"I shall answer anything you ask. But try a cigarette first?"

"I'll have you thrashed and thrown down my steps in a moment!" But as he said it he thought about how long it would take Mahesh and Sando to reach the walauwa, and then he watched his own hand reach for it and take and the rest of him bend forward as it was lit and he pulled in and in a moment his mind was all new and swoon and more was wanted and so he would give this stranger the life of one cigarette to make his case before calling for the metal-benders.

Three cigarettes later, Robert didn't believe a word.

"All these years, you've gone around as Sam Kandy?"

"Every man needs a name, isn't it?"

"Of course, but—"

"But what can an orphan left at the temple gate do but name himself?"

"Yes, but here, in this place, in a place like this, they'll never, why would anyone, how could *I* be seen to accept—"

"Yes?" Sam leaned forward, the muscles in his legs tense and trilling, breathing hard the air running through the room house village temple city/sea/dock city room house/sea/dock city street shop/sea/room rooms city/car/village house room that had been his thousand streets running as one, his twenty years coming and going in the world—Sudugama Kandy Colombo Sydney Singapore Colombo Kandy Sudugama—the headlong unstopping rush of the story he'd just told, which was somewhat more somewhat less than what it should, perhaps ought to have been, were honest accounting and not triumphant symmetry Sam Kandy's virtue because what mattered was that it worked, *if it worked.*

The very same thought had been in front of all else, four years earlier, when the ship he jumped in Sydney docked in Singapore. He had learned the destination well into the voyage, from a white man with dog-brown eyes who had come below with a cloaked camera and tried at first in vain "to document for historical purposes only the nature of this your journey." Sam, the best dressed among the shadows, hadn't tucked chin and shown shoulder like the rest, who were huddled and murmuring like cold birds behind him. Instead, red-eyed staring and shoulders squared, Sam stood squarely for the flash and pop, and then, afterwards, when the photographer had immediately and forever forgotten his existence, Sam stepped forward, asking "Where?" and showing an open hand ready to close and get to work if necessary. He knew he'd need money, whatever and wherever Singapore was.

"Give. Give me for mine, and then give me for each that you want to take or you will take none."

The photographer snorted. Sam stepped closer and the man blanched.

"No, but you see, I'm from the University."

"Give or I will take mine back."

Days later, Sam Kandy walked into Singapore, his suit torn beneath the arms from having to grab and hold historical portraits in place, his hands healthy with paper. But he arrived still burning with Mary Astrobe. He could do nothing else until this was done with. He had clothes, words, money, and he did not care what she looked like. His face was wide open as he walked upon the wharf.

"Malay Street! Malay Street! Only the best on Malay Street!"

"Flower girls for you! Flower girls just waking up from your dreams and waiting to love you!"

"Just like home! Come and meet her! Just like home!"

Any sort of man could do this any sort of way, and in this place it seemed that any sort of woman could be had. Other men fresh from the boats were walking toward the crowded rickshaw stands, not even bothering to inquire which home she was just like, only climbing out of the fried-egg Singapore sun into the shady backs of the two-wheelers and setting off for coin-fast love—French sailors in pairs, and other whites in top hats, older heavier men who insisted too loudly and for no one's conscience save their own that they needed nothing but safe passage to the Raffles Hotel; and also, really mostly, angle-bodied Chinese with slow wide village gaits that only quickened when one of the coolies called to them in some mother tongue or boys' slang, and then they too were taken and gone. But Sam only looked away, kept walking, burning. What was he waiting for?

He stopped. Coolies were on him immediately, hawking and cawing. No more, he thought. Enough, he said. Get on or stop trying at the rest of it, he decided. Get on or go back to the temple. Get on or shrivel and die to all desire. Get on or grow old man fruit. "Perfect English good time" sounded good enough. He nodded to one of them and was taken to a shophouse on Sago Street. Its main room was broken up with endless gauzy curtains, useless against the working noises within. His girl's had a slatted window and a brick wall that was mossy and damp to touch. There were slick little flowers growing in the cracks, dripping life. She was smoking on a narrow bed with a headboard whose paintwork still showed. A pastoral scene: fat sheep grazing upon a wide green, a blue sky above them full of sheepy white clouds.

She had skin like milky tea and spoke well enough to get a good price for the rest of her cigarettes and made the right noises to keep him talking telling asking long enough to charge him twice and he never so much as sat down. Instead, Sam offered her more money to meet the woman she called her Pocket Ma, who was sitting on a crate at the back of the shophouse, fanning herself with a thatched fan, chatting with another woman with a sweaty heavy chest and ragged dress, only she was standing at a table, cutting up durian. To look at them, they cooked cabbage for sailors and scared off cheap johns. But the girl had told him enough that he wanted to impress this fat old widow. Considering Sam's story as she fanned herself, the old woman began to speak English, far better than the girl's. She said she believed nothing that he'd just said about his shadow work for a great man in Sydney harbour but would let him try to prove it. She gave him a figure for every fresh brown boy he brought her way instead of their going to the Hindu operation on Orchard Road, and she gave him a far better figure than head money for every white man with a shipping contract he could bring from Commercial Square.

Three years later, Sam Kandy might have been the richest virgin in Singapore. But one day he told the old woman that he was tired of fighting the Hindus on Orchard Road for every fresh brown boy on the wharf. Besides, he knew of a crowded little island close by, where brown boys could be had with ease, boys with village-strong backs searching for ships to take them anywhere but home. And he told her that by then he also knew the right white men in Commercial

Square to secure the necessary passages. The old woman spat and shrugged. She would see what, if anything, he'd send back, and was meanwhile disappointed to lose a good earner but also relieved to be rid of him, this suited monk who always slept alone in a side room, who never took payment in anything but money.

He returned to Colombo and came to know its dockworkers very well during a strike at the harbour. He sold some of them into Singapore, making money as a sub-agent for Pocket Ma, working harder and faster and cheaper and more silver-tongued than the established shipping agents around the harbour in telling dockworkers and middle sons from the villages that for a fee if they shipped out as he suggested and then went to Sago Street they would make money too. And if they paid him a little more, he would tell them where they would find not only work but rare love behind a green curtain, fair-skinned girls who could have almost been daughters in Cinnamon Garden. When the strike ended, those who were not tempted to go to Singapore would still hold back a sack of rice for a cut, or be hungry for it at a cut price, would anyway and always need something more from the near world than blood and birth hour predicted, than jetty sweat and Pettah stalls afforded, and Sam Kandy made that, all of it, his business. Because he knew them, these young men, their every want and wish, the daily plans, the long-ago promises. He made of them what he could. But after a year of working Colombo harbour he had to go to the village. From this much trafficking in it, Sam Kandy knew the great world was not enough. He needed warrant from the village: he needed the village itself. And when he arrived, his back would not shine with biscuit tins and city things like the small world's mallis and butterfly catchers. As promised: he would arrive as no one had before him.

Sam tried schemes on six Englishmen—owners of a Crossley 19.6, a Crossley 25/30, a Morris Bullnose, a Morris Cowley, an

Austin 12/4, and a Wolseley. He was laughed at and chased off and informed on one occasion that the vehicle in question had been used by the Prince of Wales during a tour of India and was most certainly not for native hire. And yet, whenever he wasn't conducting his rice- and boy-loading business at the harbour, Sam was moving about Fort, listening for that cough and chug no bullock or man could make, his eyes sharp for the world-piercing flash that was sunlight on polished chrome. Going only harder after six no's, Sam forced his own hand. He went to Galle and then on to Matara, where he searched inland until he found a fit house for his father and then returned to Colombo and from there went to the village with papers to show and a rail ticket to give and so sent his father south, and before leaving to arrive he discreetly inquired and had confirmed that yes, the Ralahami had an unmarried daughter. Only then did he return to Colombo to visit the offices of Paulet and Son, the firm whose rice Sam had been short-loading for months.

"Before you say anything else," Henry Paulet began, standing at his desk to receive him, "and even though your suit has brought you this far into this office and it seems better than one might expect or really want, the answer, young man, is no. I have no need of a driver."

"Sir, I have not come here to see you about a position. I have come because—"

"Just where have you been to school?" Henry Paulet asked of his English, sitting forward, the first of the two occasions they met. He was crumpled and tired looking in his beige suit, like an old birthday balloon, an Englishman too long in the tropics.

"In the world, sir."

"Well said!" Paulet sat back. "That kind of answer means either you must be someone's son gone to seed or you must be no one's son and trying to do something about it. Well?"

"I know who's been short-loading rice onto your company's ships."

"So neither, or both, and anyway you're just another Judas come for his silver."

"I have not come for any silver," Sam began. "I have come about your losing money on your rice shipments. I have come to offer my assistance—"

"Excuse me, sir. Mummy said to bring tea."

Sam turned at the girl's voice and saw her roundness and he turned again to see Paulet with his head down, molesting his desk blotter as she approached with the tray. When she set it down the Englishman tensed and held his breath. Sam saw and Sam had him. *Soo sa*

"And so," Paulet coughed back into conversation, speaking over the servant girl's leaving, her free hands back of her hips, her feet beating the timber floors, her mouth muttering the breathing song her mother taught her, "take your tea, but I only have so much time in the day, young man—"

"Looks to me you have three months, at most, no?" Sam lit a cigarette, blew smoke and stared.

Paulet hit a switch for the ceiling fan. The topmost papers on the desk lifted and fell a little. Barred light came through the second-floor window. Slow fan and barred light and city noise: carters and dogs calling after people, tram bells and a convent bell calling schoolgirls to little hours, a general static of crying babies; someone was recognized and recognized back; someone else needed another malli to help carry a chest. And through all that noise Sam could hear Paulet stirring his tea; thin silver on the thin rim of a bone china cup; the wearing down of men and days.

"Just what do you propose?" Henry asked.

"That we take a drive in your vehicle, to start," Sam said.

"I need someone else's word," said Robert, pinching the stub end of a cigarette like he was born to it. "I need to hear the story you've just told me, exactly, from someone else, someone this village will trust. Then I can believe. Then I could consider."

"But I told you, I have no father, no mother, and no relations anywhere to be found—"

"Then it has to be clergy."

Sam leaned back, breathed out, his legs lost their ready life.

"It will not be clergy." It could not be. He might as well have never left the temple if he needed a monk's blessing to return to the village.

"Why not? You must belong to temple in Colombo. You are Buddhist, no? I will not sell my land to a Moor or a Christian."

"I am no Moor, no Christian."

"So you are—"

"An Englishman?"

"Mokatha?"

"If I brought an Englishman to vouch for me, then may I meet her?"

"If you can make an Englishman tell your tale, the tale you have just told me, I'll sell you the land for a bowl of rice. I'll have the chief monk sit on a low stool and keep the bowl on his head for you to eat. Wait. Wait what did you ask?"

"He holds a high office in Colombo."

"I said wait. What did you just ask?"

"Paulet and Son, with offices in Fort, Prince's Building."

"WAIT. Tell me. I said what did you ask?"

"May I meet her?"

"Meet who?"

"I understand you have a daughter, or so I have been told." Sam stood, too impatient for the speech he'd practised during the drive, save its last line. He was tense, trilling, ready; he would turn and go never to return, try somewhere else, find another way if the Ralahami asked how he knew there was a daughter—because of course to answer was to locate himself, return him to earth, to that low patch of dirt that was his father's name and house, and so undo the rest of it. But Robert didn't ask Sam for anything else save another cigarette. And then Alice coughed again.

Her servant, Latha, had also been watching, this whole time, if listening in vain. After the last cough, she had bunched and thrown the handkerchief across the threshold, the handkerchief that, like the other women in her family, she always kept at hand to wipe at her mouth before and after she spoke, the handkerchief she had been given by a now dead cousin out of a mysterious foreign-sent crate that had been sent to her cousin's no-account husband, six years before, a man who had himself lately, unexpectedly, some might say miraculously, gone from the village. When not watching and straining to hear what was happening in the walauwa's front room, Latha was looking at her girl, at Alice, whom she had raised along with her twin brother Arthur from birth. Later, Alice would scold Latha, blame her tossed hanky for his looking just as she coughed that first time, and Latha would scold back that he shouldn't have been looking at her in the first place, this stranger in her father's house. And when the girl smiled, Latha would know that all her life's squirrel work would come to this, that it had already begun, that it was, in fact, a fast progress.

Behind Latha and also watching in the inner garden was the washerwoman. She was peering through the iron grille that covered one of the courtyard windows, her fingernails raking and flaking bits of old white paint from the rods in her hands. She could see absolutely nothing from her vantage, but no woman in the village would know that when, the next day, she would squat to wash and tell of the high events that had transpired in the big house the day before, just as betel-stocked Lal would do in that evening's toddy circle. And so that night, the hundred husbands and wives of Sudugama would compare the stories they had lately heard, the men over their toddy and the women at the washing. Not compare so much as compete to recreate, or contrast, or combine, correct, dispute, deny, edit, overwrite, amend to all exaggeration, make and remake in their own image, all of it depending on the evening mood of each their own marriages. So that by the time this so-called Sam Kandy concluded his business with the Ralahami and departed, he was the engine smoke and fire of one hundred and one stories. More even.

~

As agreed, Sam returned the vehicle and driver late that night, and Paulet watched from his back window at Prince's Building to see that Sam had kept his word: that no one else climbed out save himself and the driver. The young man was already hammering up the stairs before Henry could tell him there was no need, just go.

"I trust the trip was every success hoped for," Henry said when Sam entered his office.

"It was. Thank you."

"And thank you. Now—"

"Yes, now."

"The agreement, you recall, was that I would know nothing of their whereabouts."

"Of course. Only I know where they are now."

"Very good," Henry said. The end. But why was the fellow still here? No money was to change hands. The day-long use of the vehicle and driver, following Sam's arranging the servant women's departure from Colombo, was the agreed-upon payment.

"Is there anything else then?" Henry finally asked.

"The drive into upcountry was a picture."

"Ah, I'm sure. I wish I could have gone as well."

"If you would go now," Sam stepped forward as he said it, his face suddenly hungry and Henry wanted to say *Sorry of course the likes of you cannot understand I meant nothing of the sort because one must be born to English to know its poetries can be hollow or full* but Henry said nothing of the sort because suddenly he could tell this razor was not asking that he go but telling.

"Only I know where they are," Sam said a second time.

And that was when Henry knew that now he faced the threat of two rail tickets, one-way *back* to Fort Station, from whatever black green heaven hell or limbo it was Sam had sent his servant women, mother and daughter both mothers at his doing. And so, a day later, Henry Paulet went to Sudugama and on the way was told the tale of Sam Kandy he would in turn tell some upcountry headman with an unmarried daughter. And if a recitation prize could have been given for epic fiction, it would have been given that day to Henry Paulet for his performance in the front room of the dank cool walauwa, and that night, before Henry was dropped at Prince's Building in streetlamp shadows, Sam next raised the question of Henry's pending trip to London, which Henry had mentioned earlier that day in the village when the Ralahami had invited him to the now agreed-upon wedding. If Henry was going to London, as he'd said, what need would he have of transport in Colombo? And so, naturally, Sam sought terms for the driver and the vehicle itself—whose value, as he calculated it, would be equal, if not to the cost of the house and limbo land where the women had been sent, then certainly to the price of Sam Kandy's memory.

"You must know only Englishmen can own vehicles on this island!" Henry said in a seething whisper.

"So write it in the driver's name and give him more than your blue eyes."

Eighteen years before, his servant-mother had named him Piyal, as close to Paulet as she dared, and she had refused to send him to the Eurasian orphanage. Save his eyes, the boy was otherwise all village and had been raised as one of the household servants. After Paulet bought his first vehicle, the boy had been made driver. Henry bid no farewell to him or to the Morris. He bid fond farewell to Sam Kandy less for manners than as prayer: because otherwise he fully expected to find him in the morning already waiting for him in the office, waiting now to take away his desk and pry up the timber floors and slide the windowpanes into his jacket and whatever else—his father's library, his mother's tea service, the inside air itself—was deemed closer to the original price. That night he went to his empty rooms knowing he had been short-loaded and shamed, knowing that Paulet and Son should have been renamed Pyrrhic and Pyrrhic, wondering would it have been less various shame and short-load had he paid what he truly owed and sat for an honest family portrait with his household. He decided against hiring a new girl. As he made his plans to leave Ceylon, Henry thought of the sad-faced father of the pretty village bride who had invited this pinstriped locust into his house. Who, earlier that day, had also invited Henry to return to his village, for the wedding ceremony itself, which was when Henry had been inspired past Sam's story: would that he could, but he was to be away from the island shortly. He was going, yes, back to London.

He was told, in turn, of the Ralahami's son reading medicine at the University College on Gower Street and … and … and … How the headman was biting back his words! Was the father of the bride about to beg the bridegroom's Englishman to take his other child a sack of village pepper? Or a steamed plantain leaf lumped with home rice and curry? No, Robert hadn't nearly asked him to take any village love to his son. He had nearly asked that he say nothing of this wedding, if ever he met his son in London town. But upon his saying London to the Englishman's London, the Englishman looked like he'd swallowed his tongue and so Robert said nothing more. He would instead write of this news to Arthur. But the mail was so slow. Arthur would never be able to attend, even if he had known from the start. Besides, he had exams. After making this decision, for Arthur's sake, not to tell him in advance, Robert would have begged another of his nearly-son-in-law's cigarettes, but Sam was already moving again, this time leading his crumpled Englishman out of his walauwa into his vehicle out of his village *his his his* and for all the world he was only coming back for more.

nìne

Her chin against her knees, Alice was crouched in the almirah, watching her husband through the eye-wide gap between the wardrobe's doors. He was still brushing the dirt from his jacket, just as he'd done for all those just-married hours in the vehicle, on the curving downward drive to Colombo. Seated in the backseat with enough space between them for the rest of the village to dry its garden pepper, he had brushed his shoulder and smoked and stared out his window. When they reached the rest-stop at Ambepussa, a crowd came upon the vehicle like ants upon a dropped sweet and he climbed out and said something and they gave way like blown leaves. And only then did the blue-eyed driver turn and look at her and run his hand along his own forehead. She had smiled and looked away and wondered if from his vantage, standing guard beside the vehicle far down from the wedding platform hours before, he could have seen the bridal jewellery she had worn during the ceremony, the heavy gold humility that had made her keep her head down. Head down, she did not see who'd thrown the dirt that hit her new husband on the shoulder either, that had made him turn to her and say, for the first time words meant only for her and not cigarette words for her father, "We won't stay here now. Change fast and come."

The driver was staring forward when Sam came back with cool drinks and then returned to brushing his shoulder. She wanted to tell him that the dirt was gone, that it was never so much as he was making it out to be, that anyway it was village dirt, paddy dirt, nothing more than a dried-out clod. Alice would have said more; she would have asked him if he was trying to brush the very pinstripes away, but to say this or anything else she would have to speak over the sound of the engine. Besides, Alice did not know her husband so well to make such comments. To make any comments, really.

When they reached the city, it assaulted her every sense of time and place and purpose: Colombo was a mad rushing everything and everywhere of more than two lanes; was braids of schoolgirls and coils of standing-around people and all this yelling and calling and cart dung and rows of square white buildings fronted with stalls of shiny city things, cooking pots and fish and measuring scales themselves for sale. They moved through these shocking city streets slow and fine as a queen beetle in the grass until they reached the wide road to their hotel, the Oriental Grand she thought it was called, and as they went in she tensed at the sound of her husband's heavy modern shoes on the blinding lobby floor. It sounded like a one-man artillery demonstration. Once, when she was small, Alice and her brother and father had been made to wait in their cart while some Englishmen, planter-soldiers in angry pith helmets, drilled on a scrubby green field near Mahaiyawa, where before the war bioscope films had been shown, come one come all: the Oxford-Cambridge boat race of 1909, George V tours India, *Ben Hur*. Alice had tensed and taken her father's wrist at the boom boom echo cadence of yell and shot and reload, command and fire and check targets, a roaring upon roaring that became its own echo and then, briefly, a birdwing silence. After one round, while the wheezing pink soldiers were reloading and cursing the humid air for making greased pigs of their bullets, there was an awful cracking sound from far across the brown land, followed fast by so many little beats, like some Hindu god playing the tabla. A rose apple tree was splitting apart from an earlier volley, and as it broke and dropped its fruit, the Englishmen cheered, readied, aimed, and fired again. With this last volley her hand had slipped from her father's wrist because he had turned to scold Arthur, either for too much courage or too much fear, for his readiness either to run into the field to gather the fallen apples or to run down the road in holy blue terror. In the meantime, she had to hold her own wrist.

Even if she wanted to, Alice could not have taken her husband's wrist in the hotel lobby. She had nearly to run to keep up when they walked in. He nearly knocked over a boy cooling the esteemed guests with a palm-leaf fan in the first arch they passed through. Following, she saw the boy hoist his palm again and smile at the boy across from him, who was not smiling back because he was smiling at Alice who looked down and for whatever reason, maybe an apology to everyone else, held her bangles so they wouldn't make any noise as she followed after what seemed like the only sound left in the world, her new husband's hard black heels on the hotel's hard white tiles. Alice had rarely been in a building as large as this hotel, and at least when you went to temple you went barefoot.

She stood like a statue while he studied the pages of the gilded registry book as if they were sacred ola leaves before signing, in deepest cut, across more than two lines, MR. SAM KANDY. Reminded, he signed for her as well. AND MADAM. Waiting, Alice caught her breath and better understood the good of the going-away dress he'd brought for her. After the wedding ceremony, in the walauwa bedroom that had been made the bride's dressing chamber with profuse jasmine and strung coconut flowers and lit lamps and uneaten, ant-attacked sweets, her aunties had sat as quiet as if a divorcée were present. They waited as she went behind a teak partition to step into the going-away dress with Latha's help, Latha trying to help without actually touching the foreign cloth until it was absolutely necessary, which was when she had to pull the zipper along Alice's side, the noise like his engine coming from far off, the zipper a shiny-headed snake eating itself whole. After she was ready, but before she went into the front room where the men were waiting with betel and smoking and not discussing the dirt that had hit the bridegroom in the shoulder (*Dirt? What is dirt?*), Alice faced the aunties for their approval. They were seated in a row, wearing saris their grandmothers' grandmothers could have worn. They smiled at her with sideways eyes. And after she had gone with him in the vehicle, they had gossiped about it like idle mahouts: how the cloth was crème-coloured and less than six yards and hung like a rice sack from her waist because it was meant for English hips; how shamefully fast moving had been the zipper; how wrong it was for a high-born upcountry girl to wear a dress with a zipper, which, it was agreed, was only meant for a shamefully fast-moving woman. Her wearing it was like this marriage to this so-called Sam Kandy: bad fruit that mother-eyes and wife-warnings would have withered and dropped well before blind glutton bridegrooms and fathers could pluck and eat. But in a widower and orphan house like this one, the aunties and fates both knew, a pretty daughter, an only daughter like Alice, was meant for low hanging. When she was returned to the village, alone, after a one-night honeymoon, Latha would tell her everything.

They were shown to their room and their bags were arranged and now for the first time it was only he and she behind a heavy wooden door. Sam drew the drapes, which made Alice stiffen and think of squirrels but then without a word he walked into the bathroom. Because of the drawn drapes she could not look out at last and see the sea, and in spite of the zipper dress there was nothing in the world that was going to make her wait for him on the bed, the only bed in the room, canopied in bright white and wide enough for a whole village to sleep on but still she would not touch even a corner of her own volition, and so Alice did the only known thing she could think of. She opened the almirah and climbed in and pulled the heavy doors closed with all the life in her smallest fingers. It was larger than any almirah she had been in before, and it had a funny smell, more than just clean. It smelled like opened medicine. There she waited for him.

Back home, the almirahs smelled of lime and spice and folded clean clothes. She had hidden like this many times before, when she was only a girl and not, as now, twenty and waiting, nearly a woman. How many times had she taken jaggery from Latha's latest hiding spot, cracked it into smaller pieces with her back teeth, and then spit all of it into her palm and deliberated like a village council over the order of honey-brown slivers and stones to dissolve, one at a time, against the roof of her mouth. But it was never many pieces before she'd hear Latha sweeping in the hallway and put all of the sugar rock in her mouth at once and chew like road ordnance so that when the doors opened in a rumble against the rickety joins she could smile, open mouthed, innocent. She never once hid in her father's almirah because Latha told her that it had once been her mother's. She only had to be told once. With the natural intelligence of a lonely child in a large house full of dark places, Alice knew what was off-limits for play. She considered her free passage otherwise as proof of appeasing the ghosts.

She had no idea what it would mean to appease this man she had been married to. He was handsome and he was sharp and she did not mind everything about him that meant she should not have wanted to marry him: that he had named himself; that he had no family or village behind him, or even a horoscope leaf to place beside her own; that he seemed to come from nowhere save his own motorcar; that other than telling the Registrar of Deaths and Marriages that he was for certain upcountry-born, his answers about birth date and birth hour had moved around like sea-crabs and wall lizards; that he had stones for bones when they had had to bow to the monks at the almsgiving and blessing the night before the wedding; that he hadn't thrashed whoever had thrown dirt at him, or demanded he be thrashed, but instead had taken her from the village to the city to this hotel for their honeymoon and in all this, the only thing he had touched so far was his own shoulder.

The narrow light between the almirah doors went black for a moment and then came a wash of electric city light around his white-shirt frame and Alice looked out at Sam who was looking in not at her but at the shelves beside her and she wondered should she reach out her bangled wrists to be taken or wait? Should she help him become her husband or wait to be made his wife? She did not know because the only thing she had ever been taught about being a high-born lady she had been taught by Latha placing a baby squirrel on her shoulders and waiting to see which of them moved first. All she knew was that standing sitting or otherwise waiting in the presence of a man other than her father or brother, she was to be still still still, still as a god's eye, still and perfect as the untouched, untouchable gemstone on top of the temple spire.

He had something in his hands—his suit-jacket. He placed it across the topmost shelf and looked at her and she looked down and her bangles were a little ringing because she was herself a little shaking for what came next. But he only closed the doors. He left her in there with his dirty jacket. She heard him walking about the room and then the front door closed. The door opened again moments later and he and his shoes came crashing back and the almirah doors rumbled apart again and this time he reached in for her no for his darling suit-jacket and all was closed and crashed and she could hear his footfall firing and fading down the arched hall. Eventually, Alice opened the doors herself and climbed down and smoothed her dress and brushed the rest of the village dirt from the bed-sheets and then parted the curtains and waited at the shaded window, waited and watched for what and when and who this was, whose waiting wife until next life now she was.

ten

Sam crossed York Street and stood behind a scrum of city workers gathered at a tea-stall. The rail-thin office boys and paunchy hotel uncles turned at his approach and turned back, turned in, closer together. The stall-keeper at his shoulder-wide counter stood tippytoe on an unseen fruit crate to follow their resumed talk across sipped tea and spat betel, their going back and forth over fat and lazy bosses with their ugly wives and rumoured pretty daughters; over fat hotel guests with wrongfully pretty wives but of course ugly daughters; over fat and bored English wives with husbands on circuit and ravaged kingdoms of marzipan and fondant creams for meantime company, or dangerous smiling holiday nieces; and sometimes over their own faraway waiting brides, often near-perfect strangers, or over wives sending unanswered, unanswerable letters from the village about how long more before next visit and how long more to live with witchy sisters-in-law and don't forget your waiting dowry daughter and your older-than-marriage-time daughter, your pretty daughter, your difficult daughter. Sympathy was freely poured during these late-of-day sessions, it cost less than hot water, and always the question came from somewhere young and free in the scrum.

"But uncle, and I am only asking because others like to know, is your difficult daughter so difficult because she is also your pretty daughter?"

Clapping and hooting, roaring and laughing, it all gave way to a dancing-for-drama silence, the rest of them swaying as one with expectation that family honour would now have to be defended. And it was, with an outraged father's mimed chops to the offender's neck and half-chases down the road and sometimes thrown tea and carefully worded jokes threats proposals to make the smart-mouthed beggar marry the daughter in question and see for himself just how difficult ... actually how very pretty. Before long the laughing would quiet and the replays cease and the tea be finished and then it would just be standing around in daily Colombo noise, calls for hackney carts, constables' whistles, fruit and pots for sale, the wheeze of the city's new buses built for better roads and drier air and fewer people, the curse-storms of the conductors fighting over fares, the groan and clang song of the York Street trolleys, and through this all the air itself distending like heavy-coming rain for the men gathered at the tea-stall. Eventually, one of the them would have to mark aloud what was felt by all—not time itself, but boss-kept time, marzipan-feeding time, niece-strolling time, and so the scrum would break. In pairs and alone the men would stalk back to the rest of the day, the dead inside hours of nodding and smiling, the over-starched and sweat-stained honours and devotions of work in the city, work they boasted of or lamented over in their letters home, depending on how that morning's hours had passed, or what the tea-time martyr beside you had complained of, or what was reported threatened asked for in the latest letter from the village.

"Hallo, Mahatteya, tea for you please?"

"Right," said Sam, stepping forward to the counter like he should have when he had first crossed the street. He felt strong of spirit suddenly. *Mahatteya.* How the weight of the world could tilt in your favour across the life of a word! He had been called Mahatteya, not malli: he looked like a sir, not a little brother.

Earlier that day, in the village, he had been standing high upon the wooden wedding platform and looking down upon them all barefoot upon the bare ground and squinting and smiling up, who to the ash of their fathers' fathers knew the respect they were supposed to give such time and place and people, and so were wearing their best temple white to behold the Ralahami's daughter in her bridal sari and bridal gold. One of them gave respect to the unknown bridegroom as well. The dirt that hit his shoulder broke to bits but it made the mark it was meant to: we know nothing of you, your family, or where you're from: you are matter out of place: this is dirt.

Though he'd live to one hundred, he would never know who threw it. His eyes had been long since elsewhere, locked on a latecomer among the well-wishers watching the girls of the village perform a damsel's peacock dance for the new couple. This latecomer had moved among them slow and certain, taking his time like a noon-hour crocodile, and he was wearing a yellow hat. The yellow hat from the Christmas crate Sam had sent from Sydney, from whole lives earlier. When he had come to see his father to send him south, weeks before, Sam had looked around the old dirt hut and seen nothing, absolutely nothing, from the great world beyond and decided that the crate never made it out of Colombo. It must have been breached in Pettah by some other B. who would have burned his letter before marvelling trading feasting on the hats and handker-chiefs of Sam's secret home-sent charity. But no. The crate had come home. Beyond his high-match wedding day, his own hard-won veneration, someone down there knew something of his fellow blood and soil. Or so he thought with man's supreme vanity—that your own hated fate is the turning world's axel and gravity. Because, thought the thought, why would whoever he was wear it to watch him high upon the wedding platform, save to yellow Sam's triumph? But no moment was forced, no payment demanded, no expiation given. The man in the yellow hat did not come forward during the rest of the village's respects. And so the dirt Sam was grateful for: it was something he could brush off and keep brushing off, it was right cause to step off the wedding platform and go to the big house and forgo seven days' feasting in the dry dead village for the day-long ride into the salt-loud city, a ride spent wondering would he ever be Ralahami and walauwa were his father, his horoscope, his first hut known and told? Now, finally now, with everything in place as he had wanted it, this older want—that his father have a sense of how far away his taken boy had gone, too far for any village crow to find him—had become a waiting vengeance. And far worse than any fat old crow: this was a crocodile among the mud and lilies, waiting secret and patient in its hunger, its greatest power knowing one thing more than the rest of the universe: when it would attack. And all Sam Kandy knew was that this was absolutely opposite the way life had run since he had run from the temple: this time, someone would come for him. Meanwhile it was his wedding night.

⌒

"Anything else, Mahatteya?"

"No. Right. Tea. Thank you."

"Are you sure, Mahatteya?" Something in his voice.

"Sorry?"

"Mahatteya, I have worked in this tea-stall for many years."

"Right."

"Mahatteya, this means I have been here, across from the GOH, for many years."

"Right, and I am staying in this hotel." And I want to ask you, Sam said to himself, from still another life, anything but the near past and nearing future, did you ever hear of the Ratnapura gem trader who'd tried to take a whole floor of the GOH with a dirty ruby the size of a barbet's belly? Did you hear from out here the sound of his gem hammer on the registry book? Did you give him tea when they turned him out as a certain drunk and likely thief? Did you ask him what more he needed? Did you ask with something in your voice?

"But not staying alone, no?"

"You watched me arrive in my motorcar."

"Yes. You arrived as two but only one has come."

"Madam is … she is …" Sam was biting his bottom lip. What could he make of his new wife? Her name was Alice. She was city thin and village pretty. In the car she had studied the seatback and his shoulder, back and forth, like she thought she was to be examined on one or the other. She liked to hide in hotel furniture.

The stall-keeper smiled. "Madam is … resting, because it was such a long journey, and like any good gent you have come outside to give lady her time and space before, isn't it?"

Sam nodded and sipped his tea.

"Mahatteya, this is your wedding day, no?"

"It is."

The stall-keeper leaned out and looked west, asked with his chin that Sam consider as well the later-day-light, the tea-stained redness of the sun-falling sky.

"Mahatteya, congratulations! Long life to you and your wife and many children and please, I want no money for the tea." The stall-keeper motioned Sam closer. He dropped his voice. "But now is not your wedding day so much, is it."

"How's that?"

"Now is nearly your wedding night, Mahatteya."

"Mokatha?" snapped Sam, suddenly everything in full view.

"Please, I have kept this stall across from the hotel for many years, and helped my father here since I was a boy. Can you guess how many young men, none dressed so fine as you, have come here at this hour of their wedding days?"

Sam said nothing. He should have swallowed the rest of his tea and left. He could have poured it hissing upon the ground and left. He would have flung it across the counter and left and called for the motorcar and returned and left the stall a wreck of old wood and dry leaves and bloodred puddles, steaming spilt sunset. But he did none of it. Because if he did any of it, in time there would be nothing to do but the one thing he *had* to do this day, the one and only thing that, at epic-continental thirty, Sam Kandy had not yet done.

"Mahatteya, come this way, come this way," the stall-keeper said, motioning to the side of his stall. Sam stepped around a green-stained city of old metal canisters, drooping stalks of shoeflowers, a sack of onions dropped against the wall like a drunk. The stall-keeper blocked out his front window with old crate-bottoms and met him wearing a city saint's smile, all sweet and sharp angles. "Mahatteya," the man said again, and by now Sam hated the word, heard it only as a price quote for whatever was coming next. "I would like to help you with this."

"With what?"

"That's what the bridegrooms always say."

"You know this suit means nothing. I'll give you a thrashing just the same."

"Yes, I know what you can give me. But I also know what you can give your bride!"

The stall-keeper's eyebrows moved like they were hooked to a fisherman's pole. He spread his hands across the scored surface of his counter and leaned down smiling, his face so composed that for a moment Sam worried that here was another expecting to be kissed.

"I must return to Madam."

But his feet were suddenly so heavy. And York Street itself, from here to the hotel, suddenly seemed too much for a man who'd been walking city streets like they were his own paddy banks since he was fourteen. Besides, from this side of the stall he could not see his hotel window at all: he could not be seen. He lit a cigarette.

"Aiyo put that out will you! It'll shrivel you before you can even get started. Would you like to try a little watercress in hot water instead?"

"How's that?" Sam asked.

"If not watercress"—the rest of the words came fast—"I also have tea made from the bark of a kumbuk tree. Bitter but it rarely fails ..."

He went on, trying every sure-fire remedy and success story he knew. But Sam showed nothing to watercress or kumbuk, or to the tale of an Englishman who had taken five cups of a particular concoction and had five handsome sons to show for it, five crowns of gold. While the stall-keeper spun, Sam dropped cigarette after cigarette, crushed each like this was some victory and eventually he plucked a flower from the tree beside him but memory had him here too. It was wet to touch like a Malay Street shophouse flower hanging between humid bedroom bricks, and Sam started shredding its petals between his thumbnail and first finger, petals that were either a shocked or a tired out pink-red, now splotchy Sydney cheeks.

"Ah, yes, I can also make shoeflower tea from those plants but that's for the woman, for when you don't want to marry her. It's called, you see, a cleansing tea, Mahatteya. Worried lover-boys and mad fathers come for it at dawn. Just yesterday the son of one of our finest Tamil speechmakers came and took. But not something you need today." The stall-keeper's voice dropped. "Mahatteya, also, not here, but also, I have access to yellow oleander and to an even more potent one. What another of my English customers told me is called"—here he swallowed—"*Gloriosa superba*. The Glory Lily. Not an auspicious name, at least for the madam who takes any of it. Mahatteya, do you know about these flowers?"

Sam shook his head.

"Of course not, and a bad omen even to mention on your wedding day. Now, if you don't like to try watercress or kumbuk before you go upstairs, I have durian pulp, but don't take it unless you can hold your breath like a pearl diver. Also cinnamon oil and rosewater for best-smelling breath and body. If it has been a long day of travelling for you and Madam, I recommend both. Also, look"—the stall-keeper reached out his opening hand—"for top-flight gents like you, tea made with Ceylon's strongest cardamom seeds. These are taken from the very best spice merchant in all of Colombo, his family has been selling for centuries. Mahatteya, please, know it for yourself!"

They were the right brown, but shrivelled. He breathed in just enough to remember the nature of such strength and smiled. Some poor Ismail, whether his former boss or his son or half-son, was still getting tricked or was by now tricking others by grinding fresh cardamom upon weak seeds too long out of their pods. He blew into the stall-keeper's cupped palm. It made a dirty little windstorm. The stall-keeper dropped the cardamom and it clattered like a broken bridge of teeth.

"Right," said Sam. "Strongest." He waited for the next thing to knock down. He wasn't going upstairs yet.

The stall-keeper seemed to drop to his knees but before Sam could peer over the counter the little man had come out the side entrance and rifled through a sack. Wordless, he returned to his stand, stepping back onto his fruit crate, and, staring at Sam eye to eye, showed him a long, straight knife. Right. Strongest. He sliced a copper onion in two. He tossed one half to the side and pulled free an intact ring from the other. He held it forward in the half-circle of his thumb and first finger like a squashed pearl. When in doubt for any and all wrongs and ills, take an onion, his mother said. When in doubt he'll pay, show a knife, said his father.

"Eye-slice of onion," the stall-keeper declared. His tone was now flat as blade. "Take and eat and love your bride. Take a vial of rosewater too."

"And what will this do?" Sam scoffed.

"This will do what you won't otherwise do on your own."

Immediately, desperate happily, Sam tensed and clenched his teeth and made like a man about to tear down the nearest skyline. "You know I could—"

"Aiyo Mahatteya, enough, please." He made a face like someone was taking too long piercing one of his ears. "I have customers waiting. And your bride is waiting. You could take this and go, or leave this and go. I have only tried to help you and your madam this afternoon and see what I have for my efforts." Still holding the onion slice in one hand, he showed the other, an empty palm below a shame-stained sleeve.

"So you want money for me to eat a slice of onion?"

"No, Mahatteya. I want money to forget that today, your wedding day, you had to eat a slice of onion."

⌁

He pulled open the almirah in vain. She came out of the electric-bright bathroom, where, bored far past tears, she had been staring at herself in the mirror, at the absurdity, the futility of her dress, of this going-away modern. He took her by the wrist. He led her past the bed, downstairs to the dining hall. They ate. He ate. She stared at the silverware. He ate her plate too. They went to another room and stood inside grand double doors watching English and Burgher couples glide and twirl to a music of lazy horns and drum patter, their eyes half-closed, their noses hooked to unseen wires hanging from the high ceiling. She put her hand on his shoulder and he turned looking ready as lizard if she asked him to dance but that was not it at all. Other than a little lime juice at Ambepussa, Alice had taken nothing since milk-rice before dawn and was about to fall down. Two stewards tried to help but he waved them off and took her upstairs and now there was nothing left but one bed. They lay beneath a fan going loud as a roosting tree, a starched white plain between them. She reached to touch his hair and then his cheek and Sam gripped the sheets with one hand and felt for the zipperhead with the other. Trying to split the dress open was better for his stomach churn than wondering whether onion could in fact banish memories of saffron folds and peppercorn, of ginger-root and swept butterflies. In the morning they took turns dressing behind the bathroom door. Neither spoke of the other's crying. Nor did Alice ask, why so much rosewater and onion?

For breakfast she ate two bowls of curd and even asked for part of his plate. They left the hotel and were driven to a photographer's studio where they were placed in front of a dark curtain. Sam was given a top hat and leaned on a black umbrella and Alice was seated with a shawl around her shoulders and a white parasol open in one hand and here they were frozen and flashed in formal love. Afterwards Sam had the driver take him back to the hotel, and he went inside and then he went across the street with dining room cups and saucers and brought back their mid-morning tea. They drank like touring royals as they were driven through the city to the harbour, where he kept his office in a back room above a barber's stall near the main jetty. Sam leaned forward and told the driver to take her back to the village. Upon Piyal's returning the motorcar safe and fast, Sam said, he would pay for the boy's first shave. He said this like it was the supreme prize of life and Piyal nodded thinking the drive itself was enough but he'd take the shave too. Sam turned to Alice like they were again perfect wedding-day strangers and said, "Expect me shortly and give my respect to your father." And that was all. Her husband climbed out of the motorcar onto Wharf Road and in five fast steps became the rest of the city.

ELEVEN

Nine months later, no cries had come, as yet, from inside the walauwa; no labouring woman cries, no crying new baby, no mourning women. Alice's father and her brother were waiting on the verandah. The servant was standing at the far side, studying a palm full of blown-down browned coffee blooms as if he had come upon flowers dropped from heaven itself. Later, for half a box of chocolates, he would tell Latha everything they said.

"I won't go in and see her, Appachchi," Arthur insisted, "for the same reason why you refuse. Such things are not done, at least if you follow the old ways."

"You are not to tell me about the old ways. No. And when it was my turn, when it was your mother, at least I listened from the hallway. I did not hide on the verandah like this—"

"You mean hide in Colombo, no?"

"—but that is not to be discussed now. Aiyo! What an omen to give your sister on this auspicious day! Wait. How do you mean, Colombo?"

It was a full minute between them, a father-and-son silence. They were each in morning sarong cinched below their chests. Arthur's was shock white and edged along its ironing creases with blue-grey dust; during his years abroad, where he had been sent by his father to become a doctor who would never have to return to this village, it had been folded and stacked in an almirah in his bedroom. Robert's was also fine cloth and white, but it was patterned in faint diamonds and tea stains and cigarette holes, yellow and black, like burnt wedding rings. Robert was hunched at the shoulders from age and from the defeat of recent talk with his son, and also from the defeating prospect of another birthing day in the walauwa. Arthur was hunched from the coolness that could sometimes be early-morning upcountry air, a coolness that he had forgotten from his time in the heat and dirt that was cities, was Calcutta, where he had gone to London. The young man's shoulders were also hunched from lying about medical college, from the knowledge that his father knew that he was lying about medical college and still would not relent in asking him to go see his twin sister in her first labour.

Robert made a clicking noise from the back of his mouth upon realizing that when Arthur had said hide in Colombo, this was said against Sam, who was not here with his wife in labour but of course, as usual, away in the city. His driver, Piyal, had left in the middle of the night to bring him. Robert might have agreed with Arthur, but there was an order to things. He would first catch his twenty-one-year-old son at whatever badness it was that had brought him, unannounced, eyes everywhere but level, home. And then he might see about catching his nine-month son-in-law at whatever it was he should have been caught at—whether secret city rogue or just a bad husband who, since his wedding day, had visited the village with all the frequency and feeling of a green government agent: periodically and never but pained-looking. And like a good wife, Alice had played bitter daughter and said that her husband's absences were not just because of his business in the city but also from shame, because his new father-in-law, her father, had never even tried to discover who threw the dirt at him on their wedding day. And Alice was, by old ways, right. Robert should have. But he had done nothing. The very point of marrying her off this way was to free himself from having to do such things. *What is a water glass? What is poison?*

Not just himself. When his son graduated from the Buddhist boys' college in Colombo but failed to win a Queen's Scholarship to England, Robert had spent the family's savings on his education abroad, and because by his own decree no doctor had lived in the village since his own father had fallen, his own son would not live here either, whether as doctor or Ralahami. As for the girl, he had married her off as he had. Let this city-Sam find and punish the man who threw the dirt. Let him contend with dry days and dead dirt and crops shrivelled and legions of old broken men waiting for nothing but more shrivel. Let him defend his house from the latest fish-stink moneybag and his low country chewing and his low offer. Let him chase off all the new charmers whistling through the upcountry these days, brown men in white suits speaking of the British Governors like they were brothers-in-law and batch-mates, sometimes wrapped above the waist in sarong and fine-jacketed and carrying on like the king's men of old, their secret swords apparently ready to return the land to the glory days of Sri Vikrama's Udarata. *The politics,* Robert and his villagers called those fellows. Salesmen and snake charmers all, introducing themselves as Congress one day and Legislative Council the next and National Assembly a week later and every tongue telling Robert that their coming to his village to seek his pledge of support was in fact their pledging *their support* and the support of the Crown or Congress or LC or National Assembly to him and his village. His son thought to shame him with talk of keeping to old ways as if, by 1930, old ways were anything but another slogan to be for or against in the Ceylon upcountry. Robert wanted none of it for him or his blood. And if his new son-in-law wanted justice, let him lash the dirt-throwing rogues to his motorcar and the nearest palm tree and ride. He lit another.

"It is your place to go in and see about her state," Robert said again, "because you are, for us, the London doctor." Songbird and screech filled the morning air, and now, also, tapped ash, blown smoke. "You are the first doctor to come to the village in many, many years. I do not mean for your studies to be wasted here. I don't! Where all the medicine these people want is things for cooling and mashed-up rubbish from the forest for aches and pains, and I know your studies are not yet complete, but you are already more of a doctor than betel payments and mortar mash and pouring oil in the nose, no? Aren't you? Unless—"

"Only in a place like this does the whole village have to find out whether or not the brother goes to see the sister when she—"

"Aiyo! Only in a place like this, you say. And I can hear it in your voice, what this place must look like to you, now, from where you have been and what you have become. Ruined. You are ruined for this place." And this was success, Robert thought. Shame made into freedom from the birth-village. But why, then, return, unless—"And that is why I cannot understand why you have returned like this, unless—"

"I returned," Arthur interrupted his father at the same point in Robert's speculation as he had for nearly ten thousand such speculations since he had come home from Calcutta, where, until this last failing term, he had secretly been studying in the only medical college that would admit him while, through a series of go-betweens and confectioned letters, he'd allowed his father to believe he was, in fact, studying in London, "because this is my village. I am your son, the first-born and only son of the Ralahami, and this is my village. But then I receive your letter informing me that Alice has married a motorcar named Sam Kandy. The letter arrived in the middle of exams, and I blame it for what has happened. And so I have come to see about this, to make sure what's mine is mine."

"And your exams? Your results?"

"Daddy, may I have a cigarette?"

"Arthur, why have you come home now? What have you done? What has happened?"

"What have I ever done but what you have made me do? Did I ask to become an English doctor? Did I ever ask for anything but what's mine by birth?"

"I decide what is yours by birth. And what's yours is your sister's dowry money, what's yours is the tuition and boat tickets and Parker pen it gave you. Now tell me your results and go see her in her time."

"I won't."

"You won't, or you can't?"

"I—can't."

Now Robert knew for certain. He didn't know how his son had pulled it off, the letters were always stamped from England, and Arthur seemed to have read the letters Robert had sent to the address he had given, Euston Square, London, but Robert knew. The boy must have come home on the last of the tuition money, he thought. He wondered where he'd spent the rest of it.

"Son, putha, what colour are the lorries in London?"

"I can't."

Meanwhile, inside, Latha was about to pour out the broth when she thought she heard Alice calling from the back bedroom. She had started it cooking the evening before, and by morning it had boiled down by half. A full moon night, and between fits of sleeping until dawn Alice had been breathing *Soo sa* like Latha told her to. *Soo sa* But no, it was an outside noise, some songbird or other lonely at first light. Latha returned to the broth. Using one of the showy metal kitchen things the new husband had brought, Latha skimmed the pond-brown foam from the surface of the bubbling soup and smacked it on the ground outside the kitchen door, where a cat considered it until two dogs barrelled in. Then she stretched a piece of muslin over the rim of the pot and drained the marrowy liquid into a cup that she would take in to the girl, whom she had raised from birth to bride and now birth. Alice was not lying in the same room as her mother had been, but still. Same house, same high round belly and otherwise branch thin. She would also weaken too much if the labour went too long. And so she would be made to drink this cup and would be made to drink more. Latha could also have asked Ralahami for a spoonful from his brandy bottle, which he kept in his room beside his English shaving kit and Portuguese aftershave—more things brought to the village in the vehicle. Latha had a joke with the washerwoman and with Lal, the Ralahami's servant: soon the husband would run out of things to bring and then start fastening pieces of the city itself to the top of his vehicle and drive them to Sudugama. In time the joke passed down into the village itself, so that whenever the motorcar was heard from far off, never more than once a month, they watched from their dark doorways half expecting to welcome home at last their borrowed memories and shared notions and rumours and legends of the city itself: English horses the size of elephants; Chetty men with chests painted like jungle cats; windowpanes and saltwater waves.

The brandy the husband brought a few months before would be fast-warming for the chills that would come between pushing, but Latha wanted him nowhere involved with Alice's labour. Any him. When it came to babies born in this walauwa, Latha made no distinction between memory and omen. Even a man standing in the hallway was too much. At least the Ralahami seemed to accept this, she thought; he had been waiting on the verandah smoking and talking in low voice with Arthur since dawn. Later, for nothing more than some leftover sweets, she knew, Lal would tell her everything that was said between them. Meanwhile they had not come near the kitchen threshold even to ask for their own tea. Had she the choice, she would have sent the Ralahami and Arthur to fetch the husband from Colombo in the vehicle with Blue Piyal, as Latha and Alice had taken to calling the driver outside the boy's hearing. But Alice had already sent the boy to bring the husband, who had sent the boy with the car from Colombo a few days before with instructions that when it was time, Alice should be driven down. He'd made arrangements for her to deliver at a city hospital, and if Alice thought it necessary, Latha could come too. Motorcar to city hospital and Latha could come too. Ha. Had she the choice, Latha would have given Blue Piyal a return route of her own devising, which the boy would have followed like a prayer, she knew, if only she said Alice wanted him to do it. A route that took father, brother and him, the husband, from Colombo to Galle to Hambantota, Hambantota to Batticaloa to Trinco, Trinco to Point Pedro to Puttalam, Puttalam to Kurunegala to the village. And by then, went Latha's hoping, the men of the family would arrive at the walauwa to be greeted by Alice in her old age, Alice still living.

She would not mind such slowness for the women who had been sent for either, Alice's aunties, the Ralahami's elder sister and the younger, the bride-of-next-week as she was still known in the village. They lived with their fat smiling husbands and overfed sons and fat dowry daughters in Mahaiyawa, on what they thought was the far better side of Kandy town—you could tell from how they looked and looked around those rare times they visited. Who, upon their grand fussy arrival, would take over with Alice, just as they had at Alice's birth, and at Alice's wedding, and Latha would have to play along again, play like they knew better. And she would; she always did; she never but seemed to.

"Latha! Latha aiyo, it's coming again, hurting!"

"Aney wait I am coming!" The broth splashing onto her hand, Latha rushed to the back bedroom, her bare feet pounding the bare floor.

When she reached the room the pains had already passed and Alice's head was turned to the side, her lips pursing air. Her many gold earrings, which she had insisted upon wearing for when he came, played back the morning light shining through the barred window. Latha could still remember boring the girl's ears with a lime thorn and then curing the bleeding pinpricks with the cut lime. How many times had Latha swept from the corridor into this very room so someone would find Alice hiding in the almirah, the old almirah that had been junked behind the kitchen two days after the wedding, when another, a hotel almirah from the city, had been sent in its place.

"Alice-girla, take this before they come again."

"Who is coming? When is he coming?"

"Just take this will you."

"Medicines from Aiya?" She had been born a minute after him but always gave Arthur respect as the older brother. She eased herself up to her elbows and wiped the sweaty strands of hair from her brow. Latha wiped too, needlessly, and then cupped her face, a jewel-perfect face finer than any hand save a mother's deserved to touch. She leaned in, as she had so many times, with words and a voice and a look meant to be kept between them, to keep them as Latha thought they were—themselves unto each other and then came father, brother, the rest of the world, husband.

"Mad? You think I'd let Big London Doctor come near now?

This is strength for when you need it. I put only a little garlic. Drink before they come again."

"Who's coming? When is he coming? He has to come for this, no?" Alice Kandy had never known a married woman as anything other than a visiting aunty or a bowing villager but even such passing glances were enough to know that what was hers was not enough. Nine months of it and finally, now, there was no more smiling and excusing that his work in the city kept him so far away; no more ignoring the empty chair kept daily for him at table and the empty bed beside her own; no more pretending along with Latha and the smirking envying rest of them that the gifts he sent with his blue-eyed driver and his own weeks-apart day-and-night visits were the free and fine goods of a modern married woman. He had to come for this. She turned her head, looking past the first gift, her grand GOH almirah. Until the contractions came again Alice's eyes stayed there, on the threshold that gave way to the morning-bright corridor empty of all husbands.

~

He had to come for this. If he did not, Piyal would say something. Piyal decided this again and again as he drove from the upcountry to Colombo, the Morris's lights catching nighttime walkers and wheeling bats and the quartz-coloured eyes of woken dogs and so many insects that more than once he'd had to pull to the side and wipe a translucent furze of crushed wings from the headlamps. He would say something even in the new Englishman's hearing, because she had said she wanted him, Sam, near for when baby came. And so she had sent Piyal to bring him back. And he, Piyal, would bring her husband back or he would say something, even do something, if he did not come for this. Alice, Madam, she called him Blue Piyal. Nine months he'd been her husband's driver. Her Blue Piyal. Seeing her every few weeks, he knew how many earrings she wore in each ear and the singing of her bangled wrists going and coming. He knew where, whether upon or below her growing belly, she kept her hand when she was tired or laughing or pained. He knew every glance and angled view that could be had while she sat in the back of the vehicle.

Reaching Prince's Building, where Sam had recently taken over Henry Paulet's vacated office and apartment scheme, Piyal could hear them inside, talking. But Piyal knocked and entered anyway and for the first time in his adult life, he spoke first.

"Sir, please, you must come."

Sam did not stand. His new Englishman turned in his chair.

"What, Piyal? Is she waiting in the vehicle?"

"Sir, please, you must come."

"Why *must* I come, Piyal? Is Madam in the vehicle?"

"Sir, please."

"Piyal. Is. She. In. The. Vehicle."

"No, sir. She is in the village, and baby has started."

"I told you to tell Madam she was to come to Colombo when it was time." *Latha.*

"HA!" said the Englishman, Charles Curzon. "You told your wife to be driven here to have the baby? My God, on these roads! She'd give birth in the backseat after the first bump!"

"Sir, please, Madam said you must come."

"Must come, is it?" the Englishman answered Piyal, looking at Sam, who said nothing. "Well then." He cracked his knuckles. "Of course that's the right thing to do. Shall we continue this conversation upon your return?"

"Piyal," said Sam, "tell me, did you drive through the night?"

"Yes, sir."

"That is very good of you. I will tell Madam when we reach the village. Would you like to sleep and then we'll go?"

"No, sir."

"Right. Good news. Baby is coming?"

"Baby is coming, sir."

"Right. And so I must go." Sam stood and smoothed his vest. He walked to the door. Piyal and the Englishman followed and Sam held it open and Piyal went first and Sam put his hand on the Englishman's shoulder and Piyal turned just as Sam closed the door and set the chain and they were already talking again. And Piyal went to knock and knock it down but what if he did and then said and tried to do and all of it for her but he was sent off for trying and never saw her again?

The next day, when they arrived at sundown in Sudugama, the boot crammed with toys and tins and dresses, Sam came to the room and waited for Latha to leave, who passed into the hallway with her arms full. Then he knelt beside Alice's bed and touched her forehead and told her he would have come right away but the driver had fallen stone asleep, day before, at his office door. And Alice nodded with nothing behind it, too tired for grief or gratitude, too exhausted to care whether her husband had been beside her every moment since her own birth or come just now, decades later, the twins themselves grown and married and gone. A boy and also a girl; the boy was considerably larger. Leaving Alice asleep, Sam nodded to the sideways-smiling aunties in the front room, accepted handshakes from Robert and Arthur and gave out cigarettes and then asked Latha to see the babies. He counted them, their twenty fingers and twenty toes, and he left the next morning. He had to buy more toys, toys now for two, toys for twins, toys for boys, toys for girls. And so for years afterwards, Sam Kandy's son and daughter would know him as the rest of the village did—as engine noise and parcel string, as a day's flash of love and pinstripes.

twelve

All morning and still no sign of him. For hours they'd been waiting
to escort the infamous Bracegirdle to the harbour, to make sure
he left on a ship bound for London. Sam was pacing around his
desk, circling a letter from Alice asking that he come to the village
straight away, warning that if he didn't, all would be lost. Curzon
was sitting at his, wondering what story Bracegirdle had used to get
onto the island, how it compared. Bracegirdle: the blond Jesus of
Ceylon's plantation workers in 1936 and 1937: by April 1939, old
news in Colombo. He was leaving now because he wanted to, and
such was his court-supported right as he made clear to any editori-
alist or bus conductor still willing to listen to him, but regardless,
as one of the Governor's men had informed Charles Curzon in
asking him and his partner Sam Kandy to see to the details of
departure, there was no need to take chances. May 1 was nearing
and workers' rallies were planned across the island. Dockworkers
and teapluckers and villagers were expected to gather, having been
told by outsiders who understood nothing that wasn't written for

them in some white man's pamphlet that they were the exploited poor and not simply dockworkers and teapluckers and villagers. In the meantime there was no need for ten thousand coolies to decide they had to see Bracegirdle off or make him stay and either way have high cause to stop loading ships for the day, which did no good for anyone, Curzon and Kandy included.

And so arrangements were made to ensure Bracegirdle's farewell was quiet, full, and firm if necessary, the details of which Sam had seen to while Curzon booked the island's "most famous" revolutionary a first-class berth on a London-bound ship. And if Bracegirdle took the complimentary ticket, Curzon would be newsboy pleased to tell the near world. And if Bracegirdle insisted on travelling below deck and brown, in keeping with his speechmaking, Curzon would happily arrange for that too, and keep the difference between first-class and steerage for his troubles just as, years and lives and worlds earlier, he had pocketed the penny between what he paid for the last of the day's late-edition city papers and the cut rate he then sold them for to the lovelies leaving the late ferries on Navy Pier.

That was back in Chicago, 1903, when he was still a Jewish kid called Saul Kurtz and he shared a bed with two older brothers and had to plug his nose to use the toilet because his father and uncle were trying to make cheese in the bathtub like the Italians next door. His life, until that night the letters of the late-edition headline were so big and black even his old zayde could have read it. DAUGHTER OF CHICAGO TURNED QUEEN OF INDIA! And just below that, *LEVI LEITER'S GIRL SHINES AT DELHI DERBY!* The rest of the front page was a picture of a smiling white woman riding an elephant covered in a thousand bank building rugs, wearing a dress that looked like it was made of ten thousand peacocks. When he was only six, Saul had spent his whole life's money at the World's Fair on one such staring feather. That night, he was late coming home. He would not join a crowded trolley for fear it would be crushed; the beating would be worth it to have this wild shimmery looking glass. But his onion-fingers mother only mashed his cheeks for her pretty gift. Eternal days later, when finally he found it, pressed under her pillow, the feather was frayed and faded and many times cracked along the stem. Ten years later, studying a newspaper picture of a beautiful woman robed in peacock eyes, waving at thousands, he felt connected to Lady Curzon, Chicago-born, whose father's name was Levi too.

That last night on Navy Pier he sold all his papers save one, the front page of which he studied a day later in the slatted light of a boxcar rumbling through Indiana. He also thought about how an Englishman would pronounce Saul and by Ohio he was Charles and by New York he was Charles Curzon though he went by just Charlie when he took deck-painting work on a Calcutta-bound steamer. Given a free day in Cape Town, he joined two other boys and went into the city. They got sailor drunk in a downstairs one-room bar and upstairs lost their virginity, all three to the same coffee-coloured girl. One of the others, a groomsman's son born Jim Cole in West Virginia but trying to play a touring scholar from Boston named Kolbe James, said this felt like home. Charlie and the third walked back but forgot which ship was theirs and thought this was fine and funny and by the time they were sober it was morning and their ship was gone. The third boy suddenly admitted he was from Towson, Maryland, and that before this had never been beyond the Inner Harbour. The last words between them were his thinking out loud that the upstairs coffee-coloured girl might have had a sister.

After a week of mumbling along to the rosary at a Goan-run boarding house near the docks, Charlie was hired onto an Aden-bound steamer where, it was promised, every other ship in port would be going to India. Day one in Aden, so hot and dry his throat felt like a deck-plank, the rest of the seamen went off to the bazaar but he followed the ships' officers and Englishmen and found a shop in the Crescent where he bought a chalk-white suit that he wore for the first time ten days later in Colombo, where he introduced himself to the tallest white man he could find as Lord and Lady Curzon's nephew Charles. Immediately the Englishman stepped back and bowed like G-d had tapped him back and forth with his fingers. A Ceylon Englishman bowing to a cheese-maker's son from Chicago! "No doubt you must be looking for Queen's House, yes?" declared the Englishman. Charles clipped out a "Quite," and for the rest of the day there were only introductions and apologies as nephew Charles explained that someone on the ship had stolen his bags and billfold and soon enough he saw there was no need to reach actual India.

He fenced questions for two years about his Englishness— from homesick sceptics about the location of his family's summer residences and the health of headmasters and rowing coaches; requests for clarification about positions played on the rugger field and cricket oval; inquiries after the state of certain famous gardens. In 1906 his world-beloved aunt died and to see his face no one, not even that bucket crab Leonard Woolf, had the temerity to ask anything more save whether he was going to England for the service. He was not. He gave a sombre single rose to each wife of the men he was trying to work for, work with, work. He roundly declared, "She died just as she lived," and asked that thereafter a period of silence be respected. Before long he had secured a good position in the Harbourmaster's Office. Two decades later, few of the Ceylon English still believed he was true Curzon. You couldn't but assume he was an American after watching him eat at your table. It was decided he must have been a relation on the late Lady Curzon's side, and no one could fault him for pretending otherwise. Besides, he never dared to marry into any proper English family but instead wed an Anglican Burgher girl from Mount Lavinia. Over the years he raised peacocks in his back garden and worked mostly around the harbour. In 1930 he was deputized to look into a shipping agent's racket—short-loaded rice and missing dockworkers and mariners sold by who? Where? To whom? At what cut rates? Enough to get this whoever this fellow was a white man's vehicle?

Curzon found Sam Kandy by following the Morris to a greyed wood building beside the very jetty where he had arrived years before, where, without his even having to ask, the wan-faced Tamil who ran the barber-stall on the ground floor pointed upstairs with his straight-edge, then went back to his work. Before Curzon was halfway up the stairs, Sam appeared on the landing.

"Is that your vehicle below?"

"Your name?"

"Let me ask yours."

"I am Sam Kandy."

"Ah. I see. I am Charles Curzon. Is that your vehicle below, Sam Kandy?"

"Why you are asking?"

"Because the law holds that no native may own a vehicle," Curzon answered, expertly twitching his moustache. "If you claim this vehicle is yours, either it's been stolen or paid for in ways that merit further investigation."

"It's not mine, and it's not stolen. You can ask my driver. He's downstairs, taking his first shave. I ride at the pleasure of a business partner, an Englishman."

"Ah. I see. And that is why I am here. Just who, in these things you've been doing, Mr. Kandy, is your business partner?"

"Shall we go inside?"

"Yes fine, let's go inside, where you'll tell me his name. And perhaps thereafter you shall tell me yours as well, your real one. Because we've heard much about you around the harbour and many of us in the Harbourmaster's Office would like to know who you actually are. At least if you were a Corea or a Carolis all this moneymaking of yours would make sense. But just what is a Sam Kandy? What is your real name, sir?"

"What's yours?"

A year later, they were in open business together. They started a shipping agent's firm and worked out of a free office Sam knew of, in a named building in Fort. There they collected fees from ships' representatives who were never but needful of known and strong and sea-worthy men. Sam's old office near the harbour they kept too; there they collected fees from young men lining the staircase every morning, many fresh cut and shaved while they waited (and Sam got a piece of that too): village sons sent barefoot, their best sarongs cinched at the knee and only let down just before they went in to meet the shipping agent Mahatteya; and also runaways, stowaways, middle sons, and the plain bored, all money-paying needful for someone in a good suit to guarantee the captains of the world-showing ships that they were strong and sea-worthy. And so Sam and Charlie made greater and greater sums between the two of them as the 1930s world moved itself from village to city and across the deep waters—from port to port came city-sized ships groaning with Burmese rice and German cannon, Saudi wool and racehorses, Ceylon cinnamon, British cars and umbrellas and children's tea-party sets, American cars, American cannon, crated jungle cats and sitting rooms, coca, cocoa, coke ovens, coconuts, carousel horses from Austria, Chinese tea and oranges, cosmo-politan rats and newborns, Leon Trotsky, rabbis and near-whole congregations from Riga and Kiev destined for Palestine or the Lower East Side, shaved-down Boreal forests, American salt and Kolkata salt and Gold Coast salt, Greco pillars and sacred statuary and stacked American chrome, diamonds and coffee from Angola,

Rhodesian gold and copper, tobacco, hooch, rubber, Airedales travelling in thicker blankets than most passengers, burnished film canisters of Charlie Chan, Tarzan, and … Announcing … *Garbo Talks!*, brides from Alsace for the bachelors of Fond du Lac, with father notes pinned to their coats and mother jewellery pinned in their hair, Japanese invited to pick the coffee trees of São Paulo, the Stalin Pocket Library (International Publishers, NY), thousand-pound slabs of Carrara marble ordered from Mississippi with the last of the family money to mark the founder's grave on an other-wise razed plantation, Gros Michel bananas from Colombia and the guns and bullets to protect them, typhoid, fewer and fewer player pianos, a Buddha for Wallace Stevens, Malay tin and tinned meat from Argentina, nuns, salt cod from Newfoundland for white rum from Trinidad, and also, whether carrying it all or counting it or counting on carrying it, whether fighting or sleeping or praying or trying out new names on each other while sitting around, every colour and kind of coughing hungry ready young man. The world was coming in and out of Colombo, and Sam and Charlie were making money both ways while the rest of the island, brown and white there was no difference here either, spent itself in ceremonial divination and judgment of bloodlines and birth-villages, lands held and families married into, local Anglican schools attended.

They spent more time working beside each other than either spent loving their wives or children let alone with men of their own race but still, Charlie knew no more of Sam Kandy than he did of Lady Curzon: for him these were conjuring names and lives to be lived up to, learned from, made money with, made part of his own. And when they were alone, Charlie would try to tell his subjunctive-Chicago stories of Navy Pier brawling, because even though he was by age, skin, friends, and taken name the upstairs man, and even though Sam always played along in front of others, the staring way Sam Kandy listened when they were only two gave

Charlie the notion that some former-life-Sam must have fought far more boys on Navy Pier than he could ever remember having fought himself, that for all the bright and jagged stories he could tell of himself to his partner, Charlie might as well have been throwing bottles on a Michigan shoreline already shining with sea glass.

Not that Sam ever told out himself. "What about you?" Charlie would ask. "How'd you get here?" "Where were you before?" Nothing. Head down, reading bills of lading and seaman seniority rolls or another letter from his village wife. Nothing save one October night, in 1938, when they heard crackers and snatches of "God Save the King" outside their window. Word had come from Munich, by way of London, that there would be peace for our time and the monsoon had yet to come and so the city, Sam and Charlie too, revelled this night in the good fortunes of the near world and far, revelled hard because they could tell from the air itself the time for storms was still coming. With a bottle between them they went walking along the Wharf Road to the breakwater, where the eternal sound of the world divided into its first and last chords, into crashing and the quiet that comes afterwards only to give way, always, again.

"Okay Sam, between us, for once, something! By now I've said so much about Saul Kurtz you could pick out the mezuz above my old front door! Just for once, anything. I know how names work here. No different than most places, and I've never met any Gary Indianas. So come on. Who were you before you were Sam Kandy?"

In the quiet between them there came the smatter of many more crackers, distant and muffled, as if set off beneath stacks of telegrams. Nearer were the sounds of roused birds and of sailors roaring a song against a curfew whistle that kept blowing but eventually stopped, defeated. After a cheer the song started again, one voice stronger.

"No one that any one of you could ever know," Sam said eventually, squaring his shoulders to the black lapping sea, the horizon blocked out by a parliament of moored ships. He breathed in the sour air of the listless harbour, that tang of rusted anchors and hulls, foul blooming bird- and man-rubbished seawater, all the seeping cosmopolitan bilge no one ship's like another and no ship's the same this hour as the hour before. Who was he before? To get there Sam would have to tell of things caught and burnt, driven, drowned, dropped, watched, played, picked, promised, chased, held against, hidden, heard and heard of, opened, sent, bundled and taken, taken care of, stomped, thrown, smoked, spent, remembered, remembered, remembered, earned, bought, bowed before, and crushed with his stone-hard heel. And in the next breath, he would have to tell more.

"One day, I had to be Sam Kandy. The rest I wipe from my feet."

"Yes, but when did you decide? What made you decide? Who?" Curzon was given another sip, Sam holding the bottle against his mouth. He then finished it himself, wanting the same warrant to speak ten more rare true words and, he hoped, be free of them.

"I remember things starting around the time my wife was born."

Charlie stumbled, stopped, and doubled over as if a ladder of Hindu temple gods had descended to tickle his gut. When he could breathe he tried to speak but the words themselves brought the blue fists down again. Never mind he was eighteen years older than his own wife, who was born at dawn in a Mount Lavinia bedroom while he was rumbling across Indiana in a boxcar. What kind of man dated his design from the day his wife was born?

"You know, Sam, in all these years, and I can even remember being in the office the day Piyal came to say your children were born, in all these years, have I even met your wife?" Of course he had never introduced Sam to his own wife. In some ways he had turned true English. "These years I've watched you buy her half the stuff in Cargill's and Piyal plays like he's counted the hairs on her head when I ask him anything, but from you, not a word. I bet I couldn't pick her out of a parade of two."

"Right. But maybe she would say the same."

"What, that she couldn't pick Lady Curzon's nephew out of a parade?"

"No, that she couldn't pick her husband out of a parade."

"Ha! And what do you think? Could she?"

"Where she was born, it doesn't matter what she could or could not do. She already is what she is. That's the village."

"Were you born there too?"

"We all were."

"I could have been born anywhere."

"No. That's not right. Where you're born is why you're here."

"Which is—"

"'Not payable with a plate of rice and curry,' the man said."

thirteen

He'd come at her request, right away upon receiving the letter, and he understood that they were going to leave right away—because even in the pitch black and beyond the buzzing overnight parliament of insects, Sam could tell people were missing from the huts. But first, only a cup of tea; even a common dog is given water when there's water to give. And she said no. She also said there was no time for him to hear words from her father as she had requested in the letter, and also that there was no time to look in on the children and besides Latha was with them, and before old Lal had even reached the verandah with the parcels Piyal had unloaded and passed to him, there was no time to see what he had brought and the way Alice said all of this was flat and fast, practised. Sam said nothing. Again flat and fast like a schoolgirl's recitation Alice said that if Sam had any feeling for either her father or his children they would go now and bring back their villagers before they were all ruined and gave up paddy and garden crop for speeches and never another day in the fields. They had to go to Dambulla, to bring them back so there could be someone, something, someday, to pass on. The walauwa land had been written in Alice's name upon marriage, and before sending Sam the letter requesting that he come to the village, she had taken the deed from her father's almirah, sneaking in and out of it with a small girl's expertise and leaving a letter in its place with details for her father and brother and no mention of her husband, and then she had gone by carriage to see a lawyer in Kandy town, to have the deed written into her son's name in the event of her death. Alice had decided that the Ralahami's daughter would never be the Ralahami's wife but instead the Ralahami's mother when her son turned eighteen.

"Yes," he said, "I will go now."

"No."

"No? No. You send a letter telling me to come straight away—"

"This is straight away? Had you come yesterday or even this morning instead of this—" she pointed past his shoulder at the spray of stars and quarter moon hanging above the massed black treetops.

"Yes, this is straight away when more is asked of you in a day than to wait for the servant to finish massaging your feet so she can rub more coconut oil in your hair. Yes, for a man in the city, this is straight away."

"What can you know of what it means to be in the village? To be responsible for so many—"

"And then you say no to my having a cup of tea because there is no time, because I must go and retrieve them straight away, and now you say not to go?"

"I say you will not go but that we will go. Both of us."

"You want to go to Dambulla. Right. Are you trying to make me take your brother?"

"I am going, Sam. I must go. Appachchi is too sick even to get out of bed and Aiya must stay here to watch things. I must go.

It is my duty to my father and to my son. This is what it means
to be born in this house. Are you coming? This is what it means
to be born in this house." Only when she said it a second time
did Alice step forward into the fuller light of the verandah, yellow
lanterns blazing at midnight, each a hazy ball of maddened insect
love. She wasn't wearing one of the English nightdresses he had
brought on prior visits, crème and custard and snow-covered fields
of fallen flowers, their collars and sleeves as lacy and involved as
table settings for hotel tea. Nor was she wearing one of the many
English-hipped day dresses he had given her. Instead, Alice was
dressed as of old, in a white upcountry sari of the sort her grandmother would have worn to wait in the shade beside other wives
while their Ralahamis chewed and spat their way through a council
meeting. Latha had dressed her in candlelight after the men and
children had gone to sleep, sighing and sucking her teeth as she
had wrapped her lady, sounds that were more than enough to say
that Alice had been raised to be dressed this way from day one of
her marriage. In vain. The bunching and wrappings around her
waist were like so many proud banners and fresh bandages; the
sleeves puffed and tight-cuffed in the shape of palm fronds, the
skirt itself wider banners and bandages and if Sam had looked
closely he would have seen ribbons of storytelling so intricate—
embroidered pictures of processing kings and queens and monks
and relic-bearing elephants—they made all his bought English lace
look like moth-eaten napkins. Her ears, fingers, toes, wrists, and
ankles chimed and shined with gold as she walked forward, her
head held straight from the thick gold chain running high about
her neck. The dress and jewellery, like nothing he had seen her wear
since their wedding day; her face, composed in challenge, even
command that he take her to Dambulla to find those twenty-odd
villagers who, Alice had learned from Latha who had heard from
the washerwoman who had heard from the weaver's wife who had

begged her husband not to go, had been persuaded to attend the rally by cunning pamphlet devils who had lately come to the village promising those who went a future free of sweating for walauwa people, a future of everyone their own walauwa people. They also promised free rides in bona fide modern buses for those who waited at the village bus halt at the appointed hour. And now they had to be brought back. Alice made to walk past him. He stepped in front of her.

"So you have dressed like a proper Hamine and you think going to Dambulla like this will make them weep to come home when you call them? Weep and beg forgiveness and work harder every next day in the paddy and all because of the way Latha has wrapped your sari?"

"I have dressed the way I am supposed to by birth and station and by respect for the right ways of my village and my family, the old ways. And when they see how I am respecting these, they will respect these too."

"Right. And now you want to take a motorcar to show them how you respect the old ways? Why don't you just hide in your hotel almirah until they come back?"

She did not turn and go inside and take fire from the kitchen and burn down the almirah he had given her and then make him his tea with its ashes. She would have, but she was a daughter before him and a mother after him. Duty before pleasure. She stepped forward again, her head held even higher.

"Right," he said, holding her eyes. "You may come. But I warn you, yes, people from this village might see their Hamine dressed like it was a hundred years ago or dressed like it was the day before I drove in, same thing, they might see you and right away bow and run home in the gutters. They might. But you have no idea about the others going to Dambulla, beasts and rogues, what they're willing to do to anyone, even to a high-born lady. Sometimes especially to a high-born lady, just to show what kind of respect they have for old ways. But believe it, I know."

"Yes. We both know you know."

Before she could walk ahead of him he was crashing down the steps, the sound like he was dashing every piece of the gold-rimmed china he had brought them last first-of-the-year. Alice nodded at Latha, who had come to the threshold at the sound of his going. She smiled that her resolve and dress were working as they ought to, and Latha tried to smile back. Alice turned and followed, carrying her village-made sandals while relishing the unyielding hardness and cold of the moonlit stone upon her bare feet, the rightful humility of it. A penance for eight years of accepting Sam Kandy's terms for their marriage.

Seated in the backseat, she knew what her aunties would make of her behaving this way. All modern ruin they would say. They would say it started the wedding day she went away from the village in a foreign cloth dress, seated beside unknown dirt. Still, always, unknown. One of the times Sam had sent the loaded vehicle and stayed in the city, she had asked Blue Piyal to take her for a drive along the Kurunegala Road until the children fell asleep in her lap, which was when she asked what her father had never been father enough to ask.

Where did the Mahatteya come from?

He began to tell her what he heard city men mutter and wager about Sam Kandy but she cut him off. Worse scandal than marrying nobody from nowhere might have been learning who and where he came from, which was also who and to where she had been dutiful and obedient these nine years. And like an old-time wife she had been obedient often enough to her own ends, never once asking anything of her modern money husband except sometimes a different colour size cut of whatever he had brought her or the children or her father or brother from the city on his latest visit, requests that, she knew, if never outright admitted, told him she wanted nothing more than what was on offer, only more of it. Her expectation of womanhood had been confined to one oniony night in a hotel and to nine years of the sweet-brained driver's dream-eyed devotions. But Sam's lack of interest in even securing a second son was a deliverance, or so she understood from Latha's opinion that the twins' births were a threefold miracle and that the separate sleeping arrangements when Sam came to the village were blessings for these two children, who knew their mother by loving face and word and touch. Alice could not but agree, knowing more than anyone save her brother what it meant to know your mother's love only through your father's face and word and touch.

As for her own longing that Sam know the children as something more than twin toy boxes, that they know him as something more than the sound of a coming and going engine, it had long since passed into the opposite resolve: that they be raised in the village and by the village and for the village, fatherlovecitysweets aside. She never asked what he paid for any of it, the heaps of tissue-packed clothing and the cityscapes of biscuit and beef and condensed milk tins, the soaps and perfumes and colognes in shapes and bottles more ornate than most temple stones, the stacks of cigarettes and rag-headed dolls and white wooden soldiers and paintings of wintry animals. Her brother, bitter that the land was in her name and that it was now common knowledge in the village that he was as much of a foreign-schooled doctor as she was a happily married woman, once tried to ask her questions about Sam's work, only to have their father clear his cancer-shredded throat. And so Arthur never asked again, only mumbled along his requests for his own latest set of colours and sizes and cuts for when next Sam sent, all of it tied with enough parcel string to hang herself, her children, the whole village.

The first tea-stall they passed, Sam had Piyal stop the vehicle and walk to the rear of the house and bang on the plank-barred door until the owner came cursing and threatening and then smoothing his hair and almost skipping in the dark to reach the vehicle and take the money for his late-hour troubles. Sam stepped out of the car and faced his silent wife, sipping his tea.

Hours later, nearing Dambulla, Piyal stopped again but Sam leaned forward and said, "It's rain. It will pass. Drive on. Madam says to drive on. And when we get there, the first person you see from the village, tell. Point. Madam says to tell." Alice said nothing. The world outside the Morris was bare bright sky, blowing dust, burning dry. Many people were walking past in twos and threes, their hands covering their mouths against the dust the vehicle kicked up as it stopped, or covering their mouths to keep talking with a rich man present. They were caught between two cartloads of protesters the second time Piyal stopped. This time Sam said it was monkeys throwing nuts. Alice said nothing. The twist-limbed Keena trees lining the roadway were empty of any life; what little there might have been had already been scared off by the crowds coming down the road all day and the day and night before. The people in the cart behind them were yelling for them to keep moving and the people in the cart ahead of them were dancing and clapping like the car's stopping was some kind of victory: theirs. The third time Piyal stopped, a stone hit the rear window on Alice's side and cracked the filmy pane five ways, making a claw-print out of the glass. Like some blade-footed animal had just climbed over them. Alice jumped and in the same motion turned in to Sam who by the same animal reflex put his arm around her shaking frame, crushing her sari against his suit.

With the engine cut, they could no longer pretend the chanting ahead of them was just strong wind in the trees. Hundreds of the others going to Dambulla for the May Day workers' rally milled past. The greatest number were the village poor walking in the white they otherwise kept for temple days; there were also handfuls of teapluckers dressed their best from head to hennaed feet; and, fewer still, city labourers smoking beedis, dressed in nothing other than the scandal cloth of their daily toil, pied and grimed by blood and spit and sweaty dirty fingers, everything tattered and torn by too many things to recall and where was the money to patch or buy a new anything let alone to eat or feed? All of which was why they, why all of them, had come by train-top and airless bus to rally at Dambulla. Some stared in at Piyal and Sam and Alice as they passed, others made a show of not doing so, whether from fear it was their plantation boss or factory owner, or from pride that they were part of something this day that was more powerful than any man with a motorcar. There were, no doubt, also a few who were half staring to see if any of the stones they'd been throwing at the Morris since it had first passed them had done any damage.

Alice sat up and smoothed her sari as she moved away from Sam to stare back, through the clawed glass, looking through its refracted violence for any of her villagers in the approaching crowd and wondering about what her husband had warned of before they had left the walauwa the night before. Just how many of those men would like to put their hands around her throat and shake free its gold? Sam leaned forward to tell Piyal to drive on. Sam leaned forward again and this time said Madam is fine and Madam said to drive on, and so they went.

When they reached Dambulla, Sam told Piyal to park under the tallest tree they could find in the town square, a bushy-headed talipot in full flower. The first men to rush the car were three Englishmen, cricketers who had come to town that morning for a friendly by the lake. Their faces in the windows looked far past irritated that they'd lost a fine day for their innings—they looked like terrified, exhilarated children happy to be found alive in a sudden evil snow. But then they saw Sam and Alice in the backseat, and a blue-eyed driver in front. Whatever this revolt against reason and order and white man was, it had already begun. They fell away from the Morris and decided without debate that the only right- ness remaining was to return to the grounds and wait out their fate in the well-stocked clubhouse. Provided it had yet to fall to native rot, they would wait there, fortified with gin and sandwiches and practice bats, for whatever came next.

"You saw their faces," said Sam. "Englishmen. And even they are afraid to be caught in this crowd. And still you want to get out of the vehicle and look for your villagers?"

Alice said nothing and for the second time in his adult life Piyal spoke first.

"Madam, please, Mahatteya is right. Please stay in the vehicle and let Mahatteya go."

"And Piyal will stay with you, won't you Piyal," Sam said to Alice. But he could tell nothing in her face at mention of the boy's staying with her. Meanwhile, Piyal tried to catch Madam's eye, to tell her with his staring that yes he would protect her from *all* of them if she stayed in the motorcar. More even. For years he had gone to bed sending the Mahatteya on a southbound train, just as Sam Kandy had once done to Henry Paulet's other servants. And now, in Dambulla, after the Mahatteya got out Piyal would drive the Morris anywhere she wanted, whether back to the village or down to the city and the harbour and straight onto the jetty and hammering up one of the rusted wide ramps they banged into place when they were unloading buses from London or sending elephants to the American circus and the two of them would wait there until they heard new harbour birds and then drive down another ramp into another weather, into a whole other life where, he was certain, his blue eyes would get him a brown-eyed driver and a position in a bank and her her her.

But Alice said nothing. Her face was all and only readiness to show Sam what she was willing to do herself, readiness born of her blood-rushing conviction that when she walked through this crowd it would give way as it ought to, and that soon they would be returning to the village with the shamefaced runaways trailing home behind the car. She only had to find them. She made for the door and Piyal jumped out to open it for her and Sam followed but Alice did not wait for him to go first. She walked right into the crowd, which was hot and hungry and bored, a terrible three things for a crowd to be.

fourteen

Sam made his way through the masses, trying to match Alice step for step, and failing. The others would give way no more than the span of her fine white shoulders and immediately close when she passed, before he could step into her forward wake. So much for revolution, he thought. Still, even following behind her, he was impressed, envious that she did not have to push through as he had had to everywhere he had come and gone. He was also certain they would find no one from Sudugama because they, the hundreds upon hundreds of gathered villagers, looked each and every one the same: the same round brown faces made darker by day upon day in the sun-beat fields, too dark to look or feel worthy of any greater life than another day in the same field unto death and the same for their children's children; faces that seemed near-black as good dirt against the white clothes they had worn to come here, let alone against the whites of their eyes or their bent chipped teeth those rare times they looked back at you or spoke in your presence, because otherwise these were faces that had been made constant in their downward glances by year upon year of working those sun-beat fields, and by generations of respect for the rock-face logic of blood and stars and caste, a marrow respect for those who were born of the merit of past lives into lives set above their own, whose fields they had come into this latest life to work. And so they had been persuaded to come here to Dambulla, on May Day, leaving fallow their known world, to be told why such toil and such respect were history and headmen's ongoing outrages against them, outrages to be rallied and chanted and marched against until stopped. And as one grand body they had been all day ready, even roaring in agreement. The courage that comes of hearing your voice as a thousand voices. And yet, when a fair-skinned walauwa lady wearing an old-time sari walks straight toward you and suddenly you're only one person and she's trying to catch your eye and know your face, you do what you were born to do: you break stride and drop your head and wait to the side until she passes and meanwhile you hope she has no cause to linger. And, when she's walked on, you wonder who it was in the suit that shoved by after her, his black eyes staring like a crow following a squirrel he wants the world to know is already his.

The Sudugama villagers saw her before she saw them. They were waiting their turn at a water tap where a local woman, supremely indifferent to the thirsty dusty marchers around her, was crouched on the smooth rock ledge that circled the stone-pillared spout, washing each of three naked little boys who were puffing their cheeks and chests to think that all of these people had come here to watch them take their day's wash. When one of the people from Sudugama, a weaver, saw Alice coming, dressed as she was, he remembered the walking-to-temple stories his grandmother used to tell. He was certain this had to be the ghost in the high grass behind the walauwa, the ribbon-haired Hamine of many years before, who had disappeared on her eldest daughter's wedding day some time

after no one particular villager had poisoned her husband the old
Ralahami because he had tried to send the village's men to Road
Ordnance duty. Of course, thought the weaver, the ghost was
returned to life all these years later because now, finally, in coming
here for this, the villagers were again killing the walauwa people.
But then the weaver saw Sam's dark shape walking behind her and
knew it was Alice, and his ghosted, guilty imagination collapsed as
he muttered "Amata siri." Hearing him, the others looked up and
saw her coming with the husband and cried "Apo!" and with the
next breath every single one of them began to accuse and blame
everyone else for tricking them into travelling here. They talked
over each other, their road-dusty arms chopping the air to lend
the right rhythm and threat to their louder and louder claims, all
of which ruined the three little water-clowns' washing-day performance, who whined to their mother who had before been amused
by the crowd's fighting but now broke squat to curse the whole
lot for coming to her town and carrying on like this. How disre-
spectful! she scolded, especially so near the sacred cave temples and
of course. Of course! Every one of them had the same story one
breath later: they had only come from Sudugama to Dambulla
on pilgrimage. *May Day? What is May Day?* Someone had offered
them seats in a bus and they had accepted only because it meant
they could go and come home faster than otherwise. Before Alice
could reach the water tap they were already walking away, solemn
to temple, rushing to the caves.

The tap's water was running clear and what she was wearing
was so heavy, was meant for sitting and fanning, not for searching
through blowing dust and thronged crowds and the high heat of
midday. But she could not drink because there was no time Sam
said, after ordering off the cursing local and her three boys and then
taking a long splashing sip himself, slurping the water from his flat
palm like any villager might, as if he was himself born to such low

drinking. There was no time for her to drink as well, Sam repeated, now with a fine cold throat, his hand resting on the tap's round stone cap like it was his prized pupil. And besides, how would it look for the Hamine to sip like a washerwoman?

In silence they followed the rising pathway that ran along the base of the rock face until they reached the temple's entryway, a long white verandah. The Sudugama people had long since passed inside, hands cupped full of frangipani bought beside the stall where they left their sandals in a pile like many others, each a tumbled pyramid of thin cracked leather. They went into the holy darkness complaining about the injustice of the flowers they were carrying, offerings they had purchased for far too much because their eyes were darting everywhere else in search of the bright catch of her gold bangles in broad daylight. How expensive, how wilted, how limp were the petals, like heat-sick children, and even in the shade of the temple's verandah and the candles and ledge light of the caves you could tell the flowers were already browning. Bad omen bad omen bad omen. How much better—whiter, fuller, cheaper— were the temple flowers to be had back home! How much better if they were there now and had never heard of workers' rights or been promised the future. But at least now when she found them, they would be in prayerful repose. If she found them: the caves were large and many and crowded with others in white, their palms also made into cups of bloomed once-white. If she found them: she had come with the husband and everyone knew he would never stay long enough for them to be found: since his wedding day he always looked ready to leave.

Foul that Alice walked so slowly and that he had to go into a temple now, Sam paid a smiling malli to hold his socks and shoes— the man was in fact older than Sam but had from birth been barefoot and curved sharply along the spine, born to be helped and helpful. Handing them over, Sam made it clear that he was paying for his shoes and socks and for nothing else: Alice would have to leave her sandals in one of the piles of village sandals because she had come here to respect the old ways, the stinking piled-up old ways. Dambulla temple felt nothing like the grand temple at Kandy town where he had been dropped by his father that rain-joy ginger-toed morning years before, nor was it like the small white temple by the village. And still, walking barefoot along the pebbly passageway that led to the sacred caves, his feet cool and pricked by so many little stones, he would have turned and run from this blackness of memory and devotion. Monks, old and young and even one as young as he had been, nodded and smiled like cats as he passed, no doubt waiting for him to drop his wallet and wife's gold in their beggar's bowl.

In the first cave, his heel crushed dropped flowers as he followed her in. His every necessary breath was a sweet full nausea of squished flowers, body sweat, lamp oil, Tiger Balm, oiled hair, and child's mess. His eyes suffered more: everywhere in here were Buddhas awaiting his devotion: stone and gold, seated and reclining; one was a recumbent giant; fifty small ones were arrayed in gold; and hundreds upon hundreds were painted upon the smooth stone walls. In the second cave they were seated row on row in a fading field of saffron and cinnabar lotuses, their composed faces lit up by candles and oil lamps and revealed in their greatest number whenever clouds cleared and fuller sunlight filled an archway. Room to room Sam followed his wife, burning only more to face more and more of them. They had been here, like this, for centuries, fixed upon the walls, carved in stone and gold, unchanging, no trajectory, nothing to run from, nothing to run to, only summit. Master of the world. In the third cave, arcing bands of sunlight showed more than Buddhas. There were also frescoes of brave kings and handsome warriors whose devotions and victories won them places beside the holy men. Sam ignored the images of kings kneeling before monks, their hands full of flowers and gems. What caught him were paintings of great men shooting arrows at unseen enemies, riding white horses upon crimson fields, walking upon strewn white flowers beneath copper parasols, or sitting on jewelled chairs at the centre of a fixed and jewelled world of grateful wives and loyal children and loyal servants bearing lamps on staves and pitchers of water and baskets of grain and flowers, and meanwhile, to the side, mild elephants were waiting to move the world as was commanded. These were fixed constellations of men made immortal at the height of their trajectories. Assured, arrived, served. Storied. As he walked on after his crowded-in wife to still another room, his teeth grit, his hands opening and closing like a virgin assassin, Sam wondered if Alice was really looking for the villagers. Was she in truth leading him in and out of these places to show him what he could never be? To show him so much legend upon the walls, all these fixed, these jewelled, these jurying stars?

He nearly knocked her down going into the last cave, he was walking so close behind. Not Sam, but a would-be guide. Alice had already ignored his mealy offers of a tour and then his mealier launch into explanations of whatever statuary or fresco she'd earlier passed, and she had ignored his questions as to her needs—cool drink, nicest fruit, a shaded escort from the temple to the town square whether by foot or carriage he could arrange anything to suit Madam's needs—half because she was searching the worshippers for any face that, seeing hers, would go pop-eyed and blank and so be caught before it had time to look away, and half because such was the very world she had come here to maintain, a world where a woman like Alice did not speak to a man like this. Pretending not to hear was how to deal with such things when no buffer of servants was present, nor father nor brother nor old-enough son. When, most of all, there was no husband with the presence of mind if not birth to see, step in, and send the beggar off. Yes Sam had followed from cave to cave but he was always off to himself, presumably trying to find the villagers but really looking as he did whenever he went to temple in the village, swallowed and bitten, like every moving thing inside was a scorpion, like the temple itself was a belly. She had watched him staring at frescoes like he was ready to split the painted stones. And so in the meantime Alice could only ignore the guide, which only encouraged him and by now he was convinced that Madam was looking for something that, on this suddenly auspicious day, he was self-appointed to find for her.

"Madam please if you please follow my arm to see most special statue of Lord Buddha or Madam if you please come this way Madam I shall show you most famous place where most famous queen died of thirst chained to window bars mourning the king and refusing to marry his brother."

She turned to see evidence of a wife, any wife, who so loved her husband. She followed the guide's reed-thin arm as it pointed to the barred window and she followed him to it and took in enough of his hot fast wordmeal to hear tell of a thirsty queen hanging by her wrists against this very wall for love, for love. It was a fine story and the guide was honoured to have shared it with such a fine audience. Alice smiled tightly. And only then did his words slow, like rainwater still dripping from leaves the next morning. "Madam, please, whatever you think is best. In the village I have my wife's mother and a lame brother besides my own four children."

But look at her. She was wearing clothes meant for women whose lives were so high, so protected, so intact, there was never any need that required anything so common as money. As Alice searched the low cave for Sam, the guide placed his toes upon the already dirt-smudged hem of her sari, pressing down and curling forward, letting her know her place was now fixed.

She looked down. In barred sunlight the bottom of her sari looked like trampled temple flowers. More than trampled: she saw the man's foot firmly upon it, bare and flat, knob-toed, field black. Her skin crawled to see his toes curl into the old fine cloth, to see the toenails overgrown and white as her sari had been when they had set out in darkness from the village the night before. Nails so white as to look almost fine, shaming her sari, now some low-born devil's foot-cloth.

"Sam! SAM! Aiyo Sam please come—"

The guide saw him coming before she did and, stepping forward, grandly gestured toward the archway out of respect for the worshippers who had stopped at Alice's voice and were watching to see what would happen next—save about twenty who were now looking down down down, certain they had been discovered, waiting for him to come and grab them by their hair and tie them to his motorcar and drag them home.

Sam walked right into the guide's outstretched palm, which stiffened to hold him.

"What is it?" Sam asked, pushing the arm down and holding it there, squeezing the guide at the wrist like B. used to in Pettah when a man owed him.

"Madam is—" he started, his voice wavering as he tried to twist free.

"I asked Madam, not you," Sam said, squeezing harder.

"Aiyo hurting!" the man whined, dropping to a crouch and studying the man's dusty suit. "All I am asking is small donation for telling Madam about temple."

"She has no money." His tone was as unclear to himself as it was to the guide and Alice.

"But you must be keeping it for her, no?"

"Mokatha? What do you mean, keeping it for her?"

"You are Madam's driver, no?"

Sam's hand fell and the guide fled through the archway, gone like a bat woken by a boy's rock. Sam stepped up to Alice, who felt pressure again and looked down in the barred light and the skin wasn't as black and the toes not as knobby and the nails cut back but it did not matter. It felt the same. It looked the same. This was his dirty foot-cloth. She looked up but was shocked by what she saw. His face was shattered like a child's, very like her child's, like *their* son's when he was waiting for her to tell him what he already knew: that a promise had already been broken and all that remained was his having to hear it said. She could have cupped her husband's face, but she did not. She held her own wrist instead, the gold bangles cave cool against her palms. Because what sort of man would have any cause to worry that his wife would call him her driver, to lower him so? Only the sort that could be so lowered.

He was waiting for her to say otherwise, to tell him, even if it were a lie, that she had said nothing of the sort to the guide, and then life could resume. All she had to do was tell him, just shake her head no, even look down and nod to admit yes but she did not mean it, to allow that he was her driver. Anything. But Alice said nothing. She stared back, eye for eye, silent and cold and, to him, as fixed as the surrounding stone. Sam took her by the wrist and led her from the cave, squeezing as if he was trying to break her gold. The Sudugama people followed, their heads ringing with such a story to tell, desperate now to be discovered and dragged home, whatever punishment was worth what they had just witnessed, what they could now tell. But they never would. Within the hour, a few of their heels would be bloody too, and when they reached home, two days later, and heard the story of what had happened in Dambulla as it was being told in the village and were asked what they knew, they would say they knew nothing, they had been praying in the caves the whole time.

When they were past the verandah Sam let her go and stalked ahead. He waved off the old malli who had immediately approached, his head cocked as if it had been wrenched ninety degrees, smiling sweetly, bearing Sam's shoes like holy vessels. Sam looked and looked until he saw the guide and then broke into a dead run across the bright barren plain. Alice watched him while walking toward the pile where she had left her sandals, her wrist aching and stinging as if it had been crushed in some stone beehive. She watched him give chase while her mind made mad figure eights, trying to determine if she had enough time to find the flowered talipot in the town square and persuade Blue Piyal to take her, her alone, home to the village and there persuade her father and the rest of them to roll boulders onto the Kurunegala Road before he came back. No: boulders he'd split. They'd have to move the village entirely, or at least get the metal-benders and toddy tappers and temple elephants to suspend it high above the earth, between the tallest strongest trees at the village limits, and then when he walked into its shadow—

Only he wouldn't be walking he'd be still running as he was now, here at Dambulla, and he'd run up the trunk and along the elephant's back and then along a bent tree until he reached the lifted village and he'd not stop until he was standing on the verandah, brushing the dirt from his shoulder, smoking, asking for tea. But she had to try anyway. She found her slippers just as he found the guide. She stayed barefoot, worrying the stitching while standing with the other templegoers who had gathered to watch her husband beat the guide into the ground, knocking him down and then stomping, one witness later suggested, like a bitten snake charmer. Stomping and stomping until the guide's calls for mercy became gasping mouthed words and then spit and gurgles, and then Sam kicked him in the side until the body turned over, one lung collapsed, and then Sam kicked the gasping air from the other side and the body turned over once more and the legs weakly pushed out and pulled in, pushed out and pulled in, like he was a frog on a riverbank, a newborn on a pallet, and that was when the women near Alice began to whimper for someone to do something because it's a sin even to kick a dog. And meanwhile Sam was still stomping and eventually he fell to the ground himself, his blood-slick heel slipping as it came down a last time upon the guide's pulped mouth, now a useless bloodmeal.

The crowd was nearly upon him when he stood and brushed off his trousers. Turning his heels dry in the dirt, Sam winced and nearly dropped again, one foot was so sore. Breathing hard, wiping sweat and tears and dirt from his eyes, he looked for his wife, worrying no wondering no more than wondering if she had seen. No one touched him as he limped through the crowd, but behind he could hear them, their seething plans for him. What they had just witnessed was the day's words made flesh and blood: walking away, unpunished, was one of the world's evil owners, a helpless worker's blood on his hands, his feet, the sort they had heard tell of in the May Day speeches in the town square hours before, the sort they had chanted against while they were promised that if they united in demanding justice in their fields and factories and plantations, then one day such men would fall just as they all rose up. This could be one day.

Sam walked on, seeing Alice rushing down the pathway. He could feel the crowd coming behind him. He would be trampled if he didn't run. He wondered if the last feet upon him would belong to a slick fat crow, if it would hop onto his chest when there was nothing left to do but savour his burning eyes. Burning for what he had been forced to do. He ran.

⌐⌐

Standing in the shade beside the Morris, studying chevrons of afternoon light coming through the flower-headed talipot, suddenly Piyal saw a barefoot Sam running in a hobble past Alice running in her sari and behind them every angry man in Dambulla was

chasing them, others in the town square joining the mob like metal
shavings drawn to a dropped magnet. Sam reached the motorcar
first, climbed in and closed his door and coughed, then exhaled,
then called Piyal to get in and go now, as if he was done shopping
and now they were leaving Cargill's. She was still twenty steps away.
She ran straight into his arms, Piyal's arms, and after all these years
she was so thin to actual touch, which made him even readier to—
but that was when the crowd reached them. Piyal lost his cap as he
bent to push her crying into the empty backseat because Sam had
already climbed into the front and was grabbing at the gear-box.
The car jerked away just as Piyal was knocked down, and looking up
the last he saw was so many downstriking, hammering feet. Before
a regiment arrived to disperse the demonstrators with truncheons
and boots far harder than any heels, an hour later, one of the first to
have kicked in the fallen rich man's face admitted, to himself, that
he didn't remember seeing blue eyes on the fellow who had beaten a
poor guide at the temple nearly to death, but by then enough sand
had been kicked onto the bloodied, suited body lying beneath the
talipot tree to make it any evil rich man's, and the rest were already
chanting that they could never be stopped now.

Alice dragged at Sam's arms to make him go back for Piyal and the
wheel turned sharply as he wrenched free and only just swerved
the car away from a tree and back onto the road, picking up speed.
She was sobbing and beating her chest and cursing—him, them,
her father, her village, him, this car, this marriage, Dambulla, a
queen who had loved her king to death, him, them, her father, her
village. Herself. Minutes later, she lunged forward again and Sam
pushed her back with an elbow and stopped just before another
tree and there they sat in silence. The inevitable beggars came to the
windows, as did a few strutting young men desperate to be helpful

with engine trouble, their own girls watching and laughing like champions. Eventually they all left. The brush was dense and now it was later in the day and so the world seemed to have seeped into a black-and-green wash and was silent but for birdcalls and their own hard breathing.

"What would you have me do?"

"Turn this vehicle around and go back to Dambulla and—"

"And what? The boy is dead … the poor boy's dead," Sam said into his chest, his voice suddenly, finally hoarse, and Alice sobbed to hear it and suddenly she felt wild joy—at least there was this much heart in him—and she was angry and mournful and cursed that this, this little had to be her joy.

"If he is dead," Alice said, her voice shaking, her words measured like kitchen water in a dry season, "it is on you."

"Mokatha?" Sam said, whipping around, his heart all pit again.

"It is on you."

"How, when it was you who had to come to Dambulla and not just come but come dressed in your upcountry cobwebs? What happened started from there."

"No. What happened started the day you came to my village." He made to say something. He made like he was about to get out of the car. But then nothing. "Why?" she pleaded. "Aiyo just tell me why did you come to my village? Why did you have to marry me?"

"IT IS MY VILLAGE TOO!" he shouted, finally, feeling somehow ruined and burned free of future ruin for saying it, finally, to someone, to her, to walauwa people, but now he was staring down at the floorboards. Suddenly it was impossible to look her in the eye.

"It will never be your village," she said, now calm as a cup of milk. She'd heard no confession, no revelation, only a plea in vain. "And that is on you too."

"Get out."

Alice said nothing.

"Get out," he said, terrified that he was still staring down like this, as was old ways right before a high-born lady. Terrified and now raging that the fate-roped world was holding his head in place.

She turned and looked through the dusty claw-cracked window at the road darkening with the late-day gloom of tall close trees. How long could she wait there? Could she hire a bullock cart to take her to Sudugama? Would the driver accept a bangle until they arrived and her father could pay? Would Sam have to give him the money to pay? Could she have the driver's cart loaded with the almirah and the dresses and the bright broken toys and the rest of his bloody loveshine and then have a toddy tapper climb and drop a flare on the cart as it passed so that all her husband's poison goods would vanish from the village in flames? And what if he saw and took her by the wrist and flung her on top of the bier? So be it. So be it. Her children had known their mother longer than she had, and there were still her father and her brother and Latha and a saved village for them and they didn't need to know their black-heeled father any more than they already did. And so when he took her by one wrist, Alice decided, hoped, she would take him at the other and hold him until the flames ran across her body to his and so by the village crossroads all that would be left of Sam and Alice would be blackened bangles and burnt cuff-links. So be it. Only do it as you were born to do it.

"You want me to get out of this vehicle?" Alice asked.

"Yes. Get out."

"I will."

"Right."

"Now," she said, arranging herself in the backseat with shaking hands, swallowing, "get out and open the door for me like my old driver did."

He pulled her, head first, into the front seat and then he wheeled the motorcar back onto the road. Picking up speed, it moved like a water snake because he was trying to reach over and open her door and she was kicking and slapping and asking and screaming that his mother used to wash him at the village tap too didn't she and then finally the door flung open and Sam leaned against his own to brace himself as he kicked and kicked until there was only air and if he had turned to look he would have seen a tumbling whiteness flattening out upon the black ground like a wave at night, he would have seen her crashing to mist and nothing. If he had turned to look. But he did not. There was no time. The Morris slammed into a bullock cart, missing the bullock itself and catching the cart full on. The cart driver was pitched into the brush just as Sam cracked the windshield with his forehead. The car was steaming and hissing and buried in a pile of shattered clay pots and when he pushed the door open more pots fell and shattered and wiping blood he looked for butterflies but all Sam Kandy saw before he fell was a freed white beast by the roadside eating and shitting in a perfect universe.

part three **IVORY**

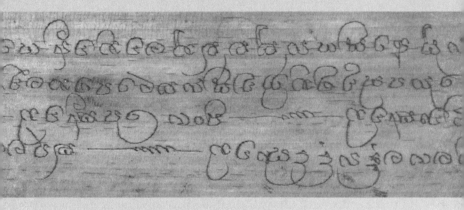

fifteen

Beyond the red brick orchid house where Sam was to meet Lord Mountbatten, British fighter planes were on evening manoeuvres. He watched them make their bored and boastful contrails, a cloud scrawl of caterpillars and tightropes hanging across the blue fade of upcountry sky. Now and then he could hear their engine drone but otherwise, in the middle of the throbbing green gardens, the noise this late of day was birdsong and bug fury, laggard's drilling and the Beethoven horns of staff cars en route to the new PX. Sam blew smoke at smoke as the last of the fighters descended, skimming along the treetops so thickly leaved they were more black than green, like an ink-bottle spilt on stationery. Like a nosebleed on a bed-sheet.

His hip was throbbing. Soon he wouldn't be just waiting but waiting in rain, the August rain of the grand procession days. Since coming from Colombo to the British command set up at Peradeniya, near Kandy town, Sam had daily made himself apparent at a first-floor office loud with clacking, dinging, screeching typewriters and with laughing barrels of American military men making jokes and love to the girls. Each time he received only apologies from a staff man who explained, with baroque patience, that the Supreme Commander had not yet returned from his meetings in London. With further apologies, he was told yet again that nothing more could be said as to why he'd been summoned, only that a cable from the British command at Tripoli had described a task requiring certain skills and Mr. Kandy's name had been raised and that only the Supreme Commander could reveal the rest, which he would, directly, it was promised, upon his return. Finally, Sam was reminded, over the lung-collapsing sound of American laughing, that by 1944 much of bottom-right Asia would be won or lost from exactly here, and so this was a very busy office indeed and a man could do his part by waiting to be told how he could do his part. By please waiting elsewhere. And so Sam paced through the Swiss Hotel's dim and echoing corridors as if hour and minute and second hands would rise out of the floor itself and take him by the ankles if he didn't stamp every one of them in place and so have at least that one victory while waiting for Lord Mountbatten.

He kept visiting the office anyway, because he wasn't about to go walking into Kandy town for a visit to the temple, and because the last time he'd been away from Colombo for more than a day and a night, leaving Curzon to run things by himself, he had lost so much. He came because he still had to visit the village before returning to the city, to learn how his son's engagement tour had fared. And he came because of a Burgher girl with sea-green eyes, second desk from the door, a hacked-in-half almirah on blocks. Not since Mary Astrobe and five years a widower.

After Dambulla, a three-cart procession had carried home the wrecked Morris and a sleeping Sam and Alice's birdcage body. It was followed by a mad potter who emptied a sack of shards at the village crossroads when Robert refused to hear his claim. On the next auspicious day, Alice's body was grand-burned upon the great green clearing. Among the mourners were those who had lately gone and come NOT FROM THE WORKER'S RALLY but as pilgrims from the cave temple. Heaving and collapsing, they grieved like palm trees in a monsoon, pulling their hair and tearing their shirts and going louder than the mourners hired in from the next village, louder even than Latha herself. Meanwhile Sam lay like a stone in a back room of the walauwa. Ten days later, he stirred. With the household called into the room and watching, he began to spit out words like bits of glass. Robert stopped him with his free hand and while he was coughing into the other, Sam waited, wondering how far he'd get on his tingling legs before the metal-benders caught him and bent his heels into hammers to break apart his face. He'd been fever-dreaming since they'd laid him here. But when Robert stopped coughing he only motioned fierce Latha to bring George and Hyacinth forward to show respect to their father. The boy dropped milk toffee on Sam's bed-sheet. The girl asked when Blue Piyal was coming back to the village. There were more bits of glass but Robert cut off his fellow widower to send the children out and ordered wretched Latha to bring in a good breakfast. Then Arthur nodded and Robert nodded and Sam was asleep before Latha returned with a plate of yesterday's rice mashed with banana and gall.

A dreamless week later, Sam was walking around the widower's walauwa as if its walls would fall on him if he stopped. Robert, who'd already decided that he had to decide the black beast vehicle and road itself were the only bloody murderers this time, asked Sam what he thought should be done with the villagers who had gone to Dambulla. Sam asked what they'd said about it so far. Told that they would say nothing, Sam said having to stay in the village the rest of their lives would be punishment enough. Robert agreed. Sam said he had to return to the city and Robert proposed the children stay at the walauwa and that Sam would come when he could. Which, over four fat war years, he did, after first finding a new driver, a Trinco-born Tamil named Joseph, and getting himself a new vehicle, a 1938 Morris Eight, painted cricket ball red. Some in the village called it a darker shade.

In recent months, Sam himself began to see bloodred when he came home. It was on sheets hanging from an RAF laundry line in the inner courtyard of the walauwa, where old Latha ordered the washerwoman to dry them because if they were taken down to the laundry rocks the villagers would start marriage talk about Hyacinth. But at fourteen his daughter was still a little girl whose father gave her dolls, who spent most of her days folded into her late mother's almirah, waiting for nothing. The boy, though, was otherwise; the bled sheets were his, from nosebleeds he seemed to sleep through. Thick, hairy, all belly and jangle, George Kandy at fourteen was far hungrier, readier, understanding of hunger than his father had been at thirty. The year before, two seventeen-year-old girls had been bathing and only turned their backs and cinched their water cloths and stopped smiling to scream blue murder when one saw the other's mother suddenly standing behind George, who had been watching them, one hand upon the man-sized boulder that marked the laneway to the village water-spout. After Robert and then Sam were informed, Robert had slapped his grandson for shaming the walauwa and Sam had come from Colombo with American cigarettes for the fathers of both bathers, cookware for the mothers, and a Meccano set to be divided between the brothers without care to match wheel for wheel or hooks with string. (The trading market for the pieces between the two houses, inevitably vicious, ended relations between the families. Both girls were then approached by older brothers who promised protection if they would only vamp past the walauwa to the water-spout one last time: fat George Kandy must have had stacks of Meccano sets in there,

and meanwhile the rest of the world had three-wheeled cars and
cranes that could carry nothing from nothing. The girls refused,
having already been given Nestlé chocolate and also nylon stock-
ings that were promptly, ravenously confiscated by their mothers,
who would never wear them.)

Six months later George tried again, this time using his own
sister's Duke and Duchess of Windsor paper doll collection. A girl
had come to the back stairs of the walauwa with mending that her
mother had done. George put aside the bundle and led her down
to the stone sluice that ran the length of the walauwa, which in dry
times was filled with brown coffee flowers and monkey droppings,
dung beetles and once-bitten, too sour fruits. There, George offered
her the dolls if she would press and hold her hand as he wanted
her to. Latha came down looking for the girl. How dare she leave
the Ralahami's mending on dirt itself! She screamed to see George
demonstrating his request and never fed him by hand again. And
so again Sam had had to come from Colombo with more cigarettes
and cookware, this time both for Latha and for the girl's parents. He
brought Bayko house blocks for this one's brothers, and (because
suddenly there were no nylons to be had anywhere upon the earth)
he brought bars of white chocolate, which disappointed, looking like
little more than lumpy milk. He also brought a new paper doll collection for Hyacinth and another for the nearly ruined girl, which was
duly, ravenously mother-taken and forever after wiped and dusted.

Father, grandfather, and uncle agreed that something had to be
done with the boy before something really had to be done for a
girl and her family. Colombo was decided against and the temple
was decided against. There was nothing else but for George to be
sent abroad for his schooling, only a long-term arrangement had to
be arranged before he went. A car would be hired and Arthur and
Robert would take the boy on a bride tour of surrounding villages.
Sam would be notified when a suitable match had been found. In

the meantime, Sam was to see about where in fact George could be sent for school in wartime, one of the things he could have been doing in Colombo these past few days instead of waiting around for Mountbatten.

Enough. He had to go. But just before he abandoned the orchid house, Sam saw two men approaching in crisp tan uniform, their sleeves cuffed above the elbow, clearly Englishmen from their straight spines and murmuring mouths, their bougainvillea cheeks. The taller one was walking as if his body was itself a standard going before a reviewing stand. Mountbatten. Sam lit up and stretched, then arranged himself into the angly receiving pose he'd been lately using at the harbour with the wartime British. These last two years, officers had been coming to see him and Curzon at off-hours, with requests that they get down still more rubber tappers from Cochin, and also with assurances that their fulfillment of said requests— if accomplished without drawing undue attention to the rubber tappers' arrivals from troublemaking Colombo labour men, who couldn't meet the demand anyway—meant that once a week, back doors would be left open for them. And so came Sam Kandy's first great wartime discovery, the stacked kingdom come that was the quartermaster's dockside warehouse. His second, its perfect match: the allowance that the State Council had started giving all workers in the city for their sugar and flour and rice. But who spends free money on sugar and flour and more rice? What Sam did not sell to the thriving foreign-goods syndicates in Pettah and did not have to split with Curzon, he brought to the village and gave to Robert and Arthur and Hyacinth and to George, who, it seemed, had been giving it on his own terms.

"Sir, may I present Mr. Sam Kandy, of Colombo harbour, a friend of our war efforts."

Sam straightened and bowed from the shoulders. He knew the British were worse than temple monks for waiting on ceremony, at least in the official hours. And this Englishman's eyebrows were church-arched. The sort for whom there were only official hours.

"Mr. Kandy, this is Lord Commander Mountbatten," said the office man Sam had daily visited, who was smiling like he'd just won a bet by baking a cake in a helmet.

Sam bowed again.

"Kandy, is it?" Mountbatten asked, amused and curious, cutting and English.

"Yes." Knowing he'd only half answered. More than a minute passed in silence, the Englishmen's smiles inexorably thinning. He knew what they were waiting for, that they would wait until Tojo himself was strolling through this garden if they had to, and Sam had to see about George and get back to Colombo.

"Yes, sir. "Indeed," Mountbatten continued, his lips returning. "May I enquire, was that your father's name as well?"

"No, it was not. Sir. My, my father—"

"Of course. Well, I suppose no man is ever born Charlemagne, is he."

"May I enquire, sir, as to why I was asked to come here?"

"Yes. Good English, incidentally. English that comes from dealing with Englishmen, I can tell, and not from just listening to them go on in an Oxford lecture hall. As to your question. First, let me say I understand that you have been the very portrait of patience while I have been detained in London. It's exactly this virtue in you and your fellow islanders, and also your support in this our great shared cause, that disposes me all the more to Ceylon's claim for greater rights from the Crown. And let me further say that while so much of Asia waits on our next endeavour, this matter between us, Kandy, is at the very top of things I must resolve. Let's step into this flower-house." Sam nodded and followed, leaving behind

Mountbatten's baker, who, glum faced, considered the sudden violet clouds.

"I cannot tell you, Kandy, how many teas one has taken in London in just such perfume," Mountbatten murmured, the air inside the steaming orchid house so blooming sweet.

"It smells to me like an elephant hold, sir."

Mountbatten smiled. Were anyone else present he would have had the fellow thrashed for impertinence. "And you say that without having met any of the hostesses in question. Do you think any of these will object to our clearing the air a little?" He gestured at the orchids, took two cigars from a hip pocket, cut them, and tossed the stubs into the potted field. Wave upon wave of hard-pinning rain began to fall, like a company of snare drummers in need of more drilling.

"Thank you, sir," Sam said, slipping the cigar into his coat pocket and lighting a cigarette. "I will save this for an auspicious occasion."

"I should say this *is* an auspicious occasion, Kandy. It's not every day a native businessman is given such an opportunity to help the effort." Bloody wasted cigar. Mountbatten wondered if it'd be chopped up and sold at the Colombo bazaar. He was fairly certain, from recent inspection, that someone, whether one of the Americans or a native coolie, had been shaving curls of wood from his caravan desk, no doubt to sell on the relic market.

Opportunity to help the effort. And earlier, *Our great shared cause.* There would be no money. But there had to be something. "As to the purpose of this meeting, sir."

"Yes. Well." Mountbatten paused, considering the aspect of something, his eyes squinting in little pulses. "Are you familiar, Kandy, with our prisoner camp at Trincomalee?"

"Yes, I've heard of it, sir. My driver—"

"Oh is he? Very good. It is, by all accounts, a model operation. Italians. A few fancy themselves gardeners, it seems. They have been trading tomatoes for cigarettes with the guards, serenading the servant girls, that sort of thing. Docile as milking cows. And it's my intention to keep them that way." He took a letter from his other hip pocket and scanned it, his eyes pulsing again. "One of our ships is to dock at Colombo harbour shortly, in fact very shortly if the lanes remain clear. I understand that you know your way around the harbour, rather too well by most standards, perhaps, but this is a time of war. Would that ours was a world where every soldier was an English gentleman, but this is not the case of course and for victory to be at hand"—here he spoke louder, as if at a reviewing stand, the pouring rain applause—"sometimes we need fists, and sometimes we need firm handshakes, and sometimes, Kandy, we need dirty fingernails."

Sam brushed his jacket.

"Good. The ship in question is the *Neptune*, a cruiser carrying New Zealand troops home from Tripoli and also, six 'special case' prisoners captured with other Italian forces when we took Tunis." He cleared his throat. These weren't his words. "'Who are to be disembarked in Ceylon and kept in extreme isolation and utmost secrecy until war's end.'" Mountbatten slapped his leg with the letter. He had to win back Asia and they'd already sent him an American, that bantam cock Sitwell, as his second, and now they were sending him these fellows. Ethiopians. What could Rommel have been using them for? "They are coming, six of them, and I'm not about to have them disrupt our operation at Trincomalee. Now I understand that in addition to your being well-placed about Colombo harbour, Kandy, you're well-placed in a village close to this command. How are you with a padlock and key?"

"You, the British army, would like me to keep war prisoners for you?"

"Special cases, remember. Only six. This is a rare opportunity to help the effort."

"Yes it is, sir."

"So we're agreed—"

"Sir, I have need of a secretary."

"Not one of our Wrens."

"No, I believe she's a Burgher girl, sir. She works in your office."

"Second desk?"

"Yes. And—"

"Really? Really. *And?*"

"It's like this. I have a son, sir."

"Ah. Of course you do. Leave the particulars with my aide before you leave for Colombo. Good day and Godspeed, Kandy." Mountbatten smiled at his pocket-watch. Half past gin. In Norfolk, in Delhi, here, at home, he thought, they always had sons.

sixteen

George Kandy craned his neck and stared into the spear-shaped branches crisscrossing above them. It was different with number eleven than it had been with the first ten: it was taking longer. The first, not counting the mender's daughter by the sluice, was a Ralahami's daughter from Maspota who bit his wrist when they started, leaving a welt like a zipper trail. With the second, the eldest daughter of the Ralahami of Mahakeliya, he pressed his forearms into the damp dirt on either side of her face, too far for her to touch when she began turning her head back and forth, eyes closed, lips opened, teeth clenched. The beads around her neck shook like a boy boasting with a sack of marbles. Was she thrashing or dreaming or reaching to kiss him? George decided to kiss numbers three, four, five, six, and seven to hold them in place. He kissed hard. Two tried to suck back their own lips, their fine-lined eyes bulging with sudden, real shock, as if this, a full mouth kiss, was the true outrage of what was being done to them. One of them kissed back with a hurried gulping mouth, a knowing mouth. She was a dark girl from

Rambawewa whose father had explained over sweets and tea and betel and cigarettes that she was actually fair as milk. Such a devout girl, she had gone to temple at noon and not waited for the servant to bring the parasol because she wanted to make puja before the chief monk took his nap. A grandmother's bridal portrait was shown; the girl was said to be her very picture and even though the photograph paper was blooming mould flowers, the fairness was indisputable, no? Robert and Arthur sipped their tea and considered the photograph and the sunlight upon the verandah, wondering why then every uncovered thing wasn't teaplucker black. Fair as milk in a tar-pot. George also studied the photo and then glanced at the girl who had earlier entered the room, as every engagement prospect did, with her eyes fixed high and distant as if she alone could see the jewel spark atop some temple spire halfway across the island. George asked his grandfather to have his uncle ask her father if he could walk to temple too: if someone could show him the way.

Almost always he'd asked to see the village temple; sometimes he asked to see the paddy. Whenever he was refused, George ate everything on every platter before him. One time he asked to play cricket with the girl's brother and cousins. Never again. George was bowled on the second ball and said he was not allowed to field in his suit. He had to wait with the younger boys on one side of the wicket while on the other the prospective bride waited behind a group of girl-cousins loud like babbler birds. After that, he only asked to see whatever it was the girl's father boasted about first: whether the thriving paddy or the temple's shining new bell, the new audience room or parapet wall or dining hall, the village water tank that, in this miraculous thriving place, was only ever broken from having to hold too much.

For the bridal parents, the boy's request was a high offence to the way things had always been done, the way things were to be done, but why stop now? They had already agreed to receive a prospective groom from a village where the walauwa people were said to be pyre upon pyre of bloody and bad omens and the villagers themselves layabout tinder, a prospective groom who came calling in dark modern suit and loud modern shoes, whose family asked for no perches but only a stretched engagement because of the boy's pending studies abroad, a prospective groom whose good name, Kandy, was a rogue's open outrage against holiness and fate, whose father was said to be serving the British at Peradeniya and otherwise would have conducted this visit himself but instead left the highest duty a father owes his son to a throatless grandfather and bug-eyed uncle and sent them here in a motorcar that had gained and immediately ruled the village with its gleaming and roaring, surpassing the best of all possible dowries. All this had already been agreed to without even looking at the boy's horoscope: not allowing a supervised walk this far into things would have been as high-born and backward as racing their motorcar with a garlanded bullock.

And so the fathers ignored their wives burning beside them and would later try to argue *What harm they were only children* and meantime made a show of staring threats at their daughters before releasing them—threats to behave as unassailably as they'd been raised to behave; threats to behave just modern enough to seem right for someday riding in a motorcar. Fathers' guilt became tyrants' commands to the chosen escorts—older brothers, head servants, and, if necessary, unmarried, unmarriageable aunts. Commands that George eventually answered, after he and she and escort had walked out of walauwa hearing, after first asking for only five minutes alone so they could speak plainly, truly, to see what there could be between them. He'd ask while pulling something out of his father-stuffed pocket, something wonderfully heavy or miraculously cold or shiny or delicate. Meanwhile, the girl, who had been warned to say nothing while beyond her mother's hearing, stared daggers in vain at the distracted escort as George dragged her into the never-so-dark trees.

On the second drive, this one going south, they had started at Galagedera, whose walauwa family kept a tusker in a clearing. The Ralahami said the elephant was royal caste, just ask the mahout; in fact such stories he could tell of the days of the kings, when this fellow's ancestors had carried princes to their weddings and to wars and then on to the water tanks of vanquished princes. Etc. George asked who could show him the way to the stall and he had the eighth on a bed of succulent leaves and dung flies while her older brother stood some hundred paces away, studying a stack of Japanese baseball cards. Ten minutes later, the three of them walked back to the walauwa. George and his dungy knees were in front, the brother was next, his head down, looking at the cards before he had to hide them. Coming up behind, stiff as a sudden old woman, the prospective bride called after her brother, demanding half of his stack—six for not telling that he'd made her go with the fat fellow and six for not telling what the fat fellow had just done to her. But before they could argue the terms someone else called after them— the mahout, smiling to be given the rest of the cards for his own forgetting. George watched and listened and could have helped. He had many more of the cards in his jacket pocket. His father had brought him a box full when he had come and told his grandfather and uncle that Japanese planes with sun-spotted wings had dropped bombs on Colombo and Negombo. George had wondered if they'd dropped these cards too. He had stacks at home; he had enough for the mahout and the brother and the girl who had even moved a little herself but she could always say it was the dung flies and sharp grass. But none of that mattered now—there were three more walauwas to visit before they turned home again.

The ninth girl was tall and slender and said to be the fastest ever born in Mawatagama. He couldn't get her down so he bulked her against a cinnamon tree. She kept pushing his face away with her bangle-wrapped forearm and so he didn't kiss this one and afterwards she slipped down and sobbed once, then sprang and boxed him hard and ran through the brush onto the laneway home. George ran after her, slower by bulk and breathless from the shot but running still because now he owed her that much symmetry. The servant girl ran too, slower because she had concealed what George had given her in the waistband of her skirt and did not want to drop it, and when they reached the walauwa first, second, and third, the girl's parents and Robert and Arthur were watching from the verandah, having come out at the noise of villagers who had cheered the girl on to victory. The mother was horrified. She sent the servant back to find any dropped bangles and earrings and called her daughter into the house, who was otherwise standing in front of her future father-in-law heaving like a laundry woman. She was taken by the ear to a back room and slapped past sobbing. Left there while George and Robert and Arthur accepted apologies and went, she fell asleep, and waking found the servant girl on her knees beside the cot, asking for forgiveness, and bargaining. Her hands were cupped to show the filigreed locket George had given her to wait on the laneway. Its inset picture was of two pale girls leaning head-to-head and smiling.

Number ten, a born-to-sob beauty from Barandara, had also right away refused, pulling back when George took her wrist, as if she already knew, and George wondered and liked wondering if perhaps he was becoming legend after only nine times, but thinking legend was nothing like its making. He pulled her wrist harder and the girl began crying for her chaperone-aunty to help, an aunty who, despite being fair, full cheeked, and well born herself, no man would marry because it was known in the village that she had been born with only one kidney. The aunty gave her niece the lacquered fan that George had gifted and told her not to cry, and that she should never mention this to anyone, and the girl sniffed, "Mention what, Kidney Aunty?" and her aunty told her never mind, only wait on the far side of the lane and pass the time by singing the pretty song they'd been practising before the visit. And then, for the first time, George Kandy was the one pulled into the trees. Meanwhile, in the walauwa, Robert asked the parents why the escort had been called Kidney Niece when she was told to walk with George and the daughter down the laneway. The hosts, hands wringing at the prospect of this burden lifted, smiled at Arthur and agreed with Robert that Thusitha, her true name, was very pretty. Robert pressed the question. After some crab-wise talking, the Ralahami said that it was his niece's pet name, that it came from the shape of a birthmark, and further that her father the Ralahami's younger brother was a rubber man in Malacca who had asked him to see about his daughter's prospects. She was already twenty-plus. Arthur was more than thirty. The Ralahamis discussed their horoscopes, Arthur's and Thusitha's, until they could hear George stomping up the steps, the aunty and daughter following behind him singing sweetly like they were going to cry. Arthur watched her enter, marvelling at the prospect of a kidney shape born to be found and kissed. George asked for a cool drink and the girl asked to lie down and then Thusitha, who was George's tenth, was introduced to Arthur, who would be her second.

When it happened over number eleven, George wondered why it hadn't happened before. More than one night a week in the walauwa, his nose bled while he slept. In the morning he would cover the bleed marks with pillows and blankets and toys—not because he was ashamed but because he was waiting. He was trying to fill a whole sheet with his noseblood because then they'd tell his father, who'd have to stay, for once, past the latest unwrapping. But taut over number eleven, the only daughter of the Ralahami of Ridigama, the pressure at the back of George's neck from holding

back the drip was taking more of his attention than the thing itself.
The blood was dropping down his throat and he could taste it, hard
and thick and sweet and unceasing, an iron tang like motorcars.
George dropped his chin and down his nose the blood dripped
and the girl screamed as it pattered onto her forehead and across
her cheek and her neck, four dark red marks on a dark red rope.
Now she looked like a child-bride playing with pottu but she had
already been made otherwise than a child and he wouldn't stop now
because he was already going and even though she started calling
for the brother, who came and so had to forfeit the chrome lighter
shaped like a Mississippi steamboat that George had promised him.
Or so George thought, in this way innocent about what it meant
to give and take promises. The brother crashed through the brush
and evaded a droopy sentry stand of palm trees to grab him off his
sister, seething "What kind of moment was this?" He forced open
George's fist and took the lighter, smashed his nose, and smeared
some of George's blood on his own shirt to show he had been
defending the family name. He dragged his screaming sister home,
the lighter hot in his other hand, which uselessly threatened and
waved off the absolutely feasting audience of villagers emerging
suddenly and everywhere like flies on uncovered meat.

～

Sam stood outside his son's room, in light the colour of hasty tea,
lamplight turned low to wake no one else. As if the whole walauwa
wouldn't be listening while he took George away. He'd sent in the
driver, moments before, and now was waiting with remembering.

"Sir," whispered the driver, parting the bedroom curtain and
coming into the hallway.

"What is it, Joseph?"

"Sir, I cannot make him come."

"Why not?"

"Sir, he says he is waiting for you to take him."

But those first few nights of his temple life had been a rage of their own remembering, of the soothing his father had given him that early early morning when they'd left the hut and he'd been carried to a cart and they had gone from the village, of how he would have asked—but why would a son have to ask his father holding him as he was, proud and promising as he was—why no branch was broken as they passed the village boundary? Of course they were coming home.

"Tell him I am waiting in the car and that we are going. We are going now. And tell him that if he does not come straight away"—Sam suddenly raised his voice—"tell him that for what he has done, believe it, I will leave him in this village and make it that he never leaves here again."

~

Father and son reached the rest-stop at Ambepussa in bright upcountry morning. They parked a short dash away from the crowd—fruit sellers and letter writers, club-footed beggarmen and spice-fingered ailment doctors, tour guides, marriage brokers, rickshaw men, coat-pocket gemologists, moneychangers—all of whom were already sweating just to stand around and call each other machang mali yakka until there was nothing left to smoke or chew. Who would only move, but move like lightning, a smiling mob of lighting, at a waving hand extended from a motorcar window. Sam almost extended his own, just to be able to wave them off when they came. Otherwise, there was nothing to do but begin, begin to be outraged. Not just by the boy's shameful, dirty things, or by the treasure Sam had had to send to the father in Ridigama, or even by his being delayed a day on his way back to Colombo to pick up Mountbatten's ivory and special cases. But, instead, begin to be outraged as the father: no more the outraged son.

"Right. And so I am to believe you wear that suit I brought you to be engaged in as your sleeping clothes? Or was it that you heard me arrive the night before and listened to our talking and dressed like this for the morning? What do you think should be done for the girl? For her family? For your own? I should give your clothes to those beggars over there and strip you down to nothing. See how you'll do in the world when you're no one's son with nothing."

Sam swallowed and wondered how long before the driver returned with water. His throat was so dry to talk like this, to spend like this. To spend like this, it seemed, in vain.

"You turn and face me when I am speaking to you," Sam commanded. "Turn. Turn and face your father or George I will turn you I promise that." His last words came out low and harder than he had expected or thought possible with his own blood: low and hard like harbour-talking. And the boy did turn, right away, the whites of his eyes showing more than only fear to hear his father speak this way, to him.

They drank the water the driver brought and then Sam laid two cigarettes across Joseph's cupped palm and sent him off. A full glass of water and still Sam's throat was drought dirt. And now, the boy was staring at him with heavy eyes and a clamped mouth, impassive, already victorious but for his eyebrows, which were softer, indecisive.

"Your Siya and Arthur-uncle have told me what they were told by the girl's father, but you will tell me yourself. If you want to do as men do, you must answer as men do."

George said nothing.

"You will tell me before we go on to Colombo, to the harbour. Otherwise—"

"Otherwise?"

"You don't ask me otherwise. I am your father, and I will …"

"Yes, Appachchi?"

Sam was exhausted. He didn't think he'd ever spoken so many such words. Family words, words that demanded of him a greater carry than any Pettah threat or harbour deal. Words with nothing behind them but everything that was his own.

"I have enough cigarettes to keep the driver over there until he smokes his lips black. We will wait here until you tell."

"Ha."

"Mokatha?"

"You will wait? Ha. You, who won't even wait in the room for me to say thank you for all your shiny rubbish? You, who has never waited? Ammi used to say—"

"You call what I have given you shiny rubbish?"

"I never asked for it."

"Ah. Right. You never asked for the Dinky cars and you never asked for the new slingshot. You never asked for anything! Right? RIGHT, GEORGE? Shall I tell you what I never asked for?"

"I think the only thing you ever asked for was a car accident."

Sam struck him across the cheek, his signet ring catching skin. He raised his hand for more if the boy dared to say her name again. But George buried his head in his lap, his hands covering his face, shaking. Sam turned to see if he could catch Joseph's eye. And while he looked for his driver he had to listen to no man seated beside him but to a broken boy, sobbing. A poor boy. His. Beside him. His. A poor boy. He was too. But was he ever to be more? Sam's lips pursed and blew, pursed and blew, louder and louder pursed and blew breaths of *putha* but before he could say *dear son* loud enough to be heard George sat up looking like some kind of madman, his nose all reddish-brown mud, tears streaking down his ring-welted cheeks. He was shaking, foaming, with laughter.

"You never asked for a son, right? You never asked! BUT CAN YOU GUESS HOW MANY I'M GOING TO HAVE? CAN YOU GUESS?"

The father never gave the son the victory of guessing how many. The son never gave the father the victory of asking where they were going, which became, after they reached Colombo harbour and George was shaved to skin and changed into a soldier's uniform while Sam smoked a cigarette, where he was being sent. After a band of Italian POWs were taken off the ship—squinting, muttering prayers and curses and head-jerking challenges to anyone who held their eyes—George was taken on with a scrum of Indian troops. The gangplank was pulled up. Sam turned and went, removing George's horoscope leaf from his coat pocket and tossing it into the harbour water, where it floated and faded unto nothing in a yellow foam that was bobbing and lapping with food wrappers and cigarette butts and, this morning, an unexpected litter of mottled pups.

SEVENTEEN

"No."

Gulls and revving transport trucks filled in the silence. And something else, too regular to be wind-made, too tinny to be animal. Made by someone. Not by something. Someone. How Sam hated English patience. Not even willing to begin a dispute until he said it, until he gave height and history and complexion their due. "No, sir."

"Yes, Kandy," the harbour warden answered immediately. "Word was sent from Peradeniya that you have already agreed. They are yours now, until informed otherwise, as are these." The harbour warden held out a rust-flaked ring dangling six bright keys, golden and impossibly small, as if to a doll-house prison.

"No," Sam said again. "No, sir." He drove his hands into his trouser pockets and did not look again into the prison-cage, into their staring faces, their heads nodding to some unheard prayer or song syncopated by the clink of bright metal knocking on iron bars.

"No discussion, Kandy. You have agreed, you have given your word to Commander Mountbatten himself. Am I not correct?"

"Right. But these are not what I, what anyone would call 'special case' prisoners. I don't know what these are, but they are not what I agreed to, sir."

"They are, I am informed, Ethiopians, who were turned over to us when we took Tunis from the Italians. Now, I shall certainly inform the quartermaster of how this business concludes between you, Kandy, and His Majesty's war effort, in terms of taking and keeping. In terms of past and present and future taking and keeping, I should say."

The two men were speaking in a corner of a warehouse mostly blocked off from common view by newly stacked crates that had come off the same ship as the prisoners, some of them already blooming mould flowers and all of them addressed to the quarter-master of Colombo, who for years now had been turning his head, once a week, when Sam Kandy and his carters came before dawn for PX crates full of—really it did not matter. It could be all the chocolate and radios of America and still, now, it did not matter. None of it.

The warden consulted his clipboard and tapped his finger six times. The triumph of official reality. "I have it right here, Kandy. This was signed and stamped at the site of first detention, Tunis, and signed and stamped at the dock of embarkation, Tripoli: 'Six special case prisoners of war, to be detained in Ceylon until further notice, under best conditions as determined by SEAC authorities at destination.' By Commander Mountbatten's hand, yours are our best conditions, Kandy. Take the keys. I have transport already arranged. It departs for your village at noon. Now take the keys, man!"

Sam walked off, breathing dust and brine and squinting in search of Italians. The warehouse's doors were now open to the city on one end and to the dark water on the other. Yellow-white morning sun poured in through the unending particulate of men at work in a wartime warehouse. The bright smoke and endless whorls of sawdust and fannings made him near blind but he felt a sudden and great lift from his sudden, great resolve: that he would not. He would take every last one of the Italians instead, set them up in the walauwa itself if necessary. But he would not be a keeper of men like those others, men who could neither curse nor challenge nor keep quiet of their own resolve. He would not keep them, not that way. He would not.

The warden sighed and followed. The coolies and perhaps even the stove-stomach quartermaster himself would now see him trailing after a native like he was some fussy shopkeeper trying to settle a bill. He did not like this kind of dealing with the locals. It was exposing. It lowered everyone. He would have almost kept the Ethiopians himself, but that would be a whole other kind of lowering. They'd been delivered the night before by men from a New Zealand cruiser, in a tarp-draped cage like some kind of circus attraction. The deckhands had grimaced as they pushed it, he'd thought from the toil of rough ship rope and brine-pocked trolley wheels kedging along the grit floor. But as the accompanying officer presented the transit document and the keys, the deckhands composed themselves solemn as pranking schoolboys to watch him, the harbour warden, remove the tarp and inspect the prisoners and make sure the count was right. He'd jumped back, dropping the clipboard and the key ring. The accompanying officer was already walking back to the ship. The deckhands departed shortly thereafter, having waited in vain to be asked what the prisoners ate. The warden was left by himself, on his haunches, his hands drumming the floor in search of civilization, watching them watch him feel around for his clipboard, pity and fear and puzzling wonder occupying the air between them as thickly as the cloud legions of electric-drunk bugs that swarmed every night when the overhead lamps were switched on to hum until dawn.

"Kandy!"

Sam turned from his vain listening for the lilt and gutter of Italian mutter and curse. The warden stopped with a stutter, righted himself, and immediately held the clipboard in front of Sam's face like a tablet he was daring him to break.

"Where are the others, sir?" Sam asked.

"The others, you say. What others? Are six of *those* not enough for you?"

"No. The other prisoners I watched come off a ship this morning. I will take—"

"You will take and keep, Kandy, what His Majesty's Government requires you to take and keep. The war effort does not proceed via your vantage. It's barely proceeding via ours of late. Now keep your word, man."

"And otherwise, sir? Do you really think I will keep these fellows so I can take more mosquito nets and Horlicks candies from the PX?" This was not the man who lately had lied about his only son's age to obtain a spot for him in a regiment of Indian soldiers transiting through Colombo to the Italian front. Holding here, against becoming the keeper of caged Ethiopians with padlocks driven through their lips, was everything, was not balancing or defeating or holding back but obliterating everything else.

Meanwhile, the warden did what his schooling and blood told him to do: he smiled himself deaf and blind to Sam's counters and left.

"No," Sam called out after him. But the warden kept walking. Sam followed. "I did not agree to this when I met your Commander Mountbatten Sir. You cannot force me to take them. It's not, it's not right." Sam spoke with vehemence, with the impatient innocence of sudden virtue. He was outraged, shocked, and also pleased that the rest of the world failed to see things the same way.

"But I can. And I shall. You have already given your village's name to the Commander's aide, who in turn has given it to me. In two hours these fellows will be on a transport truck to"—here he flipped through his papers, victory assured by signed and sealed reality, his index finger scaling down script—"yes, Sudugama."

"No. I cannot, I cannot give my word for their safety, for what will happen to them in the village, what will be done."

"Good God, man, why have I been chasing you all morning trying to give you the keys? No one in your village will have any reason to fear."

"No. It's not them I mean, not the Kaffirs—"

"Ethiopians."

"It's not the prisoners who will do something in the village. It's what the village will do to them."

"That's your concern, Kandy, and all the more reason for you to take the keys or I shall have no choice but to leave instructions with the transport driver to give the keys to the first villager he meets. Are we understood? Are we understood?"

They'd reached the prison-cage. The prisoners were still clinking, a golden glint playing about their black faces, their glum, padlocked mouths. He would not keep them and now there was nothing to be done but keep them. But he would not take them to Sudugama, at least not right away.

"Right. How are they fed?"

The warden waited, smiling tightly.

"How are they fed, sir?"

"Very good. Glad you remain a man of your word, Kandy. That's the sort of thing we reward, as you well know." He cleared his throat. "Now this will be the last that we, meaning you and I, ever discuss this matter. You will be contacted by another party regarding their next transfer, which is to occur when command deems conditions suitable. What remains is to sign here, Kandy." The warden counter-signed and patted the document like a good boy's head. It would be dropped in an oil barrel and burned minutes after the Ethiopians were taken from the warehouse. They were never here.

"I have to speak with the transport driver. How are they fed, sir?"

"You'll find him in the depot on the south side of the warehouse. Ask for the man waiting to make the upcountry run. Here are your keys. The padlocks themselves, I understand, are new. The fellows were found already padlocked, but with Roman lock-and-key, which have been duly replaced with our own. Good day."

"As to my question, sir?"

"You mean how these poor chaps are fed?" The warden flipped through his pages, found the answer, tapped it smartly, and looked up. Smiled. "As of now, Kandy, they are fed by you."

~

Sam heard Curzon's voice while he was still on the stairs. The office door must have been open. Curzon was ordering someone out, it seemed, in vain. Sam wondered how a beggar had come this far into the building and also how much of Curzon's English he would have understood. Curzon's voice was sliding around, from highest-pitched pique to gutter-toned curse before pirouetting, screeching back up again. Sam couldn't remember when last he'd heard him scale about and lose himself this way, this much.

Over the years, Curzon had graduated from playing at a Ceylon Englishman to remembering nothing else, to insisting on it. By 1944 he had grown fine and fat as a spinning top; his wife, a fair-skinned Mount Lavinia Burgher, had taken to referring to her own family as natives; to dismissing dress-wearing women from prominent Colombo families as "zipper nonas"; and to pining with other fair Cinnamon Garden wives for the English goods of their girlhoods. She also complained, especially when Sam had disappeared those months only to return one day as if from a downstairs shave, with a scar on his forehead and no car and no wife, that the black harbour-work Curzon had been doing in the meantime was not what a man of his station was meant for. His was a name known throughout the Empire. He had two prefect-certain sons at Royal and a daughter who captained the hockey team at St. Bridget's. He decided she was right: all he was ever meant to be was elsewhere than this. When he had made enough, they would close the Colombo house and take to hill country and find a good green estate. He had been stashing away errant export coupons for years. He would be a high-grown planter at Nuwara Eliya and she would become a plantation madam and they would have a trout stream and milking cows and he would never have to sight that salt-blue water again, save whenever it was that the war ended and the children left for Oxford, or Cambridge. In the meantime, there was money to be made. City warehouses were filling up smartly, goods waiting redistribution; more and more rubber tappers were needed from Cochin; a reliable letter-drop address in Singapore was asked for; a caravan-sized desk was wanted. And so Curzon kept his own daily appointments with titled men in the city, passing on untitled queries to Sam and otherwise confining himself to the Fort office, to reading and rereading damp planters' memoirs until the heroic memories became his own, so that all that remained now was to shift triumphant and forget.

When Sam reached the second floor he rested his hand on the newel post. A woman's voice was answering Curzon's. Sam passed into the office and she turned and Mountbatten was also a man of his word. When last he'd seen her, in the British office at the Swiss Hotel, her long ladyfingers had been playing sonatas on her Royal, her face calm and smooth and oval and fair, yes ivory; her eyes had been open and considering, her small round mouth about to say—but it had been a busy office with a war to win, etc. But here, now, having words with Curzon, her face was the colour of battered tusks; her brow was broken up with colliding fault lines, and her eyes, narrow as if spat at but now widening, were more cat than sea green. There was more than recognition in those eyes. Not surprise, more like mild outrage that he had left her waiting this long, like this, with *him*. She was a fine long body in an ankle-length dress, white with gathered and strewn dark flowers playing across it, the cloth flowing down from the waist. There was some kind of yellow smudge, there, but no matter. The cloth hung fine upon those sudden, slashing hips and rose to a sweeter rising. And her throat, blushing too, like a fine vase smudged.

"Kandy," Curzon began sternly.

"Charlie," Sam countered with an off-hand voice, finished with this.

"Char-lie!" the woman repeated, suddenly bright as a morning bird, her hands on her hips, her eyes studying Sam's studying hers.

"What in God's name, what is this?" stammered Curzon.

"I already told him, sir," she began, looking at Sam, her hand trying to cover that yellow smudge, "that I was sent!" Her pleading English was servant's sing-song, but her mouth was red like flowers, like petals floating on milk. "I told him, sir, that I was sent to you as a—"

"This, this, this young woman tells me she was sent here, to us, by no less than Lord Mountbatten himself!" Curzon smirked. "No doubt," he continued, feeling suddenly winded, "she must have heard our name while you were up there. Chased off for God knows what and now she's come to Colombo to con us instead. My God but do they think the war makes nodding asses of us all? Claims her name is Ivory but refuses to say her good name, which says enough. She informs me she is to be our new secretary, on Mountbatten's orders no less!"

"Sir please, I was sent to you as a special—"

"Enough!" Curzon bellowed.

"Sir please I was sent—"

Sam held out his hand and she stopped speaking. He walked toward her. Eyes studying eyes, mouths pursed. He showed her to the door and as she crossed the threshold Sam whispered "Wait."

The door clicked shut. Sam turned. Curzon considered his partner's set staring eyes, the set mouth. He knew at least this much after thirteen years of working beside Sam Kandy: what had just happened was part of a plan he did not yet know about. How much hill-country green, Charlie wondered, how high up, could he and his wife have if they left the city tomorrow?

"That woman is not our new secretary," Sam said.

"I thought as much. Mountbatten!"

"That is correct."

"Sorry?"

"Yes. She is mine."

eighteen

"Meet Madam Kandy."

The walauwa fell so quiet you could hear the new servant boy already running home, the sound of his bare feet like some bored fruit seller passing a mango back and forth between his palms. Meanwhile, in the front room, his hands cinching his sarong at the knee, Robert did not ask her to sit. He rocked and swallowed his coughing because if he tried to speak it would have been yelling and were it yelling it would not stop until his throat croaked out of his mouth onto the floor like a burnt frog leaping from a funeral pyre. He would not have it end this way. He would not die for scandal in the front room of his father's father's father's own hand-built house because his motorcar son-in-law had just gone and made a milk toffee love marriage. They were, Robert thought, supposed to be widowers both. And where was George? Where was George playing hell now? Was he in the back of the loud green monster that had followed Sam into the village? The village that was, and suddenly Robert felt his blood, he felt fierce about it, still *his* village?

The Ralahami turned, staring back Latha, who was about to bring Hyacinth into the front room to greet her father, wearing a new white sari. The girl had crossed into womanhood in the month her father and her brother had been away. But Latha had heard Sam too and was already backing away, one hand covering her cursing mouth, the other covering and turning her young lady's face. She was also, of course, craning, straining to see her, this sudden Madam Kandy, standing there beside him like the devil's white shadow. A new woman in the walauwa. A woman that she, Latha, had not raised. Wearing a sun hat meant for true fair skin, a two-piece dress and shoes from anywhere but here, her hands on her hips, hips—this woman was more shined-up betel spittoon than temple jewel. If they, the husband and his new wife, if they stayed here more than an hour, Latha decided, she would keep Hyacinth in her bedroom for one hundred years.

Meanwhile, the only noise in the world was that sweet mad patter: Lalson, as everyone called the new servant boy even though he was twenty-five, running home as he had been taught, his legs swinging in such close succession from his feet touching every stone step. One of the first lessons the boy's father, Lal, had taught him before giving way, when his own coughing from years of reviving the lives of the Ralahami's crushed cigarettes became too much, was that even if the Ralahami were calling for you with his head on fire, you still had to show respect. You had to touch every step, going up and going down. Before his son went to the walauwa in his place, Old Lal also told him to palm passed-over betel and half-smoked cigarettes; to take boxes brought from the city before the kitchen or the laundry woman could; to ask for tea first and then answer Latha when she asks what you just heard them say on the verandah; to mark where a toy or bauble sits and only take what hasn't been touched between two Poya days; to bring the Ralahami tea and cigarettes whenever he coughs like this (here Old

Lal demonstrated). Most importantly, to come home at least once a week to see your father, to bring him palmed cigarettes and betel and boxes for your mother, because having already deposited every family possession in one of Sam Kandy's discards, even the onions, she had now almost covered every wall in the hut with the flattened richness of Cargill's cardboard. And when you come home, to tell everything in the walauwa that's been said, whispered, bought, brought, broken, taken, cooked, thrown, cried about, coughed at, and cursed. And, finally, never but come straight away if ever there's birth death or marriage in the big house.

And so the boy rushed from the walauwa to his father's hut, passing the crowd gathered around the green army truck that had followed Sam into the village and was now parked at the village crossroads. A crowd so focused on the truck that none had noticed Sam's latest ascent, ten minutes before, his hand at a bare fair elbow. A crowd which, whether from whole cloth or half truth, recalled memory or borrowed, had been made gloriously one in a sudden bout of divination, an asking and answering that was unto itself generative and affirming, sceptic and disputing, all of it only to make more of the same, to keep it going, the telling.

What was in the truck?

There was much in this question for men old since used to the rattle and vroom of Sam Kandy's coming and going, men by now bored of believing that the rest of the world would inevitably emerge from the boot of Sam's car. This was a sudden new roaring, a war-green monster with a black mouth in the back, which had stopped at an immediately auspicious hour on an immediately auspicious day in October 1944, beneath the water-print fade of an auspicious moon, and was now parked only a walk away from where they had all been born and married, would die and be burned to next life. It would be a sin for the back gate to swing down and what emerge?

What?

Inside were British soldiers, come to take the village boys to fight the Hitler war. No, inside were row on row of Japanese, them come to take Ceylon; the white driver was a dupe, a decoy. Yes! The Japanese had come to defeat the British at Peradeniya and knew that this was the place to start; they must have heard of the village's famed Road Ordnance victory against the British, years before, from the new monk at the village temple, who had studied abroad, in Siam or was it Burma, which might as well have been Berlin or Japan. Who was no monk but yes a Japanese agent, a pilot!, his beggar's bowl a flying cap, his scholar's specs goggles, and inside the truck was a Japanese aeroplane, its wings folded up like a Vesak lantern. Aiyo no! Madness! It was so much simpler. Inside were a thousand field Tamils got down from Madras to take over the Ralahami's paddy fields. In that much dark for that long, by now there could be two thousand field Tamils waiting to take over in the fields and take our huts and garden pepper and declare themselves upcountry since before the days of Sri Vikrama. No. All lies. There was only one reason Lalson had just run to his father's hut. The walauwa must need Old Lal's carrying help. Because inside the truck was George Kandy, returned from his latest engagement tour, now so fat his father needed an army truck to bring him home.

"No. You're all wrong."

The speaker this time was the village weaver, not the village weaver's wife, who could go on like she was seven sisters, but the weaver himself. He could have heard something when he went to hang new cane tats across the walauwa windows the week before, after Hyacinth had crossed. And so for the first time in their glorious mongering, the crowd became a windstorm of threats and pleas each to all to be quiet so they could hear the latest certainty. Inside that truck, the weaver declared, were all the cooking pots and chocolates of Ceylon, all the paper dolls and aftershave the father could buy or steal, a collection that explained the latest absence; it took even Sam Kandy a month to get it all. And all of it was needed—not in Sudugama, but in Mahakeliya and Rambawewa, in Galagedera, Mawatagama, Barandara; in walauwas full of ruined daughters and sobbing mothers and outraged fathers from here halfway to Habarana. George's engagement tour route. The invocation of known places, not more conjuring words like *Berlin* and *aeroplane*, was the modest champion, collapsing the wild fine rest of it.

And so they neared the back of the truck, expecting to find cooking pots shining in the darkness. Two young men came forward, two of the three boys who, one vellum-sun morning in 1929, had chased a Morris Minor fireball down the lane. One of them dropped on all fours at the muddy bumper so the other could climb onto his back and look in, their having agreed in advance that the positions would reverse at the count of ten. But the first fellow didn't get to peer past the count of five, which was when Old Lal and Lalson marched past. Without breaking stride Old Lal called into the crowd for the metal-benders to follow. Everyone did. And only when he saw the village stream toward the big house did the truck's driver hop down and knock twice on its side for the prisoners' handlers, two sons of a Pettah seamstress, to open the gate and, as instructed, let it drop without banging. While they got the Ethiopians down, the army driver smoked, shaking the key ring in his other hand, trying to remember which way down the crossroad Sam had said he would find the empty hut where they were to be deposited.

~

Inside the otherwise silent walauwa, the sound of foot on stone was now much louder, was now like a lane of bored fruit sellers. Lalson was returning along the steps, following his father. Heavier and slower and behind them were the metal-benders. The rest of the village was gathered below, at the twin boulders, where they were frenzied with fresh fecund telling about why Old Lal had walked so straight and serious, why the metal-benders had been called along, what or better still who were they going to take from the walauwa and throw into the back of the army truck. Hearing their approach and beyond them a murmuring crowd, Sam knew it was time for the day's next business. Taking Ivory at the waist, he turned her away from his stony father-in-law and idiot-smiling brother-in-law and walked out onto the verandah wondering, hoping, needing the whole village to be waiting there with clumps to throw. His suit would show all, would encourage more, he thought. And he did not worry about any man in a yellow hat. In fact, over the years, when no crocodile ever came for him, Sam decided it must have been a heat shimmer, a hot mad dream on his first wedding day. On this, his second, the only question was how to get the village yelling loud enough for when the army truck drove off. But he knew how.

In the city, she had asked for the whitest cloth Sam could find for her wedding-day dress, and he had said nothing. The shoes and hat she picked out at Cargill's, her dress copied from a creased catalogue print she had shown him ten minutes after Sam proposed marriage one evening in the office, two weeks after Charlie Curzon had left for the day never to return, and a long, respectful hour after Ivory had interrupted a dictation to say her parents were both dead and she had no other family on the island. And she had accepted, right away and without much excitement, more impatience, just the same way he had proposed. They exchanged toothy, congratulating smiles. Then pressing his hand into hers Ivory had shown Sam the design as if she'd had it in her palm all the two weeks and one hour they'd known each other. Sam had it made for her by a Pettah seamstress whose eyebrows showed she thought it was more than absurd: the jacket with its row of fish-eye buttons and plunging neck like some scoundrel man had split it open before it could be worn; a sharp-gathered waist; and then the skirt, too short by at least two hands from above the ankles. She wore it that dawn, to appear before the Registrar of Deaths and Marriages, who, unshaven, had married Sam and Ivory on the front step of his office without once looking up from his vow book.

Lal and Lalson and the metal-benders met Sam and wife just before the three final steps to the verandah. Looking up, they watched them emerge from the noon-hour maw of the verandah. Everything about her was so white. The sun was white too, at least what was throbbing through the spear-leafed green and pouring down the lines of the walauwa's staggered orange-red roof tiles in a blinding wash. It was as if, as it would be told in the toddy circle that night, she had been poured down beside him. Only much later, when descriptions of both the new wife and the army truck's coming and going were exhausted, were the metal-benders asked what Sam had also looked like from so close. And they answered, being the first men of that long day, from meeting the truck at Pettah to outside the Registrar's door to the rest-stop at Ambepussa to the walauwa, to notice that Sam Kandy had been wearing a full white suit. In fact he had chosen off-white because he did not think it would look so bad after they started throwing their dirt.

But no one threw anything. The villagers staring up at them, at her, were shocked silent for a moment. But then they knew who and what kind of affront, how many affronts, this was. Meet Madam Kandy. Their answer to Sam presenting his new wife was total, was outraged, and it was loud and long enough to bring the Ralahami and his son from the shadows of the walauwa to stand on the high step behind Sam and Ivory, without coming forward any farther. It was also enough to annihilate the sound of the now-emptied transport truck leaving the village and turning onto the Kurunegala Road, where it was seen off by seven saffron-clad monks who had been watching it all from the other side of the road, three old ones frowning to appear solemn and four boys waving with mad longing to leave too.

Fifteen hours later, Arthur felt Sam's hand against his mouth. Thrashing his face back and forth to break free, he was pushed more firmly into his mattress and held there, trying now to bite enough fingers away to call for help.

"Arthur!" Sam seethed, pulling away his sudden throbbing hand. Wanting to wheel around and knock him in the jaw with the key ring. But he was needed.

"MOKATHA?"

"Damn quiet will you!"

"*Mokatha?*" Arthur squinted in the silver moonlight that came through the edges of the window tat above his bed. "Sam-aiya?" His brother-in-law had come to his bedroom in the middle of the night, the middle of *his* wedding night. More than that: his brother-in-law had come barefoot, in sarong.

Bunching it between his legs, Sam took Arthur at the wrist and pulled him up and put an iron ring in his hand, its little keys falling between his fingers. Arthur quickened.

"What are these for?" he whispered.

"Come and see," Sam said. He had already kept the Ethiopians longer than he had wanted, fifteen plotting days in back of B.'s old stall in Pettah, for which he had paid well the widow seamstress who occupied it now, and also paid her two sons to keep the prisoners dry and fed and no morning noon and night attraction for the city. He'd also paid the English transport driver to return to Pettah at dawn for the upcountry run and, before they left the city, to witness Sam's second marriage, and finally to leave the key ring in a pile of dead timber beside his family's old hut, where the prisoners were taken and left while the rest of the village was, earlier that day, distracted.

"What is it?" Arthur asked.

"Just come and see will you." And then they could return to the city, he could return to the Oriental Grand. And if that tea-seller so much as looked across York Street as he walked his wife into the hotel, Sam would burn his stall down. Only he would do it the next morning. Because he had been aching certain for three weeks and a day now that no onions would be needed this time; that there would be nothing and no one to un-remember. All that remained was the return drive to Colombo, before which was this black of one night's work.

After Arthur changed into his oldest sarong, as instructed, they padded through the kitchen and down the steep back stairs of the walauwa. Arthur was to lead them where they were going, because Sam Kandy had to say he could not find it himself, the empty hut a few down from the village crossroads on the great green clearing side that no one had taken over since its old widower had disappeared years before. Sam said they had to reach the hut without anyone's seeing them. Arthur agreed like this was a boy's game and, having counted the keys on the ring Sam had given him, grinned at the idea of six vehicles waiting for him and his soon-to-be bride. He was amazed. He had only told Sam about his own engagement hours before, over boiled eggs and cuts of cold chatty roast that Sam had brought from the city in a plaid hamper. It was a wedding feast for the whole house, but no one else in the walauwa would eat, not Robert who remained in his room for the day, not Hyacinth in hers with Latha soothing her and staring daggers at the curtained threshold, and certainly not Ivory, who had been left by her new husband in the farthest back bedroom, where for hours she sat rigid upon the bed, waiting with cigarettes and a water glass and with worrying her buttons and blaming this devil place for the creases and smudges on her wedding dress. They had been married since dawn. He had never mentioned a daughter either.

Dogs barked as Sam and Arthur neared the hut, but it was not a mad warning of rogues, it was a warning to them. Meanwhile, anyone watching their progress would have seen only the bent-over shapes of two village husbands in old sarongs, midnight drunks sneaking about for more pot arrack.

"Magee Amma!" Arthur breathed when they went inside and Sam lit a match. What little furniture had been there was long since stolen, and the old home smells were gone from years of vermin and mould. The prisoners, shirtless but wearing once-white sarongs and seated on the dirt bare ground, looked up. They were sleepy, bored. So many had already entered the hut and looked at them that day.

"I cannot, what am I, what are these—"

"No. You already have agreed, Arthur. See who is holding the key ring."

"But—"

"No. You are a man of your word and you are soon to rule this village, isn't it?"

"But where can I keep them? What are they, yakkas? Aiyo, how to feed?"

"I am told they can eat and drink with their mouths like that and that they like fruits. They are called Ethiopians."

"Aiya ... what did you do with George?"

"He has gone abroad."

"London?" He said the word like a bug had landed on his tongue.

"Yes, George has gone abroad like you did."

"But even if I take them to the old cave behind the walauwa you know the village will find out. Appachchi will find out. Aiyo, my new bride will find out! You cannot leave them here. What kind of man! Your daughter is here!"

"What colour do you want?"

"You say they are called Ethiopians. I say you are a yakka."

"What colour?"

"You are the devil's own son."

"What colour?"

"Or is George the son?"

"Arthur, what colour motorcar? Decide. Then you can send it to bring your bride home. Decide."

"I like black," Arthur muttered, defeated at motorcar and now wondering which men in the village he could trust to help him bring them to the village founder's cave, how many cigarettes he'd have to give for their silence. Sam slipped out of the hut while Arthur was doing the figures, neither of them knowing how many villages within a day's walk would have already heard of Sudugama's man-eaters one day later, when Sam was long since gone to the city, to the rising, the slashing, all of it.

nineteen

He was one year married before he had to admit what had been breathless blank and collapsing true from their first night together: he had been so very wrong about why he had to marry as he did, where he did, the first time. In 1929 Sam had thought it was the birth-village. A boy's idea. He had been thirty and he had gone home to triumph with a boy's idea. Now forty-six, he had lived this past year, the whole of 1945, at the Grand Oriental. On their second night in the hotel she'd told him that so long as they remained there, they remained in honeymoon, and then she pressed her heat and cradle bone again against him lying there breathless blank and collapsed, and eyes closed murmuring Sam had agreed. And this past year he had daily worked and waited for it, had nightly sought in curtained darkness, was discovered, was each and every time gloriously defeated by what he now knew was the world's true first best where. Which was his now, which had made the rest of what Sam Kandy had and did and went after mere adjunct to its ongoing possession.

Ivory laughed at his wonder noises afterwards, when he lay beside her like a starfish and she was propped up on her elbows, her back pressed against a dark wooden headboard shaped like a great headless bird ascending. She liked to remind him that he had been married before and had a daughter and so obviously must have had some idea, no? Her face never showing any colour no matter how thrashing things had been moments before, she would make him tell again of his one night with Alice. She never tired of it. Yes she had her Mills & Boon books but she liked the Alice story more. She liked how she could make him show her their wedding night, how Sam and the first wife had lain like boards beside each other in the honeymoon bed and how, after some time had passed, one board had turned over onto the other and waited there, then slipped off.

Never once were things the other way. Never once did Sam ask how from the very first she could do it all so well, the guiding, the commanding, the soothing. These were, among other things, taken as given. Those other things: her name, her family, her birth-village. How she came to work for the British at Peradeniya if not how she left. Why she had asked that the wedding-white canopy be removed from the bed when the boys came in to turn down the sheets that first night, why she never wanted to see the hooked-nose couples dancing in the ballroom after dinner, and why always first the chamberpot. She only liked to tell of how she had had to come to Colombo. There had been confusion at the rail platform in Kandy town, about her papers. She was supposed to have travelled to Colombo in the car reserved for office natives in His Majesty's employ but was sent in error to a fully native car. Only then did her face flush and her brow break, propped up beside him in the bed and telling of having to sit so close to so much village life for so many hours, the open windows blowing bugs and hot country into the still air that was itself bloated from all those packets of home cooking, and from the crying babies and sleepy children asking for more sweets, the humid woodsmell of their handicrafts and their garden spices to sell in the city without need of any crooked nephew go-betweens, and also with incense, foot sweat, cooking oil and coconut oil, underneath which was the rust and blah of coughing old men. She parroted how the woman seated beside her had complained through hours of her husband's sleeping that Ivory was so thin the first time she turned a corner in the city she would vanish without so much as a letter home, just as her own daughter had vanished, which was why she and her husband, who coughed rust at his mention, were now going to Colombo. The woman insisted on sharing her food because Ivory seemed to have brought nothing and then she leaned over and actually fed her from the bright wet mess of rice and curry opened on her lap. This Ivory had to show him, every time. Her long fingers pulsing air, she shoved and shoved a mouthful of nothing down Sam's mouth, the motion shocking and jerky and when every time he turned his face to the side her fingers followed, reaching into his mouth like some fat dancing spider. Her cat-green eyes wide with both achieved and expected outrage, she needed him to turn away, to resist just as she had, just as anyone would, and yet the old woman had persisted in trying to feed her, which was why there had been that yellow stain on Ivory's dress the first day she had come to the office. A clump of jak fruit curry slipped from her fingers and both had looked down and the husband leaned over and inspected and only then did the woman stop and turn away and speak not one word more the rest of the journey, as if only then did she realize that Ivory was wearing a dress no village daughter could wear, that Ivory was riding in a car never meant for her. She told him she would never forget that train. She seemed to have no memory of herself otherwise.

But she could be gluttonous for his.

When she wanted it, she would sidle down from her elbows and reach for him with her legs, play him slowly with a foot. Ask him to tell. And so was rubbed away Sam's resolve that he would have only a forward life. For once, when asked, Sam told truly of his past. Of course never of his crow's past and temple squirrel past and not much about Alice save bed boards and never once, not so much as a breath about George, but he told her some nights of B. and B.'s stories and of the butterfly-stall if not of B.'s mutton or the Malay girl with the raven hair. He told her Ismail's stories and of the elephant hold to Sydney, its sweet black pungency, and of ball throwing about the harbour and of his shining silver Astrobe life high above the city. He told of Pocket Ma and of pig-trading for Hindu workmen in Singapore and of returning to do the same and more in Colombo but never of Dambulla and whenever she wanted to hear of it—either she intently did or seething did not—he told of Sudugama's two-faced ways and of Curzon's, about which they often laughed together, triumphantly, and he told of Mountbatten and one night showed her the cigar and she smoked it like a fat customs agent and Sam knew this was not her first. Eventually, he even told her about the Ethiopians who for the past year had been kept by Arthur in Sudugama, hidden in the village founder's cave in the high grass hills behind the walauwa, though she refused to believe her wedding day had gone off with cannibal savages so close behind her bridal train and she liked to declare they would be at home in that bloody old house and village and Sam had agreed because touching her hip he was ready and this was noted and then she gave him whatever sweet or cold and tough fried pastry was nearest and sent him from the bed to the chamberpot and when he returned and was ready she would make him tell one more thing, of his one night with Alice, show again how they had lain like boards and there, holding his breath, Sam waited without moving until she moved, until Ivory rolled on and began another sweet hammering rush to oblivion.

He got fat. She encouraged him to sweets and rich meats when they went to breakfast and to dinner downstairs—kidneys on toast, meat kedgeree, mutton with beans; battered mutton in a brown sauce, frikkadels, piquant steak, and on Fridays fried fish in Sauce Robert, all of which she ordered for him. After meals Sam ate meringues and trifles and pastry horns filled with whipped cream and jams, platefuls of fondant creams as if he was some Circuit-working Englishman's bored sow wife. He was certain the waiters must have joked about it in the kitchen. But where were they in the middle of the night? Herself, she only took tea, or tea with a breakfastcup of egg and milk soup in the morning; in the evening it was more soup, sometimes a plain omelette, and once a week she asked for Angels on Horseback: she would eat all twelve oysters and always need more slices of lime and she would leave the briny fried bread for him.

Midday in the city, ravenous as he had never been before, Sam began to queue at roadside stalls near the harbour, or in the backstreets of Fort, waiting in his suit for packets of rice and curry behind beedi-smoking carters and tar-black dockworkers and rail-thin village boys themselves trying to stand around like city men while, as he knew well, they were secret hopeful that this latest food-stall might sell something that tasted anything of home. Sam obviously did not join the eating rows in the shade but he could not be seen ordering a lunch boy to bring such a packet into Prince's Building or even to his harbour office. And so he had to take his common rice and curry in open air while trying to keep it to himself, like a dog frantic at finding a pile of hot good fortune in the street. He ate crouched down and turned in, facing whatever sudden free space he could find in the midday heat of the weekday city, whether against the cracked wall of an English church or in the phantom entryway of a building half-built or half-demolished or in the fickle shade of the broken mossy seawalls and bird-marked monuments of Ceylon's old gone conquerors.

As requested, he brought sweet fritters and fried combs and short-eats to the hotel in the afternoons. The phonograph would be playing fast blaring American music and she would take the food out of its oily vellum packets and arrange it all on a plate spirited from downstairs, dipping her finger in the fritter syrup or nibbling off the ridge of a fish patty while he closed the curtains and took off his jacket and shirt and hung them in the almirah without ever looking in. When he turned around in trouser and banyan she would present the cold shining crud and he would stand there silently in the middle of their room, eating until he could eat no more, breathing loudly with the effort, his forehead beaded with sweat, and when he was finished he went to the chamberpot and then washed his hands and face and neck and returned to her naked save an abused facecloth. And then they could begin.

She said she liked it, the new roundness of his belly. She would inspect it some nights, pat it and say she felt like a king building a private little temple on his body, her lush grounds. He tried to turn over or say otherwise; he could have taken her wrist and bent it back, snapped it off even and then slapped her smiling blaspheming mouth with her own hand for making of his own body a sacrilege she could never know. But she would keep patting, looking and waiting for him to do whatever it was he wanted to do, saying nothing but the way she looked at him, breathing fast as he began to breathe fast she was daring him to see what he could do, wanted to do, if he could do it. But then she would look down, past her stupa, and smile with victory and rolling on whisper all that remained now was to find the jewel for the spire.

Sam would have made of their room world enough, world enough would have been their bed, or whatever part of it was in use when they were joined, but every month came a bill, and even though she never left the hotel she liked the seamstress to come from Pettah every few weeks with good bolts and needle and thread. Meanwhile,

Sam was using the Pettah stall again. Now, October 1945, the world was still needful but in reverse. The war against Japan had suddenly finished. Around the harbour, two months after the August bombs, he heard men, local men, still speaking of what had happened, their opinions, sympathies, pride diverging. Sam liked the British response more than all this betel talk: now was no time to worry over what had happened. Now was time to move on to what was next: offices to shut and so much to rubbish—tropic-ruined desks and paper and books, cabinets, lamps and chairs, potted meats and untouched jars of Christmas-sent jam.

Meanwhile, these same Englishmen became needful and sudden lovers of true Ceylon notions, for their wives and mothers and mantelpieces. And so, through Sam, British wants and discards met Pettah goods and wants. First, he set up an operation in the seamstress's stall for fences and buying agents sent to Pettah by native planters and businessmen mad for northern wood and banker's lamps, heavy desk blotters, music cabinets, Walter Scotts in indigo marbled hardback, country church prints and solemn hunting scenes to hang upon their huna-studded walls. Next, Sam sent word through Pettah and Pettah sent word everywhere: the war British were leaving and did not want to leave empty-handed. An ironworking shop near the quartermaster's warehouse was cleared out. The lower ranks of the departing English went in for handiwork from the village: devil masks and palm-sized charms that carried pithy biographies of warding off and healing powers, brass ashtrays shaped like coiled cobra tails or held up by trumpeting elephants, cuff-link and earring dishes carried by faceless coolie stickmen or contemplative primates, weak gold chains dangling semi-precious stones for girls to win back, pillboxes made of buffalo horn for wives taking unmentionable medicines. Behind an arched doorway was an anteroom for the officer class. Crate-bottom boards displayed heavy, ornate suriyas dangling from bronze chains that had once dangled from noble necks; boar and leopard pelts awaited unchallengeable stories of their provenance; in a far corner, under sheets sat a stone lion head and cracked free moonstones and assorted segments of stone frieze brought to Colombo from the ruins of the old interior kingdoms, all ideal for English gardens.

A note came from the village once every two months, and Sam would take a taste from his operation and send it there. He never went once to Sudugama himself in the first year of his second marriage. He only sent his driver Joseph with bootloads of canned food, foreign cigarettes, and war-orphaned northern wood and shine, and also with instructions to tour around the old coughing Ralahami as he pleased for one full day before returning. All was sent in answer: to formal word of Arthur's engagement, and then of Arthur's marriage, and, seven months later, to word of a new baby. With that third shipment he also sent some leftover tatters from Ivory's dressmaking, as a welcome to the walauwa's new servant girl, Pathy. After thirty-seven years Latha had left the walauwa, laughing wildly, the very same day Arthur's son was born. Sam also sent to the temple for Vesak and, though late, he sent for Hyacinth's crossing and for her birthday and for the anniversary of the accident, and with every shipment to the village he remembered the Ethiopians for as long as it took to buy six new sets of banyan and sarong, which were also sent, addressed to Arthur. When Joseph returned to the city, Sam asked him how things looked. "Good, sir." The letters sometimes said otherwise, as when Arthur wrote that his son's birth had been blighted when Ralahamis from nearby villages, the same villages visited on George's engagement tour, came to the walauwa demanding justice for their ruined daughters, who were now brides without grooms and mothers to bastard sons. Arthur wrote that Robert was too ill to receive anyone, more ill with the noise of each of these visits, and so Arthur had sent the fathers off with threats and cigarettes and his own metal-benders and could Sam send more cigarettes next time please. Arthur never mentioned the Ethiopians and never asked where was his promised black Morris, and Sam would have worried why the British had not yet come to him for their prisoners, it was war's end, and why his brother-in-law was not so keenly asking for his promised reward. But Sam Kandy's going time was better spent going elsewhere.

⌒

On the first anniversary of his second marriage, it changed. Sam blamed Latha. The morning of the anniversary he went to the office in Fort to bring something for their dinner, a fading frayed menu card whose items he had copied onto the back years ago in deep incisions. He planned to instruct the hotel to make it, all of it, for them that night. But he never went into the office that morning. Latha was there, waiting for him. Latha, at his office, standing outside the door, squinting in the smudged windowpane light of daybreak in the city, wearing a village sari and flat-as-leaf village sandals and carrying an old Cargill's shopping bag like she had been cut from the page of one chronicle and child-pasted onto a page from its successor. Not in the walauwa not in the village but in the city in Fort in Prince's Building in front of his door: Latha. This went against nature itself, as if a tank crocodile had just swooped down from a branch.

"*Mokatha?*"

"Mokatha? I should speak here for all to hear?" she scoffed back, squinting worse than the last time he had seen her, the handkerchief dabbing her mouth. She was old now, slow, her skin had darkened around her clouding eyes and wattled about her neck and the arms. He followed her chin, which was motioning toward the tall narrow office door.

"Mokatha?"

"Ah. Fine. Why should I think that your new boutique madam would have made your manners any better. You would have me discuss it here so all of Colombo can hear. Right. Your father-in-law is to die soon."

"Why did Arthur send you to tell me?"

"Not even your eyes blink to hear it," Latha said, smiling thinly, as if something was just confirmed. "And Arthur did not send me. Arthur does not know I have come. Arthur is, I am sure, scared to tell."

"To tell what?"

"You've grown fat now, isn't it! What has she been feeding you?"

"To tell me what? What."

"Arthur is scared to tell why Ralahami is to die soon. What has happened."

"But you are not scared."

"No." Stooped, swaying, showing her village teeth, she eyed him back.

"So then tell and go."

"You would have me tell standing here, like this?" She breathed out loudly and bobbled her head. Something else confirmed. "Right. Your father-in-law went for a walk in the high grass behind the walauwa." She waited, studying him studying her. "He said he wanted to see the first place in the village, the old cave, one last time, and he asked Lalson to help him climb the hill but of course, you know, you know what Lalson said. He said he would not go to the founder's cave and tried to tell Ralahami not to go either but how can a servant tell such a thing? So Ralahami went, Lalson followed, and when Ralahami reached the cave he saw them. He saw all four of your fellows, fell back, and knocked his head on a rock. Since then he has even stopped coughing and asking for cigarettes. He is on the bed. He is to die soon."

"Four, you said."

"Yes, I said the Ralahami your father-in-law is to die soon."

"But all four, you said."

"The whole village knows. They have known from the beginning. Other villages even know. Since you came with your new madam and left those fellows in the muspenthu hut."

"What hut?" Sam asked in a hard voice, but hard the way a bug sounds hard underfoot.

"What hut? Ha. The only hut fit for such devils. Believe it. I know," said Latha.

They were only two, the rest of the building empty of Royal bells and footfall this early. Latha. After so many years of mocking him by looking only to Alice when he came to the walauwa, she was now standing here and mocking him outright, in his city, in his building, outside his door. Blocking it. Mocking his old misfortunate hut too, if truly so.

"Arthur told me you have left the walauwa," Sam said. "Why have you come here to tell me about the Ralahami?"

"Because," but here, suddenly, Latha faltered. Something had been touched by his question and he could tell that if he kept asking the same question she would break and go, but all Sam did was look down while Latha mouthed air at his question, like a fish on sand. She had already said all that she had planned to say to him. She had come to the city after fifty-seven years in the village, thirty-seven serving its highest blood, an omen blood, a dying blood, all of which she had witnessed and so now had dying eyes herself and would serve no more. She had decided to see Sam as her last duty by the walauwa and also because then there would be at least one known face, even his, in the city, but also because she thought she would have at least some triumph after sixteen years of his devilry. To tell him that she knew, that everyone knew, other villages even, about his black-and-gold padlock men. But here, now, more: from the start of their talking Latha had so wanted him to open the door and let her sit a moment somewhere without rogues and beggars and sick men all walking the same lanes, none giving way. She would even make the tea herself, for both of them, if only he would do the very least for someone from the village, no less someone who had hand-fed his wife from birth and then hand-fed his children the same and never once asked directly for any of his city shine but was now standing before him in need like she never had been before, because she had been standing since coming to the city alone and unknown by every passing face. And all Latha wanted was tea and ten minutes to sit and sip it and then she would go back into the crowds and look for the place called Pettah. She would see what kind of new life could be had for the price of two golden earrings she had long ago decided Alice would have given her anyway.

"But Hyacinth must miss you, no?" Sam asked, looking down. Not the hammer question he had wanted to ask. It was now everything to keep this as only talking. Because suddenly, of all things in the universe, Sam wanted to go to her, to his mother's old cousin, the walauwa's eternal governess, the hated old woman. Who in a moment would turn or he would, and then would be gone the last known of the old blood, his blood, however forsaken, however thin, however spat upon, faded, rusted. But he would not. It had to be so, he wanted it that way, he had to: everything done to him and taken from him, everything he had taken and done demanded that it be so. And more: Sam Kandy knew from a year's worth of prior nights that all would be forgotten by day's end anyway, those hips, those eyes like quartz.

"Hyacinth is a young lady now," Latha finally answered. "You will get her a husband soon. There is nothing more that I can do for her." But there was no venom in her saying it. She was soft from the first true thing Sam Kandy had said in sixteen years, that the girl would miss her. The first kindness too, in his voice, she thought.

But in vain. He'd made no move to open his door and give her only ten minutes. Truth, yes, but no cup of tea.

"You have not been to see Arthur's son, have you," she said.

"No."

No tea. No mercy then. "Do you remember George when he was a small fellow? How big he was? Where is George? Where are you keeping him? Under another of your padlocks? He should see the new fellow too, no?"

"Why?" But as he said it he knew why. Sam took a step toward her but then he turned and hammered down the stairs loud enough that he could not tell, no one in the city could tell over such crashing, what Latha was claiming down after him, what words and sounds were her last before she went down into the city herself, where she would never be called by name again.

twenty

Sam waved off Joseph and the vehicle. Instead he made his way by
foot along Lotus Road, where there were enough beggars, sick men,
and sellers to step over shoulder by and break past, enough to make
a man feel like he was still moving through the world of his own
volition. Even a forty-six-year-old grandfather. He walked the same
route for two hours, trying to empty all of it there, the worry and the
plotting and the outrage over what was asked of him now, from the
village, from his sent-off son, from his well-kept walauwa people,
from the British when they with their own rage for right numbers
would demand why he was returning four prisoners and not six. He
pounded out his worry and plotting and outrage through successions of layabouts and eventually curious doormen until enough of
them knew to give this mad stomping Mahatteya a wide margin and
so Sam Kandy could claim victory, but now there was nothing to do
but go to the room and tell her he had to go to the village.

Only, she wasn't there, waiting for him, when he came back.
He did not know where his wife had been for the middle hours

of their anniversary day. And now he did not know what she had been doing for all the middle hours of their first year. But he would not ask because asking meant having to match her answer, meant having to know her as something other than one hundred warm pounds of milk skin without history or family or plans to get either, with only requests that he eat as she asked and go to the toilet when she wanted. A perfect year.

When, endless hours later, she returned, Ivory immediately smiled to see him waiting for her. He asked nothing. He stood and said that he was going to the village the next day, that he had no choice but to go to the village, that his father-in-law was to die. Her face was shocked, then blank.

"But why do you have to go there? Your wife's father is already dead. You have known this for more than one year now."

Sam wondered how she could already know, and by the third time she said it, he was certain of the source of her knowing, which also had to be the reason for her absence from the room. It had to be. Ivory must have somehow met Latha in the time it took Sam to walk from Prince's Building to the Oriental Grand. There could be no other reason, and because he was this certain he would not ask her to deny it and so, instead, they went downstairs for Angels on Horseback, which, silent as a windowpane, she neither touched nor put before him. Back in the room, she didn't tell him to use the chamberpot either, and so Sam went to bed on his anniversary night expecting nothing. He decided the village would answer for that too.

They lay beside each other like boards until she began asking again and again that one question. Again and again Sam said nothing. Eventually, suddenly, Ivory shot up and shut the light on her side and he did the same on his and in the fan-droning dark he could feel her moving beside him, not onto him yet but all elbows and great pumping legs, like she was a frog swimming for its life. When she stopped, she began to breathe in and out, loud and long like sea blowing, and he went to touch her nightdress and could tell she had shimmied it past her belly and here at last, he thought, was forgiveness, return, obliteration. He touched her cool bared skin, its wonder-bending promises. And so Sam let down his night trouser and waited. But she only kept breathing like sea blowing, like she was a schoolgirl readying to take a jump, and then she reached for him, saying nothing, cupping his face, pulling him closer and she wanted him to climb on her this time and as ever she guided, commanded, but then she pushed down his shoulders and kept pushing and he was too confused then surprised then curious then absolutely shocked and horrified as she held him in place by his hair and after how many minutes she arched and hummed, a long sweet falling note, then let him go, and fell asleep. He sat up and looked sharply for her to stir, like a dog looks to be noticed after a trick, but in vain. Instead, Sam crawled beside her and stared at night shapes until he fell asleep. And in the morning, having studied night shapes for hours, he washed and spat and spat and spat and just as he bent down to tie his shoes, all that new belly folding against his ribs, she asked him again, as if never before, as if nothing had happened, that same question.

"But why do you have to go there? Your wife's father is already dead. You know your wife's father is already dead. You have known for more than one year."

"Mokatha?" Sam finally demanded, walking over to the bed. How could she ask now, after that? How she could she ask anything more of him?

"But why do you have to go there? I know—"

"How do you know he's already dead?"

"Because he is my father! Because I am your wife now! Because I told you both my parents are dead more than one year ago, before you asked me to marry you, and you tell me she died how many years ago and still you have to go to her village and see to her father. But I AM YOUR WIFE. What you do for your wife you do for me."

"You are jealous, Ivory," Sam said slowly, angrily. She was breaking the arrangement. She was showing her blood and history.

"Not jealous. I know I have nothing to be jealous of in that village or in this marriage. I only want what is mine, Sam."

"When he dies, the walauwa becomes mine and then I am Ralahami and you are—"

"NO. I told you I would never go back. I will never stay there and be some bloody teacup queen of a teacup village. I cannot believe someone like you, dressed as you are, living here, now, speaking English and listening to a music cabinet, even uses those words anymore, let alone makes like you have always wanted it, like you spend days dreaming of it while working the paddy, wearing nothing but the same amude your father and his and his and his wore. Ralahami. Hamine. Walauwa. All old magic, useless tricks. That is not what you should want. That is not what I want. That is not what is mine."

"What do you want? What do you think is yours?" he asked. Did she really think she could tell him about the village? Did she actually believe centuries of mud and hanged stars could be conquered with English medium and a music cabinet?

"Did you hear me, Sam? Did you? I said I want the same as you do."

"Ah. Right. You tell me what you think I want."

"One year married I know, believe it."

"What?" But his challenge sounded tentative, was too full of immediate longing that all be forgotten and forgiven, if only she show him what they both knew he wanted. She laughed.

"Same as I do."

"Ivory, this is the last time I shall ask. What? Tell me what you think I want. Tell me what you want." Desperate hopeful in spite of himself.

"I want more."

Downstairs, Sam ate breakfast alone, declining the plate of crèmes and jam pastries and feeling wretched and triumphant for it. He told Joseph to take him to his harbour office, where he took a shave from the barber downstairs and paid him to tell anyone who climbed the stairs, whether a white man or a Greek from one of the ships or a brown boy from the village, that he would return and take care of it in two days. He sent Joseph for fresh banyans and sarongs, four this time, and then he went to see the English, to tell them that in two days he would bring the Ethiopians to the harbour as promised. If asked how many prisoners he would have to tell, but otherwise he would gamble that in their packing for home, the prisoner transfer sheet the warden had shown him triumphantly the year before was already at the bottom of some crate at the bottom of some ship already long past Gibraltar. But Sam had no idea just how mad had been their leavetaking. He went into the quartermaster's building and found nothing, the murky-shaped, ashen nothing of reclaimed space where a week before had been crates full of civilization. And though the grand trident doors were partly open on both sides and it was a bright day without, the emptied warehouse seemed to brown down all light. Now it smelled of old oil and of last night's cooking fires still smoking, of morning piss, beedis, cold tea thrown at the dogs. Now ragged little men were lying about where once were daily stacked and un-stacked whole economies. There was no one here.

"Where are they? Where did they go?" Sam said to a beggar digging a trench in the floor with his finger, who did not stop even when Sam dropped a divinely bright coin near his hand. "Now look at me will you."

"Two questions, Mahatteya, but you only give once?" the man observed, still digging.

"Here. And here is another. And another. Now answer me and I will give you more when I am done asking if you can tell me something."

"They went. They went away."

"I will kick you flat as those coins. And I will take them back too. Now tell me something as if I am more than a blind man. Have they all gone?"

"Not all," another voice answered from the other side of the grand doors. The beggar in front of Sam turned onto his back, covering the money Sam had dropped, waiting for Sam to either leave or stomp him down until the coins could be seen shining again. He did not seem to care. He was staring up at the electric lamps the British had shut off when they left, which were now roosting perches and spider maps. On days when the doors were open and there was sea-blowing, a bird's egg would sometimes fall, or wild skeins of web would trail down, whole lives' worth of work in vain.

"Last night, Mahatteya, they were still loading in the harbour," the voice called out.

"They are always loading in the harbour," said Sam as he crossed to the other side of the doors, to an upright beggar sitting against the warehouse wall. "You expect money to tell me that? Next you will tell me the sun comes in the morning and goes away at night and again hold out your palm."

"I don't ask for money, Mahatteya. I only mean to say they were still loading prisoners last night. Did you bring your fellows?"

Sam studied the man's face. He was gaunt and especially black around the eyes and ragged-dressed as the rest but wearing loose-fitting sand-coloured boots, the laces gone to some other purpose. An Englishman's parting gift.

"You worked here."

"Yes."

"So you, you remember."

"Yes, I remember when you came and took those Kaffir fellows."

"Ethiopians. Do you know where the warden has gone?"

"War has been good for you, no?" he observed, tapping his own notion of a belly.

"I will give you better than those boots. Tell me where the warden has gone."

"I told you, Mahatteya, I ask for no money. I am a patient man. And I do not know where the warden has gone, only that yesterday they sent off the Italian prisoners. One of them stopped on the gangplank and cursed the crowd and people started dancing a baila because his cursing sounded like a song, and even the English clapped for him and the Italian fellow of course spat as he turned to go but he was smiling, everyone was, because war is over and everyone is going home."

"Except you, it seems, unless you were born in this warehouse."

"I told you, Mahatteya, I am a patient man."

"Patient for what?" Sam asked, even though he was certain another warship departed with every word passed between them, another known Englishman gone, another hour it would take to reach the village, where once were six and now were four, which meant at least another two hours away from Ivory who was waiting in the room or not waiting in the room but waiting where, and was she waiting with her knees up, and would this be for the whole second year of their marriage?

"I am patient, Mahatteya, for what comes next. For who comes next."

"And who comes next?"

"I listened all the years I worked here, Mahatteya, sweeping in the canteen and up and down the rows three times a day because the English thought they could govern our dirt too. I swept anyway, and I listened to the English talking about who was coming when they left. Someone will take over this island from the English and take over this warehouse and all these other beggars will be cleared out and I will work for them, whoever they are. It won't be the Japanese anymore. But otherwise? Who can tell? Most of the English said it will be the Americans, but others said it will be the Red Chinese or the Russians or our own people even. But one thing is certain, Mahatteya."

"What?" Sam asked, already peering through the door at the ships in the harbour, his ears desperate for more Italian singing.

"Can you spare cigarettes, Mahatteya? Foreign brand."

"Right. Here. Now tell."

He motioned for Sam's lighter, lit, and inhaled deeply, then blew luxuriant spumes against his own body like some kind of private benediction. He tapped the ash beside him very carefully, as if he was feeding someone. The smoke spread into the murk.

"Tell, I said!"

"Whoever takes over, Mahatteya, won't take your black fellows."

Sam turned to go.

"Aiyo Mahatteya cigarette please!"

"Aney Mahatteya cigarette please!"

"Apo Mahatteya cigarette please!"

He kicked over the fellow lying on the other side of the door, squatted and took back his coins. He left the others fighting for the cigarettes he dropped in his wake as he passed through the grand doors. Looking across the lane, he saw the True Ceylon goods store he had been stocking since war's end. There was no queue of departing English, only the slumped counterman staring at the dividing line of sun and shade thrown down by the warehouse across from them. He looked south and felt better. He could still see queuing green metal and tan uniforms consulting clipboards. They were still loading. But he had only four men, and there were three hundred and sixty-four days until his next anniversary. And so he went on to the village, counting and counting undefeatable numbers.

⟋

Robert's funeral bier was set atop a rude-stacked square of dried-out logs and rosewood and sandalwood branches. It went up right away, as if with its passenger's relief, so fast that Arthur ducked at the air-walloping whoosh as he walked away from lighting it. Even though many in the crowd also ducked at the sound, all were certain that as the first public act and first village memory following his father's cremation, this was no good omen for the son. When he rejoined the first line of mourners, Arthur spoke to Sam, who was standing beside the senior monks who had taken seats in the front row where they chanted at the bier and chatted behind their palm-leaf fans.

Sam knew what Arthur was asking but made like he could not hear. He wanted him to have to ask over the sound of his father's roaring-away body, over the sound of the wailing mourners hired in from another village, to see if Arthur would in fact try to beat those sounds with such a question, standing there with his father-less shoulders already broadening. Sam now knew why Arthur had never once mentioned the motorcar in the letters he sent from the village. It had nothing to do with Arthur's fear of losing two of the prisoners—three, as of last night. Arthur's not asking yet had everything to do with the overwrought patience of an adult son, patience and patience and then absolute insistence for what was promised him, because now it was at last his to do with as he pleased. And Sam, whose hip was aching more than his feet from standing beneath slate-grey skies on the village's great green clearing for the first time in thirty-six years, finally answered, after Arthur asked a third time. Both men were loud enough to be heard over the burning and so were chatted about behind palm-leaf fans.

"When will you bring me my motorcar?"

"What motorcar? You owe me three men."

"You would call them men? You, who left them like that, to be fed and washed and kept like that? It's a sin. And you are not even staying for the almsgiving, are you? And where is your new wife? It's a sin. All of this."

By now the other mourners could hear, were listening and whispering and reporting and inventing from row to row. "And what," Arthur continued, "do you think the Crown Agent will say when he comes and finds out about *your* Ethiopians? You cannot think the walauwa will be yours too."

"Do you want it? Or do you want a motorcar to ride out of here? Give me the deed—"

"And then? Then you'll give?" But Arthur's voice was defeated, his shoulders already sagging with having to return to the walauwa where he could only wash himself with limes for so long before his wife would ask when was the vehicle coming, and how long after the mourning and almsgiving before they could visit her village and show the new baby as he had been promising they would, promising in candlelight when she let him search again and again and again for that famous birthmark.

Sam pressed his hand against his hip just as it began to rain. The monks disappeared behind black umbrellas. After a brief consultation, they processed to the temple single file. When they left, the rest returned to the village, certain that the rain, its timing, its effect, whether an overdue cleansing or quenching or drowning, was anyway auspicious. The rain was a judgment upon the Ralahami or upon whoever would be his successor, and anyway not on the villagers themselves, who only needed dry clothes and hot tea and the rest of the day to talk about it all. Sam and Arthur were left alone before Robert's bier, soaked, neither talking, both watching and listening to the sodden cremation and each near certain the village was his now and trying to convince himself that this was what he wanted—all this ash and hissing.

As expected, Sam went directly to the car where Joseph, staring forward, had been waiting with the engine running. Sam went feeling certain beyond his thudding heart that the funeral smoke and rain and remembering were why a yellow hat just caught his eye, that this wasn't, at last, the crocodile come for him. He climbed in beside the driver and, turning around for a moment, counted the little black men in the backseat, and then they all went, one two three four five, to the city.

Instead of going to the harbour, as instructed, Joseph stopped the Morris in front of a short-eats shop in Borella Junction. Standing in its threshold was a metallic woman worrying the pirith thread on her wrist while wordlessly directing a traffic of dogs and beggar children and men in motorcars. None of whom, the old woman included, stopped to watch Joseph climb out of the Morris, remove his coat and cap, and place both on the seat, by which point the questions and commands issuing from the passenger side were commands and then threats, threats made of the blade and gutter words Joseph always knew his boss kept in his fine pockets. The sort of words that made him feel right to resign like this, stopping the vehicle full of cannibals in front of a short-eats shop and not in front of the dress boutique over which he and his mother lived.

Cursing, Sam climbed into the driver's seat vowing never to hire another, suddenly realizing how little he knew the city to drive through it himself. After four times passing the same man and son standing in the middle of De Soysa Circus hawking a silver-mounted toilet mirror that caused three blindings and two accidents that day, Sam found the artery that led to Wharf Road and the harbour, where, in his approach, he could still see the great grey ships filling with green metal and steamer trunks. When he arrived, the newly painted gate remained closed, though for how many years had he known the men in the guard booth, all of them, knew each their preferred brands of smoke and drink and aftershave. Sam honked. He switched on and off the bug-lathered headlamps. He honked again. Eventually, one of them came to the vehicle—a handsome fellow, tall as English, who drank Old Monk and smoked Woodbines and wore Musgo Real—and when he waved the car off Sam thought he was motioning him toward another entrance, that perhaps a queue of Wrens or warplanes were on the side of this gate. But then the fellow slammed his hand on the hood and all four inside jumped at the sound.

"Mokatha?" Sam demanded, stepping out and slamming the door shut loud enough to make the guard jump too. Only he did not.

"Entry barred. Military business only."

"You know what kind of business I am. Now open the gate."

"I am not to open the gate except to persons and vehicles on the list."

"And?"

"And you are not on the list."

"Right. It was Old Monk and Woodbines, no?"

"No. You are not on the list anymore." The guard motioned him back to the Morris. But Sam did not move.

"What is this?" he asked the universe. Deed gone, driver gone, gate closed, and was she in the room, was she in the hotel in the room in the bed waiting and if so waiting how for what? But he could not know or return to the rest of his going until he was absolved of these men, these three remaining men. He knew from asking Arthur that one of the prisoners had died in the intervening year from unclear sickness; and that one was thought kidnapped for rival spectacle in a neighbouring village. The third Sam knew himself had been outright killed in the village the very night that Sam had arrived to take them back to the British, by village men with arrack-red eyes who had decided to avenge the fallen and sudden beloved Ralahami. Before blue light the next morning, among the sandalwood and rosewood bundles, someone had carried the limp black body and flung it onto Robert's bier.

A second guard walked over, a short fat fellow with little dangly arms who liked molasses whisky, the brand didn't matter. He was stern-faced but began smiling with the boast he would make against his taller partner when they returned to the guardhouse, because upon sighting him, Sam rushed back to the Morris. The squat guard thought he'd chased Sam off, until he turned to see the gate opening for a Flying Ten Saloon. Sam went straight at it. He did not hear the guards' whistles or the other car's horn as it swerved and he did not see the curdled white face at its rear window or the guards sprinting after him into the harbour compound where for years he had come and gone and picked up and dropped as freely as a frigate bird and only when he was inside and could see no open ramp did he stop, surrounded moments later by dust clouds and whistling men. He opened the back door and pulled them out and when the guards stopped calling for their mothers and the Englishmen stopped calling the heavens good Sam asked where should their prisoners queue. But one of the Ethiopians was too impatient for the answer. He ran, tripped from the atrophy that had been his Ceylon life and for the first time in years his gums bled around the padlock. He began frog-crawling toward the water but well before reaching it a guard cracked him with a rifle butt—a real sixer! his fellows would toast him afterwards, when the crazy

Mahatteya shaking the key ring before impassive white faces had driven away with the other two black fellows. The Mahatteya who could now convince no Englishman at Colombo harbour that he had ever been there before, that he was only returning their own spoils, that he had been trusted with the prisoners by no less than Mountbatten himself, that all was written down and so had to be real, which was finally conceded as a fair point, but none could find any such records on their clipboards and the only counsel given, because pity if not guilt endures past official memory, was that Sam might have more luck depositing his fellows at the Puttalam salt plains.

Sam drove on, first to Pettah, where he had the seamstress hang cuts of heavy fabric along the back windows. She told him people would think he was driving a funeral car or touring around royals or Muslim wives. Next he went to the hotel, bringing along the seamstress's sons to watch the vehicle, the men, until he was ready to go to Puttalam. He gave them enough cigarettes to reach dawn and told the front desk to send them tea through the night. Then he went upstairs, to the room where yes she waiting for him. But Sam walked into a completely different marriage. He shut the door and they were again man and wife but both were suddenly, starkly aware of how little they knew of each other beyond their body parts. When, later, they were lying in the bed, Sam told Ivory that he had to leave again the next day. He told her to have things ready because they would be moving from the hotel when he returned. She did not ask where but she did not jump through the window either. She did not move at all. She did not move even when he began to, when wordless he climbed onto her and sprung open her knee-knocked legs and then, to her surprise and his, wretched shocked his, Sam put her hand in his hair, squeezed the fingers full and waited, breathing ragged, hovering over her face, waited until she pushed him down.

twenty-one

By February 1948 he would have padlocked his own mouth. He would have padlocked everyone else's too. People were suddenly acting as if they cared little for foreign goods. The harbour itself was loud with village boys returning from the Italian campaign, calling themselves veterans and standing drinks on promise of pound-sterling pensions. There was a four-month madness of young men asking for passages to Australia when terrifically ambiguous notices had been posted in Colombo announcing openings on Queensland sugarcane fields for anyone with plantation experience (four months because that was how long it took the first batch of misery letters to reach Ceylon). Otherwise, more and more mothers were keeping their middle sons back from the great ships. Soon there would be no need to go abroad to get enough to become enough to come home again. Every day, 1947, 1948, was another day until independence, another day until they were their own for the first time in anyone's remembering, in anyone's father's father's remembering.

Meanwhile, the Englishmen who still ran shipping offices in the harbour had no plans to leave. The lizard-splayed walls of their Cinnamon Garden homes displayed prints of Midland country churches and solemn oil portraits of titled and long-dead uncles, but also more recent family triumphs—the mounted heads of Sambar deer, boar with tusks like old mower's scythes. These were Ceylon English cured of homesickness by movie reels of blitzed London and, after the victory, by gloomy letters whose good cheer was rumour of the clothing ration coming to an end and reports of baked snoek and beans, mashed turnip and snoek, snoek piquant. Staying in Ceylon, with impeccably Oxbridge natives taking charge, these Englishmen sensed that more than pride and the propriety of skin and accent would be needed to maintain them under any new, local dispensations. Propriety of association would matter too. And so they turned thin-smiling amnesiacs when Sam Kandy came calling at war's end. For a few months he tried their offices in vain, and then for a year he tried lower down, in the brine-smelling warehouse near the ships themselves, only to find that even the brown men who ticked items on and off cargo manifests had become remarkably straight-eyed and austere—they were practising patience, certain that their English directors would soon leave for home and leave intact, waiting, their library tables and gin and gin trolleys done in local calamander, their bloodstone seals and lineal sextants set up like holy vessels on side tables.

Sam Kandy had no such patience, no such need for another man's bloodstone. But he would not return to his old short-loading days, to mucking his shoes with dock slick while flashing whatever staple or cheap shine turned a dockworker's eye and made him Sam's own carter. That was a younger man's game, a minor man's game. At least people still needed salt. When he'd first gone north to Puttalam, the year before, Sam had thought the Englishmen at the harbour had been making a joke in sending him and the Ethiopians to its salt plains—only in such whiteness could black men be freed in vain. Eventually he found the man in charge, fat as Sam and just as brown skinned but with a yellow-gold cross hanging from his neck. Sam brought him to the Morris and pulled down the curtains and asked him to look in the back and the man, Peter Rodrigo, looked in and crossed himself and stepped away and crossed himself and accepted one of Sam's cigarettes and asked how he obtained them, the foreign cigarettes. Never once did he ask anything about the Ethiopians after Sam said they had been left behind by the war British. And so they had started dealing. Rodrigo said they could stay if the padlocks could be removed and they did not run or try to eat anyone but were willing and able to carry and stack like the old-time Kaffirs already in his employ— who had been carrying and stacking and telling rosaries close by the salt plains of Puttalam long since the orange-headed Dutchmen chased Coutinho and Menezes and their soldiers home to Lisbon, leaving behind clerks and priests and fishermen and half- and quarter-blood sons and also their servants, who had been baptized before leaving Fort Jesus against the native devilry in which they were found and first taken from Mombasa, some watching their departure from the granular white water where three hundred years later what attenuate remainder of their many times crossed blood and skin and singing was working that same white water for a man who was himself, if only in name, an attenuate remainder of the blood that had come and gone on the same such ships. In return, Sam was only asked to listen to Rodrigo tell of how strong and true was Puttalam salt.

He had Sam taste it to agree that it was stronger than Hambantota salt and truer than Kolkata's. More: Rodrigo said it was still prized in Portugal, that stories from centuries before were still told of its preserving qualities in the bellies of the great ships, that exhumed missionary saints found in perfect state were known to smell of Puttalam salt. Besides which, any man could see how plentiful were

Rodrigo's beds and how needful was salt island-wide, war or no
war, British or no British. But Rodrigo Salt Works (Pvt.) was only
a small operation sending north to Jaffna and inland. The southern
hook of the island, down the coast from Colombo, was dominated
by the Hambantota outfits. If there were someone who could break
him into Colombo, Rodrigo would be willing to share the profits.
Sam gave him another cigarette; a whole pack. The Ethiopians
woke, many hours and cigarettes later, without incident, having
passed out when the padlocks were first removed. They began
stretching their mouths silently, like the very, very old. They were
dressed in the banyans and sarongs Sam had brought and given tea
they dribbled to drink freely and then Sam appeared before them,
for the last time, his mind already back in Colombo with salt and
Ivory but also, for a moment, spinning, raging, to know how little,
save four deaths and the loss of his own harbour privileges, had
come of his virtue-making with the Ethiopians' years of confine-
ment. His own. They were led away by a gang leader in need of
new men, to a low wide shophouse that stood behind the salt-filled
godowns. They departed him weak legged and flabber mouthed,
squinting at the sun and sea and salt that here was all one terrible
brightness.

New, a year later, no longer the Ralahami of the harbour's
backrooms, and the Ethiopians made into another man's carry, Sam
had nothing to do save tasting grains and counting manifest sheets
at his desk in Prince's Building, before going upstairs to the dusty
rooms where he had moved Ivory the year before. Not dusty so
much as un-dusted because the girl Ivory had hired, mud brown
but thin and pretty of feature, seemed hired to do nothing. And
because she was hired to do nothing save sit with Madam and listen
as Madam reread a year's worth of Mills & Boon books, Sam paid
her to tell him what Madam did when he had to go to Puttalam,
or to the village. The servant girl's reports were, of course, singular:

Madam went nowhere today. Loyal reports, worded by Ivory herself no doubt. And Sam knew. Yet he kept paying and listening, believing that Madam went nowhere today because if he did not believe then what kind of nights would there be between them, what next would he have to do, what next would he have to do.

He was too much by himself these days belonging to others, he had too much time to make figure eights and zeroes of memory and prospect, of why he kept giving her tufts of his hair before even she could reach. Of how it could end. It had to. No Curzon at the desk beside his, no driver, no father-in-law coughing in the front room. Not that he ever had to say anything to any of them, but they had been blood-and-bone stays against what he was now doing with the long, long hours of going back and forth from the city to the bright flat plates of Puttalam, the shock-white nothing of accumulate salt in the shallow seawater that washed onto an island about to be free, an island never and never to be his.

⚊

When he returned from still another such trip on February 4, 1948, Colombo was in revel. Crowds were hooting and cheering for cooking fire oratory and toddy rebuttals over whether independence won without blood would be independence taken away with blood; over whether this would now become again the nation it had been for so long and was ordained always to be by blood and Lord Buddha, or whether it would have to be shared with the Tamils and Muslims and Christians; over whether new anthems or old anthems would be sung and in what tongue, tongues; over who would try to bite off the other fellow's tongue first.

"What has happened?" Ivory asked excitedly as he walked into the kitchen for water.

"British are going," he muttered, wiping his mouth. He'd grown a beard in the last year, to return the abrasion. Staring in the mirror, it looked like he'd caught it from her body, as if her body was consuming him at the join. But how fine she was still, standing before him dark eyed like rain in deep forest, mouth still like a flower.

"I want to see!" Ivory knew bankers and their wives, office-seekers and their sons, would also be in the streets this night. They could see her passing in the triumph of a motorcar. She also knew she could leave the rooms now because she could tell how strong still was his need for her, for her body that way, that she make him do it that way. She was no longer afraid that if she left he would shut the door and open it only to close it again, as happened last time, with the last one. The first one she'd left was a Chetty banker with wife and children who had set her up, at nineteen, when she was still called Hilda Stevens, in the top floor of a house on Magazine Road, within walking distance of his own. The terms: she could stay and have whatever she wanted if whatever hour he came she would be there waiting, drapes closed, with cigars and something for him to eat on hand, and otherwise growing only paler and more perfect. He had called her his ivory. One night he came in, full and drunk after a director's meeting, and passed out on top of her, his body collapsing and collapsing even after he was sleeping until, collapsing more, she smelled it, as burning hot it trailed down through his legs onto hers and she had reached for the side of the bed and pulled herself free and smeared, washed herself, washed herself raw, then filled his valise with the dresses and vials he had bought for her, and left.

The second, who caught her perfume as she waited to be danced with one night in the Grand Oriental ballroom, was as wild for it as Sam was, as needful in some of the same ways. But he had had not let her back into the room when she had gone away to the Holy Family convent as they had agreed she would when, a few months into their time together, she began to show and had refused his offer of shoeflower tea for cleansing. "Reducing," he called it. It was a baby girl. He was a Colombo Tamil, the son of a speechmaker whose only son could never marry a Burgher girl if he wanted to be someday an office-holder—let alone marry a Burgher girl who professed to have no parents and said her name was Ivory. She knocked on his door after her months at the convent and eventually he opened it an eye-space, sudden-cured of his need for her body and making strange like he did not know her or the mud-brown child riding her hip. She knocked until the child began crying and then another fellow came to the door and made it known that if she did not go and never return he would make it so she and the child went and never returned, anywhere. And so she went back to Holy Family, agreed to call the baby Mary, and meanwhile was taught elocution and shorthand and to type. She left the child there because she was fair enough to find work in the English offices when the war came and then in the office at Peradeniya, where the laughing Americans proposed marriage to her morning noon and night only honeymoon first baby. But then Sam Kandy came and she was told to report to him in Colombo and she went and first saw her daughter and then him, who married and kept her and after leaving the hotel had unknowing kept her daughter as well, whom Ivory had retrieved from the convent and called a hired girl, whom it was she used to visit when she left the hotel room for the afternoon during her first year with Sam, who it was that now gave her mother the money Sam paid her to tell him that today Madam went nowhere.

She knew he thought she was going with other men. But with Sam there was more: she could also tell he could not stop treating her as his nightly plate and making like it was her wanting it, even if she only wanted to try it once to punish him and also because of a Mills & Boon passage that had long confused her. But no matter. He kept coming for it and making like she was taking him by the hair and pushing him down. And however long that needfulness persisted did not matter. The girl, her girl, was already on the home side of the door. Ivory had decided they would stay here for good only if he never returned from wherever it was he went, whether stabbed or shot or eaten for whatever he daily went for and whatever he did and kept to get money. Otherwise they would go once he had given the girl watch-and-tell money sufficient that they could depart, mother and daughter, and live elsewhere in the city, without need ever again of men or convent care. Such were their whispering plans at night, each consoling the other for how long more until their days and nights were truly their own.

"I want to see!" she insisted, not just because bankers and speech-makers' sons would be there but also because how she longed for this, for an evening's freedom from these rooms, from Sam Kandy and Madam.

"They are not going just now, Ivory. They have announced they are giving up the island."

"To who?"

"To Mr. D.S. and the other politics men and their men."

"And?"

"What?"

"When will there ever be such a night again? And on such a night, you want to wash and have a cup of tea and sleep? Truth?"

"What else do we do at this hour?" He was daring her to correct him, to be the one who started what would have to stop, be stopped.

"I want to see. I want to go. I have to. Don't you?"

"I have to do everything that I do. You don't know. But not this, I don't have to go stand like a street boy and watch old rich men give the island to new rich men. But you want to meet them, right? So go."

"You would let your wife walk the streets by herself, at this hour?"

"You know the streets well enough, no?" Sam scoffed.

"Which means what?"

The servant girl was standing in the doorway looking at no one.

"I want you to take me," Ivory said when Sam said nothing.

"Take you how? You mean here, now, in front of her?" Wounded sounding and wretched hopeful but more: forcing, begging her again to start what had to be stopped. Ivory motioned the servant girl out of the room, away from words never meant to be heard by daughters.

"I want you to take me to see the celebrations."

"Why? Who is out there that you have to see?" he spat, feeling the jealousy juice out at last, fresh life for pent needs beyond its own. "Right. You would like to see him, with me standing there watching."

"I am not asking you to stand and watch anything. Take me in the vehicle. The whole island is outside while I wait day after day in this cobweb palace, only allowed to go from room to room."

"I never said you had to stay here. You told me, remember, you told me, from the first, all you wanted was in the room."

"Yes, and you told me that you would not go back to the village. And that we would stay in the room. That you needed to know nothing of me but what happened in the room, and I needed to know only the same of you."

"The war is ending, Ivory. Money does not come as it used to. Nothing does. But tell me, are you going to leave me now, unless I do what you want me to do?"

"You do only what you want, Sam."

"This is not what I want. If I did what I—"

"Aiyo tell."

"You want me to tell you or show you?"

"I just want you to show me the city. I am not asking you to walk with me. I am only asking that you take me—"

"Wait." His heart was crashing.

"What?"

"Wait. What do you want me to do?"

"I keep telling you, Sam, I want you to show me the city."

"You want me to take you in the vehicle?"

"Of course. How else?"

"Because, you say, I am your driver. Say it."

"You are my husband."

"No. Tell me I am your driver and I will take you."

"Sam—"

"No. Right. I am your driver. I will take you."

His face, his eyes, his words were serene, old since composed in untold history. He did not wait for her to chant it with him. He did not have to. It had already been said. It was already done. Sam took her and went.

He returned the next morning, driving through a city quiet of its revels and waking to a day that looked and felt like any other, only this was the island's first day made its own in any known remembering. He came back with torn knees and salt stains on his shoes like the marks of gone spirits. The hour spent in Puttalam had been unchartable, starless, no moonfall on the black water. Dull as broken bone had been her salt bed. No one could have seen him there, kneeling at his own vengeful penance. But reaching his office, Sam knew God had seen and sent his. Blue Piyal was sleeping against his office door, in certain flesh and blood before him. He was village-dressed but the body and face were the same, the same age even as when the boy had fallen at Dambulla, and when he woke at the sound of Sam's shoes his eyes were just as damning blue.

"Are you Sam Kandy, sir?" the revenant asked, getting up.

"Are you, what are you?" Sam asked, his hand working his downstrike scar.

"I am Henry B. Paulet."

"No. That cannot be. You are not Henry Paulet. Henry Paulet is dead and gone to England. You are, are you, you are not. Piyal?"

"You are right, actually. I am Henry B. Paulet but I go as Bastian. But where is Piyal-aiya? Achchi told me to ask you, if you were here. You are Sam Kandy, no?"

"Achchi. Who is your achchi?"

"She has lately died. She was called Manel. She said she used to work here and so did you, for the Englishman I was named for, and that you sent her and my ammi to live in Matara when Ammi got sick. Achchi said that when she died too, I was to close up the house and take the money to buy a rail ticket to Colombo and to look for you, starting here, and that you would help me, or Piyal-aiya would. Where is he?"

"I don't know."

"So then you will help me, sir. You are Sam Kandy."

"What do you want from me? I need no driver. I need nothing." He was too exhausted to join the universe already laughing at him. He had been made free only for the drive back from Puttalam for the next pull.

"I only want to leave the island."

"Leave the island?"

"For many years, I have wanted to see the world." He'd practised on the train. "I am—"

Sam held a hand up, removed a pen from his pocket, took a piece of paper from the boy, and wrote down the name of a rival shipping agent.

"Thank you, sir. I promise I will come back to—"

"Go. Now."

Their talking brought the servant girl from the rooms, where she had been waiting to hear her mother's step since the night before. She came downstairs and found only Sam standing there, eyes closed, his head against the door.

"Sir," Mary said. "Sir. Please."

"What. I don't want tea. I want to sleep." Eyes still closed. He would sleep right there. He would dream of nothing, no heels hammering down, no known faces.

"No, sir. Please, where is Madam?" Mary asked.

"Madam. Madam?" he said it like a word from a lost age. *What is Madam?*

"Yes. Where is she? Where is Mummy?"

Sam went away seeing nothing, hearing nothing of her crying. He felt nothing nothing nothing, wanted needed asked for nothing but what he had just gone to Puttalam and accomplished, become: an island freed from memory and prospect and other such rule. Long waited for and sudden changed and what was before what was now what would be next did not matter because Sam Kandy was already far from all such reach, unbeholden, unjoined, floating out under a moonless, star-gone sky, like a body that would never be found floating in brine and black water.

part four ROSE

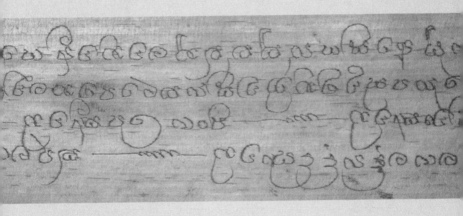

twenty-two

"But he will return. This is Sam Kandy's village, no?"

The thin men who'd stepped out from work-stalls and sagging awnings to block his way bobbled their heads. He could have revved and gone but instead he cut the engine. They watched him without approaching. He unzipped his leather jacket and stretched his arms, breathing deeply as he turned, considering Sudugama. This was the village always told of under the crow tree, the village long since imagined, from long ago hoped for. Its air was no rivalling oppositions, no rise and fall of enemies, as in the city, but the timeless accord of all living: it was cooking fires and the clarity of recent rain; it was greenness, so much greenness, the spread of paddy and garden things put to dry; everywhere were spearing and curving and hanging-down leaves smattered through with the white light of clear day; in the air was fruit and incense and balm and oil and yes under it all for certain was good dark dirt, the dirt from which all came and to which all goes. All was thriving. This was what he had come back for, from actual Munich's grey air and grey light like the world was always at the end of day. And what he heard while he breathed in Sudugama was likewise hope's reward. Never mind Munich, this was nothing like his boyhood life inland from Matara, his life under the loud Mara tree. Here were troops of sweet birds calling and answering, squirrel and monkey chatter, mothers calling for children answering. The highest sound was no constable's whistle or train shriek but the bronze peal of the temple bell from across the main road; the lowest was not black whispering about his blue eyes and brown skin when he went with his grandmother to the market but the steady thwack of washed clothes on drying rocks, itself a kind of strong pulse. It was a thriving, all of it.

None of the villagers knew where Sam was or when he would return. They did not mind not knowing, because of what had been arranged during his absence years: a doctor now visited fortnightly, smelling of Dettol, not bark and root and the last patient's left-behind betel sheaf. More: Sudugama was soon to have its own government school. There were Poya day deliveries of kerosene for every man with a family, and tins of brick-shaped meat, so pink and modern. Since 1956, an American movie was shown for a day and a night once a month in the Dansala hall. His fine screaming red bike aside, they did not want this fellow, whoever and whatever he was, to ruin all of it. Because if he reached the walauwa and spoke with Arthur, who could tell what Arthur would tell him, or what Arthur, the Ralahami-in-name, would do?

"Then can you tell me who in the village knows when he is coming? The walauwa people must know, no? Wait. You like my bike? Who likes my bike? Who wants to sit?"

The man in the faded yellow hat passed through the gathered crowd just as Bastian was lifting the third beaming boy onto the Heinkel's red leather seat. Hunching forward to take the black handlebars, the boy was smiling and squinting, his glorying mind roaring across endless open road. His father stepped forward to watch within catching range, just as the others had when it was their sons' turns, watching and squinting and smiling just the same as their boys. For going on ten years now Sam Kandy had sent kerosene and American movies, yes, but he'd let a man-eater ride in his motorcar before any village boy.

"Where are you from? Who sent you? What business have you with this village? Who sent you?" asked the man in the yellow hat, who was Arthur's driver and had been named to the position after travelling to Colombo with his son years before, where he had met with Sam Kandy, met him again.

"I am Henry Bastian Paulet. Bastian," he answered, lifting another boy onto the bike, a boy who at eleven was already a champion tree climber. The boy landed on the red seat in a perfect squat and had already raced past Jaffna town, speeding north by northwest like some kind of machine-age monkey prince jumping islands on his way to conquer India before the man in the yellow hat, Bopea, answered Bastian.

"Who has sent you?"

"No one has sent me. I have come."

"To see who?"

"You know, or else you wouldn't be talking like this."

"Who?"

"Sam Kandy."

"He is not here. He has gone."

"I know. But I cannot find him in Colombo. I was told to look here. I was told this was his village."

"Who told you?"

"The barber."

"Right. Well you have come and looked in vain. So why are you still here?"

"Because I am waiting for him. And because I think there are more boys that would like to try the bike, no? Or try a second time?" Small black-thatched heads nodded, were proliferate: every time a boy climbed off he ran to tell brothers and cousins and even long since sworn enemies to come quickly. A group had already gathered in front of the scooter, respectful and proprietary the way boys can be with sudden-found treasure or an injured animal. They wanted to wipe the bug lather from its headlight, to polish the mystic emblem bolted below it, a great-winged bird taking flight across a chevron of silver letters.

TZIRUOT

"I have no money to give you," Bopea said.

"Aiyo!" Bastian laughed. He looked past Bopea to the village men, as if for sympathy at the absurdity of the suggestion. "You think I have come all this distance for money?"

"Then what? What? Do you owe him money?"

"I owe him something, yes. Not money, but something."

"Then show. Tell what you owe and leave it with me and he will get it. Otherwise go."

"What I owe is to Sam Kandy. I will give when I see him. I would like to wait for him to return. If you say I must go, I will, but I will come back until I meet him."

"You cannot know when he will come. No one knows when he will come."

"But he will. That is enough. I will wait."

"How to wait? Here now, you listen to me. I am not going to—"

"What distance?" a voice called out, interrupting.

"What distance?"

"Yes, tell what distance you have come!"

"Aiyo, tell what distance!"

The calls kept coming as Bopea, muttering, stalked back to the walauwa where Arthur and his son were crouched and watching from the verandah. Where, inside, were Arthur's kidney wife and his niece, sweet Hyacinth Kandy, officially listening to the music cabinet Sam had sent years before, just after independence.

Meanwhile, below, Bastian was standing in front of the bike, legs planted, one hand on a handlebar. Boys were pushing each other spans apart to stand just as he was.

"You want to know how far I have had to come, to come here?"

Decisive nods, no bobbling this time.

"But you must all have work, no?"

Decisive laughter. The day's work had been done for hours. Or it could be done in the hours to come. Or tomorrow. The paddy had been thriving for years, obliterating memory and omen hunger even more than the kerosene and movies did. These days you could carry a crying baby along a paddy bank and by morning the dirt would have shot green.

And so Bastian cleared his throat, breathed, and told. And that night, after he had been called up to the walauwa where he was doubtless telling the same story, in the huts of Sudugama he was retold. Fathers and sons, older brothers and younger, all trying to tell the story to trick their women's hearts just as theirs had been, just as that other mother's heart had been, in actual Munich. *Submersible.*

⌒

One morning in 1948, eleven years before Bastian finally came to Sudugama, he had bought a cup of useless station tea and a cone of green gram and gone to see Sam Kandy, who gave him a paper to see a man at Colombo harbour. Bastian soon had his papers to be a deckhand on an oil tanker (Kuwait/Colombo/Rangoon), but the harbourmaster refused to sign his release to the ship. Without so much as looking at Bastian standing inside his office door, he declared to the rest of the boys waiting outside that as of that morning, no citizen of Ceylon could be released for work abroad without first showing a school certificate. None of the boys in the queue had a certificate in their packets. None of the boys moved anywhere save one spot forward when Bastian left a few minutes later. Each of them was certain, as vaulting young men need to be, that he would be the exception, the one whose paper the harbourmaster would be convinced to sign, whether from believing in the boy's promise to go and come like none before him; or for mercy, to hear tell of father death, mother sick, village drought, village sick, and then day upon night upon day of bullock and bus, barefoot and train top in blistering sun, through monsoon rain and rogue's alleys before reaching the harbour, and all to go and come like none before him. And if still denied, that didn't matter: this was Colombo, there had to be someone set up nearby who long since knew to copy the harbourmaster's signature, in whose veins ran the blood memory of every harbourmaster's signature, Sinhalese British Dutch Portuguese. Either that, or the true harbourmaster would sign the paper upon the boy's return with his school certificate, because that same forger would no doubt have known of this new edict before even the harbourmaster did and so already be waiting for the boys with a stack of embossed papers: of course Royal and St. Thomas, and also Ananda, Nalanda, St. Antony's and Trinity, St. Joseph's, St. Thomas', St. Peter's, and even Maris Stella: all that was needed was the proud graduate's name. And the fee. Not payable in promise or saddest story.

But Bastian needed none of that: he left the harbourmaster's office that morning with his papers signed because the harbourmaster had chanced to look at his face while showing him to the door, only to close it and sign his release asking nothing telling nothing knowing nothing because Englishmen in the tropics tend to make exceptions for brown boys born with blue eyes.

And so Bastian joined seven other new boys on the tanker, bunking with a Tamil fellow from Jaffna town who said he was shipping out to reach his mother and father—they cleaned houses in actual Munich and had sent him a letter saying that if he could reach Germany, he could attend hotel school. The ship was Greek save the eight of them and two of ten original Burmese boys, the only two who hadn't jumped ship when the tanker last reached Rangoon. The brown hands' daily work was scraping the deck free of the chips and slivers of the last paint job so the next could be done by the waiting, watching Greeks. The listing deck. The listing deck that needed scraping on hands and knees. Who would think a ship larger than some of their villages could rise and fall from side to side like a devil dancer's shoulders? Who would believe the far deep sea itself could be all such chop and churning when from shore it looked like indigo stone? The eight Ceylon boys were all first to sea. The Burmese fellows were by now used to it and never once looked up at the others' retching. The Greek sailors made sympathetic faces and mimed that they had once been so sick too, and they even washed down the deck afterwards, when the boys were lying on their sides, rusted scrapers in their open palms, mouths burning hot and wretched, eyes closed waiting for any kind of land or for someone else to be the first to call for his mother. The second time they were seasick, there was no mimed sympathy. The Greeks washed down the deck and the boys' mouths, then their faces, their hair, their whole bodies until they crawled back to work. By the fifth day it was only Bastian still getting sick and the Greeks were tired of spraying him and so sent word to the captain, who came and saw and took pity on blue eyes never meant for deck life. Even a little English blood could ruin a fellow for hard work in open air. He was put to work in the galley, carrying fish and potatoes from the pit and scraping and peeling until they reached Kuwait. And while they were docked in its harbour, and the other boys fished from the deck at dusk, drinking beer while comparing casts and catches with the Greeks and together calling out useless jibes challenges and questions to the passing brown dhows, Bastian never fished once. At night, asked why he was coming to the cabin so late, he would only tell his mad-as-wife bunkmate that the captain had asked him to do something. What betrayal! After even giving Bastian his parents' address in actual Munich! At breakfast the next morning, the others called him the captain's compass polisher. But all Bastian carried for him were cases of beer and wine, and also arrack and ouzo, gin and whisky and molasses whisky from India, all kept in a room off the galley that he had never noticed as anything but another rusting green door. Each night, he carried the crates along the starboard side to the bow and down a flight of stairs to another little room. And on the third night the captain told him to bring all of it onto the landing and he pointed to the flat black water, which began to break up at short distance as it began to surface, rising with blinking red lights and a man standing in its water-beaded glass top. The captain had been selling to the princes of Kuwait for many years, trying when he could to get the specific gins and whiskies they asked for, but they always bought all of it, never once—

Wait.

"Wait."

"Wait!"

"Wait wait wait wait wait" the villager men finally sang one after the other, all at once, hands up, some smiling, others looking sceptical, shocked, outraged to have listened this long and believed the whole of it until now, until that.

"Mokatha?" Bastian asked, broad and innocent as blue sky.

"No, you tell us."

"You don't believe that Arab princes buy Indian whisky?"

"Aiyo, stop playing the fool! What was it you say came out of the sea? Red lights, glass top, man standing in the glass top. All lies!" They had to demand that he deny it, their picture-making with his story. But there was nothing in their voices save laughter and hope that this stranger was no liar, that here was no loveshine, that for once the wild dreaming of men born to live dream and die far from the marvelling world be true, triumphant, their own triumph.

"The captain told me that for years the princes would send pearl divers to collect the bottles," Bastian continued, "but after one of the princes was named head of the Naval Force he bought it from the British without first asking his father, who did not mind the cost, only what six of his sons were discovered using it for when they returned from the tanker that night and there at the dock was the king and the other six sons, who were devout and also had never been given rides. The next morning the captain was brought to shore. He came back and told me he was being sent from the country and that I was too, that he would cash me out less the cost of the ticket he had already bought for me, because we were to fly from Kuwait to Beirut and from there he was going home and he said he would get me onto a ship going back to Ceylon. But I did not want to go home just yet. I wanted to go to—"

"Apo go to a boutique on the moon! What was it called?" one of them pleaded, the others nodding as he spoke, their faces righteous and wounded with waiting this long without asking.

"Submersible. They came up from the water in a submersible."

Bastian waited while they tried out the word, each to himself, their faces lost to the work of fitting word to picture, then fine and calm and smiling. Submersible was exactly right.

"No boutique on the moon but I decided to try for actual Munich," he continued. "When I started in Beirut, I had two hundred dollars. Twenty dollars for YMCA hotel, ten dollars for food, then another ten dollars for a bus ticket to Ankara, then five dollars to Istanbul, and, for an underground tram to the Europe side, one dollar. And on that side, believe it, is a street where pretty girls stand all day and night in glass boxes. They only close the curtain when a chap goes in."

"One hundred dollars gone!" someone called out to a thunderclap of hands.

Bastian bobbled. They asked for more. He said he knew that to reach actual Munich he would need new clothes and a school certificate. He found a uniform shop where he bought the same kit that he saw a scowling boy wearing while his mother and laughing sister inspected him. Then he bought the largest piece of cheese he could carry and spent almost the rest of his money on a ticket from Istanbul to Munich on the famous London Express. Two dollars left. On the train he traded seats with an old man who wanted to be anywhere but the car full of schoolboys going abroad for the first time. They were a few years younger than Bastian but dressed much the same. When the train was stopped at the Austrian border and the car was emptied beside an endless field of goldenrod, a teacher taught them to say *Die Studie* and Bastian said it just as the others did and was sent back to the train, where from his seat he watched four Indian fellows dressed like Indian fellows and pleading like Indian fellows being led off by two guards. Before Munich he was more than once scolded and stared at by teachers wondering why he was not sitting with the rest of the students. All he would say was *Die Studie Die Studie* until actual Munich, where in the station he traded his last two dollars for two marks with the first man willing to do it, who was the first black man Bastian ever saw, who wasn't AWOL jack he just wanted to go home.

"Truth?" one asked him.

"Yes, I tell you he was truly black, blacker than—"

"Ah ah okay. Only you have gone such distance, so many places, and that was the first black you saw?" another asked. The Sudugama men became bored cosmopolitans.

"Yes," Bastian said. "Why?"

Sudden wry smiles and sideways eyes and they each had a story that could rival *submersible* but they were of one mind about village secrets—they could be told and retold for years but only for known ears and shared dirt.

"I went to the bus terminal and took out the paper with the address of the Jaffna boy's parents and showed it until someone put me on a bus, now no money, and I showed the paper to the driver who pointed to a seat and we drove and drove from square to square and it's getting darker and darker and this isn't like back home, no? These are Germans." He stepped closer to them. They stepped closer to him. He lowered his voice. They leaned in.

"*These are Germans.* I can't turn to the fellow beside me to ask where I should get down. But soon everyone else has got down from the bus and the driver keeps driving and we come to another square and it looks like all the others but then he stops and opens the door and points. His finger is showing me these buildings, all the same brown squares, like giant chocolates, but he tells me to get down and goes and now I'm left alone in actual Munich and I don't see any Jaffna Tamils. What to do? An old woman came to the bus halt eventually and I showed her the paper and she takes my wrist and we go to one of the buildings and we stand just like this in front of the door, beside a board that was green and rusted like ship doors, only with little black buttons running up and down and she keeps pointing at it and at me and finally she takes my finger and pushes one of the buttons and it starts ringing and I thought they had tricked me and taken me to a police station and I told her *Die Studie Die Studie* and she took my finger saying *Gleich Gleich Gleich* and then the door opened—"

"Police!"

"No!"

"Then?"

"A Tamil fellow comes and screams and pulls me to him and kisses my head and takes me down the hallway calling for his wife and she comes running and crying but then she goes back into the room and comes back still crying too but now spilling a cup of milk. She gives me the milk and she's about to put a vadai in my mouth too and now I'm crying but then she drops the vadai and calls the husband to come away from me and he takes the milk before I can finish it and asks whose son are you and I say nothing and they go and now I am standing in the hallway and the only other person is a German boy who's opened his door. He's looking at the vadai on the floor and watching me to see who'll get it first."

"Aiyo why? After you had come so far to see them!"

"Who?"

"Your daddy and mummy!"

"Not mine."

"What do you mean, not yours? How when you went so far to find them?"

Before Bastian could answer, Lalson broke through the village men and told him that the Ralahami was waiting. He nodded and climbed onto his bike, kicked it to life, and rode forward slowly, the servant bounding ahead. He saw an old red Morris parked beside the twin boulders, and then the stone steps leading to the great house itself. Looking up, he saw a man and a boy recede from the verandah. Following them toward the dark threshold he saw something else glinting, then gone. A bangle. Whose?

Meanwhile, behind him, like lit candles, each man remembered one after the other how far gone they'd been moments before, listening to the stranger. They broke away, planning how to tell their wives the story that night and see if they would think the same, that in Munich it had been this fellow's parents. Bloody Tamils rioting in Colombo and taking all the jobs abroad and can't even give a poor Sinhalese boy a glass of milk in a distant country.

"Right, they weren't his parents. But how did he come back to Ceylon?"

"What men, are you blind? He came back on his motorbike."

twenty-three

Everything was as he'd left it ten years before, black or green or dirt. The piled shells and drying laundry, the cooking fires and busted thatch were all as these had always been, would always be. The dogs were still barking blue murder and daring him, tempting him to brake or reverse, but he drove his Hillman Minx on through the crossroads without stopping. Sam Kandy was sixty years old. He squinted more than stared now, but he needed no spectacles to see the red motorbike waiting there beside his old Morris, the two parked like older and younger brother under the walauwa, under his walauwa high above his village, even if he had no lawyer papers saying so. Now, as never before, he needed it to be his, not for the taking or keeping but for the staying, living. Him. Here. Where, these last ten years, never once was a fuel can or film canister sent back unopened; never once was a stethoscope or music cabinet or toy soldier or stuffed dolly or stuffed envelope refused.

In April 1956, when the harbour and the city suddenly turned all patriotic saffron and Sinhala only, Sam went to Trincomalee and worked as a native proxy for quiet Americans who'd taken over an English airfield to fly planes back and forth from Indochina. They had their own warehouse kingdoms come. But then one day in 1959, the Americans left. And even if no one was, Trinco Tamils were not Sam's people. He returned to the city only to discover that Colombo harbour was now fully closed for business to all save blood relations and devout Buddhists. And Sam Kandy was not born to the first and would not bow low enough to be the second. Meanwhile, the greater city was useless with strikes and rallies and even his barber was charging double the old rates. There was nowhere left to go. He bought a new car and went that night, the moon hanging before him like the heel smudge of some passing god. On his way to the village he wondered about the balance of the stars, about why it was set always against him. And now, greeting him upon his return, a bright red motorbike, another man's machine. He was too old to knock it down.

The first time he tried, he only kicked it into the old red Morris. The second time, he slipped and fell down. He stood and brushed off, then took the bike with both hands, pulled it away from the old Morris, righted it, and considered it. Yes, it was very fine. Then he pushed it down to the ground and looked around, his face desperate shameful and daring proud; desperate to see if anyone had been watching, daring them to come forward with a claim against his. A sixty-year-old seven-year-old. Sam's lungs hurt, he was heaving so much from the effort, from breathing more than just outrage about this bike, which had not been brought nor sent here by him but bought with all his sweat and running while here, high upon the world, they never had to move save when the servant swept under their feet.

Sam wondered where Bopea and his yellow hat were, why he was not waiting for Sam when he arrived, why he had not sent word that this motorbike had been bought. He wondered how much

of his money had gone into it. Arthur must have ordered it from
Colombo, from the warehouse of some new minister's nephew's
cousin who in the latest election had helped put down a riot, or
start one, or put up a poster or tear one down for its English or its
Tamil blasphemies, and thus was now the High Commissioner of
Imports, whose first order of business of course was to celebrate the
nation's prosperity by ordering German motorbikes for the whole
family and no problem he could get one more for an upcountry
chap with a good upcountry name who made his inquiry on the
back of a fat envelope that had been filled by Sam's sweat, a chap
who agreed that upon delivery he would pry off or paint over any
foreign words before using it on Ceylon roads and anyway not to
worry he would only ever use it to bring the village temple's chief
monk to and from schoolboy recitations of the *Mahavamsa*. It was
very fine. It would be Sam's now too. He almost pulled it up but he
stopped himself, straightened his back, and stood to the side. It had
to be righted, yes, but not by him. It was his place to want it so, to
have it done. If he were going to stay in the village he would have to
follow village ways. Waiting to be received, Sam began to imagine
it: at last, day-after-day in the village. Cough awake and call for tea,
then take a wash and a shave, dress and come to the front room
and take more tea, listen to the Radio Ceylon news report and to
the cocks crow and to the temple bell sound and to the sound of
the boy washing the vehicle below. News report and tea finished,
next would come vehicle inspection, smoking a cigarette while
checking for mud and smudges as the boy stood to the side, rags in
hand, smiling and hating, waiting to be released by the pinstriped
Ralahami's nod and grunt. But there would always be missed spots
and only when they were gone could the boy fetch fresh water and
new rags and wash the other vehicle, because both were Sam's.
And when it was all done, he would return to the walauwa and
take his breakfast while listening to the next news report and now

there were only twelve hours more to pass until he could sleep and twenty-two hours until his next morning tea, until another day of taking a wash and a shave and dressing to descend and tell the boy to wash it again.

What triumph.

"You should have told me you were coming," Bopea called out as he approached, putting on his yellow hat like an amulet while eyeing the fallen bike.

"I should have told you. I should have told you? I should go from here and fly to Russia and bring your son back and still it will cost less than this thing that I have paid for and never been told that I have paid for." He kicked more dust at the shining bike. After the servant boy washed both vehicles and the bike, next would be Sam's shoes to shine.

"Aiyo, what am I to tell when I don't even understand myself? And leave the boy alone because he must be having more exams." Bopea's son had been in Moscow studying for ten years now. No word yet of return. Over the years, he'd sent his father occasional mimeographs of graded work and degrees earned, all of which hung in Bopea's hut. The first degree was framed over a woodcut print of Sydney harbour. The second degree papered over a young Queen Victoria.

"You are to do what I tell you to do. And I have told you: tell everything that happens. That was our agreement."

"Right." Bopea smiled like an old noon-hour crocodile. He cocked his hat. "But our *first* agreement was about what I remember."

Sam had almost asked for mercy, mercy from memory rather than from Bopea's grip, when Bopea had come to the harbour office that morning in 1948, a few months after the island's independence, knocking and entering before Sam could say come or come later and then Sam said nothing because there, standing before him, finally, was the man in the yellow hat. He was a village man about Sam's age, dressed to come to the city the way village men do, in his good sarong that he only now let down to his feet.

"I don't know you," Sam said, too quickly.

"You do. Only you won't remember."

"Go. What do you want? Go. I'll give you a thrashing. What do you want? Go."

"You know this hat, no? You sent it. Many years ago, you sent it to the village."

"This is the last time I will tell you—"

"You're fatter than you used to be but I know you. And I knew your Appachchi and it's like this:"

Before Sam could catch and thrash and throw him, Bopea met him in the middle of the office and took him at the forearm with one hand and with the other began turning the skin on his forearm.

"Now you know me? Now you remember?" Bopea laughed. Sam should have laughed with him, with the universe laughing at him, here, about to drop to his pinstriped knees on a wooden floor in the middle of his own office in his city, biting his lip like a seven-year-old. Found and returned, returning, returned past even salt stains and accidents with a bullock cart. Returned to the great green clearing itself, to an age before the rest of it, before even *only a little bird, putha. Soo sa*

"Let go of me."

"And?"

"And tell."

"What?"

"LET. GO. OF. ME."

When they were both seated, Bopea talked twenty years of waiting to talk. He asked and answered his own questions because Sam would say nothing to any of it, to Bopea's recounting his wonder, that day in 1929, when Sam stood on the wedding platform, ignoring the dirt thrown at his shoulder to stare at Bopea in his yellow hat walking through the wedding crowd, and then ran back to the city. Bopea had in truth only worn it that day because it was the first auspicious occasion fitting the hat's own grandness that followed upon the departure of the man who had given it to his father years before. All the things from that mysterious crate had been given in discharge of various debts in the village. The particular terms between Sam's father and Bopea's father had been long since forgotten, but not their source. Bopea told Sam it had taken him time to piece things together, that he was not so smart as his son: first, why the old man had disappeared, who Bopea had always thought would never have gone farther from his own hut than whichever was the next hut he was begging or borrowing from; and second, how then this new fellow had come as he came, to try for the Ralahami's daughter and the whole village could tell what the pinstripes and loud car and absurd name tried to tell against, that he was village too, only which one he would never tell or why he chose to come to this place, or why he came when he came, or why he had stared at Bopea in his yellow hat—and then Bopea began remembering, deeper into the past, wondering if this was that black crow boy who had disappeared one day, long before. And, Bopea continued, even if he was not so smart as his own son, still he had studied Sam's coming and going for years. He had studied a face that was, save his first wedding day, always so void of pity for the rest of them that he passed in his motorcars full of gifts for the walauwa, a face void of pity even for his children after his wife their mother had died, void as that boy's had been who had dropped Bopea back in that useless turtle pond years before, void of pity even for himself though he had had to bite his lip the first time Bopea had burned his arm and beat him down on the great green clearing behind the village.

"So now you must only have one question left, no?" Bopea asked.

"Yes."

"So?"

"So answer it."

Bopea then said what Sam could already tell, could probably have known from that first day they'd fought: that he, Bopea, was a patient man, a very patient man. He asked Sam to think of how many times since Sam's first wedding day he could have told against Sam or told Sam himself, told that he was known and known to have been not just a low-caste paddy worker like the rest of them but low-born right there like the rest of them and not just low-born right there like the rest of them but low-born to such a fellow as his father had been, long since known in the village for only sweating and moving when someone came to his hut to collect.

"Just tell me what you want," Sam seethed through clenched teeth, clenched fists. Tell how much of what and then stop telling, stop making me want to stand and defend my father's name never worth defending.

"First, do you admit?"

"Tell me who else knows."

"So you admit?"

"Tell me who else knows."

"No one else, I swear on my son's life. If everyone knew, then my knowing would be useless, would be just another jungle paper nailed to the jak tree tomorrow morning, no?"

"Then tell. How much."

"So you admit."

"HOW MUCH."

"Right. I want nothing like that."

"Then go to hell."

"I'll go and come straight away."

Bopea returned, minutes later, with his son, a thin boy in his early twenties smelling of bay rum and holding a book, always holding a book. While his father was upstairs, he had taken his first proper shave at the barber-stall below. Bopea told Sam that the scholarship examinations were to be held the next day, at the Public Library, Edinburgh Crescent, Colombo 7, that the monk who had long tutored his son at the village temple had told Bopea's son and then Bopea that the Russians were coming to Colombo to give full university scholarships to top-flight boys. The monk said he was certain none of the Royal-Thomian types would sit for anything but Queen's Scholarships to Oxford and Cambridge, let alone go to the Public Library if it wasn't a British Council event. The only thing was to get an admission ticket to the exam, and the monk did not know how an upcountry village boy with only a temple teacher could.

"But I knew straight off who would get him one," Bopea said, beaming, staring at Sam, his arm around his son. "I knew the most generous man of the village, Sam Kandy, would want to help the smartest boy in the village, no?" Immediately Sam understood the game and he played it well, had to keep playing it after the boy sat for the exam and won the scholarship and needed another ticket, this time a ship berth to Madras and from Madras by train to Calcutta and from Calcutta to Moscow by plane (Dum Dum/ Aspern/Vnukovo) and of course a Parker pen and proper, heavy clothes because no one wears sarong to lectures in the Russian snow. Before the boy left, he wanted to return to the village and tell the monk his results, give the monk alms in his late mother's name, then drink a cup of good heavy milk and break a branch and go. Sam said if Bopea knew to drive or was willing to learn, he could take the boy to the village in Sam's old red Morris, the car that still smelled of Puttalam, of blackwater saltwater, the car that could be Arthur's, and let him paint it black with his money if he wanted. After a driving lesson along Wharf Road, there came their second agreement, which carried across Sam Kandy's absence years: after his son was sent off to his studies, Bopea would become Arthur's driver and Sam's man in the village. He would report only to Sam, meeting him where and when Sam said to and bringing to the walauwa and village what Sam decided to send and telling Sam who if anyone came looking for him and what if ever anything had happened since their last meeting and telling also whenever Sam's name was heard in the walauwa, telling what was said, what was whispered, bought, brought, broken, taken, thrown, coughed at, and cursed. Whenever and whatever, and this bloody motorbike lying in front of them was not grown in any paddy field.

Sam glared at Bopea glaring until they heard the hammering of modern shoes upon the stone steps.

"There. You hear? Your latest blue-eyed fellow is coming. It's his bike."

twenty-four

Ten years later, thirty years later, the same blue eyes. Sam's mouth opened and closed like a caught fish. But after a few moments he nodded, less at Bastian than at what Bastian's being here now meant, could mean, if not had to mean. Sam nodded more vigorously, taking a new measure of those old jurying stars, of how time and men, time and means, could constellate and shatter and constellate again, and not always forever more against you as Sam Kandy, great shattered shatterer, had long since been certain. What vanity! It was, for now, a freeing thought. And so, after Bastian righted his bike, the two men climbed the stone steps, one in front of the other, and Sam told Bastian to wait on the verandah and he went into the walauwa first, nodding after ten years at Arthur and Thusitha, at Hyacinth, at the servants waiting to the side. They were staring at the floor near his feet. Embarrassed to receive him dressed in their daily sarong and home skirt and blouse, or respectful? Or considering whether to queue and bow low and give ten years' respect? But then he looked down as well, just as a boy, bowing low, started running a die-cast toy car across Sam's black shoes. Running it hard, then looking up and disappearing. This was Dudley, who was called Arthur's son, when in truth or Latha's talking this was Sam's grandson, one of the thirteen George left behind in Ceylon.

"Welcome, Sam-aiya, after so long," Arthur said, half standing, his voice all boom and quiver. "And where is …" He could have said lawyer George Madam Ethiopian. He said none of it and Sam's face showed none of it, and no one in the room minded the withering away of ten years' fear and curiosity.

"Sam-aiya," said Thusitha, amazed her husband had not already yielded and called him Ralahami, "you must have had a long journey. Would you like to take a wash? Would you like tea?"

Sam said he would take tea now and take a wash later. And when she asked if tea should be sent down for the driver too Sam said there was no driver, that he had driven himself. And when they asked if Lalson should go down to empty the boot Sam said there was nothing to carry other than one suitcase and a shaving kit. Sam lit a cigarette and told them that he had come to stay. He remained standing. The room wondered if he would motion for Arthur to give up his seat, an oak-panelled armchair that Sam had sent from the city. All of them, Arthur included, wondered if Arthur ought to invite him to sit in one of the other chairs he had sent, for which had been rubbished stools and benches turned out long ago from village wood by village men for village headmen. Sam included, all of them wondered if Sam would accept Arthur's invitation and if so what then, what meaning, whose? Whose victory? He remained standing.

"For how long?" Arthur asked.

Sam said nothing. He was studying Hyacinth. She was not so pretty as Alice had been, but not so proud either. Her face was rounder, fuller, sweeter. His daughter was what, thirty years old now. She was not even a young woman. He had been sending her dollies for thirty years. He nodded at her.

"Appachchi," she said, coming forward and giving respect. Then she stood, stepped back, and looked at her father. No, she looked just over his shoulder, past him, onto the verandah. Searching to see if he was waiting there with his stupid hope, or had he already gone?

"Shall I have him called in?" Sam asked her, now knowing why Bastian hadn't done anything save righting his bike and following Sam like a tail, then waiting outside just as Sam commanded. Was this what it would mean to have a son-in-law?

"Who?" she answered, her voice high and hollow and everyone listening looked away, pitying the girl, her poor acting, their mouths each whispering *Who* one hundred more believable ways, a roomful of quietly mad owls.

"Right. Who. Right." Sam finished his cigarette. "Lalson!" he yelled, making all of them start, because Lalson was already in the room, standing within arm's reach. "Bring the betel and then tell the visitor he may come in." Sam walked to the empty chair beside Arthur's and dragged it across the tiled floor to the centre of the room and there he sat waiting to receive his daughter's suitor, arranging himself like some bemused king.

Thirty minutes later, Bastian stopped telling. He waited for Sam to answer. And he looked over at Hyacinth who, like a proper high-born daughter, would not look back at him but only sidelong at her listening, now considering father, and otherwise at her feet, properly lost in the sylvan inlay of a toe-ring. At thirty, Hyacinth Kandy was long pitied and envied her father's indifference, which some thought came of her looking like her mother, and which others, Hyacinth included, thought was just indifference because she was not her brother and so never once gave Sam, gave anyone really, cause for anything more than that. She did not think this day would have come. She was still unsure whether her father even understood this day had come for her, that she was even in the room and if so, that he, Bastian, was in the room not only to say thank you to him, her father, for his getting him that first passage out of Colombo harbour but also to ask him about her, to ask for her, for her hand. She was and had been for twenty years too old for dollies and at thirty she should have been at least ten years too old to be married. But then this fellow had come and as of today had passed nearly exactly thirty auspicious days in the village, days spent walking with her and always with her nephew near and never but in highest light, listening without looking at him tell of yellow apples and of snow, its bluish colour in a field at night, how it became its own kind of yellow under streetlamps; its sound underfoot like schoolboys grinding their teeth at night. But unlike her mother and brother, Bastian had stayed here *because* of her father. And now it was her father who could give his assent and then horoscopes could be read and a time set and a visit to the chief monk made and then onto the poruwa they could go, and then, then he, Bastian, could stay truly, and Hyacinth Kandy would no longer be the sweet unnoticed girl sitting at other people's meals in her very birth-house.

Sam's ears were burning. Not from the story of going and coming—which Bastian enjoyed telling too much, which he told too much of—or even from hearing in that story the size of the dowry this fellow was going to expect, to keep making as if he were the only blue-eyed brown boy ever to have visited Sudugama. No, Sam's ears were burning from having to hear Bastian's audience make such sounds—pitying, wondering, shocked, worried, confused just as the Munich Tamils had been confused. How many times had they heard it? This latest telling ended with Bastian saying he had come and waited to give Sam his thanks for giving him his start into the world, which made Sam's ears ring, strain to hear more. But that was the only moment in the story that the walauwa people made no noise about.

"So now you have said thank you," Sam said, finally. "And you have thanked these people, my relations, for letting you wait like this, here, to tell me."

"Yes. Of course, Mahatteya." Bastian turned his head. "And thank you, Ralahami."

Arthur nodded gravely. Sam blackened. Called Mahatteya. Called Ralahami. How stupid. How fatal, to let Arthur be the one to be thanked, to be so named as he was thanked. Had they, Arthur and Bastian, planned this before Sam had come? Would Bastian next ask for a dowry and before Sam could answer Arthur would offer it from his own pettagama and steamer trunks filled by Sam's thirty years' running? And then Arthur would walk to the temple with Bastian to see the chief monk?

"And now that you have said thanks, you shall go," Sam declared.

"Actually, Mahatteya, there is more," Bastian answered. He had been practising this speech too, at night, sleeping beside the boy in the back room, across the hall from where, for the rest of his days, he would sleep beside his wife, were it granted that he could stay.

"Right. You say there is more," Sam answered. Something had to be done. He had been in the village for one hour and already it was upon him to show that what was here was his to give or his to deny, his to defend.

"I also want to say, Mahatteya, that of all the places I have been to, this is the best place. This is the most beautiful place. I would also like to say, Mahatteya, about your daughter—"

"Where is your horoscope?" Sam barked. "Where are your parents?"

"What do you mean?" Bastian asked. "You know—"

"What kind of house do you think this is, what kind of people do you think we are, that you can come and stay and tell grand stories and make like you are something other than a vagabond?" Sam stood and walked across the room, toward him. "And while

I have been away you have mooned with your bad omen eyes and fooled these village minds into thinking you have come down from Buckingham Palace itself on the devil's own motorbike to seek my only daughter's hand and when I grant it the morning after the wedding you will be gone and so will every piece of my gold."

"No! I ask for no dowry, I only ask, about your daughter—"

"GO! I don't need another driver. Making like you are no orphan, no servant's son. No Englishman's bastard born to drive other men. I don't need another driver."

"Aiyo," breathed Thusitha, looking over at Hyacinth shaking in her chair.

"Stop this, Aiya," tried Arthur.

"A bastard born to drive other men, I say."

"I said stop this!"

Now Sam had to keep going and he leaned down on Bastian, muttering it again and again. Yes Sam's blood was running fine and hard and true and who said a sixty-year-old man couldn't shatter the constellations? "GO!" Sam commanded.

"YOU GO!"

"Mokatha?" Sam whipped around, but Hyacinth was already looking down again, sylvan lost, would say no more. No one said anything else while Bastian went to the back room and gathered his things, Dudley pleading in vain to know why as Bastian then walked again through the front room frieze. He looked a last time at Hyacinth, who for the first time held his gaze. She nodded once and looked down again. Before dawn the next morning, she met him at the bus stand, climbed onto the back of his bike, and they went. Smoking a cigarette and leaning on the stone ledge of the verandah, Sam Kandy watched his daughter go. Then he called into the house for tea and went down to watch the servant boy wash his motorcars.

twenty-five

"Yes! Yes you must! Please, Father Marcelline, please bless it before he comes. You know Daddy is coming home. HE IS COMING JUST NOW!"

Rose had to yell at the priest. Laughing screaming children were twirling noisemakers while running back and forth between the glass-box statues of St. Anthony and Our Lady that marked the far ends of the church square. Meanwhile, passing cars and trucks were honking at the crowd gathered in front of a fresh-painted cement mixer, either because the crowd was taking up too much of the main road or because the drivers knew the crowd was gathered because Xavier Joseph De Moraes was finally coming home.

While the rest of the family had spent the morning packing the vans and picking their outfits for the journey to the airport, Rose had made sure that lagoon crabs had been brought and the pork set to roast and lights strung between the houses in the compound, that the floors of their own house were washed and the bronze polished and the dogs washed and the vehicles washed and polished and the flowerbeds fixed up. She had even ordered her mother's squirrel cages cleaned. Born to be giants and fed like their dogs, the squirrels never tried to escape. Instead they lay about making nasty screeching noises, arguing like a parliament of fat women. Rose hated them. She loved the peacocks her father used to keep, before he went against Mrs. Bandaranaike and then went from the island, leaving one of her brothers in charge of his birds, not her. The peacocks were dead within a year.

But now there would be birdsongs in the compound again. At lunch she had ordered the kitchen girl to keep rice for the pedestal in the side-garden, where her father liked to take his morning tea watching the birds take their breakfast: green parakeets and yellow bulbuls, sometimes a pair of spotted thrush. There should have been new peacocks also, but the brother who should have arranged for their return instead had spent the last few days driving around Negombo with his friends, trying to assemble the world's loudest sound system. In the meantime, Rose had done everything else, for years had been doing everything else. Not only because she was the eldest and remaining unmarried daughter but because her mother, Vivimarie De Moraes, for reasons no one knew and none dared to ask, stopped running the house during her husband's absence years. She had left everything to Rose, save feeding the giant squirrels. Now, upon word of his return, Vivimarie had called for her dress-maker and made plans to publish the results of three years' novenas not just in the *Catholic Messenger* but also in the *Sunday Observer*. The rest remained for her eldest girl to do, a girl the rest of the family had long since assumed would grow old minding other people's children, the lone De Moraes daughter who, according to theories related to her shortness, her most Portuguese of noses, and the telltale length of her second toe, had never been asked after by families with suitable boys.

She allowed herself a cup of tea only after the rest of them left for the airport—her mother, her mother's brothers and sisters and her father's brothers and sisters; her own brothers and sisters and their children; her cousins and her cousins' children; school friends from three generations; and also, cramming and hanging on and sharing corners of seats, boys armed with epic lists of the many things they'd done for Mr. De Moraes's family while he was away. Together they went in garlanded vans down the Negombo Road. They wanted to be in Ratmalana at least four hours early and then wait in the grassless park outside the airport. The De Moraeses packed for the journey like they were going north to Madhu Church for the Assumption Feast: they brought coiled effusions of extra garland, guitars and lap drums, two radios, rosaries, rosewater and Tiger Balm, breviaries, Enid Blytons, Mills & Boons, Sando from New Generations, Sando's father Andrew who owned Portrait Studio 3A Mangala Road, bottles of Pathma's Asian Rose talcum and English Lavender too, flasks of Brooke Bond tea, jugs of water, bars of Zellers fruit, Zellers fruit-and-milk, Zellers plain milk and introducing new Zellers milkcracker chocolate, cricket bats and a badminton set, Maliban cream crackers, Cow & Gate baby formula, tennis balls, a simple pavilion tent, and a full meal for at least twice their number. Everyone dressed up to go to the airport, but waited with newspapers and canteen tea. This family would go like pageant, as usual, and wait, as always, like carnival.

Meanwhile, her own tea finished, Rose had wanted to arrange a blessing, and so she'd gone to the church square which, two days after Christmas 1965, with the village's most prominent man about to return, was its own carnival. And so of course Rose had to yell at the priest: The band she'd hired, New Horizons featuring Sando from New Generations, was nowhere to be found but younger boys, denied noisemakers at the church door when everyone was exiting vespers, were playing hell behind the bass drum, trading turns hammering down on the footpedal with their hands. *Tho tho*

tho But never mind the noisemakers and the bass drum booming like the world's own pulse; it was little different than most holy days in the De Moraes family universe. In truth Rose liked the noise: it let her yell with best intentions, with a necessity not her own, at the family priest who was refusing to bless her father's welcome-home present.

"No. I will not. This is scandal and madness," Father Marcelline insisted. "I am not going to bless something that your own father knows should not be blest. Wait and see, child, how he will come and before even taking tea or a wash, paint over it himself. In that way, he is a good son of the Church."

"Father Marcelline, Daddy is in all ways a good son of the Church, no?"

"And I'll not have holy water mixed up with all this paint!" the priest yelled and so did not hear her last question. Never mind the money Xavier Joseph De Moraes had given the Church over the years, how many feast days he'd footed, how many Walk Rite kits he'd bought for cripples, how much he'd given for the Beggar's Palace alone: he had also promised his support (his name, his money, and, if necessary, trucks from his cement co.) to the 1962 coup plotters in the name of defending the Church, its schools, and its clergy from the rising temple and from the rising sangha that had weepy Mrs. Bandaranaike's ear and were trying to be her eyes and mouth, her arms and fingers, her fists. Her father had made this promise, as Rose and everyone else knew, after speaking with Father Marcelline, who, after the coup failed, turned amnesiac and would not even give him a St. Christopher's blessing the morning he left home. Some thought he had gone to Rome or to Tuticorin, others said he was hiding out in the old Portuguese fort on Mannar Island; a few believed he had gone to Lourdes itself.

He was coming home, at last, because the charges had been dropped against all of the men named in the attempted action against the government. And still, the family priest would not appear at the homecoming rally planned at the top of the church square, would not even shake a few drops of holy water at the Leyland Comet cement truck that had been bought to celebrate Xavier Joseph De Moraes's return and also announce the company's own return to competition with the big Colombo firms. After the acquittals had been announced, Rose's brothers decided that the company would be just as proudly Christian as Farook Concrete was Muslim and National Agglos and Cement Elephant Cement Co. were Buddhist. And so the new lead truck's mixer had been painted with two images, but they had run into each other when some fool had climbed into the cab and turned on the mixer before the portraits had dried, striping the mixer itself and purpling Christ's crown of thorns and Mary's starry veil. The truck's cab at least showed perfect red roses on its doors. Underneath, in fresh stencilling, it read LOURDES CEMENT CO. (PVT.).

"But it's not Daddy's fault they turned the mixer on before the paint dried, Father, is it? He didn't even ask for it to be painted."

"Wet paint or dry paint how can I be seen to bless such a thing? It is blasphemy!"

"Right then. Thank you, Father. I will send Daddy your best and we will see you at Mass." Rose turned and went, walking fast through the crowds. She found another priest, a young Chilaw fellow who knew nothing of anything here save the name of the most prominent family in the parish, whose eldest daughter asked him to bless Xavier De Moraes's new truck and what was he to do but find his holy water? Rose led him through the crowd and he decided to be blind about the paint job. (Afterwards, he went to the parish house where already how many old women were queued to tell Father Marcelline what he'd just done!)

A boy on a Bajaj beeped and threaded his way to Rose and the cement truck to tell that a line of vans were coming down the road followed by two first-class cars, banged up, old, but first-class. Were these ministers' vehicles? Rose gave the signal and the blessed mixer started up and every head turned because now there was nothing else in the world save the magnificent double roaring of engine and mixer, Jesus and Mary making solemn revolutions.

⌐⌐

Nothing he could say do pay promise forget or threaten now could change that it was his fault. Ceylon roads were governed by one rule: never hit the fellow in front of you. Even if the fellow has stopped suddenly on the airport road; especially if the fellow is your own man driving one of your vehicles and you've hit him just as he's hit the van in front of him. He could not pay for any of it. December 1965, Sam Kandy was out of money. His last source, short of opening a Pettah of his own to sell his own things to his own villagers, had been the salt concern up the coast, but it had failed the year before, after Puttalam burned for seven days in creedal fury. Sam listened to reports on Radio Ceylon and a month later Peter Rodrigo sent word that the operation had been ransacked in three languages and in the name of at least four gods and now Rodrigo Salt Works (Pvt.) was part of the Ceylon Salt Board. He'd released whatever workers hadn't already run off and was now himself migrating to Australia. Meanwhile, the village paddy profits went to Arthur by old precedent ties, temple-sanctioned precedents, which Sam was too old now to try to break, and when Sam finally demanded money, Arthur said that everything Sam sent during his absence years had long ago gone to maintaining the village and the walauwa. Right. Pools of sunlight and monsoon came as they liked through the walauwa's roof, more every season, and the village itself needed a new water tank five years ago. There was no money to fix anything, according to Arthur, only the old true promises of merit for next lives and good meals for the workmen who more and more expected something other than old true promises and noon-hour plates of rice and garden curry for their sweat.

And then, one day, came remarkable news—Arthur's son had won a scholarship to England, no school anyone had heard of in Colombo, the boy hadn't even applied, but no matter. Within days, Arthur had Bopea drive him to the city, where he arranged their papers and bought Air Ceylon tickets for himself and Thusitha and Dudley, and because he had expedited the passports with yet more of his secret hoarding and kept the rest to set them up in England when they arrived and he had to tell his son the truth about the scholarship, truly now there was no money left in the walauwa. Sam drove down to Colombo separately, to make sure at least this much was true, that Arthur and Thusitha board the plane with the boy. The last he saw of them was at the departure barrier, where they were writing their names and addresses in ALL CAPS on sheets of paper and affixing them to their suitcases. Arthur said he and his wife would return in ten days, after settling the boy, but he had stayed his son's hand against breaking a branch before they'd left the village for the airport. (At last, he would reach true London.)

And so the empty walauwa was at last Sam's, and returning he would knock down all remaining walls so they could not taunt his final days with their blankness, unwritten and lizard-splayed save where hung the pictured dead. And when the time came, he would make his funeral bier right there, in the finally bloodless walauwa made a fitting size full of fitting memories, rotting with all those fine fitting things that were fit, in the end, everything was, in the end, only to burn to ash and blow away, at last freed. There was nothing more to the world save that final triumph, or so Sam thought as he drove away from the airport, before he hit and was stopped. When he stepped out, a whole village surrounded him. He could just see Bopea ahead, likewise surrounded, and still more people emptying out of the vans beyond, the women making the sign of the cross with beads in their hands that they kept kissing as if they were long-lost wedding earrings. These were like no people Sam knew. They were fatter yet faster moving than upcountry people, their hair just as oiled but done up in American waves and fins. They gave no ground to pinstripes. They did not seem even to notice. If only he could kick out and go, but would these people think he was kicking or dancing? Would they give way or join him? Or would he be joining them? Looking ahead, hearing it before he believed it, Sam wondered, What kind of people bring guitars to a car accident?

twenty-six

After following the convoy from the airport, so many fenders and bumpers scratched, so many headlights and taillights shattered, Sam and Bopea were brought to a Negombo church square already teeming with more of the same people. The driver of the van that Bopea had hit came to them with bottles of Lion beer. Sam declined. Bopea took both and, suddenly full of festal courage, followed his new friend into the crowd. Standing alone, Sam listened to welcome-home speeches from members of the business community and from the president of the Negombo Bharatha Association, and to a series of solemn, absolutely shouted recitations of Shakespeare by uniformed schoolboys. All for a man who looked about Sam's age, but with broader shoulders and softer eyes and a straighter back, dressed in a much newer suit, white, and he wore it with a white shirt and brown-and-white shoes. He told the crowd he was glad to be home and thanked God and our blessed Saviour and all his dear friends for watching over his family while he was away. To great applause he said that patience always pays, and then he climbed into the cab of the Jesus-painted cement truck and turned on the mixer and every boy tried to join him and soon all you could see was the gold of his watch, his heavy wristlet, his rings, as he waved to the crowd that waved back until the night's first crackers were lit and then everyone clapped and covered their ears, shaking their heads at how loud and how many were set off, how many! Three years away, the company all but dead while he was gone, a fleet of hired vans to have repaired, and see how much money De Moraes still could burn!

To Sam it was sterile smoke, empty noise. He pitied the fine suit crushed inside the truck cab. But later, in the family compound, the man seemed not to care as it crumpled still more from all the hugging and waving and clapping and singing along. Sam watched and listened and tried to understand what kind of world this was, what kind of Saturn-upon-Mercury could so command its mad joy. Eventually De Moraes removed his coat and tie and collar, and then, to applause and like-minded gestures, his shirt and shoes. Sam thought at first he was behaving low, like a hired driver at the end of day, or like a man would when alone in his bedroom just before sleep. But then Sam watched De Moraes move through the compound in his banyan and bare feet, so many always gathered around him as he called out to others and drank and was fed by endless old women's hands, joined one dance and led another, the steps coming to him as if he'd just walked in from the Brown's Beach Hotel. There was no space between him and them, none given and none demanded. Here was a man elaborated into a crowd elaborated into a man. Sam watched all of it from a side-garden, standing beside a barren bird pedestal, smoking and turning down how many invitations to join meals, Jim Reeves songs, rosaries, thanksgiving novenas, carom, crackers, darts, epic retellings of the extraordinary pile-up on the airport road, new meals, the same songs.

Sam's children didn't even send him triumphant crates from wherever, from whoever, they now were. And when he went walking through his village these past five years, he was given wide but glowering margins by men and women who hadn't seen a movie or a fortnightly doctor in five years, whose children were still without a government schoolmaster and whose paddy sweat wasn't paying for a new village water tank but apparently for airplane tickets to London, and all of which was Sam's doing even if they could tell he too had been lately lowered. No more did he go and come from the city with bootfuls of loveshine, no more new wives or vehicles; he didn't even know anyone to get a phone number for the walauwa while across the main road at the temple the chief monk could trunk-dial all the way to Colombo. The most Sam could imagine now was his own bier, that it burn higher, longer, grander than any before it. All his sixty-five years of steel and pride, fever and speed, would make a grand plumage of rich black smoke that would be seen across the island before all of it fell upon the village green, conferring upon that blackbird field its right recompense. What triumph that was to dream of, and Sam finally did dream when night became the blue before morning and he was too tired to keep watching Xavier De Moraes keep going and so he left the dark-lit side-garden, not knowing he had been watched the whole time. Sam lay until morning on a cot in a spare bedroom somewhere deep in the compound, where, eventually, drunken Bopea was brought and dropped and stretched out against a wall like a warehouse beggar, snoring but still holding a bread-ring in his hand. There Sam waited through the rest of the night in a broken sleep broken by the roaring life outside his window, by still more firecrackers, and yes by envy for all of it made into the vain consoling firedream of his own someday great burning. And when Sam went outside the next day there he was, already awake, in fresh and pressed clothes, clean shaved and sipping tea in the side-garden. There he was, watching birds light upon a stand that, barren the night before, was now full and brilliant with gathering green and yellow and a fine blue-feathered fellow as well. De Moraes was standing beside a girl who must have been about Hyacinth's age, only she was holding her father's arm, and she was looking at her father, and she was smiling.

Xavier saw him approaching from the lane between the two houses in front of his own, a stranger in scuffed shoes and a fine suit not black anymore so much as black sheen, under which was a white shirt whose collar was wilted and splayed. He pitied the fellow his wearing it, the needful pride you could tell he took in still wearing it, in the years and years of proven expectation that others would give way to the cut of the cloth itself. But his eyes weren't so challenging anymore, his step not so hard. He was favouring one hip, more from the habit of pain it seemed than from pain itself. His hair was smoothed back by hand, his face salted with old man's stubble. A tired old bird. During the party, one of De Moraes's drivers had befriended his driver and asked him a question about his boss for every drink and ring of breudher cake he wanted (the fellow ate like he'd never had butter on bread before). By the time the driver was carried to a room, it was clear his man wasn't a minister or a minister's man or a rival cement company's agent or a debt collector; he wasn't the phantom father of a phantom daughter demanding money for a phantom baby phantom-fathered by one of De Moraes's sons. Other than shaking his head to all such queries, all the drunken driver would say of his Mahatteya was that he was called Sam Kandy. He said the name like that should have been story enough. De Moraes had never heard of him, but even to watch his approach, he could tell whatever threat this threadbare man could have posed had long since passed.

"Good morning!" he called out.

"Good morning," Sam said.

"I hope you enjoyed our party last night. I am told your driver certainly did, no?"

"Yes, he is my driver. Right. Thank you. About my vehicles—"

"Fine vehicles they are. I saw both this morning in the car park when I was coming from Mass. But not so fine just now, no? Rose darling, do you know what this gentleman managed to do yesterday? I am told he managed to bust one of our hired vans and two of his own vehicles on the airport road. One man, three vehicles, all busted. Remarkable, no?"

She nodded at her father. She did not look at Sam. What kind of unmarried daughter looks at a stranger before her father? Having already looked at Sam the night before, having watched him smoke in her father's garden.

"What's more remarkable, Rose darling, is that I think he's come to ask me to pay for it."

Sam said nothing.

"But you see he is a gentleman! He won't speak until proper introductions have been made, isn't it? Right. I am Xavier Joseph De Moraes."

"I am Sam Kandy."

"Yes, I know that."

"How do you know?" There was formal suspicion in his voice, but more curiosity and also, barely, pride.

"Your driver. Where are you from, Mr. Kandy?"

"That's right. He is my driver. And I am Sam Kandy."

"Yes. Are you from Colombo?"

"He is my driver. And I am Sam Kandy. And both my vehicles, my old red Morris and my new Hillman, are damaged because your vehicles stopped on the airport road."

"What you mean to say is that you hit your own vehicle and your driver hit one of our vans. Do you expect me to pay for all of it?"

"What would a headman and a gentleman do?"

"Yes, a headman and a gentleman would offer to pay for what he has done. Do you agree, Mr. Kandy?"

Sam looked away, thinking now of home. Home! Because at least upcountry sun was merciful at first, burning away the morning mist upon the fields and then throbbing through the trees before it came for you at the break of day. Here there were trees too, but they were palms, bushy-topped nepotists with their shade. Squinting in bright morning, Sam could find no great ramparts of skyward green surrounding this town, this compound, this wide house, this blooming side-garden, these people standing in full sun asking him questions to catch him yes, but catch him how and could he catch them first could he even, still, catch? Sam said nothing.

"Do you agree, Mr. Kandy?" the man asked again. "Because you see, I was in the front van and when we stopped, my van hit nothing."

"But they are all your vans. All of this is yours, no?"

"No, Mr. Kandy." De Moraes smiled. "All of this is hers, is theirs." His hand extended toward the many-roomed house behind him before sweeping to show the other houses surrounding them, all many-roomed. "And I am hers too. I am theirs too." Sam could tell the man had said such things before. Yes, but there was more in his voice than the obvious ploy this was. There was also pride and relief, certainty, certainty of place. "And that is why," De Moraes continued, "I shall ask my daughter to decide. Rose darling, who should pay?"

Her father had asked her that question at eight and nine, at ten, twenty, twenty-five, and now, at thirty. He had never kept an office anywhere but in the family compound and sometimes, when men would come to see him, strangers dressed either much better or much worse than he was, Xavier would call one of the children to stand beside him and meet this nice gentleman. Then he would tell the man that all was theirs, that he was theirs too, before asking the child, *Darling, who should pay?* The first few times, Rose and her brothers and sisters and cousins would race to his side when he called. But as the prize became more widely known and won—it was either a single sweet or the latest found peacock feather, and only after the purgatory of standing around while adults spoke and then answering a question from Daddy while the stranger never once looked at you—the older boys would not come from their cricket when their father called, nor would the younger boys abandon their chance to retrieve boundary balls and then heave their whole lives into the ball's flight back to the bowler. And when they realized there were no boys to race, the girls would not leave their games of netball and French cricket, either. And so eventually it was only Rose. She always went, not only because leaving netball and French cricket were no great trials for her, not only because going spared her sisters bottom slaps and her brothers thunderclaps and later because they were auditioning wedding bands and picking bouquets and fabric for going-away dresses and later holding crying babies and busy threatening their own children to eat or sleep: Yes to all of that, but Rose went most because she could not stand her Daddy calling and no one coming, his waiting in vain, and she loved to hear him tell that all belonged to her, that he did. And so, by twenty and well past twenty, her father had long since called for her and her alone. And while her sisters were called about boys, Rose was called and asked the question she'd been answering her whole remembered life. *He should pay, Daddy.*

Only this time Rose was not so certain, so ready. Joyful yes that her father had come home, but she was thirty. This morning, with her father at last come home and taking his tea in the birdsinging side-garden with the world again right and full, only now did Rose know that she needed more than a father. Her sisters' houses, her cousins', even her mother's squirrel cages: they teemed with life. And she had been sleeping on the same cot since she was ten. She had slept there also the night before, after watching this sudden new stranger smoking in the side-garden, shaking his old handsome head according to whatever principle also governed his wearing a worn-down suit her father would have long ago given to the cook's husband. Standing there like that. The poor fool.

"I shall give my answer tomorrow," Rose said.

"Tomorrow?" her father gasped.

"I cannot go and come from my village in one day," Sam warned.

"Then you shall stay," said Rose.

On the fourteenth morning, Sam was already waiting for them in the side-garden. Xavier could tell what his oldest girl was doing, what she wanted. At least, by that morning, he was willing to admit to himself, if not to anyone else, what had been evident to the whole watching world on the prior mornings Sam had come, walking faster each time and by now in scuffed shoes that were daily spit-shined, an old suit daily stone-pressed, his hair combed into a crest and his creased face shaved clean of its salt. And each time Rose told him to stay until tomorrow and the next morning he would walk even faster, faster, faster, until the fourteenth dawn when Sam was already there among the birds lighting upon their pedestal, smiling at Rose who was smiling at him as she had never before smiled at anyone, not even, no, not even at her father when he called and she always came. But how many girls this fellow had smiled at, Xavier could not tell. How many rich men's daughters? And yet, Xavier could tell he was not smiling with extortionate plotting but with nervousness and bliss and idiocy, with the joy of a girl smiling at him, and in this alone was the fellow like a young suitor, a proper suitor, a hopeful groom for Xavier De Moraes's eldest daughter.

After lunch on that fourteenth day, father and daughter left the compound. Rose's mother had been on the other side of the house, feeding her dandos, the only ones in the world whose chatter did not stop when she came near these last thirteen morning-noon-and-nights. Now, at last, on the fourteenth day, Vivimarie thought, as she followed the beehive of her husband's Austin driving out of the compound, he was doing something. Ask him to support action against Mrs. Bandaranaike, the trucks are running. Tell him to fly away when the action fails, the bags are packed. But it was two weeks before he'd do something for his daughter's good name, his wife's, his own! But because she was speaking neither to her husband nor to her eldest daughter at the time, Vivimarie De Moraes did not know that Xavier drove with Rose to the Grand Street Church in Negombo. At that midday hour the church was mostly praying widows and napping madmen. Kneeling together, father and daughter prayed opposing prayers and lit opposing candles until Xavier was noticed by a priest walking past their pew. Others soon came. Soon there was a crowd congratulating him on his blessed return and apologizing for Father Marcelline's not blessing the truck, which they would have been honoured to have blest if only asked, and meanwhile, just as she would when she was a girl and her father was caught to such talking, Rose followed the churchbirds wheeling between the great white rafters above them. She prayed that her father's heart would not harden, and she prayed about Sam Kandy, for Sam Kandy, that she was right about Sam Kandy: that he was what he seemed to be from the first she had seen him, standing alone in the side-garden that night her father had come home: that he was not even God's lonely man: that he was no one's: that he had been no one's for so long he would stay day after day only to hear her say *stay another day*. Rose had never known a man to step taller, faster, finer because she, not she and her father not she and her sisters but she, Rose, was standing there waiting for him. She was herself too old to wait any longer.

"Rose darling, there are so many suitable boys—" Xavier began, after they left the church and passed through the beggar's gauntlet to the car.

"No, Daddy, there are not so many boys waiting to marry a thirty-year-old girl."

"You come from a good family, a known family, Rose darling. I will make inquiries—"

"Now you want to make inquiries? Why, so you can find me a fat Bharatha widower with a good name and a house full of small fellows, who has seen me with my sisters' children in the church square and been told by the parish widows what a good daughter I am and so wants the same for his children, the same for him?"

"When you were younger, you never once asked that we make inquiries about any boy. Your sisters did. You never asked." He sighed. "Darling, also, you were never asked about, darling. I am sorry. I am sorry. But you never said anything and so many years have passed and all this time we have thought—"

"What, Daddy, that I would be happy for the rest of my life to get a sweet from you when I say the other fellow should pay?"

"Aiyo Rose, I have only come home." He stopped the car beside a fruit stand whose seller, an old woman in ragged purple, smiled scattershot teeth in vain.

"This is not the time and this is certainly not the man! I have only come home!"

"I am very happy you have come home, Daddy, but you are not the man either."

"This is murdering your poor mother!"

"But when I give her more grandchildren?"

"You think you can have children with this fellow! You want to make me a grandfather with someone else's grandfather! This is madness! He is my age! How can my sweetest smartest girl suddenly be so stupid? What do we know about this fellow? What if he is already married, if he has children older even than you? He is my age! We cannot know what he wants from you, from us, from me. I have more than just rivals in this country now, don't forget."

"And you think some enemy has sent an old man to take away your only unmarried daughter? What kind of rivals are these? But you can find out about him, no?"

"Yes. Well, I don't know. Who's to say?"

"Will you try?"

"No, Rose, I won't. I am your father. You are my daughter. This is my family. No."

"And yet you will try all for country, you will try all for church, for concrete, for everyone else in the compound. You will not try once, for me?"

"But what have I told you, for so many years, darling? I am yours! Everything here is yours! And you want to give all of it to an old man in an old suit who crashes good cars and won't pay? How in the name of God and our blessèd Saviour, after seeing this fellow for five minutes these last fourteen mornings, can you think you are ready to see him every morning noon and night for the rest of your life?"

"I am."

"When just on the other side of a parapet wall down this road, you have everyone? There is nothing sadder than an unknown man, Rose. Believe it, I know. But the whole world is there for us, for you, and it always will be. We cannot know if this fellow will get in his car and go the moment I fix his fender, or if he will go in five years, with all your wedding gold, if he lives that long."

"Do you think he's a rogue, Daddy?"

"I don't know what he is. What I know, Rose darling, is that now, again, you have all of us. Why would you take him over all of us? How could you?" her father asked, his voice at last failing.

"Yes, I have all of you," Rose answered carefully. Knowing that if ever she was to be more than a daughter now would not be the time to cry in her father's arms. "And you have me. You have all always had me, and I have always had you, and I have been happy that way. I am happy that way."

"Then why are we even talking such madness? Send the fellow off tomorrow morning. I will even pay for his cars. And then we can look into this properly for you. Patience pays."

"No, Daddy. I have paid too much patience while all of you have learned what more there is. And I don't, I, I never have, and very soon I never will."

"But aiyo why does it have to be with this fellow?"

"Will you make the inquiries if I tell you?"

"Yes."

"You give me your word you will send someone to find out about him?"

"You have your father's word. Now tell me why it has to be this fellow."

"I shall tell you tomorrow."

━━◞

After they returned to the compound, Xavier called trusted men to the car park. Minutes later, Vivimarie learned the instructions: get the fellow's driver drunk again, get the name of the man's village, go and make all necessary inquiries. That her husband was even considering this made Vivimarie fall martyr. Attended by aunts, sisters, parish allies, she didn't leave her bedroom for three days, where she meanwhile stormed heaven to know what she'd done to have a daughter treat her so, let alone a husband come home after so many years and marry off their eldest girl to an old man whose only known people were a drunk driver and two busted motorcars. A few mornings later, the inquirers returned and reported that no one in the man's village would speak, whether for or against him, that they would only point to the walauwa where he lived alone: no wife, no children in there. The next morning, the old fellow was invited to the verandah for tea. He was allowed to sit across from Rose in her best dress for twenty minutes while Xavier sat beside her, trying not to tear his newspaper in half, and just as she had done with all the other suitors for their other daughters, Vivimarie watched from the dining room with a pearl rosary wrapped through her fingers that was, this time, apparently, useless. And so when Rose and Sam sat together that morning, the rest of the shocked near world knew a courtship had begun. If not why, if not how, if not, really, even with whom.

Two nights later, men came for Sam. They were certain this was extortion. They came most of them drunk, carrying broomsticks and cricket bats, bottles, belts, crackers, and messy torches made of old banyans and kitchen rags soaked in kerosene and wrapped around lengths of suriya wood. They called him out, loud and threatful and tearful, lyrical like Hindi movie heroes. Rose heard from her window and ran past her mother standing in the threshold of her own room to ask her father to stop them. Xavier stayed on the bed, also listening. Rose said if he did not go, the blood would be on her hands, her hands. Her mother came into the room and, as her first words to either husband or daughter in two weeks, she told Xavier to stop them. When he was certain of what his wife was actually saying, what she was assenting to, Xavier dressed and went. Rose asked her mother why. Her mother told Rose that Rose had a stupid heart and a stupid father for listening to her stupid heart but no daughter of hers would have blood on her hands. God did not make daughters to have blood on their hands. Then, in a different tone, Vivimarie said, "God did not make wives to have blood on their hands either."

While mother and daughter were speaking, Xavier ordered the useless torches doused before the whole compound burned down. Then he went in to see Sam, who was sitting on his cot. Bopea was standing at the far end of the room. Both were smoking. Robert saw Sam's suit laid out on a chair beside his bed, the shoes underneath, ready for another morning.

"Mahatteya, please," Bopea pleaded with Xavier, "I am only the driver. My son is studying abroad. Aiyo please, I am only here until the vehicle is repaired."

"You don't deserve my daughter, Kandy."

"I don't deserve anything that's come to me in this life."

"No, not anything. I don't know what you deserve and don't deserve because I don't know you. You aren't known. You don't deserve my daughter."

"No. No, I don't."

"Then tell me one reason I should stop them from thrashing you."

"I can't."

"Truth? You can think of no reason? None? What kind of man are you? Every morning you are asked to stay another morning and you won't even ask me to stop them for her sake?"

"I need to ask you for that, for her sake?"

"NO!" Xavier yelled, a good father trying to be a good father and defeated and trying, trying to make of this defeat a triumph. Never mind the mob was his own flesh and blood and he would be standing at its head save the blood that then would be on her hands, her hands. But what father ever thought any fellow deserved his daughter? And at least this one was old enough to admit the same. God help her. He left the room and told the crowd to go. The next day, Vivimarie told Rose that she would convert the old fellow and that the children would, of course, be raised in the Church. She also told Rose how many of her squirrels had been drowned in Negombo lagoon that morning, in bags tied around collars of Lourdes cement. Rose asked her to repeat the number of squirrels her mother expected her now to match. Vivimarie smiled and wished her daughter good luck and Godspeed, then called for her dressmaker.

No crowd gathered again in the compound until three days before the wedding. For the engagement dance, the great drum was brought out and heated and a dozen women were called from the parish and given cloth and jacket to play it until the crackers were lit. Xavier took Sam round to meet all of them who weeks before had wanted to hammer him but now offered baroque toasts and congratulations, sweet words about Rose, manly questions about the upcountry land he was said to hold off the Kurunegala Road and about his cars, lately repaired. In the end, De Moraes had paid. No one called it a dowry, at least not in his hearing. He said he paid because he wouldn't have his eldest daughter driven to her wedding in a brand-new vehicle—the Leyland cement truck was outfitted with a fine rounded Burgomaster chair for the bride, its mixer garlanded and repainted bridal white—only to be driven home in a wreck. There was no wedding Mass. Not even Rose's mother could persuade him, or was it plead with him feed him pray with him pray over him pray about him catechize him threaten him threaten to pray more feed more plead more catechize more, to convert. But the family had insisted on something more than fifteen minutes in front of the Negombo Registrar of Births and Marriages, and Rose told Sam that even if he would not convert he could at least kneel beside her for the vows. And he did, Sam Kandy knelt, with wan Bopea looking on from the groom's pew, the lone pew reserved for the groom's side because Bopea was the only person who attended the wedding from Sam's people.

The rest of St. Anthony's was full of De Moraeses, save the back pews where sat the parish widows who attended every good family's wedding, only this time not only to see how decked in gold was the bride, or to cry during the presentation of the bouquet to the Virgin, or to cry during the Ave Maria. Of course they did all of this at Rose's wedding too, glad the eldest girl, a very good girl, her father's girl, was at last getting married, if not as she should have married even if she was short and thirty: to a known Bharatha boy from a known good family, a boy with blood and a name that went back across the salt-and-pearl water to Rig Veda times, whence first their people had come to Ceylon. But no, Rose De Moraes married no Bharatha and no boy. And so this time the womenfolk of the parish sat in the back pews for the wedding mostly to see if the story coming out of the De Moraes compound in the days before the wedding was true: that Xavier De Moraes had left his smarts abroad during his exile and Vivimarie De Moraes had drowned her tongue with her giant squirrels, because otherwise how to explain Rose's groom, how old he was, how unpeopled, how un-baptized, how universally unknown save the name he gave, the cars he crashed, his driver, his suit, his rumoured village. But now Sam Kandy was known again in the world, was known beyond his own conceiving, was a smiling grey groom standing on the church steps beside his triple-decker new wife, and she was smiling too.

twenty-seven

And so came the age of cement, of Christians, of Christians and their hired vans and Leyland trucks and guitars and miraculous medals that, over the years, would be discovered on the common ground of Sudugama like the parted shells of fine silver nuts. And from the first day Sam Kandy brought the De Moraes family to the village there also came the age of children, children in the walauwa and in the lanes, children challenging the village boys to footraces before the village boys could even tell they had been challenged. In turn, the boys of Sudugama challenged the invaders to a cricket match. The visitors won the toss, calling miraculous Mary over miraculous Joseph, and then ran back to one of their ten thousand vans and returned carrying actual cricket bats and tins of tennis balls whose every wondrous opening was an occasion for awed silence, for every boy to wonder if this was what the world itself had sounded like when it went from nothing to the stars; what it would sound like when to nothing it someday returned. Soon the green-black branches surrounding the rude village oval shook with blasted sixers and bounding fours and the gardens of Sudugama became studded with strange fruit. The batsmen were too gallant or was it impatient for the balls to be retrieved and why should they be retrieved when standing in the shade were younger cousins and little brothers dying, absolutely dying, to throw in a replacement to the scowling bowler. The visitors ran up an impossible figure for plank bats to answer, for anyone, even Don Bradman, to match. But these weren't walauwa children. These weren't old Sam Kandy children. When their inning was up, the visitors let the Sudugama boys use their bats, and so came an age of eternal friendship, all in the first hour of the first day.

⌁

He came home with a Negombo bride in July 1966; he came, it seemed, with all of Negombo itself. A few of the village men stopped wondering where Bopea was when they recognized one of the drivers in the caravan as among those who had come some months before, asking about Sam. Those who were questioned then had been surprised at how suddenly numb were their tongues, how heavy their lips. Were they protecting Sam because say what you will, he was at least more village than the men asking after him? Afterwards, in that evening's toddy circle, which was again hosted by Lalson on the walauwa verandah because no one had lived for days in the big house except the servants, it was agreed that Sam Kandy was being held somewhere while his story was checked out. Bopea must have been held too, apparently, poor proud fellow in his yellow hat. By the end of that evening's toddy, the majority held that Sam Kandy must have owed someone significant and owed him significantly and at long last, after so many years of his city life, five years after his city life had ended, his collection time had come. A minority, well, really only one fellow, a tabla player, insisted that Sam was being considered for a minister's post, less because he truly believed it than because he was, like his father before him, a stubborn drunk. But that night no one thought, no one could even conceive, that someone had sent questioners to ask about old Sam Kandy because he, the sender, had a daughter.

Months later, when Sam climbed out of his Hillman and went to the other side and opened the door, smiling the whole time, the women watching already knew what he'd gone and done before the men within their hearing knew there was anything more remarkable here than the dozen Gipsy trucks queued behind Sam's Hillman. The village women wondered with limed innocence if poor Hyacinth had shrunk in her absence years, and only then did the men look away from the Gipsys and their bulging canopied flatbeds to see the young woman on Sam's arm. Only then did they search their memories and fail to find anything of Hyacinth Kandy's face in this young woman's, and so one or two declared with superior and stupid innocence that this was not Hyacinth and were woman-told with honeyed innocence that of course it had to be Hyacinth, because who else would a sixty-six-year-old widower be squiring toward his house, save his very own daughter? When, eventually, *finally*, their men understood what Sam had gone and done, again, the village women then noted how this latest Madam Kandy was walking toward the walauwa. She was moving with more care than her city shoes warranted, with the kind of care a woman only takes once: when it's her first. Her first what? one man asked but he wasn't answered. The question itself, that late in the hour's revelations, was considered beneath any woman's notice.

The caravan left a few days later but not before a visit to the temple. While the rest of them waited in their vans, playing Jim Reeves songs and fencing with fruit sellers, one of Rose's brothers went in to speak with the chief monk. Sipping clammy tea, he was made to wait in a damp-smelling Buddhist hallway lined with Buddhist things: monks, namely, but also darkwood cabinets full of slapdash plenty, books and brass plate, brass statues, brass lamps topped with brass-cast roosters and temple flowers; palm fans that looked older and more dried out than the oldest Palm Sunday crosses hanging behind the holy faces in his mother's house; pied pennants, ola leaf scrolls tipping into each other like sleepy drunks and ruined columns, left as if their consultation was interrupted one hundred years ago and never returned to by the monks who were themselves captured in the formal portraits propped up behind it all. Eventually, the chief monk came and sat in a schoolmaster's chair across from Rose's brother who, reaching up from a child's chair, presented him with an appointment calendar and a desk diary and a sheaf of plastic book covers before beginning to explain why his family had come to Sudugama.

"You are here because others won't come, no?" the chief monk interrupted, keeping the calendar and diary on the ledge of the cabinet beside him, where Rose's brother thought they would remain unto dust. The chief monk handed the book covers over to a younger monk, who handed them on to another, and then another, until eventually they came to the youngest fellows in the temple, the Samaneras, who took them behind the temple buildings and conclusively determined that the book covers could float, flip, and be made to flap like birds if not wheel like bats, and in the end failed to convince as airplanes.

"Sorry? I am here because I was hoping—"

"You don't need to tell me why you are here, or what you are hoping for," the chief monk declared. "I know. I know *he* is hoping I will forget how many years he has lived across the main road and motored past this temple and never once stepped foot or sent until now. Now he sends some office goods."

"No. I am not here for Sam Kandy. I am here for Rose Kandy."

"Mokatha? What is Rose Kandy?"

"She is my sister. And as I was trying to tell, she now lives across the main road, with him. She has married him. Yes, I know"—Rose's brother smiled at the monk's shocked face and the monk did not scowl away the sympathy because even if he hadn't seen her in the seventy years since he'd taken to robes, he had a sister too. "We have only come here to help her settle," Rose's brother continued, "and I see that there are things that are needed for the walauwa and the village too and my father—"

"Your father's name is?"

"Xavier Joseph De Moraes, of Negombo."

"Negombo."

"Yes. Negombo, where he is the owner of the Lourdes Cement Company."

"Negombo. De Moraes. Lourdes. *Your* family has come here, to the Udarata, to Sudugama, to the temple."

"Yes, my sister has."

"And no one has told me and no one has asked me," the chief monk observed loudly, and his attendant monks shook their heads vigorously, hoping that for sharing his outrage they would not be asked afterwards why none hadn't already informed him of the old devil's latest devilry, instead of his having to hear it from a Negombo cement man, a Christian. "But you also said cement?"

"I did."

"And?"

"And there are things in the walauwa and the village that need repair. The walauwa's steps, the water tank, and also gutters to be poured for the lanes and sluices behind all the huts. My family will do all of this. But there is no telephone in the walauwa and I am told that—"

"Not just in the village and the walauwa is cement needed."

"Sorry?"

The monk made a disappointed face. Rose's brother right away knew his father would be making the same face were he here and watching him fail to understand that of course cement would be needed here too. Here first.

"Right right. I was about to say the same. And so shall I trunk-dial to Negombo?"

〜

Standing on the verandah a few days later, Sam heard a cement truck coming down the main road toward the village—like some giant working his pestle into a mortar full of road ordnance. Sam went to the stone railing and yes the villagers were coming into the lane, leaving their dawn lives of cooking and tea and puja to see what it was this time: first looking up to see if the noise had split the moon and then looking down the lane toward the main road, wondering what was left in the world that he had not yet brought to the village: what there was that could be louder even than a caravan of De Moraeses. He smiled. Since he had married this third time, Sam Kandy had been smiling, smiling terrifically, idiotically, shamefully; smiling at last like a malli by the roadside. Because what else was there to do, this late, save smile and smile back, talk a little about the day before or the day to come, tell how he was feeling and ask her the same. One thing else there was: to tell. To tell Rose of how many inside lives and outside lives, of how many joins had been tried and broken, tried and broken. And if he did tell, tell all of it, then what would be left, after she left? One thing else: to tell the cement truck, a fleet of Lourdes cement trucks, to still come to the village and drive up past the crossroads and past the walauwa and past the old founder's cave and there queue, position the chutes, open the drum-hatches and only stop when the village, all and all and all of it including the old man in the old pinstripe suit lying in one of its old huts, was covered and gone. And then at last he would be a triumph to beat all others, because even smoke fades away. But if the trucks came and poured cement over all of it, then Sam Kandy would forever be the slab Ralahami of an endless flat world, the eternal stone headman of a hard grey sea.

So why tell anything instead of smiling along, agreeing along like a sweet greyed malli who'd been given this unearned newness of life, this newness that she was giving him, that he had given her even at sixty-six, this newness she wanted to give him and the walauwa and the village, none of him or them deserving. And yet she gave. But she was giving *them* too? From the verandah, Sam watched the cement truck turn off the main road, turn away from him, the walauwa, the village so undeserving. The cement truck turned into the temple grounds, toward the temple less than undeserving. Sam went into the walauwa, calling for Alice to come quickly he said Rose come quickly, Rose come quickly.

"The cement truck has turned into the temple."

"Yes. It's going there first, and then coming here."

"No it's not."

"Yes, it already is."

"Mokatha?"

"What?"

"Yes, exactly, what?"

"Seven months married and this is when it happens?"

"This is when what happens?"

"This is when your face more than smiles?" When his voice, his staring eyes, she thought, turn so hard. Seven months married and now, Rose could imagine her mother telling her, now, when he's got you in the village and we, your people, are a day's drive away. Now, darling, he stops smiling. Right now, Rose thought, they'd be taking breakfast in Madhu. They'd be gathered under a white pavilion tent set up in front of the old fine church, and her mother would be asking an unknown little boy to tell her the seven gifts of the Holy Spirit, a boy who'd only slipped into the tent already mad with children in hopes of slipping out with a fish bun and maybe one of their badminton racquets.

"Why is the cement truck going to the temple?" Sam demanded.

"Because the temple needs cement."

"How do you know that?"

"Because my brother had to go to the temple to call Daddy to send a truck—"

"And the chief monk—"

"Yes, he has asked for a little work to be done."

"Ha. A little work. Ha. Right. You are a Christian. You don't know. He probably wants a beggar's bowl poured for himself, one that would fit the whole courtyard."

"And how, husband, do you know that?"

"Believe it, I know."

"Daddy has greater reasons than you to send a truck anywhere in this country except to the temple, and yet he allows it. And do you know why he allows it?"

"How can you think your father has greater reasons than your husband?"

"How can I know otherwise? Can you tell me otherwise? Or shall we keep living as we have been, as if you were born on our wedding day? I have never asked, Sam. Most of my relations think I am a fool for never asking. Tell me, am I?"

"You are my wife."

"And I will be your wife even if you tell me I am a fool for being your wife. That is holy vows. That is love, this." She patted her swelling belly.

Sam said nothing.

"Will you tell me another day? When the cement truck has come and gone from the temple and the village and the walauwa?"

"By the time the chief monk is finished with the cement truck," Sam said, his face cloudy, his hand reaching out for her, touching that swelling newness of life that called him to stop his vengeful symmetries, to stop saying what he still had to say, "this child is going to be old enough to do what his father is too old to do now."

"Which is what?" Rose asked, feeling for once foolish for deciding to pretend all these months that you can marry a sixty-six-year-old man and make like he's historyless, like he's only a smiling sweet adjunct to your own hope for a purpose beyond forever daily answering your father's questions and minding your sisters' children, a purpose that would take you away from the useless last plot of land in the family compound to upcountry grandness—echoing, dripping, dusty old gone grandness awaiting its restoration. Its redemption?

"I was twice married before you."

"And you are telling me this only now?" She was not surprised. She wished she was. A jungle paper had been slipped through the bars of her bedroom window a few days after she had come to the village, a mad scrawled boast, or was it a warning? *Don't think you're the first lady of this house. You're only the one he's let live the longest.* She had folded the note into an envelope marked Should Anything Happen, which she put in an envelope addressed to her family in Negombo and hid in the back of her almirah for a day, then removed, reread, tore, and burned in that morning's cooking fire. She had married him. *He* was living now because she had married him.

"I was never asked before."

"Then tell."

"My first wife's almirah is in the bedroom. My second wife's music cabinet is in the front room."

"No, tell me more than that."

"Right. I am twice widowed."

"Twice. How?"

"They died."

"Two, you say. How?"

"Car accident."

"Both?"

"No, the other drowned."

"How long ago?"

"Lives ago."

"No. We each are only one life. How long ago?"

"The first, in 1939. The second, in 1948."

"That's all?"

"No. There are children."

"Living?"

"Yes. A son and a daughter."

"How old? Here in the village?"

"No. They are not in the village. They are about your age, I think."

"You think? Where are they?"

He looked at her. He looked away. She nodded.

Two more Kandys trying to be historyless. Would she be too, one day? Would she have to, want to? "Why are you telling me these things now?"

"You will hear these things and other things before the baby comes. That's the village."

"What other things?"

"No. No." Sam rubbed his forehead. He swallowed. He swung his heel back and forth upon the morning-cool floor. He looked everywhere but at her until, after how many birds and squirrels and dogs had informed each other and the rest of the world of their day's ambitions, Sam Kandy confessed. "I don't want to be widowed again."

Their first child was born in September 1966: a girl baptized Rose-Maria and called Rosemarie. The second, third, and fourth were girls too: Vivienne-Maria, Charmaine-Maria, and Elizabeth-Maria, called Vivimarie, Charmarie, and Lizzy-girl. The fifth girl was named Blossom-Maria and called Blossmarie and was also born without curse or great motherblood lost in a walauwa bedroom, but she was not baptized in Negombo, as were her sisters. She was born in April 1971, a few months after Sam and Rose built the first set of new bedrooms onto the big house, and hours before a group of boys with village skin and university mouths marched into Sudugama chanting against the enemy government and the enemy British before chanting against the old enemy walauwa high above them, which, the fellows lectured the villagers, had been carried for years on their toiling backs, had been floating for years upon their blood and sweat. The university boys caught no village sun on the rusted blades that rose and fell with their chanting and lecturing. They made it no farther than the crossroads, where they were turned away by village men, the oldest among them wondering if Dambulla had come their way this time, the youngest unmoved by the marchers' invitations demands pleas jeers threats jeers pleas demands invitations to cross the lane and join them. Theirs was the kind of thing best joined in a smoky canteen or crowded common room, not steps away from the hut where you were born, not steps away from the men you were born to stand beside and now asked to stand against. And so all of the villagers chased them off, wielding their own rusted blades and mammoty sticks. Retreating, one of the university boys demanded to know why the village was protecting the walauwa that could never protect them the way they deserved. He was answered by a palm-sized shard of cement whirring past his ear and hitting one of his fellows in the back, who turned and showed a gun. The villagers dropped their blades and sticks and many more hand-sized pieces of cement broken off from the many blocks that had been twice-yearly supplied to every villager in Sudugama since Rose-Madam had come. Only now what? The fellow holding the gun had never held a gun in front of others before; it had been given to him by his former chem lab partner, who had joined a group of JVP boys in sacking a police station near campus the day before. The whole world knew what came next fell to this fellow to decide, but he didn't even know how many bullets the gun held, how many it now had. Certainly fewer than there were men standing in front of him. There were other villages on this road. They went.

When the villagers returned to the crossroads, old Sam Kandy was waiting there, his arms full of daughters. They told him it was nothing, it didn't matter, it was nothing. *What is a gun?* They asked him if the new baby had come yet. He smiled. They smiled and shook their heads again, at old Sam Kandy's year-after-year feat of elaboration, of such giving and getting, which impressed them more than any chrome or other such long-since-rust-taken-loveshine he'd brought to the village in the years before. Sam knew they were flattering him into forgetting his question. He swelled with the knowledge of it, what they never before had done for him or any other man who had walked down from the walauwa and asked the matter among them, what years of assured water and good growing and a great deal of smoothing, levelling cement and laughter, child's laughter heard in the walauwa itself, had done; what Rose had done, kept doing, for *all of them*. Giving without counting, without demanding, without considering first what was leaf- and star-cast by each their birth-hour heavens.

By 1971 he had been married to her for five years and they had five children and he'd held each in their swaddling clothes and so felt the warmth of life's bawling newness in his trenched hands, fresh blood in Sam Kandy's hands. He would hold each and look over at Rose who was already looking at him, at them, tired but smiling at her handsome old un-lonely husband. Sam and Rose smiling at what they had given and been given, wondering if they were yet too old to hold more such abiding, to give and so gain another true warrant. In time again they would try. And so, down at the crossroads, Sam smiled at the villagers' question, which they asked to protect him from knowing more than a seventy-two-year father of five needed to worry about. He adjusted the squirming girls in his arms and told them that yes Rose-Madam had had another girl, and she was named Blossom-Maria. "Blossmarie!" said one of her older sisters.

Later, Rose was told more than Sam and so refused to leave the village until that July, when her family made its annual one-week stop in Sudugama on its way to Madhu Church for the Assumption Feast. She decided to have the baby baptized at Madhu and this time Sam came as well, and he also came when they baptized the twin sixth and seventh girls at Madhu, which was when they were living no longer in Ceylon but in Sri Lanka, because one morning in 1972 Ceylon was decreed banished from the island, only to be found alive and thriving in London and Dubai, Scarborough and Brampton, where it became the watchword of conjuring emigrants ignored by their television children; and then came Rose and Sam's eighth and nine and tenth girls, and then the eleventh—which was when the first Maria was given in marriage to a good Bharatha boy and settled in Negombo, near the De Moraes family compound; and with Arthur in London long forgotten and Alice's long-ago letter granting deed to long-gone George long gone in the belly of insects that themselves had long returned to dust in the long-closed office of a long-dead lawyer in Kandy town, the first-married daughter and her husband were also given a parcel of walauwa land for a holiday house; the same was done for the second and the third and the fourth—after which these first and second married Marias had their first and second children and meanwhile came Rose and

Sam's twelfth and they were written up in the *Sunday Times* and *Sunday Observer* and Rose was photographed pregnant and holding a grandchild and then came their thirteenth, all of whom were also baptized at Madhu, but not their fourteenth and last, Xavier Joseph Maria, who was called Zamarie and named in memory of her grandfather, who died a month before she was born, "peacefully, in his sleep, a holy death," as went the notices that ran in all the English dailies while the *Catholic Messenger* reported that the meal given in his name was the grandest in living memory, which Rose read about and saw pictures of because Bopea finally came home, after Xavier died, and brought Rose the clippings. She had been too pregnant to sob beside his casket and so Sam went and came with some of the older girls and then their fourteenth was born, in July 1983.

The timing seemed right—they would have gone to Madhu and had an Assumption Day baptism—but the Kandys stayed in Sudugama until almost the mid-August feast day itself, listening for the latest news of the trouble in Colombo, hearing from village talk that the trouble had come to the upcountry too. There were none in Sudugama, and while of course you talked for years against upcountry Tamils when you were in toddy circles and standing around the carpenter's shed and walking back from the fields, against their field blackness which was also Indian blackness, and against their old treacherous, poisoning queens who, as the schoolmaster and the temple had been teaching since 1956, had so weakened the last four kings of the Udarata that the British came and took the island with ease from already-defeated men. There was likewise talk against their blue devil temples, their Shiva love, above all of late against their demanding ballots, schools, first-class positions for their people, and not demanding in Sinhala or even English medium but in their shipbottom Tamil. These were not our people. Still, there were also days you talked against your wife's relations, but that didn't mean if someone gave you a can of petrol and a knife and asked you to join in you would. If twenty asked you to join, and none of you knew any of you, it might be different. But this wasn't the city.

When the trouble finally seemed over, Rose said they should still go to Madhu, even if her family in Negombo refused. And so the Kandys set out for the shrine in two hired vans. They moved fast, far too fast along the Vavuniya-Mannar Road, no need this time for roadside stops beside other vehicles likewise defeated by the pilgrim traffic ahead of them. According to their ages, the girls complained they hadn't had any road sweets or road toys, lagoon baths or smiles from any roadside Romeos. Their caravan was stopped only when they were very near Madhu, by two army jeeps parked in a chevron across the main road. A soldier came to the window and told the lead driver who turned and told Sam that there was trouble ahead, on the far side of Cheddikulam. Word was sent to Rose, riding in the second van, and word was sent back: Our Lady was waiting. Sam told the driver who told the soldiers who shook their heads until these mad fools actually gave them money and then, still shaking their heads but now counting the bills, the soldiers let them pass.

After driving through a ghosted Cheddikulam, the lead van came across two Tamil boys on push-bikes lolling back and forth across the main road as if it were long since theirs. As the lead van neared, honking, more boys began walking out of the bushes, un-slinging dead men's guns and raising mother's knives and jogging at them, waving them down, now running. The vans turned sharply and while they sped back toward the other checkpoint Rose baptized Zamarie from the vial of holy water she kept in her purse and then gave the screaming wet child more Cow & Gate formula to stop her crying and told the rest to stop their own screaming and crying and pray rosaries instead. Meanwhile, in the other van, Sam watched the boys coming at them, boys like none that he had ever known in his own hard-running days. They weren't queued in a shipping agent's office waiting to go out into the world and take what they could of it. They were already taking from the world, and all the world they wanted was here and now, was this line of road, this common patch of wind-tossed green. And if they could not keep it, then no one else would. Sam knew more: he knew he was too old to run anymore, but going home from Madhu in the safe, crowded van, he did not mind. At eighty-four, Sam Kandy had run enough, had taken and spent and broken and been given far more than enough to know what kind of races were run and won in vain. It was late, he was weary, yet he knew.

twenty-eight

The decision was made not to sell tickets to Sam Kandy's funeral. Sudugama itself was closed to the public for the day. Tour operators and upcountry hotels were informed and the evening before the cremation, two village boys went along the Kurunegala Road in a pickup truck to collect the nameboards that had been lining the way to and from the village these last fourteen years. Across the top of each it read ALL WELCOME / WILLKOMEN / AUYBOWAN and beneath was promised AUTHENTIC TRAD SRI LANKAN VILLAGE ATTRACTION 5 MI. AHEAD / 4 MI. / 3 MI. / 2 MI. / 1 MI. / 500 FT. / TURN! / PLS. COME AGAIN! Over the years more words were added, in curlicued and filigreed and bold black strokes. HANDICRAFTS, SPICE GARDEN, BUTTERFLY HALL, TRAD DAMSEL DANCE, TRAD MASSAGE, TRAD FIREWALKING DEMO, TELEPHONE, ELEPHANT RIDES, ELEPHANT HOUSE, ICE CREAM, SNAKE CHARMER, TRAD HOROSCOPES, GIFT-SHOP, TRAD LUNCH THEN WESTERN LUNCH then finally TRAD + WEST LUNCH, RESPLENDENT CLEAN TOILETS and eventually, when terms with the chief monk were reached, GUIDED TEMPLE TOURS. By 1999, there were

still more letters: A/C, USD, GBP, & DEM, then EURO, then VISA AND
M/C, and also postcard-sized renderings of the Union Jack and the
Stars and Stripes and the Deutschlandfahne and the Lonely Planet
logo and the Sri Lanka Tourist Board's seal of approval.

The village first opened as an attraction in 1985, as a compromise
between Rose and Sam and the villagers, who had sent a delegation to the walauwa the year before, a day after the first and last
Sudugama Annunciation Festival. On their way to the big house,
the delegation had to pass the glass-boxed blue Virgin that had
reigned over the village crossroads for two weeks. Bouquets of dried
roses were tied with wires around her feet, and she was attended
by papier mâché angels hanging down from the bulb-lit top while
still more bulbs lined the edges and back wall of the box. The effect
was like an electric waterfall, or the entrance to a Foreigners Only
nightclub in Colombo. Yet there had been no opposition to the
scandal of this Mother Christ buzzing and beseeching in a true old
upcountry Buddhist village. There had been no opposition because
there was no saying otherwise: the village had done very well in the
eighteen years since Sam had brought Rose to Sudugama. They, the
temple included, were living lives finer lit and firmer walled than
their wattle-and-daub and lamplit fathers and grandfathers ever
had. To all who stayed in the village had finally come better lives
than the rutted bloodcourse of their meritless history, but there was
something in that blood and history that had been offended by the
festival, something other than pride of temple.

Rose had invited her family, etc., to the village to pass the Feast
of the Annunciation because there would be no going to Madhu
that year, given the country's situation. Afterwards, the village
delegation informed Rose that her family's coming was not the
problem. It was the etc., it was all the other pilgrims who'd come
from Negombo and from Mount and from Chilaw, who stayed in
tents and pavilions on the great green clearing where stall-men sold

wood apple chutney and kites and shelf upon shelf of bright plastic guns, cars, weeping Virgins, and washing bowls.

Now no one minded the caravans lining the lanes whenever Rose had a baby, or when they visited for school holidays or before going on to Madhu in July in the years before the trouble, just as no one said anything, not even in the cement-smooth temple was anything said, when every second Sunday a Catholic priest came from Kandy town and said dawn Mass for Rose and the Marias in the walauwa's inner courtyard and then stayed to breakfast and said grace before a true old upcountry meal. Speaking softly, out of respect for Sam, who seemed to be sleeping, the delegation asked Rose please to agree that no one had ever said anything about any of it, that her family had never but been welcomed in the village.

"But now?" Rose asked.

"Aiyo, please agree, Madam."

"Agreed," Rose said. "But now?"

"Madam, they looked in our houses."

"Sorry?"

"They did not stay in the clearing. Your pilgrims came into the village and they looked in our houses. They asked how we made things, what we made, where we slept. They looked in our houses. They looked at our wash. They watched us make puja, make tea. Madam, they watched us eating. Your family has never done that, just as we have never looked in their vans, isn't it? But these other people, they watched us eating."

"What men, they meant no offence," said Rose, imagining what these fellows would make of Negombo compound life if a face in a window was cause for a delegation to be sent. Back home, pregnancies could be announced before even conception. "They must have liked to see some of the old ways still going. I know my family likes that when they come. Our daughters tell of it in Negombo."

"Yes but Madam your people have never treated us as if the way we sweep the house is something to watch."

"But what if it is?" Sam asked, awake.

~~

A week later, a meeting was called to discuss what parts of the old-time village might hold attraction for visitors. The meeting was held in vain. The people of Sudugama thrashed each other's memories of what was old true village. And so, no choice. A professor was called. He was a very short man. He flared his nostrils as preface and conclusion to his statements. And when he was not telling them about the strange damp of a rainy day in Aberdeen, where he'd given a paper last year, or the familiar heat of stepping off the plane in Gainesville, where he'd given a paper the year before last, he smiled at their efforts to dispute him on certain aspects of *Temple Paddy and Paddy Politics: Ceylon's Upcountry Village Life, Pre-1948*.

In time workers came and cut a fine wide roadway from the village crossroads to the great green clearing. Here the village was rebuilt in small. Sudugama became a charm bracelet of itself, of old-time huts with side-garden plots winding down from a water tank beside which was a pile of washing rocks. The huts were broken up by godowns fitted with cadjan roofs; to one side was the notion of a paddy field at whose edge grew rubber and areca nut and kitul; on the other side were a car park and a trenchline of bathroom stalls. Buddhas were liberally installed. The new village crossroads was dominated by a little walauwa that was erected across from a canopied stage where a bride and groom would stand and where damsels would dance their numbers to traditional music played on hidden cassette tapes because the professor thought the local tabla men did not rate. The night before the village opened for business, the paddy workers revolted, refusing to appear in loincloth before strangers. At remarkable cost, white swimming trunks were rushed in from the nearest hotel gift shop, which the paddy men tried to save for more auspicious occasions than pretending to their mud work, until they were threatened with replacement. Those villagers not selected to be villagers became ticket-takers and staffed the refreshment stand and the craft tables. The professor arranged for a rotation of his graduate students to work as guides. Three of Rose and Sam's sons-in-law agreed to move their families from Negombo. One would be the chief managing director; another would be the operations manager; the third would handle the money. The outraged Marias still living in the walauwa, those of a dangerous age for public life, were strictly confined during operating hours, where they had to mind their nieces and younger sisters. And when she was not running the house, Rose helped her husband prepare for his own duties. Twice daily, Sam Kandy played the Ralahami.

What was left of Robert's own clothes turned out to be an old moth's feast found at the bottom of an almirah drawer. To the professor's specifications, items were purchased from a traditional upcountry costume shop in Kandy town, which sat between a bookstore and currency exchange office on the first floor of the Queen's Hotel. It rented out headman's costumes for weddings, family portraits, twenty-first birthdays. It was also pleased to ship worldwide upon request, whether to London or Dubai, Scarborough or Brampton. Before each performance, Sam was wrapped above the waist in a heavy white cloth that reached his bare feet and was topped with a broad crimson band, over which was placed more red—a crimson-and-gold belt whose buckle was no smaller, no heavier than a child's head and filigreed in golden leaves that made a courtyard around a crimson field of golden temple flowers. A pillow had to be fitted around his sunken old man's waist to give the necessary effect of a village in prosperity.

While the professor's graduate students over-explained to their tour groups in their loudest BBC English, villagers would come for audiences with the Ralahami in the little walauwa. They would pantomime shows of respect and be shown to graded stools by the servant, played by old wan Bopea standing behind him with a sun-shaped palm fan slumped against his shoulder. Raising his hand, the Ralahami would then direct the servant to give the petitioner a sheaf of betel or accept his offering of rice or coconut, fruit or spice. After the betel was sagely prepared and solemnly chewed to loud live tabla (at last, work for the spurned drummers), Sam would render pantomimed decisions to their pantomimed disputes, pantomimed commendations to their pantomimed reports, grant his panto-mimed permission to their pantomimed requests to burn a field or marry.

With the audience trailing behind him, cameras snapping like grasshoppers, Sam would then make his rounds, first nodding at the bowing smiling women dressed in their best home-cloth, who then returned to their sweeping and winnowing; next witnessing a solemn family make puja before their home Buddha and give their solemn first son a glass of first milk on his eternal first day of school; then inspecting the smiling potter and weaver squatting in their chequered sarongs and squinting at their work, the shirt-less carpenter leaning into his plane, the grinning metal-benders clowning with trick-bent rods. Lastly, Sam checked the health and promised wealth of the rice paddy farmed by shy-looking little men in bright white swimming trunks. He then led the audiences back to the village crossroads before walking back to the walauwa proper where he was changed, took a wash, and lay on the bed until his next call. The audience was meanwhile invited to enjoy a tradi-tionally rigid wedding ceremony followed by a traditional village damsel's dance while drinking thambili water through bright plastic straws. King coconut refreshments were offered at the beginning and end of all tours and were complimentary. A few years into the venture, when Rose's cousin Jerry Fernando replaced the professor, they were sold separately. Everything was.

The first time he came, Jerry immediately saw how much better the operation would run with proper facilities, as supplied by his father's firm, Resplendent Clean Co. (Pvt.). He could also see how much money Rose and family were losing, which he explained when he was allowed to address a directors' meeting in the front room of the walauwa proper. By only charging admission, he pitched, they were missing how much more money the visitors would be willing to give over, to buy their own traditional drinks, their own leaf brooms and engraved pots and pirith strings and grinding stones and winnowing fans and washing bowls and betel-chewing sets, not to mention spice packets, vials of pure village toddy, devil masks, home-cloth curtains, and jute sacks of pure village rice small enough to fit in carry-on luggage, never mind what they'd pay for elephant rides, snake charmers, garden remedies, and Ayurvedic massage. Making a face like he'd just stepped in something, the professor noted a series of geo-historical inaccuracies in Jerry's list of proposed souvenirs. In turn, Jerry informed the meeting that he'd just received a first-class certificate from the Ceylon Hotel School. As to the question of inaccuracies, he agreed and said the villagers could make a few display items, but the best way to ensure quality and satisfaction was for all items to be brought in from Colombo warehouses. The professor smirked that he thought Jerry's expertise was in toilets. But the air in the room had already turned. No one laughed. And so his voice going higher and louder, the professor said he would not cite his own numerous degrees but he did wonder why the far more salutary possibility of offering a selection of historically sound pamphlets was not mentioned and then he concluded, his voice now whistling, now exploding like a bombed teakettle, that he had grave reservations about turning a project so true to his years of scholarly care into some Pettah stall Disney World!

"Exactly!" said Jerry and the professor left immediately, returning for his graduate students the next day. In time, they found more rewarding work with a proper folk-culture museum in Koggala.

"If you want to make money," said Sam in his wake, "build a butterfly hall. See how many come then."

⤚

And they came. Colombo people went mad for the place. In this village there were no cousins urging that you stay the night and sleep in the room with the new fan, begging that their middle sons be put up in your phantom spare room in your phantom big house in the city so they could get phantom computer jobs and how can you refuse any of it, how can you, because who can forget when—and so would begin the great chronicle of good deeds and black deeds done for and against—and that was why you never went to the village unless someone died or was married, because in the village no one forgets, there is nothing to forget, because in the village everything always forever is. Whereas at Sudugama, history and memory and butterflies were conveniently located and reasonably priced, and also reachable by safe roads lined with newer rest-stations and only a few army checkpoints.

And they came. People from villages up and down the main road, who had grown up on Sudugama's Sam Kandy stories. Some paid the S/L national rate and took the tour and always had a question for the guide that they mumbled only to each other, about when the tour would show the traditional village's traditional motorcars and traditional cannibals; others simply hung around in the shady parts of the car park, cadging cigarettes and asking drivers trying to nap under newspaper sunshades about the size and strength of their engines, waiting for their friends to come from the tour and tell how much they were charging for the bronze pot that kept the old murdered Ralahami's ashes, and which bright Barefoot curtain hid all the dead Hamines, and which pedestal Buddha held back those ten thousand Negombo Catholics.

And they came. British and Germans, and also Australians and Japanese and Gulf people and Malays, and even a few Americans and, though rarer and rarer by the 1990s, the odd pathologically anglophile Indian. All of whom loved Sam Kandy's Sudugama for being what, from afar, it could be, the lovely spot it must be, yes the garden of the world, the trees full of big lazy leaves to float on, the Cinghalese lobbing around in the sun in *dolce far niente*. Paid to be photographed doing village deeds on the hour and otherwise not doing a hand's turn all day. Just waiting there, staring, smiling while they were considered by pale visitors carrying canvas bags and sipping bottled water and at last able to see exactly where a boy would sit in defiance of municipal orders.

And they came. Emigrants returning with their television children on summer holidays. They came and found at Sudugama the Ceylon they always dreamed of remembering from their grey northern lives: sunny and beautiful, bird mad, green and clean, clean bathrooms, actual queues, an A/C gift shop filled with brass bowls and sequined prints. Better still were the villagers themselves, their shy smiles and un-benefited teeth, their mumbled requests for foreign stamps and addresses, their smallness, even the men so slight as to make any last-picked brown boy in Cambridge or Sydney feel like a true champion to be photographed beside them. And when the emigrants went to leave, calling the driver to come and take the bags and get the water jugs for hand-washing, a final blessing: no beggars in the car park, only more little men in cheap slacks and T-shirts and Bata slippers smoking in the shade, men who never studied like they should have when all of them had been village boys, and so now could only watch as those who did study left the village again, while they remained here, weeds in this the garden of the world.

⌒

Sam let Bopea do the afternoon show after the first year and stopped doing it altogether three years later, when he turned ninety. Bopea did both shows until he died at ninety-two without ever seeing Moscow, at which point Jerry Fernando hired a tragedian from Colombo to play the Ralahami, a fellow who, a year later, persuaded Jerry to hold auditions for a Hamine. Sam never saw the woman they brought in, another Lionel Wendt player from Colombo, because by ninety-four it was enough for his hip and heels to go and come from the verandah. When he wasn't lying on the bed or called to walk around the kitchen table clearing his throat to make the children eat, he went to the verandah. From there, because of how many abandoned huts had been flattened and trees cleared to make car lanes, Sam could see what had once been the great green clearing, how much had since been wrought upon it. Now and then he was joined in his watching by one of the Marias, other times by Rose, with whom he had been fighting as old married people fight since 1983, when they had come back from Madhu and she had told him about baptizing the baby in the van and then asked if he would be baptized, if he would come to the Church for the sake of his own soul and the ease of her nightly prayers. To which he said, year after year, that coming to her was enough, which sometimes made her smile, and sometimes made her curse, and always she prayed for him.

When even waking became a triumph, Sam wanted to talk about what was to be done. As we all do, Rose made as if he was talking madness, but by ninety-six, ninety-seven, she could tell he was already elsewhere, his face either determined steel or drooling gobs of old sweet spit, pained or surprised, proud, stern, angry, blank, smiling—and all unto himself. When he was ninety-eight she asked him where he wanted to be buried, and he said he would not be buried, that of him and his body what deserved to stay upon this earth was already here, was here fourteen times over. He said when the time came his body should be burned on a bier in the car park and then a meal given at the harbour office. What harbour office. She sent word to the village men, who began collecting the wood behind the walauwa. At ninety-nine, he said the feast could be cigarettes or even just jaggery, one hard miracle popped into every beggar boy's mouth. Only no monks should be called. On that he insisted. Rose said you couldn't keep monks away from a funeral any more than you could keep crows away from a beggar's feast and Sam said yes, monks were no better than crows, always waiting to feed unless you ran them off first. Rose told him church or no church he should not die with a bitter mouth. And at one hundred, he told her he did not mind who came, who stayed to feast. Only, when they laid him upon his bier, he asked, in a now puny, not yet exhausted voice, that he burn brighter, louder than just woodsmoke. And then, one evening in July 1999, he was called to make the children eat, in vain. Sudugama was closed to the public for the day. The bier was built and packed, the caravan came and the village, both villages, went to the car park and sat behind Rose and the Marias, who sat behind the monks, who claimed the first row. Who, when the bier was lit, muddied their saffron diving for cover as Sam Kandy shot the heavens in flames full of firecrackers, bright streams and busted rainbows roaring and screaming and chasing all the birds from the still green trees.

acknowledgments

Colombo: Ajith Goonawardene, Mrs. Sybil Francke, and the people of Boyagoda village.

Toronto: Ivor Boyagoda, June Boyagoda, Bruce Westwood, Charles Foran, T.H. Adamowski, and Nicole Winstanley.

The author also gratefully acknowledges the support of the Ontario Arts Council and Ryerson University.

Beggar's Feast

Readers Guide

"And so he was taken to robes and shaved to skin to begin a new life of desire and suffering, defeat and triumph, from which would come another, and another, and another, and then, at last, after one hundred years of steel and pride, fever and speed, another."

In the tiny Ceylon village of Sudugama, a boy is judged by the vagaries of old traditions and superstitions, the selfish vanities of family, the very whims of nature, and is found wanting. His fate so capriciously determined by others, the boy is remanded to a life in the temple, where systematic degradation and abuse at the hands of the monks inspire him to quite literally strike out into the world in a quest to satisfy his overwhelming appetites, his unquenchable desires, with no apologies, with no fear of reprimand, on his own terms.

So begins *Beggar's Feast*, the rich and detailed second novel by Randy Boyagoda, author of *Governor of the Northern Province*. More than just the picaresque story of a man who drives himself to fortune and infamy, *Beggar's Feast* is a fascinating exploration of a hundred years of life in Ceylon, in the dusty village and in the bustling city, in the caves and temples and in the markets and offices, from war to colonialism to independence. There to witness all of this change is that village boy, who boldly takes the name Sam Kandy and sets off to claim the world as his own.

His journey takes him to the back stalls of the marketplace and below the deck of a steamer ship. He works behind the scenes in a Singapore brothel and commands a gang of young cheats and pick-pockets in Sydney. He schemes his way into the import/export business, taking advantage of everyone and everything at his disposal, using and abusing all those unlucky enough to cross paths with one Sam Kandy.

But his ultimate destination in all things is the village. Sam's return to Sudugama is heralded by the screaming roar of a motorcar and a sur-prise proposal to the Ralahami's daughter. Now easily insinuated into the village's ruling family, Sam sets out to exert his will and exact his revenge. Births and deaths follow in his wake, as does empty generosity and murderous violence. Over long decades of change and strife, wealth and despair, Sam cannot fully understand the depths of his anger or the depravity of his actions, and is truly challenged only by the strong wills of his three wives—tragic Alice, manipulative Ivory, and redemptive Rose—and the realization that in this beggar's feast of a life, "where you're born is why you're here." ∎

Q: Since Sam Kandy is such a larger-than-life character, I was surprised to learn that he has a real-life inspiration in your family. What is the story behind the distant relative who served as the template for Sam? How have your relatives reacted to the book and its infamous main character?

The idea of this novel came by sheer chance one day in August 2007. I was in Sri Lanka to do a reading from my first novel. The day before I left for Toronto, I was walking through an aunt and uncle's house in Colombo and came upon a grand wardrobe called an *Almirah*. It was made of burnished teak, the doors inlaid in black, endless intricacies. I told my uncle I thought it was very beautiful.

"Thank you." he said. "It was my grandmother's. She was murdered."

"Murdered?"

"Yes, by my grandfather. They married, had two children, and then he killed her."

"What happened to him?"

"Nothing." My uncle shrugged. "He was a big man in a village in the Ceylon countryside in the 1930s. No one touched him. No one touched him when he killed his second wife either."

"Really?"

"Yes. A few years later, he married again," my uncle said, holding up three fingers.

"And he killed that wife too?"

"No. He had fourteen children with her, became an international shipping magnate, and lived happily ever after."

My uncle's grandfather, as I came to learn, was born to a bad horoscope in a village in Sri Lanka in the early 1900s. The custom at the time, for parents facing the prospect of a son fated by the stars to a life of no good, was to leave the boy at a Buddhist monastery. My uncle's grandfather was left that way. He absolutely hated it. At thirteen, he ran away from the temple and made his way to Colombo, where he stowed away on a ship to Australia. He lived there through the 1920s and became a man of means. He fell in love with a Sydney girl and was trying to marry her when he received a letter from his father informing him that his mother was dying. He left Australia and returned to Ceylon, to the village, only to discover his father had tricked him into coming home, having arranged a marriage for him based on his success abroad. That was to his first wife. Then came the second. Then came the third. When I asked again about the *Almirah*, my uncle told me that it was given to him by an aunt, one of the fourteen children from the third marriage. She didn't want it in her house because family legend has it that anyone who accepted something that belonged to either of the murdered wives went mad soon afterwards. And so the *Almirah* came to him. The next day I started writing this novel against a dashboard on the way to the Colombo airport. The book developed as I returned to Toronto, and after further trips to Australia, Singapore, London, and Sri Lanka again, where I went to Boyagoda, my family's ancestral village in the island's highlands and the village that became the basis for the village that features in *Beggar's Feast*. ∎

Q: What cultural and literary inspirations influenced the writing of *Beggar's Feast*?

Gabriel García Márquez's *One Hundred Years of Solitude* and William Faulkner's *Absalom, Absalom!* rank highly. I was actually reading Márquez's masterpiece on the flight over to Sri Lanka when I discovered the family story that inspired the novel, and so I was already attuned to the possibility that writing about a small, out-of-the-way place in the fullest possilble way could wonderfully reveal that place's connection to the world at large and, also, the universals of the human condition as experienced through family life. Faulkner's novel is a passionate and intense exploration of what it means for a man to make something of himself when the world around him tells him he's nobody. I created Sam Kandy in just such terms, and the ambition, violence, and secrecy that characterize his life in turn suggest the further influence of two notable characters from recent television series—Tony Soprano, of *The Sopranos,* and Don Draper, of *Mad Men.* In fact, in a CBC Radio interview about the novel, Shelagh Rogers suggested that Don Draper just might be "the Sam Kandy of America." ∎

Q: In discussing the character of Sam Kandy, many critics have made direct comparisons to such literary and cinematic icons as Jay Gatsby, Duddy Kravitz, Tristram Shandy, Richard III, and even Charles Foster Kane. What are your thoughts on these comparisons? How do you think Sam, at the height of his career, would have fared against Citizen Kane himself?

I've been flattered and even humbled by these comparisons, and also, in a way, amused: It's great to discover a character's family tree when you didn't realize its full membership even while you were creating it. These are characters that I have a great deal of affection and sympathy for, and it's not surprising in retrospect that Sam Kandy inspires others to invoke them. As for Charles Foster Kane vs. Sam Kandy, now that's a cage match I'd pay good rupees to see! ■

Q: You're a frequent contributor to *The Globe and Mail*, *The New York Times*, *The Walrus*, and *Harper's*. How does your non-fiction writing influence your fiction? Which do you find more personally rewarding?

I've always balanced my fiction and non-fiction writing. Together with my academic work, they provide me with an always-vital interplay of ideas, stories, themes, and images. I find all of these very rewarding, but I'll admit there's nothing that compares to the feeling I get when I'm full-on writing fiction. According to my wife, I often hold my breath when I'm really immersed in writing a story, and she knows I've finished a good sentence when she hears me exhale. ■

Q: In writing the novel, you obviously spent countless hours in Sam Kandy's occasionally blood-splattered shoes. How did it feel to live with that character for such a long and intense period?

He was good about leaving his shoes on the porch when they were bloody, so I didn't mind at all. ■

Q: While Sam's character elicits sympathy from the reader in the early section of the novel and then again at the end, for most of the book it can be difficult to identify with him. What were the challenges in writing a character who can be unsympathetic at times?

The characters who are most fascinating to us aren't those we can easily slot into discrete categories of good and evil, but the characters who are a complex and shifting combination of these eternal opposites. The challenge in writing about a character like Sam is to be true to his nature, no matter how awful it is at times. In other words, it would have been easier—for me as much as for my readers—if I gave Sam an "out" and explained away his less savoury dimensions or didn't bother including them. The result might have been a more likeable character but frankly not a character who was nearly as interesting to write about and, I hope, to read about. ■

Q: Though Sam is somewhat redeemed late in life through his marriage to Rose, he never seems to openly admit any guilt or culpability in the deaths for which he is responsible, nor is his character punished to satisfy the demands of a traditional narrative. Did you consider toning down his murderous actions or adding a more classical redemptive catharsis in order to satisfy the reader's expectations?

Sam Kandy isn't the kind of man you'd find on *Dr. Phil*. There's no weepy confession in this novel because that kind of stuff wouldn't be true to the realities of who he is, where he is, and the age in which he is living. Readers might expect, and even want that Sam be punished, and I think in many ways he is. That said, in the end, redemption and love conquer despair and vengeance. Who wouldn't want that for someone, even for Sam Kandy? ■

Q: While the events of the main narrative are often quite bleak or dramatic, the novel also has a fine vein of dry humour and satire. What do you feel that humour brought to *Beggar's Feast*, and was it difficult to maintain that balance?

I brought everything I had as a writer to the telling of this story, and as such satire and humour were natural elements. I never tried for any kind of balance. The particular emphases, whether on something serious or sad, funny or joyful, always made sense with where the story was, where it had been, and where it needed to go next. ■

Q: How did the experience of writing *Beggar's Feast* differ from that of your first novel, *Governor of the Northern Province*?

I wrote my first novel in three months, based on a short story I'd published in *The Walrus*. The experience was fast and fun. It took me almost five years to write *Beggar's Feast*, and the experience was obviously not nearly as fast, but often it was far more fun. The first novel I wrote as a newly married man. The second novel I wrote while my wife and I started a family. As a result, there were times I was typing with a baby sleeping across my arms! The dirty diaper dimension of such writing experiences, admittedly, was less fun. ■

Q: You were born and raised in Oshawa, Ontario, and weren't exposed to Sri Lankan customs or culture growing up. Was it difficult to capture the traditions of the Ceylon culture? What do you think your Canadian perspective brought to the novel?

While I was working on the book, I was surprised to discover just how much exposure I'd had to various dimensions of Sri Lankan culture, in spite of how little I seemed to encounter it growing up in Oshawa. In terms of a Canadian perspective, I'm not sure of how meaningful that was to the writing of the novel. What matters more is the perspective I bring to it as a passionate and serious reader and lover of stories, including family stories like the one that I heard in Sri Lanka, the one that inspired the novel in the first place. In fact, a few years later I was back in Sri Lanka and did a short reading from the novel at a literary festival. This was shortly before *Beggar's Feast* was published by Penguin Canada. I was nervous about how the local audience would respond to this outsider's representation of their homeland. Afterwards, a few readers approached me. I expected criticism but they said, "We don't know how you did it, because you've never lived here, but you got it, you got this place right!" For all of the success and accolades the novel has earned, that compliment just might be my favourite. Now, the only question, will I hear the same someday in Oshawa, when I write *that* novel … ■

DISCUSSION QUESTIONS

1. Considering Sam Kandy's lifetime of scheming, hostility, violence, and murder, it would be almost charitable to describe him as an anti-hero. What are your thoughts about Sam as a character and as the protagonist of the novel?

2. The picaresque novel traditionally functions as a satirical critique of society and features a main character born of a low class who succeeds in the world using roguish means. Discuss how *Beggar's Feast* functions as a picaresque novel and Sam Kandy's role as a picaresque character.

3. While Sam is the main character of the book, his story is driven in some ways by the women in his life. Discuss the ways in which Alice, Ivory, Rose, and Latha propel and influence his story.

4. The novel explores a century of Ceylon's history and cultural development using extensive research and rich detail, not to mention a fair amount of skepticism and satire. What are your thoughts on how the traditional customs and culture of Ceylon are depicted in the novel, as well as the transformation of the village into a tourist attraction?

5. Sam's marriage to Rose marks a distinctive change for his character, in both emotional and behavioural terms. Do you feel that he has experienced a sort of redemption for his violent past? Do you believe that he is capable or deserving of redemption? Does Sam ever pay the price for his cruel and murderous actions?

6. At times, the novel makes light of the villagers' superstitious attitudes and rituals, and yet, the astrologer in the opening chapter quite accurately predicts for Sam "a future tattooed with empty houses and empty marriages" as well as "hunger, poverty, rage" (page 3). Discuss the roles that fate, religion, and superstition play in the village and in the life of Sam Kandy.

7. "One day I had to be Sam Kandy. The rest I wipe from my feet" (page 124). For Sam, as well as other characters like Ivory or George Curzon, one's past can be changed or discarded to suit the times or the task. Discuss the fluid nature of identity as it pertains not only to these characters but to the tumultuous history of Ceylon/Sri Lanka itself.

8. What does Sam mean when he says "Where you're born is why you're here" (page 125)? What do you feel is Sam's true relationship with the village? Does he love it or hate it? Why does he return to Sudugama when his success could have taken him anywhere in the world? Or was his success only a result of his single-minded focus on the village? Do you feel the meaning of his statement changes at the end of the novel?

9. Discuss the symbolic and thematic importance suggested by the frequent references to such animals as squirrels, crows, elephants, and butterflies.

GLOSSARY OF TERMS

Amata Siri – a bad word, an oath, used only by uneducated people or those from the slums

Amma – mother

Appachchi – father

Apo – father, also used often as an expression of frustration or disappointment

Baba – baby

Beedis – a tobacco product similar to cigarettes

Betel – a chewable leaf, similar to tobacco

Hamine – the Ralahami's wife

Machang – a pal or chum

Mahatteya – sir, a title of respect from a lower person to someone of position

Malli – little brother, used both affectionately and pejoratively

Mokatha – what, used often in an animated way

Musphenthu – bad luck

Pirith – the chanting of Buddhist scriptures

Poruwa – a ceremonial wedding platform

Pot Arrack – a distilled alcoholic beverage favoured by poor people

Pottu – a bindi, or the circle dot on the forehead

Poya Day – a monthly Buddhist holiday

Puja – worship

Putha – son

Rajay – kingdom

Ralahami – the headman of the village

Rambutan – a fruit similar to lychee

Sadhu – a wandering monk

Thambili – a king coconut

Vadai – a spicy deep-fried donut-shaped snack

Walauwa – the manor house or plantation estate owned by the village Ralahami

Yakka – devil, used colloquially to suggest a ne'er-do-well